Obsessed

USA TODAY BESTSELLING AUTHOR

IVY SMOAK

To my husband, Ryan.
You're the inspiration for James Hunter.
And it always makes me laugh when you say you're #TeamTyler.

Part 1

Chapter 1

Tuesday

I stepped out of my car into the falling rain. Some days were hard. I was used to that. This happened to be one of those days. The kind that just kept getting worse. I side-stepped a group of students walking on the sidewalk and my foot landed in a puddle.

For fuck's sake. What was I doing here? I loved teaching. But I could teach anywhere in the world. What the hell was I doing in Newark, Delaware? It was a question I kept coming back to. Being here was supposed to make me happy. At first it did. I settled into a routine that worked for me. But now? It felt like I couldn't breathe.

I shook the water off my shoe. It was the first day of classes and I had slept through my alarm. That's why I was in a bad mood. It had nothing to do with Delaware. Or the rain. Or the lack of meaning in my life.

Get a grip. In fifteen minutes I'd be teaching my first class of the semester. I wasn't sure I had ever enjoyed anything more than teaching. Why couldn't I just focus on that? But instead of feeling excited, I felt empty. A feeling that I was all too familiar with. I'd felt empty pretty much my entire life. But I didn't understand why I had the feeling again now. I had everything I wanted. *Finally.* Why didn't my brain understand that?

I needed coffee. That would fix my mood. I was just tired. I hadn't slept well since the summer semester let out a few weeks ago. Having no obligations was something that people usually looked forward to. I wasn't one of those people. Vacations weren't something I looked forward to in the slightest. I needed constant distractions, not time to let my mind wander.

I was exhausted. That was it. A coffee that I didn't have time to grab would certainly fix all my problems.

"Hi, Professor Hunter," a girl said and waved as I walked past her. The girl next to her puckered her lips and gave me sex eyes.

I didn't have time for this. I was used to the attention around campus. Although I tried my best to ignore it. Or at least shut it down as fast as possible. "Have a good first day of classes," I said without even really looking at them and then continued walking. Last spring I had been pretty sure one of my students was stalking me. I almost had to file a restraining order. Not engaging was for the best. Besides, it took too much energy to try to be nice especially when I was in a foul mood. And I seemed to always be in a foul mood recently.

"You too, Professor Hunter!" she said from behind me. The other girl giggled.

I sighed and didn't turn back around. I had no interest in dating my students. And they clearly didn't know anything about me, or they'd be running in the opposite direction rather than batting their fake eyelashes at me. Despite what my brother thought, hooking up with a co-ed was not why I took this job. At all.

I pushed through the door of the little coffee shop on Main Street.

The door slammed into someone, splashing coffee down the front of her... I swallowed hard. For just a moment I was transfixed by the droplets of coffee that cascaded down her chest, disappearing beneath her tank top. But then I heard the thud as her cup landed on the ground and it pulled me out of my trance. Just as I was about to force my eyes to her face, she started to slip. I grabbed her waist to prevent her from falling.

"I'm so sorry. Are you alright?" I asked. I took in the flush of her cheeks. The way she melted into my arms. And the fact that she didn't look up at me at all. Her eyes were firmly rooted to the ground.

"I'm fine," she said. "It wasn't hot anymore."

I wanted to ask her why she was carrying cold coffee around, but I bit my tongue. It wasn't any of my business. I should have immediately stepped back, but I couldn't seem to drop my hands from her waist. And the more she melted into me, the less I wanted to let go. *Look at me.* She kept her attention on the ground. The blush of her cheeks intensified the longer I held her. I had no desire to ever let her go. I leaned in a little closer. She smelled like something floral that I couldn't quite pinpoint. But I had a feeling that I could figure it out if I got even closer.

The buzz of the coffee shop eventually registered in the back of my mind. People would recognize me here. Did she recognize me? I slowly let my hands fall from her waist, wishing that I didn't have to. "I'm afraid I've ruined your shirt." *Stop staring at her chest.*

She stepped back and spread her hands over the stains on her blue tank top, clearly not realizing that she was basically feeling herself up in front of me. And I couldn't peel my eyes away.

"Oh, crap, I have an 8 a.m. I don't have time to change," she said in almost a whisper.

I couldn't bear to watch her flounder. Even if I did find the blush of her cheeks intoxicating. "Here." I put down my satchel and pulled off my sweater. It was too hot today for it anyway. I didn't realize it outside, but the coffee shop was certainly stifling. Fortunately I was wearing a dress shirt underneath my sweater. And just like this girl, I didn't have time to go back and change either.

"That's okay. I can't take that." She laughed but it sounded forced. "I'll be fine." She stepped to the side so I could pass. Her cheeks flushed even more when I didn't move.

She was finally looking at me. I could have gotten lost in her blue eyes. And her red hair was calling for me to sink my fingers into... *Breathe.* I looked at her backpack. She had just mentioned having an 8 a.m. She was clearly a student. "I insist. First day of classes." I shrugged. "You'll want to make a good first impression."

She took the sweater from me. "Thank you." Her voice was so quiet.

I studied her as she pulled the sweater over her head. Her thin waist dipped down to a luscious... What the hell was I doing? *She's a student.* Luckily the sweater covered her ass so I had to stop staring. Her eyes met mine again. And then it was like she couldn't look away. Like she couldn't manage to look anywhere but at me. For just a moment it felt like we were alone. The coffee shop disappeared.

"I'm sorry, I have to go, I'm going to be late," she said.

I wanted to ask for her name. For her number. Anything. But I pressed my lips together so none of what I was thinking would come out. There was nothing to say. I was a professor. She was a student.

She smiled and then walked out of the coffee shop. I stared after her. My baggy sweater, a pair of black leggings, and bright red rain boots. She somehow made the combination look like the sexiest thing in the world.

I shook my head, dismissing the thought. But it was hard to forget that for just a moment, while she was in my arms, it had been easier to breathe.

Chapter 2

Wednesday

It had been another restless night. But for once, I wasn't plagued with thoughts of my past. My dreams had been consumed by the timid redhead from the coffee shop. All I could focus on was the blush of her cheeks and those bright blue eyes.

She wasn't necessarily an undergrad. She easily could have been a grad student. Or maybe she didn't even go here at all. She could have been on her way to work. But who referred to going to work as having an 8 a.m.? And only students carried backpacks.

Grad student. That's what I was hoping for. The possibilities didn't matter in my dreams, though. I dreamt about wrapping my fingers in her hair and guiding her lips to my...

Breathe. I had woken up with a hard-on and I was regretting my decision to not relieve myself. I walked into Smith Hall and made my way up the stairs. I needed to focus on the class I was about to teach. But no matter what I thought, my mind kept running back to her.

Why hadn't I said anything to her when I had a chance? I could have asked her if she was a student. Or at least asked for her name. For some reason, I'd completely shut down. I'd been captivated by her face. The blush of her cheeks. Why couldn't I get her out of my head?

I stopped outside my classroom and pulled my hand down my face. I needed to stop obsessing. We ran into each other once. I was never going to see her again. Which was for the best. She was most likely a student, probably an undergraduate one. I sighed. I had a class to teach. That would at least be a good distraction from her for the next 50 minutes.

I opened the door to my classroom and walked in. The room immediately fell silent. I dropped my satchel on the desk and turned to my new students. This was one of my favorite parts of teaching. Setting the initial tone for the upcoming semester. Seeing all the new faces and some old ones. "Welcome to Comm 212 - Oral Communication in Business. I am Professor Hunter."

When my eyes scanned the room, all the air left my lungs.

There she was. Sitting in the back row of my class-room right next to a window. She was staring out the window, not even listening to me. The sun shining through the window made her hair even brighter. It practically shimmered, drawing all my attention to her.

Fuck. Me.

She slowly turned. And made direct eye contact with me. The color immediately rose to her cheeks.

For just a second, it felt like I couldn't breathe. Like someone had punched me right in the gut. Any hope I had that the girl from the coffee shop wasn't a student was gone. I cleared my throat and forced myself to look away from her. "I know that most of you are seniors and have waited until the last minute to take this class. I haven't met a student yet who was excited about Comm. Heck, I don't even like teaching it."

Light laughter broke out amongst the students. I kept my eyes off the redhead, even though all I wanted to do was stare. If she was sitting in this class, she was most likely a senior. At least 21, maybe even 22 already. I tried to dismiss the thought. It didn't matter that she was in her twenties, she was still a student. *My* student.

"Seriously, we have to teach this class on a rotating basis. I'm not even sure I'm qualified. I promise it won't be as painful as the rumors have made it out to be, though. I tend to grade rather easily so there's no need to be nervous when you're giving speeches." I was rambling. I could feel her eyes on me. It was so hard not to stare. "But I like to jump right into things. I'm going to take attendance. When I call your name, please stand and tell me one interesting fact about yourself. Then I'll stop torturing you and you can all leave class early." I needed to get out of this classroom. I needed to get away from her. I needed time to force myself to stop thinking about the vision of her from my dreams. "Not so bad, right?" I looked down at my class list. Okay, Raymond Asher."

I stole a glance at the redhead. She was staring at me in horror. I winced and turned away. Why was she looking at me like that? *She's upset that you're her professor because she wants you too.* No, she was probably just embarrassed from the other day. Clearly. Her face was crimson.

A boy in the middle of the classroom stood up from his desk. "Hi, I'm Ray. Hmmm, one interesting thing about myself? Well, I'm pretty good with the ladies."

"Yeah right, Ray," the girl beside him teased.

He tried to kiss the girl on the cheek when he sat back down, but she pulled away.

What a pompous prick. "Well I can tell we'll all be enjoying your speeches," I lied. "Ellie Doyle?"

A girl stood up in the front of the room and began talking, but I tuned her out. Every now and then someone would say something funny. Or they would be so unbearably awkward that it was better that I wasn't paying attention. I was just waiting to see what *her* name was. I read through the list on autopilot. I needed a name for that perfect face. A name for my dreams. *Jesus.* I sat down behind my desk. Just thinking about her was making me hard. What was I, twelve?

I looked down at my list for what felt like the millionth time. This wasn't going to be her either. "Tyler Stevens?" I said.

I had to be getting close. I was near the end of the list and she looked so nervous.

"Penny Taylor?"

No one answered. *I guess that's not her.* "Penny Taylor?" I asked again, ready to cross the name off my list.

She slowly stood up. "Hi everyone, I'm Penny."

I watched her cheeks turn pink. I wanted to wrap my arms around her and tell her she had no need to be nervous. Instead, I stared at her. *Penny.* It suited her. As soon as I heard it, I couldn't imagine her name being anything else.

"Unfortunately, you'll need another of me for my thoughts," she said and quickly sat back down.

"Weird," some girl scoffed near the front of the class. A few other people around her snickered.

Fuck off. That had been the most interesting answer I had ever heard during one of these exercises. I hoped my smile reassured her. "A penny for your thoughts. Well I guess I'll have to bring my piggy bank with me on Friday." I forced my eyes away from her. "Mia Thompson?"

But the clanging sound of metal made me snap my eyes back to her. The boy sitting next to her had just tossed a penny onto her desk. He leaned over and whispered something to her.

My pulse slowed as I watched their exchange. I was tempted to yell at them for talking during my class. But that wasn't why I was upset. I wanted that boy to stay away from her. What was his name? I scanned the list. *Tyler Stevens.*

"Class dismissed," I said as soon as the last person went. But that didn't shut Tyler Stevens up. He talked to her for a few more moments before winking at her and leaving the room.

As soon as he was gone, my eyes landed back on Penny. Her face flushed and she looked down at the ground as she walked toward the door. There was a small, tense smile on her face as she passed by my desk without looking at me.

I stood up from my chair and reached out for her before my brain could tell me to stop. My fingers grazed down her forearm.

I saw her shiver from my touch.

It was almost like I had the opposite reaction. If felt like she had shocked me. And that feeling of being able to breathe easier returned. "Miss Taylor, I'm sorry again about your shirt."

She folded her arms across her chest. "Oh, no, I'm sorry."

I tried not to laugh. "Why are you sorry? I was the one that hit you with the door."

"I just meant, about taking your sweater. I'll bring it back."

"No rush. I have quite a few," I gestured to the one I was wearing. It was identical to the one I had given her, except it was a different color. I had put it on because I had been thinking of her this morning. And all last night. And all day yesterday.

She looked up into my eyes. My fantasies from the previous night wanted to escape. My eyes wandered to her lips. Her perfectly kissable lips. It was like they were begging for my attention.

"I didn't realize you were a professor," she said.

I smiled and forced myself to stop staring at her lips. Maybe I was right about why she looked shocked to see me walk into the classroom. Her flushed cheeks. The way she was staring at me. *She wants me. She wishes I wasn't a professor.* The thought was numbing. It didn't matter if she did. She was my student for Christ's sake. "It's more fun when students think of me as their peer. I believe it fosters better learning." It was the most professional answer I could think of.

She didn't say anything. She just stared at me and then suddenly looked embarrassed. "Well I should probably go. I'll see you Friday, Professor Hunter."

I was used to my students calling me that. I had been a professor for a while now. But there was something about the way *she* said it that affected me. I could just imagine her moaning it when I was on top of her. *Stop.* I nodded to her as she walked away. "Miss Taylor."

After she exited the room, I realized that I hadn't even handed out a syllabus. So much for setting the tone for the semester.

Chapter 3

Wednesday

Breathe in. Breathe out. I tried to slow my breath and focus on it like my therapist had instructed. *A deep breath in. A slower breath out.* But there was a reason why I was running instead of meditating. Or doing the yoga Dr. Clark suggested. One thing I liked about the life I left behind in New York City was the fast pace. It was hard to just switch that off because I was in a new state. And I tended to like to do things fast.

I ran on the brick path around the green and tried to focus straight ahead, even though my eyes wanted to wander. Normally I liked to run where the students weren't. During the day meant a run on Main Street because the restaurants weren't frequented as much until nighttime. After dinner meant a run on the green because students were done walking to classes for the day. I avoided the free access to the University gym altogether. I'd only made that mistake once. And I usually skipped the one in my building too, because it was a little easier to breathe slowly when I was outside. That was one great thing about leaving NYC. The air was cleaner. So Main Street and the green were my main options, at the designated time to avoid students.

But today I was spicing things up. A run on the green as soon as my classes were done. Which meant there were still tons of students walking around. But I was only focused on finding one.

My eyes wandered to the students sitting in the grass studying and playing frisbee and… I narrowed my eyes. I was pretty sure there was a group of them doing yoga. Dr. Clark would have been thrilled if I told her at my next appointment that I did yoga on the green with some of my students. I shook away the thought. Honestly that was probably the last thing he'd want to hear. I was supposed to be focusing on myself. That was why I'd moved here in the first place. A fresh start.

And yet, I was scouring the green, not breathing slowly like instructed, hoping to find a flash of red hair. I hadn't been able to stop thinking about Penny since class. Well, really since she first ran into me yesterday in the coffee shop. If I was supposed to focus on breathing slowly, it felt like I needed to be around her. She made breathing feel a little easier. I just didn't realize that I had been suffocating before I ran into her.

Breathe in. Breathe out. It was even easier to breathe just thinking about her. The way she'd looked at me with her big blue eyes after class. *"I didn't realize you were a professor."* Her words had caught me off guard. I didn't want to be her fucking professor. I wanted to bend her over my desk and... *Breathe.*

I pushed my fingers through my sweaty hair, removing it from my forehead. What the fuck was I doing out here? I didn't know Penny's schedule. Maybe she had a class right now. Or maybe she liked to go to the library to study. Or did she prefer to stay in her dorm? Or maybe she lived off-campus, which made this run even more pointless. Well, not exactly pointless. Because exercise helped distract me. Specifically running helped.

I turned the corner and headed back toward Main Street. There were things that probably helped distract me more than running. Sex for one. I was pretty sure that would be the best distraction.

"Professor Hunter!" someone called.

I turned to see one of the girls leading the yoga session jogging over. *Oh fuck me.* Not just a random student. It was Kristen Dwyer. I kept running, trying to pretend I hadn't heard her. I'd had her in one of my classes last semester. She was extremely bright. And most definitely had ulterior motives when she came to my office hours all those times for extra help. She didn't need extra help. But I'd offered it anyway because it was my job and tried to ignore the way she looked at me. I kept trying to ignore it even though she just kept showing up like this. It had gotten to the point where I thought she might be stalking me. I'd almost filed a restraining order and now I kind of wished I had. Or that I'd at least stuck to my normal routine and not run on the green in the middle of the day. I was asking for trouble.

"Hi, Professor Hunter," she said as she eased into a pace that matched my own.

"Hi, Miss Dwyer," I said without really looking at her. I'd already run five miles and she was an athlete herself. Outrunning her wasn't an option.

"I'm so bummed that I don't have any of your classes this semester," she said.

"Mhm. I'm mostly teaching senior classes this year."

"Oh. Maybe next year then?"

I didn't respond. I just tried to pick up my pace. Sure, I knew I was being an asshole. But she was a student. And I was a…professor. I sighed and wiped the sweat off my forehead. I needed to keep reminding myself of my own profession. But not when it came to her. There was another student that was preoccupying my mind. And not in a professional manner.

"Are your office hours still the same this year?" she asked.

"Yes, but they're only for current students." I glanced at her out of the corner of my eye. She was tall and thin and male students tended to drool when she passed them in the halls. But physically she reminded me a lot of my ex. That was a reminder I didn't need.

"Oh." She shrugged like she didn't care. Or maybe like she didn't plan on listening. "Do you want to do some yoga?"

I looked over at her again. I had a feeling she wasn't talking about normal yoga. More like yoga in bed. Naked. "No. I need to get home."

"Are you sure? It's a great exercise after a long run. It's really good for your joints. And flexibility."

It was possible that she wasn't flirting with me. That it was in my head. But then I glanced over at her again and she was staring at the front of my shorts. *Jesus.* "I'm sure. Have a good semester, Miss Dwyer." I picked up my pace, despite my aching muscles, and ran away from her. And I had the oddest sensation that Penny was the one that should be running. Running away from me. I started running even faster.

When I thought I finally lost my stalker, I pushed through the door of one of the small stores on Main Street, completely out of breath. A moment to catch my breath in here would be good, just in case Miss Dwyer was still hot on my trail. I walked through the store looking at all the random items to decorate a home with. I had plenty of empty shelves, but I didn't need any décor. I leaned past one of the shelves to glance outside. There was no sign of Miss Dwyer. I was about to make my way out when a small ceramic pig caught my eye. *"You'll need another of me for my thoughts."*

I pressed my lips together. I'd told Penny I'd bring a piggy bank on Friday. At the time I hadn't been serious. It was just to let her know I'd understood her joke when the other students had snickered. But actually bringing a piggy bank would be a nice gesture. A friendly one. Possibly even an appropriate one. I wanted her to know that I was listening. That I cared about what she said in class. Fine, maybe the gesture wasn't that appropriate. Especially since it was equally as easy to picture her smiling at me during her speech as it was to envision her smiling up at me naked in my bed.

I walked around the store a bit more searching for a piggy bank, but there wasn't one. Then I searched another store. And another. And another. Slowly making my way down Main Street, trying to find the one thing that apparently wasn't available anywhere. I'd never owned a piggy bank growing up. And I was pretty sure I hadn't touched any change in years. I was the last person that would know where to find one. But once I set my mind on a task, it was hard for me to stop.

At the end of Main Street, I looked up at the last possible store to look in. A dollar store. I laughed. And I'd certainly never been in one of those before. But there was a first time for everything. I walked in and a bell jingled above my head. Was that to notify employees of shoppers coming in or out? Certainly it was for people coming in. Because no one could steal that much valuable inventory from a dollar store.

I shoved my hands into my shorts' pockets as I roamed through the disorganized aisles until suddenly I found one. A tiny pink piggy bank. I lifted it up. It was perfect. And my bad vibes toward the store disappeared. Hell, this store had everything. I caught my reflection in a small mirror. I was a disheveled mess from my run. It was hard to imagine I'd ever been in New York at all. The suits. The money. Honestly, I looked like I fit in hanging out in here. Not just the dollar store. But Newark. I smiled to myself and looked back down at the piggy bank. Or maybe I was losing my mind.

The cashier rolled her eyes at me as I pulled out a credit card to pay for the dollar piggy bank. For a moment I was debating whether I should stop by the bank to get some pennies to fill it with. But I had a feeling the bank teller would have the same reaction as this cashier. Besides, what would I do with a roll full of pennies?

By the time I walked back out on Main Street it was dark. I'd been wandering around for hours in sweaty workout clothes searching for a piggy bank for a student. I looked down at the paper bag. *God damn it.* I'd turned into the stalker.

Chapter 4

Thursday

I could hear music blaring outside. For such an expensive apartment, the walls seemed rather thin. I turned off my computer and glanced out the window at the rowdy students. It was raining. Again. When I was in college, I wouldn't have let a little rain keep me from a party either. But that was a long time ago.

I stretched my arms above my head. There were no papers to grade or anything else to distract me. My lesson plans were already written for the next few weeks. None of that was on my mind though.

Penny Taylor. I was tempted to look her up in the school directory. But what did it matter? She was in my Comm class. Which meant she was a senior. Which meant she was off-limits for two more semesters. There was nothing else I needed to know.

Why didn't that dismiss her from my thoughts? If anything, telling myself I couldn't have her made it even more impossible to push the thought of her aside.

I needed fresh air. I stood up from my desk and walked out into the hall. I ignored the empty walls and lack of any decorations. There was no reason to hang images of people that weren't here. That wasn't a cure for loneliness.

I laughed. There was no cure for being lonely. Was that really why I was fixated on Penny? I pulled on my jacket. She wasn't exactly the person to help me if that was my problem. Before pressing the elevator button, I grabbed an umbrella.

Besides, it was better when I was alone. I exited into the parking garage instead of the lobby so I wouldn't risk having to socialize with anyone. It was definitely better when I was alone. I stepped out in the rain and opened my umbrella.

The sound of the rain against the fabric of the umbrella was soothing. I didn't move here to find a girlfriend. I was here for a fresh start. I walked down Main Street, trying to clear my head. Now that classes had started back up, I was going to be fine. Or at least focused. I sighed. Who the hell was I kidding? The only thing I was focused on was a certain undergrad.

And then she was there. I blinked, assuming I was imagining her. No, that was definitely Penny walking a few paces ahead of me. Her red hair was unmistakable. I should have turned around as soon as I saw her. I needed distance from her if anything. Instead, I increased my pace.

She was dressed in a ridiculous sparkly blue miniskirt and a pair of heels that were way too high for her current state. She was stumbling down Main Street, obviously drunk. All I could focus on were her long legs. The rain on her skin almost shimmered as much as her skirt.

I knew I shouldn't. I knew talking to her outside of class was the last thing I should be doing. But I couldn't let her walk home like that. It was my responsibility, as her professor, to make sure she was safe. Right? "Miss Taylor, is that you?" I called.

She stopped mid-step, like hearing my voice froze her. "Um...no. You have the wrong person," she said and quickly started walking again without even glancing at me over her shoulder.

She still looked wobbly in her heels. And clearly she didn't want me to approach her. I knew I should let her go. But I couldn't. What if she fell? *Or worse.* Someone could take advantage of her. It happened on college campuses all the time. She needed my help. I needed to keep her safe.

Again, I knew I should let her go. Instead, I started jogging up to her. I wasn't some frat boy creep. I'd help her get home. I wouldn't even touch her. I'd be a good professor, helping out a student in need. That was it. "Penny, stop!"

She turned around and stared up at me. But her eyes didn't stay on my face. They slowly wandered down my body, like she was drinking me in.

She's drunk. She doesn't know what she's doing. But I just stood there, letting her do it. I liked her eyes on me. Besides, it gave me a moment to stare at her long legs again. And her... I swallowed hard. She was wearing a white tank top. In the rain. *Fuck.* What was she trying to do to me? I forced my eyes back to her face.

"Professor Hunter, I'm sorry..." she let her voice trail off and folded her arms across her chest to help hide her breasts.

Professor Hunter. What was it about the way she said it? It just sounded sexy falling from her lips. And wrong. So fucking wrong. "You like to apologize when you've done nothing wrong," I said. I was the one doing something wrong. I couldn't stop staring at her. I stepped forward to prevent myself from ogling her. And to get her under my umbrella to keep her dry. Mostly the keeping her dry thing, of course. I tried to tell myself I had no ulterior motives for being closer to her. I gripped my umbrella tighter so I wouldn't touch her.

As soon as I drew closer, I saw the mascara under her eyes. And her beautiful blue irises were surrounded by red. She had been crying. Had I been too late? Had someone already hurt her? I resisted pulling her close. That was the last thing she probably wanted. And the last thing I should do. "Is everything alright, Penny?"

"I'm fine," she said too quickly for me to believe her.

"Then what are you doing out so late all by yourself?" I did care about her safety. I truly did. But I was also curious about her being alone. I thought about the boy that had talked to her in class. Were they dating? Was she dating anyone? And where the hell had she come from? A party? A date? What kind of prick wouldn't walk her home?

"I could ask the same of you," she said.

"I was just going for a walk."

"Me too."

I laughed. She drew a little closer to me and her arm brushed against mine. She wanted to be closer to me. But I'd promised myself I wouldn't touch her. She was probably just cold from the chilly rain.

"Are you cold, Penny?"

She nodded up to me.

I handed her the umbrella as I shrugged off my jacket. I held it out for her. She hesitated for a moment before slowly slipping one arm in and then the other. Had no one ever helped her into her jacket before? What kind of pathetic men had she been dating?

It was none of my business. I took the umbrella back and held it above both of us again. "Well you really shouldn't be out alone this late, Penny. Especially in those walking clothes." *Walking clothes? What the fuck was I even saying?*

"Neither should you."

I laughed. I was pretty sure jeans and a t-shirt were more appropriate in the rain than her outfit. Her skirt barely covered a thing. I had to tear my eyes away from her to prevent myself from pushing her against one of the brick buildings and kissing the sadness off her face. *Jesus. You're her professor.* "Is your dorm near here? It would make me feel much better if I escorted you home."

"I live in Sussex."

"This way then," I said, and placed my hand on the small of her back for just a second. I immediately removed it. What happened to not touching her?

We walked in silence for a few minutes. Every now and then she'd stumble slightly and I'd have to touch her again. I didn't want her to fall. It had nothing to do with the fact that it was hard to keep my hands to myself. And each time we touched, I kept thinking that it didn't feel wrong. Even though I knew it was.

What would she do if we wandered off the path into the green? If I pulled her on top of me in the wet grass? How would she react if I kissed her neck? If my fingers slid up her skirt and gripped her firm ass?

Breathe. I was trying to protect her. Clearly she only needed protection from me. I kept my eyes trained straight ahead and willed myself to keep my fucking hands to myself.

"I'm not good at giving speeches," she said, finally breaking the awkward silence my wandering thoughts had created. "I feel like I should just drop your class."

That was the last thing I wanted. I could control myself. I didn't want to stop seeing her. Having her in my class was the only way that was possible. Because this was probably the only time I'd ever see her again outside of a classroom. *Probably? Definitely.* It was definitely the only time I'd get with her outside of class. The thought made me was to reach out and touch her. *Stop.*

"I wish you wouldn't," I said. "If you ever need extra help, I have open office hours. I really am a fairly easy grader for Comm." I could picture her coming to my office. Locking the door behind her. Asking me to help teach her. *Breathe.*

"It's going to be extra painful when you fail me, though."

"Why extra painful?" I knew it wasn't just me. She was probably picturing my hands on her too.

"Because you...I mean I. Well, you're..." she let her voice trail off.

It didn't matter what she was going to say. I was her professor. "Well it does seem that you aren't great at giving speeches." I laughed even though I didn't find it funny. Was she stumbling over her words because she was drunk? Or because I was making her uncomfortable? Or was it because she was nervous around me because she wanted me too? I took a deep breath. "Like I said, you can come by any time." I forced my eyes back on the path as we continued to walk the length of the green.

"Have you been a professor here for long?" she asked.

"Not long at all. I do love it here, despite how much it rains. Besides, you never know what you'll find during a long walk in the rain." I smiled down at her. I had officially lost all control. Now I was blatantly flirting with her. She was drunk though. Maybe she wouldn't remember this in the morning.

Before I even realized it, we were standing outside her dorm.

She stepped out from under my umbrella, letting the rain fall on her. She was a fucking vision. My eyes traveled to the tops of her breasts. The way the rain glistened on her pale skin. I could so easily imagine licking each drop of rain off.

"Here," she said and pulled off my jacket.

I shook my head, pushing the image away. The fabric of her wet tank top clung to her skin. I didn't want anyone else to see her with her wet tank top. I wanted the image to be mine and mine alone. "No, you can keep it."

"I've been stealing all your clothes. Soon you'll have nothing left."

"That does seem to be your plan." I smiled at the thought of her wanting me naked.

"I insist," she said and held the jacket back out to me.

I reluctantly took it. It was late. Hopefully she'd get back to her room without anyone seeing her.

"I'm not in trouble, am I?"

What? Scolding her was the last thing on my mind. Although now visions of spanking her... *stop.* "You're a senior, you're of legal age to drink, and you're allowed to wear what you like. Why would you be in trouble?"

She paused for a second. "You're right. And I was only walking, after all. Thank you for escorting me home, Professor Hunter."

God. I could feel myself growing hard. The wet tank top. The way she said my name. I wanted to devour every inch of her. I was so fucked. "I'll see you at 8 a.m. sharp, Miss Taylor."

"It's a date." Her eyes got huge and she threw a hand over her mouth.

A date.

She turned quickly away from me and fumbled with the sensor pass to open the door.

I practically groaned when it clicked. I didn't want her to disappear. I wanted this moment to last forever. Because this was the closest I'd ever get to her. A date. If only she knew how much I wanted that. More than that. I couldn't stop thinking about how sweet her lips would taste.

She turned around for one last moment and our eyes met. I didn't acknowledge her date comment. She had nothing to be embarrassed about. Didn't she see how much I wanted her too?

The door closed with a thud. And all I could think about was how I wished I was on the other side with her. I wanted her to wrap her drunken arms around me and beg me to stay. I wanted to call her mine for just one night. One night. That's all I was asking.

I sighed. I really was a shitty professor.

Chapter 5

Friday

I splashed water onto my face. It felt like I hadn't slept in a week. Last night I should have just fallen asleep and dreamt of her like I'd been doing every night since we'd met. It was wrong, but it was innocent enough. I wished I had done that.

But the wet tank top. The way she said my name. The way she looked at me. It was too fucking much.

So I had thought about her when I wrapped my hand around my stiff cock. I pictured her lips around me. Her moaning Professor Hunter over and over again.

It was wrong.

I knew that.

Yet I came faster than I'd like to admit.

And now I was losing my mind. Just thinking about her again was like torture. I needed to dismiss the thoughts of Penny Taylor from my mind. She was off-limits. Period. I had one moment of weakness. It wouldn't happen again.

I quickly got dressed, not bothering to dress professionally. Maybe if I could get her to stop looking at me in *that* way, then I could stop staring at her in awe. And I was pretty sure I just wanted her underneath of me because I knew I couldn't have her. Her thoughts probably aligned with mine. So today, I wouldn't look like a professor. I'd look like the way I felt…like shit because I hadn't been sleeping. Because thoughts of her kept me up every night. I grabbed my glasses off the nightstand. They wouldn't really help my cause of not looking like a professor, but my eyes were too tired to wear contacts. I walked out of my room.

"Long night?" my housekeeper, Ellen, asked as she set down a plate on the kitchen island.

"Why would you say that?" It came out defensive. I instantly regretted my tone. It's not like she knew what plagued my thoughts. She had no idea what I had done last night.

She laughed, never one to be affected by my moods. "Dear, you look like you haven't slept a wink. The glasses. Whatever you have going on there," she added and pointed to my hair.

I ran my fingers through my hair as I sat down at the counter. My hair had gotten wet last night and I hadn't bothered to try to tame the curls. I knew I looked ridiculous. That's what I was going for today. Because if Penny stared at me with her flushed cheeks one more time I was going to fucking cum in my pants. "It's Friday. None of my students will care if I look a mess when they're suffering through hangovers."

"To the contrary, James, you look very handsome. Just a little tired is all."

Great. I was hoping I looked like a disheveled mess. I took a bite of my omelet and immediately felt a little better. Ellen's cooking had a way of always calming me down. "This is delicious."

"I know." She walked over to the fridge. "Anything in particular you want me to prep for this weekend?"

I shook my head even though I knew she wasn't looking at me. I couldn't even help my mind from wandering. What did Penny like to eat? *What the hell am I even thinking?*

"I'll make a lasagna for you."

"I can fend for myself over the weekend," I said.

She turned back toward me and put her hand on her hip. "You know perfectly well that you don't know how to cook a thing."

"That's not exactly true, Ellen." I took a sip of my coffee. "I know how to…"

"Yes, your signature dish. Dear, you use sauce from a jar. *A jar.* That hardly counts as a homemade meal." She smiled at me and turned back to the fridge. "Besides, the agreement was that I wouldn't work weekends as long as you let me make you a few things ahead of time that you could reheat. I don't want you to starve. Or eat takeout for every meal."

I didn't mind takeout. But she was right, I preferred her cooking. And I knew she thought it was her job to take care of me. I relied on her way too much and we both knew it. She was my chef, my housekeeper, and really the only friend I had in Delaware.

I finished my coffee and stood up. "I'll see you on Monday, Ellen. Have a nice weekend."

"You too, dear. And just give me a call if you need anything."

I didn't respond. Even if I did need something, I wouldn't call her. I had given her the weekends off for a reason. She was my only friend here, but I was certain I wasn't hers. Besides, who could stand me for a whole week? I could barely stand myself. And the thought of Ellen quitting on me made my chest feel tight.

I grabbed my jacket from last night and a whiff of Penny's sweet floral scent hit me. I closed my eyes for a second. She smelled like cherry blossoms. That was it. Cherries. And sunshine. *Get a grip.* No one smelled like sunshine. I just missed the sun from the last few days of rain. That was all.

Luckily today the rain had stopped. I kept my head down as I walked on Main Street. I needed the fresh air, but I didn't want to have to interact with any of the students. That was my new motto. Just...stay away from them at all costs. No fraternizing.

By the time I reached Smith Hall, I felt re-energized. I had a class full of eager students to teach. And I was going to help them excel in Comm. Nothing else.

I opened the door to my classroom and kept my eyes focused on the front of the room. If I didn't look at Penny, it would be like she wasn't even there. I put my satchel down on the desk and took off my jacket before her lingering scent on the fabric consumed me.

I put my hands into the pockets of my jeans to remind myself to keep them to myself and stared at the front row of the class. *Stay focused.* "Doesn't everyone look alert today? So, I think the best thing to do is probably hear about your nights." *What the hell is wrong with me?* That wasn't on my lesson plan. The words had just slipped out. I wanted to know if Penny remembered last night. I quickly thought of how I could spin this ridiculous assignment. "The more comfortable we are with each other, the easier it will be to stand up here later in the semester and give fantastic speeches. Everyone up to share?"

Some of my students groaned. I wanted to see Penny's reaction. But I knew it was better not to look. *Breathe.* My eyes refused to listen to reason though, and they wandered over to Penny. She was staring right back at me. I had tried to look a mess today, but she was staring at me like I was anything but. I immediately dropped her gaze, sat down, and pulled out the class list from my satchel. I went through the names on autopilot, barely registering their responses. The first few people swore they were just studying. Some people mentioned that they weren't lame and had gone partying.

I stared at the roster, hating the name even though I didn't know the kid. "Tyler Stevens?" I tried to hide the disdain from my voice.

Tyler stood up. "Honestly I got drunk and made a fool of myself. I was with this smart, beautiful girl, and I probably blew my shot with her."

Penny turned away from him. Was he the piece of shit that made her cry last night? I was going to kill him. The paper crinkled in my fist. First fantasizing over a student and now wanting to murder one? I let the list drop to the desk. This was going to be a great semester.

"Sounds like an unfortunate series of events," I said and turned my attention to Penny. It looked like she gulped. I heard Tyler sigh as he sat back down, but my gaze didn't leave Penny's face. This was the only time it made sense for me to stare at her. I wasn't going to miss a second. "Penny Taylor," I said.

While she stood up, I pulled out the piggy bank from my satchel. The one I'd spent hours wandering around Main Street to find because I'd apparently turned into a stalker in my free time. It was special treatment. Special treatment drew attention. But I still bought it. And I still pulled it out for her to see. Hopefully everyone was too hungover to notice. "I came prepared today," I said. "You'll have to trust that I have some pennies in here." It was a lie. I didn't have any pennies. She was the only Penny I wanted.

Her cheeks turned rosy as she looked down at the piggy bank and then back at me. "I went for a walk in the rain with a stranger I met at a coffee shop."

I raised my eyebrows. She remembered. And she was more confident than the blush on her cheeks implied. Bolder. Sexier. "Sounds rather enchanting, Miss Taylor."

"It was."

Would she be horrified by what I did after our late-night walk? Knowing I masturbated to the thought of her in her wet tank top and the way my name fell from her lips? *God those lips.* I couldn't pull my gaze away from her. But it was time to call on the next student. The moment was over. Hours searching for a piggy bank had led to one minute with her. It was worth every second. I looked back down at my paper and called the next name. But I didn't hear a thing anyone else said.

I stood back up after the last person recalled their dull evening. "Well, it seems as though we have quite a few interesting characters this semester. And now I have a feel for things that you can all use improvement on. Speaking of which..." I rummaged through my satchel and pulled out the syllabi I'd forgotten to hand out on the first day of classes. But I was glad I did. It had given me a chance to get closer to Penny. Even though I knew I shouldn't. Even though every bone in my body was telling me to stop.

"I forgot to hand out the syllabus on Wednesday," I said and pulled the top packet off and dropped the rest on a boy's desk in the front. "Take one and pass it."

The boy grabbed one and handed the stack to his neighbor. As the papers began to cycle, I sat on top of my desk. "So your first presentation isn't for a few weeks, but you'll probably want to at least pick a topic soon so you can start mulling it over. All you need to do is pick a person that has inspired you in some way and tell us all about it. But please, I'm tired of hearing about everyone's grandparents, so try to think outside the box. And next week I'll start talking about how to give effective speeches, so you'll definitely want to incorporate that advice. Any questions?"

A girl in the front row's hand shot up.

"Yes?"

"Do we need your approval for our topic?"

"Not for this one. For later projects though, yes. But if you do have any questions you can always email me. My email is on the syllabus. And my office hours are listed on there too, if any of you have any questions or need some guidance on an assignment." I stared at Penny. She was the only one I wanted to take me up on that offer. The things I could do to her on my desk... *Stop.*

The two girls in front of Penny looked way too excited about my private office hours. I ignored them and watched as the pile of syllabi ran out right before reaching Penny.

She looked up at me, staring at the syllabus I was holding in my hand.

I smiled. What she didn't realize was that this one was special for her. This morning I'd told myself that I'd be better. No fraternizing. No socializing whatsoever with students. But I'd altered this syllabus last night. And technically it was the only other one I had. "Any other questions?" I asked and waited for her to raise her hand and ask for the syllabus I was holding. But...she didn't. She just stared at me. Maybe she wanted to approach me after class instead. Alone time that I was craving too. Or maybe she couldn't bear the thought of raising her hand and asking for it right now. I could tell she was shy. Bold and shy? I was starting to wonder if it was a lethal combination. Regardless, it meant we'd have one more moment today. And I wasn't upset about that at all.

"Okay then," I said. "Make sure to brainstorm this weekend. If you have an idea in mind on Monday, then my advice will be more beneficial. Have a great weekend."

I heard the pull of zippers on backpacks and feet shuffling. I waited for the class to empty out. And while waiting, Tyler started talking to Penny as she packed up her backpack. I couldn't hear what they were saying, but I hoped it was an apology for whatever shit he'd put her through last night.

She didn't look happy about the conversation, so I was surprised when she handed him her phone. It was like I was watching a horror movie playing out in slow motion and I didn't want to see the rest. I looked down at the syllabus and flipped to the page where my office hours and email were. I'd made my note to her hard to miss.

Miss Taylor,

I hate to think that you make walking around in the middle of the night a habit. But if you find yourself alone in the rain again, please do not hesitate to call me if you feel you are in need of an escort.

- J. H.

152-726-0133

An escort? What had I been thinking? That made my innocent gesture sound not so innocent. Maybe this was a mistake. I could just tell her that I'd bring her another syllabus on Monday. Or to just get a copy from her new friend, Tyler Stevens. I should be pushing her toward other people, not drawing her closer to myself. That was the right thing to do. But Tyler? He'd done something to make her cry. He was the reason she was walking around in the rain late at night in a white tank top. I trusted him less than I trusted myself.

"Excuse me, Professor Hunter?" Penny said nervously.

I looked up from the pages. I hadn't realized we were alone in the room. "How can I help you, Miss Taylor?"

"I didn't get a syllabus."

I knew what I was about to do was wrong. I'd written the note in a moment of weakness. But it could be a good thing. If she was ever in trouble, she'd call me. I'd help get her home safely. End of story. I was just trying to help. And even though I was hoping it would be more than that, I handed the syllabus to her anyway. "Well here you go then."

She gave me a small smile. "Thank you."

"So a walk in the rain with a stranger was a highlight to your eventful evening, was it?"

"It was the only good thing about last night, actually."

Mine too. "I had my suspicions after you referred to this class as a date."

She placed her hand over her eyes, and then slowly let it slide down her face. "I thought I had dreamt that." She looked completely mortified. And beautiful. God she was so fucking beautiful.

"I didn't realize I had made an appearance in your dreams, Miss Taylor." *Wrong.* It was the wrong thing to say. And yet…it didn't feel wrong.

"That's not what I…I mean you didn't. Well I meant…"

I laughed, knowing we had to end our conversation. Students for the next class would be walking in soon. And I had another class to get to. "Have a good weekend, Miss Taylor. Maybe on Monday I'll ask everyone to share a memorable dream they had over the weekend."

Her jaw actually dropped. The door creaked open and students for the next class started walking in. "Professor Hunter," she said as she quickly turned and walked toward the door.

My eyes wandered to her ass. She was wearing jean shorts that were short enough to kill me. If she bent over I was pretty sure I'd see parts of her I'd only imagined in my dreams the last few nights. I closed my eyes. I was losing control. And if there was one thing I knew about myself, I had a hard time getting that control back once I forfeited it.

Chapter 6

Sunday

I glanced at my phone again. I'd thought that maybe Friday night I would get a call from Penny. I pictured her in the rain again, waiting for me to walk her home. But the call hadn't come. So I'd pictured it again on Saturday night. It was all I could think about. But…again she didn't call. Now it was Sunday and my phone had no unread messages or missed calls.

Maybe she hadn't read the syllabus yet. That was the best-case scenario. Had I ever bothered to read my syllabi when I was in college? I couldn't remember, so probably not.

The worst-case scenario? She'd seen the note and reported me to the dean for being inappropriate. Either way, I would eventually get a call. Maybe she should report me. The things I had thought about doing to her…

"James, are you expecting a call?"

My eyes gravitated back to Dr. Clark. He was giving me a hard stare, and I realized he had probably been trying to get my attention for some time. I cleared my throat. "Hm?"

"You keep looking at your phone."

I slid my cell phone back into my pocket. "It's nothing. Just a work thing." A lie. A bad one at that. But what was I supposed to say? That I had been waiting all weekend for a student to text or call me? That it was the only thing I was looking forward to anymore? That it was the only thing I could think of? None of those answers were appropriate. I knew I should be talking about this. That was why I was here. To talk about my feelings and whatever. But I had no desire to be judged right now. I knew what I was doing was wrong. I didn't need him to tell me that.

"A work thing?" He raised both eyebrows. "On a Sunday? That seems a bit odd in your profession."

"Really, it's nothing. You have my undivided attention." He most definitely did not. I couldn't remember the last time I had been so distracted.

Dr. Clark put his notebook and pen down. "It's not about giving me your undivided attention. It's about you wanting to be here. It's about showing up for yourself, James. Putting yourself first for once in your life."

"You're right, I'm sorry. Lay it on me, Doc. I'm…present." I figured he'd like the meditation term.

"Great." He picked his notepad back up. "Let's move on then. How are the breathing exercises going that I gave you?"

I only really used them when my mind wandered to Penny. I was hoping that if I could focus on breathing maybe I could unfocus my mind on her. But it wasn't working. I couldn't stop thinking about her. Reminding myself to breathe around her did at least stop me from grabbing her and kissing her though. So it was probably working better than I realized. "It's easier when I run."

"It is easier with exercise. Speaking of which, how is the yoga going?"

I laughed. "I'm not doing yoga."

He wrote something down in his notebook and I frowned.

I hated when he wrote stuff down. I pressed my lips together so I wouldn't say anything else notebook worthy.

"How do you know you don't like yoga if you won't even try it?"

I had tried it. I'd tuned into a workout channel on TV and given it five whole minutes before I decided it wasn't for me. Everything was just so slow. If I did that for an hour I'd be bored out of my mind. But Dr. Clark wouldn't view five minutes as trying. I shrugged. "I have tried it. And I prefer more fast-paced exercises. Running, specifically. We've already talked about this."

"We have, but I was under the impression that you'd give it a real go. The whole point is to introduce new activities into your routine. Things to preoccupy your mind. And the best part about yoga is that it will facilitate your breathing exercises too. It's a win-win."

He wanted me to be able to control my thoughts. But I was in control of them. I thought about the phone in my pocket. *Most of them.* "I don't need to do yoga. I've been good. Really. And I have a very set routine."

"During the week, sure. But what about the weekends? What were you doing this morning?"

Thinking about that phone call. "I ate breakfast, went on a run, looked over my lesson plans for the week."

"And what are you planning to do with the rest of your afternoon and evening?"

I had nothing in mind other than obsessing over that phone call. But there was no reason for Penny to call me on a Sunday night. At least, I hoped not. Partying on a Sunday night was a bit extreme. Not that I was one to judge.

"Ah, the pause," Dr. Clark said. "Idle minds, James. Idle minds lead to nothing good and we both know it. Do yoga tonight."

"You're relentless."

"It's my job. And this time when you try it, give it more than five minutes."

He was a freaking mind reader. I sighed. He was also the best in the business, which was why I was sitting here. I basically paid him to read my mind. "Deal."

He nodded. "But reminding yourself to take deep breaths has been helping in general?"

"Mhm." *I guess.*

"Because we could also revisit the rubber band…"

"No, I'm good. Really." For a few weeks when I'd first started seeing him he'd made me wear a rubber band around my wrist. I was supposed to snap it whenever I lost focus on the present. I hated that damn rubber band. All I did all day was snap it. And if I put it on now? Penny was all I could think about. It would be slow torture.

"Okay, back to your work thing, then. What is that really about?"

It was the one thing I didn't want him to read my mind on. "Like I said before, it's nothing important."

"We've spent a lot of time together in the past several months. You've never been distracted by work before. Are your classes going well this semester?"

"Yes."

"Our time right now is supposed to be a priority. So what work thing could possibly need your attention on a Sunday afternoon then?"

Penny. There wasn't really any use in lying to Dr. Clark. He'd eventually get the truth out of me anyway. I knew my thoughts regarding Penny were wrong. And I also knew Dr. Clark would tell me that. Of course he would. So I might as well rip the Band-Aid off. Maybe him telling me I was being inappropriate would finally shake this girl out of my system. It was one thing for me to know what I wanted to do…it was another thing entirely for someone to stare at me accusingly. Screw it. I already thought I was a monster. I'm pretty sure he did too. "It isn't work…exactly. I gave my number to someone." I was trying to find the right words to describe Penny when Dr. Clark cut in.

"Oh, is it a colleague?"

Well, that seemed a hell of a lot better than a student. Dr. Clark's mindreading was a little off today, but I was thankful. "Yes. And I've been waiting all weekend to hear back from her." This was a conversation I could get on board with. I could certainly talk about my "colleague" for the rest of my session. Talking about Penny was a hell of a lot better than debating the merits of yoga.

Dr. Clark nodded. No smile. Just a simple nod, which made me think the next thing he said wasn't going to be good even though I hadn't even mentioned the student thing. "What are the school's policies about dating fellow faculty members?"

Probably more lenient than the ones regarding dating students. "I don't know. I'll have to look into it."

"James, I'll be honest with you. I don't think you're in the right state of mind to be in a relationship."

I hadn't been expecting that. For some reason I thought he'd be happy for me. But Dr. Clark and I weren't friends. He wasn't here to tell me good job. He was here to help me get my act together. "Who said anything about a relationship?" I said it as a joke, but still no smile from him. Yeah, he could see right through me.

"Do you think maybe you like this colleague of yours simply because she *is* off-limits?"

Huh. Did I like Penny simply because she was off-limits? Honestly...maybe. Possibly? A temptation for something I shouldn't do...it wouldn't be the first time. Dr. Clark and I both knew it. But then I thought about how it felt easier to breathe when I was around Penny. It wasn't about wanting something I couldn't have. If anything, it felt like wanting something I didn't deserve.

Because I could have Penny. I knew I could have her if I wanted. But I definitely didn't deserve someone like her. *Innocent. Sweet. Happy.*

"I don't think that's it," I said. "I was attracted to her before I realized she was a…co-worker." For a brief moment when she fell into my arms, before I saw her backpack. Before she showed up in my class.

"You really think you're ready to enter into a healthy relationship? One based on honesty? Complete honesty, James?"

He didn't say it, but I knew he was referring to the fact that sometimes I wasn't even honest with him. And he was my freaking therapist. I didn't have an answer for him. Was I ready? Did it matter? I couldn't be in a relationship with a student. "I want to be ready. But I don't know if I am. Aren't you supposed to tell me that?"

Finally he smiled. "That's what I'm trying to assess. You'll need to tell her about your past. Everything."

"That's a great way to end it before it even begins."

"I'm not talking about telling her on the first date. But before it gets serious."

Serious? I couldn't let it get serious. So that wasn't going to be a problem. Penny and I would always just be a student and her teacher. Minor flirtations maybe, but nothing more. "Yeah…I can do that."

"Great." He closed his notebook. "I say go for it."

"Really?"

"You've isolated yourself from your family and all your old friends. You've been alone in this town for far too long. This is the first time you've joked during a session. And I've never seen you smile this much."

I felt the curve of my lips. I hadn't even realized I'd been smiling.

"Whoever this woman is, she's clearly good for you."

If only you knew. But there was truth to what Dr. Clark said, even though he didn't have all the facts. Thinking about Penny did make me smile. I felt like joking again. Smiling again. If only she really was a colleague.

There was a knock on the door.

"Ah, our time is up," he said. "Same time next week?"

"Yeah." I stood up.

"You'll have to let me know what she says when she finally calls you. And she will."

I pulled out my cell phone and looked down at the blank screen as I walked back out into the reception area. Dr. Clark was right, Penny would eventually text me. From the outside I was a catch. But if she ever found out about my past? My secrets? The worst-case scenario would definitely ensue. She'd run straight to the dean. I'd get fired for fraternizing. Penny literally had the evidence in her syllabus. And I would never get another second chance at starting over. At least not as a professor.

But it felt good to be smiling again. I just wasn't sure that happiness was worth the risk.

Chapter 7

Monday

I did my best not to look at Penny as I walked into my classroom. But it was impossible to miss the extra makeup on her eyes. Or the short skirt. Or the fact that I was pretty sure she was trying to slowly kill me.

She didn't need that extra makeup or a skirt that short to get my attention. She looked gorgeous even in one of my sweaters and a pair of rainboots. But then I had the numbing thought that she wasn't trying to look good for me.

She'd never texted me, which was for the best. I knew that. I'd told myself that over and over again last night. For a moment my mind wandered to our last conversation. She mentioned dreaming about me in passing. And I'd teased her about it. I dropped my satchel, and then the next thing I knew, words I hadn't meant to speak were coming out of my mouth.

"Today I thought it might be fun to talk about a recent dream we've had," I said. *So much for my lesson plan. Again.* I smiled, trying to dismiss the thought. I'd already dug my heels into this topic, so I might as well get the information I was seeking. "And I'll kick us off." I tried to think of an appropriate answer. Anything to derail this train wreck of an assignment. But I could only think about one thing. *Penny.* I'd been lying to myself all weekend, trying to pretend she meant nothing. I'd been lying to my therapist about Penny too. And for once it would feel good to be honest. The truth would mean nothing to my students. Well, except for one.

"Ah, I remember one." I put my hands in my pockets, thinking about my latest dream. The dream that had been haunting me for the past week. "Last night I dreamt that it was pouring outside. And I just had this feeling that I was waiting for something to happen. Something exciting." I leaned against my desk and tried not to look up. I tried so fucking hard not to look. But I couldn't resist. I needed her to know I was thinking about her. Just one glance. How much harm could it do?

I locked eyes with Penny. And in that one second, I knew I was completely screwed. Her throat made a weird squeaking noise and her cheeks grew red. But she didn't look away. She stared back, and for some reason that made me want her even more. If we had been alone, I'd... *Breathe.*

I turned my attention back to the rest of the class. No one seemed to notice that I had been staring at her. Or that she had been staring back at me. The rest of my students were oblivious. Most of them probably weren't paying attention to me at all. If they were, they would have seen it. They would have seen how fucking much I wanted the gorgeous redhead in the back row. They would have known I wanted to devour her. That I was growing hard just thinking about it. *Breathe.*

I tried to focus on the rest of the students' dreams. A few of them were funny enough to make me laugh. My therapist was definitely right. I was happy. For once in my life I felt carefree. My eyes landed on Penny's name on my roster. Finally. I wanted her to flirt back. I wanted her to be brazen. Like it was just the two of us in this room. I needed to know if she was thinking about me too or if this was just in my head. "Penny Taylor," I said.

She quickly stood up, her skirt riding up higher on her thighs. A necklace plunged between her breasts, disappearing beneath her tank top. God, I was jealous of that necklace.

"I've actually been having the same dream now for several nights." She tucked a loose strand of hair behind her ear. "It's always raining, but there's a man there holding an umbrella above the two of us so that we don't get soaked."

Her gaze finally met mine. And for a moment it was just us. It felt right. But also wrong.

"And he kisses me," she said.

So fucking wrong. It was exactly what I wanted to hear. So why wasn't I happy to hear it?

Someone in the room laughed and Penny quickly sat back down.

It felt like all the air had been sucked out of the room as I watched Tyler lean over and whisper something in her ear. I turned away. I had a class to teach. Not whatever the hell I was currently doing. But the way I felt when she turned to Tyler gave me a pretty clear picture of why I was bothered by her dream. It was because I could never have her. I'd never get to kiss her. Taste her. We'd only ever be in each other's dreams.

I walked over to the board and picked up a piece of chalk, being careful not to snap it in my hand. *Breathe.* I wrote the word "emotion" on the board and turned back around, hoping that I looked composed. "The best advice I can give you is to make your speech personal. You want to draw emotion from your audience. You want to hook them." I made a fist to emphasize my point.

"That's why this first speech is easy. You're all speaking about someone you admire, someone who has helped shape who you've become. It's personal. Make your classmates aware of that. Don't ever be afraid to show emotion."

I looked out at all my students, making sure to not let my eyes focus on Penny, and tried to think of a way to make everything about today's class make sense. I was all over the place. And if I didn't get my shit together, one of these students might complain. I'd be fired for something other than sleeping with Penny. Which seemed like a waste. "Many psychologists will tell you that there are hidden meanings in your dreams, but I've never seen it that way. They're quite black and white. The first thing that comes to your mind when you think of your dream is what it truly means. And it's emotional." I looked at a boy on the opposite side of the class as Penny, trying hard not to glance at her. "Fear." I looked at the girl who had snickered at Penny. "Anger." And finally my eyes landed briefly on Penny. "Desire." I couldn't help it. *Breathe.*

"So when you think of who you're going to talk about, figure out the emotion that they make you feel." I glanced at the clock. *Thank God.* "And I will see you all on Wednesday." I walked away from the board.

A girl in the front row quickly got up from her desk and walked up to me. She started asking questions about all the upcoming assignments. She went on and on even though all her answers were in the syllabus. I tried to stay focused on her questions instead of watching Penny slowly gathering her things. I could tell she wanted to talk to me. That she was delaying leaving.

But I couldn't dismiss the student in front of me. It was better that I had a distraction. Better that I didn't have time to flirt with a student.

Yet, I watched Penny as she got up and walked past my desk. *Look at me.* She'd flirted with me in class. Blatantly. *Look at me.*

I tilted my head so I could see her better over the student in front of me. We made eye contact for just a moment. I couldn't tell her to wait. That I wanted to talk to her. Needed to talk to her. I raised my left eyebrow, silently willing her to come over to me.

Instead, she broke eye contact and walked out the door without a word.

And that was for the best. I knew it and yet...I didn't want that to ever happen again.

"Professor Hunter?" the girl in front of me asked.

"Yes?" I should have known her name by now. I made a good habit of learning my student's names, but I was drawing a blank.

"I asked when your office hours are."

"I mention it in the syllabus. Look that over today and if you have any more questions you can ask them on Wednesday, okay? But I have a feeling it'll cover everything you've been wondering."

"Oh. Okay." She looked dejected. I should have felt bad for shutting down an eager mind, but I knew she wasn't talking to me for educational purposes. Or else she would have asked me a real question. Something at least a little insightful. And she wouldn't be leaning forward so much, making her breasts practically spill out of her shirt. I'd dealt with this behavior before with my stalker.

"Anything else?" I asked, trying not to sound too rude.

"Um." She twirled a loose strand of hair around her finger and leaned forward slightly. She was wearing a shirt that showed off her toned stomach. Tan skin, long dark hair. She was attractive. But I wasn't attracted to her. I had my eyes set on someone else.

I glanced back at the door. "Well, then. Definitely check out that syllabus." I grabbed my satchel. "It'll have all the answers you're looking for." I started to walk out of the room.

"I hope you have a really great day, Professor Hunter," she said to my back as I retreated out of the room. The way she said it sounded dirty. But not in a good way.

I took a deep breath as I made my way outside. There was a reason I kept my distance from students. I did not need awkward encounters like that. But being with Penny had been anything but awkward. And the way she said my name was dirty too...but in a really fucking great way. It was just further proof that I shouldn't fraternize with students. It was a bad idea. But sometimes bad things felt really good.

Chapter 8

Monday

I was currently lying in corpse pose, staring at my living room ceiling. Dr. Clark would be happy with me at my next session. But I wasn't doing this for him. For some reason I liked this one yoga pose. Just the one. The rest of it was slow ridiculousness.

Corpse pose. I let the name roll around in my head as I kept my body completely still. Maybe I liked it because I spent most nights doing the same thing in the comfort of my bed. But lying on the hardwood floor? It felt fitting. Like it was my punishment for wanting to fuck one of my students. I turned my head to look at the floorboards. *Maybe I'd fuck her right here.*

Breathe. The word to help distract me didn't stop my train of thought. It was one thing when I wanted to cross the line. I was taking strides toward learning how to control myself. But the fact that Penny wanted to cross the line too? That made it feel real. It made it feel possible. And I could picture being with her that much more easily.

Penny Taylor. She seemed so innocent. But she did in fact want to cross the line. Her response in class was proof of that. *"I've actually been having the same dream now for several nights. It's always raining, but there's a man there holding an umbrella above the two of us so that we don't get soaked. And he kisses me."*

Yeah, I was going to fuck her right here. *Breathe.* I was great at making bad decisions when properly tempted. Maybe she was like that too. Full of bad choices. We could be bad together. I could feel myself growing hard. *For fuck's sake.* "It's corpse pose," I said into the empty room. "You're supposed to act like a corpse."

Me reprimanding my growing erection did nothing. There was a tent in my sweatpants that wouldn't be going anywhere anytime soon. I'd found that the best thing to do when I thought about Penny was to get her out of my system as fast as possible. Unless I wanted to sport a boner in class. I pushed my pants down and wrapped my hand around my hard cock, picturing her hand instead. Her mouth. Her parting thighs.

I'd provoked her response out of her today. I'd told her I'd dreamt that it was pouring outside. That I had the feeling that I was waiting for something exciting to happen. She was the exciting thing. I stroked myself faster, picturing her beneath me on the hardwood floor.

And then my phone buzzed.

Shit. I sat up from my broken corpse pose, my hand still on my cock. I was about to remove my hand, thinking it had to be Ellen texting me, when I saw that it was from an unknown number. There were very few people who had my new number. I grew even harder as I clicked on the text.

"I enjoyed our first date. But you stood me up today."

Penny. I smiled to myself. Was she referring to the fact that I'd had another student to talk to at the end of class? I'd hardly classify that as standing her up.

I ran my thumb along the pre-cum at my tip. *God.* I'd been waiting for her text. And now that it was here? It felt like she was in the room with me. Staring at me. Would she like watching me touch myself? Would that get her off? Seeing how hard I was for her? I started stroking myself again, picturing her in the short skirt she was wearing in class today.

I typed out a response with my free hand. "Miss Taylor, that was never my intention." I kept my response as clean as possible. Telling her I was as hard as stone and thinking about her? Not yet. That would depend on her response. And God I hoped her response was dirty. Maybe she'd tell me what she was wearing. Maybe she'd flat out tell me that she wanted me.

I closed my eyes, figuring it would be a while before that response came. That was the game, right? Text and respond half an hour later like you weren't just sitting next to your phone?

And I'd be done soon and my mind would be clearer. I pictured her lounging in her bed. Maybe her hand was inching up her thigh. Pushing her lacy panties to the side. Swirling her index finger around her wetness. Soon it would be my tongue.

My phone buzzed again. I glanced at the screen.

"You dreamt about me."

All I do is dream of you. I stroked myself faster as I responded to her. "I can't control my dreams, Miss Taylor." And I couldn't. Every time I closed my eyes I saw her. My favorite dream? Her calling me Professor Hunter and dropping to her knees. Her skirt riding up her thighs. Her lips wrapping tightly around my shaft. My cum dripping down her chin. Her greedy tongue licking up every last drop.

Fuck. I grabbed a tissue, catching stream after stream of cum. *Jesus.* My breath was ragged as I removed the tissue. The evidence of my wanting her was enough to fill a few tissues.

My phone buzzed again.

"I don't want you to," her response read.

She was asking me not to control my dreams. If the text had come in a second sooner…maybe I would have told her about my dirty thoughts. About how hard I wanted to fuck her. How I was thinking about her being here with me in my apartment. Hell, maybe I would have gone and picked her up so that my fantasies would become a reality.

But now I was sitting alone in my empty apartment with a tissue filled with cum. And my arousal had been replaced by guilt. A pit of guilt in my stomach that was growing by the second.

Penny didn't need a man like me in her life. I stood up and tossed the tissue in the trash. She needed someone good. Someone with less baggage. "Trust me, you do," I texted back as I walked into my bedroom. I needed a hot shower. Or maybe a cold one. Something to rid me of this day.

"I don't trust you," her next text read.

I turned on the water, trying not to let her words affect me. She was the one that reached out to me. She was the one that started this conversation. So why was I the one that felt like shit?

But she had every right not to trust me. She didn't know anything about me. If she did, she wouldn't look at me with lust in her eyes. She'd be running in the opposite direction. I needed to push her in that wrong direction.

I shot off another text. "Miss Taylor, are you in need of someone to walk you home?" That would shut the conversation down. I'd already gotten what I needed tonight anyway. She was out of my system.

My phone buzzed. "I wish that I was, Professor Hunter."

I tossed my phone onto the vanity and stepped into the steaming hot shower. I wasn't sure how long I stood there, but eventually the water ran cold. And I knew I was lying to myself. Penny wasn't out of my system. I couldn't wash her away as easily as I wanted. I turned off the water and let it drip off me.

But if I acted on my feelings? I'd lose everything. The risk was too high. I needed to give her up.

As soon as I thought about it, I could hear her voice in my head. *Professor Hunter.* Nothing had ever sounded so sweet. I took a deep breath. Giving her up didn't seem like a possibility either.

Chapter 9

Wednesday

I felt her absence as I walked into my classroom. Usually it was easier to breathe as soon as I stepped into the room. But today? My eyes flitted to the back of the class as I put my satchel down. Penny's usual seat was vacant.

I hadn't heard from her since the last text she sent. Her responses had been all over the place. Flirtatious one moment. Pushing me away the next. She was at war with what she wanted. But I wasn't. All I wanted was her. I looked down at my roster, wondering if she had dropped the class. I'd have to print out a new one this afternoon to see.

It would be for the best. I knew that. And yet...it was the last thing I wanted. I glanced at her desk again and noticed that the one beside hers was empty too. *Tyler Stevens.* Were they together right now? I drummed my fingers against the desk until someone unzipping a backpack pulled me out of my thoughts.

What the fuck was I doing? I had a class to teach. The world didn't revolve around whether or not Penny and Tyler were going at it like bunnies. *Ugh.*

I straightened my glasses and wrote the word "emotion" on the board again. I needed to drive this point home or else I'd be listening to awful speeches for the rest of the semester. A door creaking in the back made me turn around.

Penny strolled in solo and plopped down into her usual seat. Tyler was still nowhere to be seen and I couldn't help but smile. I hadn't been sleeping well. I never slept well. But the past few days I felt like I was waiting. Waiting for a text from her. Waiting for a call from the dean with my termination. Just…waiting. And it was a relief that Penny was here. Although, she wasn't all seductive stares and rosy cheeks today. She was staring at me rather defiantly.

I tried to ignore her as I underlined the word "emotion" on the board. "Today we are going to drive this point home. And first we are going to share what emotion we are currently feeling." I needed to know why she was staring at me like that. Had she just shown the dean our texts? Or was she pissed at me for some reason? "And say the word in the way that the emotion has affected you. For example, if I was upset, I'd probably frown a little and say it in a rather pouty way."

Most of the class laughed. I glanced at Penny again but her expression was unreadable. "Very well," I said. I called out the first name and went through the list.

"Tyler Stevens? Absent," I said to myself and made a note on the roster. Maybe he was the one that had dropped my class. *Hopefully.* "Penny Taylor?"

She stood up quickly. "I feel foolish." She closed her eyes and it felt like my heart stopped.

"And frustrated," she added. "Foolish and frustrated." She sat down without looking at me.

Her emotions affected me more than I thought someone else's could. I could feel her frustration. *With me.* I tried to think back to our conversation. She'd told me she didn't trust me. She had ended the flirtations. She… my mind stopped. *Oh.* She'd also said that she wished she was in need of someone to walk her home. And I'd never responded. I was angry at myself the other night. Ashamed of what I'd done while I was talking to her. I'd never even thought to respond back. *Shit.*

Penny kept her eyes on her desk for the rest of the class. I had to make this right. I hated seeing her upset. But when I dismissed class, she grabbed her things and snuck out the back door to avoid me. She might as well have slapped me.

***

I paused outside my next classroom and typed out a text. Penny being upset with me was an easy out. She could stomp out whatever it was we had before we even explored it. But I didn't want an out. *Right?* I stared at the unsent text. "Now I know how it feels to be stood up. Lesson learned."

Even though I was trying to practice self-control, it was hard when Penny was on my mind. It was like she helped me focus. But all my focus was trained on her. I wasn't sure if that was a good thing. My thumb hesitated over the send button. I breathed slowly, trying to concentrate on something besides her. Trying to find some semblance of clarity. But I couldn't think about anything else. Was sending this a bad idea? I mean, I knew it was a bad idea. But would I regret it?

"Are you going to the staff meeting tomorrow?" someone asked.

I turned to see one of my colleagues standing next to me. She was closer to my own age. Pretty. A much more suitable companion. I wouldn't even have to lie to Dr. Clark. But I'd met her a few other times and couldn't even remember her name. There was nothing there. I pressed send on the text, slid my phone into my pocket, and gave whatever-her-name-was my attention for a moment. "Yes, I'm going."

"We should head over together. I can stop by after your office hours tomorrow afternoon."

"Yeah, sure. I should probably get to class."

"Great!" She lightly touched my arm. "I'll see you tomorrow then!"

Professor Kean! That was her name. I was relieved for a moment for remembering, but it disappeared when I saw that her smile was so big that it looked like she'd crack through her red lipstick.

Crap, did I just agree to a kind of date with her? I dismissed the thought. Walking to a staff meeting wasn't a date. She was delirious if she thought it was.

She was still smiling at me like a psychopath.

I'd shut that down hard tomorrow. Until then, I just wanted to be away from her. "Yup, tomorrow." I retreated into my next class.

But teaching wasn't a relief today. Because as the minutes ticked by slowly, it became increasingly clear that Penny wasn't going to text me back.

Chapter 10

Thursday

"Are you sure there aren't any extra credit options?" Noah asked as he leaned forward slightly and bit his bottom lip.

You've got to be kidding me. It was bad enough that most of the female students flitting through my office hours didn't have any real questions. Now I had to worry about my male students too? "I'm sure, Noah. Classes just started. There's no need for extra credit when no grades have been assigned. And if that changes, I'll make sure to mention it *in class*." I hoped he got the hint. *Also, I like women. One woman in particular.*

I tried not to grimace when Noah kept looking at me seductively. I picked up my headphones instead and gestured toward the door. "See you in class."

Noah sighed and stood up. He bit his bottom lip again, like that was somehow going to convince me to switch sides.

I focused my attention on my computer screen, even though it was off. *Leave. Leave. Leave.* Finally, I heard his footsteps. I breathed a sigh of relief as he left the room.

Sometimes I wasn't sure I was a good professor. If I was, maybe I'd have real questions during my office hours instead of whatever the hell that was. Or maybe I was such a good professor that none of my students had any questions. I pulled on my earphones. That was a much better option in my mind.

***

The last half-hour had flown by when I didn't have to entertain any students' ludicrous flirting. And my office hours were almost over. I was going to make it to the end without any more awkward encounters. I paused from my work and rolled up my shirt sleeves, loosened my tie, and even undid a few of the top buttons. *Much better.*

I had written down a few ideas of how I could convince Dean Vespelli to let me cancel office hours for the remainder of the semester. He'd probably say no. But it certainly wouldn't hurt to ask. Besides, office hours were a little old-fashioned. If a student had a question for me, they could easily just email me. Now that was an option I could get behind. I could promise Vespelli that I'd answer every email within a few hours. It's not like I had anything else to do when I was at home. Honestly, it would make my nights go by faster.

There was a knock on my door.

What now? I was almost free for the day. Free to go home and do whatever I wanted. Which meant staring at my phone waiting for Penny to text me or thinking about her in some other illicit way. As soon as I finished this office hours proposal, I'd go back to focusing on how exactly to go about seducing a student. Willfully.

I looked up and everything about me wanting to cancel office hours flew out the window. *Penny.* I could handle the rest of the harmless flirting from other students if it meant I even got a minute of Penny in this room. But with her standing in the doorway, the space suddenly felt too small. Intimate. Perfect. I pulled off my headphones and set them on the desk.

"Miss Taylor, come in," I said. It would have been more professional of me to tell her office hours were over and to come back another day. I knew I couldn't trust myself around her. And yet...I was inviting her in anyway.

Clearly I wasn't very professional. For just a few minutes, I wanted to be alone with her. I needed to be alone with her. I walked over to the door and closed it behind her. Every bone in my body wanted me to lock it. But that was inappropriate. I turned to look at her. Those big innocent blue eyes were staring back at me. Yup, definitely inappropriate. I shoved my hands into my pockets so I wouldn't lock the door. Or worse…reach out and touch her. "I didn't expect to see you."

"I didn't expect to be here." No smile on her lips. No reaction to being alone with me at all.

I'd fucked this up before I'd even gotten a chance for it to begin. "You're angry with me."

"I'm not." She pulled off her backpack and leaned against my desk, looking way too comfortable in the confined space.

Jesus. I looked down at my watch to prevent myself from walking over to her and pushing her down on top of my desk. I'd been dreaming of doing just that for days. *Breathe.* "My office hours are almost over." I didn't actually want her to leave. But as the seconds ticked by I was losing more and more restraint. She'd look perfect with her legs parted, her back on the middle of my desk.

"I tried to come the other day when they first started, but you had quite the line."

I ran my fingers through my hair and watched her eyes follow my hand. She liked when I did that. *Noted.* I walked over to her so that we were only a few feet apart. "Part of the duties of being a professor." I shrugged, hoping to keep the conversation light. I didn't want her to run away. What I wanted was to run my fingers up her thigh… *Breathe.*

"Right." She picked up her backpack and pulled out my gray sweater. "I came to return this."

For some reason the idea of her giving me my sweater back felt like an ending instead of a beginning. And this was not going to be the end. I let my eyes trail from the sweater slowly up her body, until our eyes locked. Her face immediately flushed. No, this was definitely the beginning.

"You can keep that," I said.

She shook her head. "It's yours."

"Certainly it looks better on you." I knew it for a fact. One of my sweaters paired with some leggings and rain boots? The image did something to me.

She placed the sweater on my desk.

I closed the distance between us, reached around her, and picked it up. Her body was so still that it didn't seem like she was breathing. I grabbed her hand and placed the sweater on her palm. But I didn't let go. I kept her hand cradled in mine as I stared down at her. And I felt more aroused in this simple touch than I had in years. Fucking years. I wanted to pull her against my chest. I wanted to taste her lips. But it was too soon. I didn't want to scare her away. This was a game of cat and mouse. And I was definitely the cat, because I was seconds away from devouring her.

"It's a gift, Penny."

"I like when you call me Penny."

Breathe. Her alluring cherry scented perfume invaded my senses. Or was it her shampoo? Or just...her? Usually it was easy to breathe around her. But today I couldn't think about anything but her legs spread wide on my desk. And that thought was dangerous when my door was closed. When we were all alone. When I was on school property. *Shit.* "Miss Taylor, you should probably go."

She glanced down at my tie and I imagined her pulling it, drawing my mouth down to hers. Instead she gripped the desk with her hand that wasn't trapped in mine and leaned back ever so slightly. Her breathing grew shorter and more sporadic. And I knew that she wasn't going anywhere. I was going to have her on my desk. And she was going to beg me for it.

But then a knock sounded on my office door.

Damn it. My hand instantly fell from Penny's, and I took a step back. I stared at the ground for a moment, trying to clear my head. All I could think about was the fact that I wish I had locked the door. When I looked back up at her, I still felt that same heat. That hunger. I needed her. I needed her like I'd never needed anything before. My eyes drifted to the sweater. *Take it back.* I needed her to keep it. For some reason, if she did, it meant that this wasn't over.

It was like she could read my mind. She picked up her backpack and shoved the sweater back inside.

I smiled to myself. I had Penny just where I wanted her. I walked over to the door like I hadn't been about to tear off a student's clothes and opened it just as Penny pulled her backpack over her shoulder.

Professor Kean walked in. I had completely forgotten about the faculty meeting. And I'd definitely forgotten about walking over with her. She was wearing a charcoal pencil skirt and matching blazer. Her high heeled shoes made her almost as tall as me. And her bright red lipstick just made her look...unnatural. Her sophisticated ensemble did nothing for me. All I wanted was to see Penny in my sweater again, staring up at me sweetly, if not a little apprehensively.

"Ready to go, James?" Professor Kean asked, and then she spotted Penny. She glanced down at her watch. "Sorry, I thought office hours were over. I can wait outside." She smiled at me.

"We just finished up," I said. "I'm ready to go." I tightened my tie as I turned back to Penny. "See you tomorrow, Miss Taylor." I said the words without really looking at her, because if we had made eye contact, I was worried I wouldn't be able to control myself. No, I *knew* I wouldn't be able to control myself.

Penny walked over to us. "Thanks for your help, Professor Hunter."

God, I love when she says my name like that. I tried not to stare at her ass as she walked out of my office.

"So sorry about interrupting," Professor Kean said with a laugh. Which made no sense, because what she said wasn't even funny. She proceeded to touch my arm.

I pulled my arm away and watched as Penny disappeared from view. Professor Kean was saying something else to me, but all I could think about was that I had been so close. So freaking close. And I wasn't sure if it was a good or bad thing that we'd gotten interrupted.

The professional part of me was thankful that Professor Kean had walked in. But the rest of me? I was still a man. And the part of me that wasn't worried about my job was really pissed. I'd almost had Penny. Right here. I'd been seconds away from kissing her. Touching her. *Damn it.*

"Are you okay?" Professor Kean asked as she touched my arm again.

"Fine." I grabbed my satchel, again making her hand fall from my arm. I didn't want her to touch me.

"Rough office hours? I'm always telling Vespelli that we don't need to sit here for hours. I barely ever get any students stopping by. And when I do, it's always just a simple question. Email would suffice, don't you think?"

Now this was something I could actually talk to her about. "I was just thinking that myself."

"Really? We should bring it up at the meeting today."

"Yeah…maybe." Did I really want office hours to be cancelled? Office hours could mean more one-on-one time with Penny. Time I was aching for.

"What, don't tell me you're scared of the dean? He's a big softie."

I wasn't scared of Vespelli. But I did want to remain on his good side. Because I was going to sleep with a student. It wasn't even a question anymore. It was just a matter of when it was going to happen. And if Vespelli ever found out…I wanted him to like me. As a backup plan so that he wouldn't unleash hell on me. I didn't expect anyone to ever find out though.

"I know he's a big softie," I said. "I just don't want to step on his toes."

After all, Vespelli had done me a favor by giving me this job. I wasn't qualified. And I certainly didn't deserve a second chance after what happened in New York. He'd taken a leap of faith on me.

"But who ever got anywhere without stepping on a few toes?" she asked as we made our way downstairs.

I shrugged. Not me. I'd created a handful of enemies in my early twenties and I hadn't cared at the time. But my life wasn't as black and white as it used to be. "Keep your friends close and your enemies closer. It's a saying for a reason."

"And what am I? A friend or an enemy?" She smiled up at me.

An enemy. Everyone at this school was an enemy. Because any one of them could potentially betray me once I finally got Penny where I wanted her. Even Penny herself. But this was the perfect opportunity to make my intentions clear as far as Professor Kean was concerned. "Friends," I said. "That's all I need right now."

"Well, at least I'm not an enemy," she said with a laugh. But this time she didn't touch my arm. Hopefully that meant she got the hint. "Any chance you want to go out for drinks after this, buddy?"

Or maybe she hadn't gotten the hint. The addition of the word "buddy" didn't convince me. "I can't, I have plans." It was a lie. I never had any plans. Just a routine, and it was better if I didn't break it.

"Maybe some other time, then."

I walked into the room where the meeting was occurring instead of answering her. We sat down in the back because it had already started. I looked around at all the other professors. All the ones that knew how to keep it in their pants.

Anyone else in my position would follow the rules. But I wasn't like everyone else. There was a reason I was going to therapy. There was a reason why I'd stopped talking to everyone from my past. There was a reason I was alone. And it all went back to the issue of self-control.

As Vespelli droned on, I pretended to snap my wrist with an imaginary rubber band.

A few professors laughed about something Vespelli said. I could feel Professor Kean's eyes on me. She probably thought it was odd that I hadn't laughed. But I wasn't paying attention. And nothing about the situation I was in was humorous.

I was spiraling. I thought I was getting better. But with Penny? Whenever I saw her, all my self-control went out the window.

Chapter 11

Friday

It felt like I was hungover even though I didn't drink a drop of the scotch I'd poured myself last night. And the last thing I wanted to do was step into my classroom right now. I needed to go for a run and let off some steam. Or take a nap instead of staring at my bedroom ceiling for five hours.

But the real reason I was standing outside my classroom door was because there wasn't any part of me that was being reasonable anymore. My head, my heart, my cock...they were all pointing in one direction. One of those things quite literally.

Penny was like a drug in my veins. And I knew I needed to get her out of my system. Maybe this weekend. My dick stirred at the thought. I had her number now. Surely one night with me would be more alluring to her than a night with the boy she liked to sit in the back row with. One night and we could both move on. That's what we needed.

I ran my fingers through my unruly hair and straightened my glasses. But first I had a class to teach, because that was my job. The fact that I had to keep reminding myself I was a professor was troublesome. I was officially losing my mind. God, I just needed one taste of her. One taste and I'd be able to move on. Right? I looked down at the jeans and tight black t-shirt I was wearing. I didn't even remember putting them on this morning. Probably because I had been up at 4 am. So much for looking professional.

I pushed through the door and did my best not to look over at Penny. I needed to get through one lesson plan without fucking it up. "Today's assignment is an easy one," I said and sat down on the edge of my desk. "Let's talk about our weekend plans."

Usually I gave an example, but I wasn't going to tell my whole class that this weekend I was planning on seducing a student. In every way I'd dreamed about. I was going to literally fuck her out of my system. Instead of delving into those graphic details, I called the first name on my roster and listened intently to their responses.

For the first time this semester I actually felt like a good professor. My students seemed less nervous when they stood up one by one to talk. They were starting to feel comfortable in this environment, which was what I wanteded. Maybe my crazy spur of the moment topics hadn't been so bad. I was feeling good about myself until my eyes landed on the next name on my roster. "Tyler Stevens," I called.

He stood up, but his eyes stayed focused on Penny. He smiled down at her while he spoke. "I will be spending the weekend wallowing in my room, because this girl I'm crushing on is too busy to hang out with me."

I smiled to myself. So she wasn't even planning on hanging out with Tyler.

I was itching to finally make eye contact with Penny for the first time today. I'd been a good professor for the past half hour. I was allowed a break in professionalism. "Penny Taylor," I called.

When she stood up, I felt my jaw drop. She was wearing my sweater, a pair of leggings, and her rain boots again. Just like the first time we'd met. Just like I'd imagined her wearing as I stared at my ceiling last night. I quickly closed my mouth and looked down at the roster in my hand. I'd told her she looked better in my sweater than me. And she decided to prove that today. I had her just where I wanted.

"This weekend I'm going on a double date with my roommate and her new boyfriend," Penny said.

A date? I winced. *So much for having her right where I want her.* My plans for this weekend disappeared. She was seeing someone. Just not Tyler. Who the hell was this other guy? I wondered if his name was as stupid as Tyler freaking Stevens. God I hated that kid.

"But I'm absolutely dreading it," she added before sitting back down.

I wasn't sure why she added that. Had she seen my reaction? Did it even matter? I kept my eyes on my roster and called the next name.

When I finished listening to the other students, I wrote "lust" on the board in all caps. For God knows what reason. I was supposed to be talking about preparation and how important it was. People planned out their weekends well in advance. And I was going to relate that to planning out their speeches well in advance. But now "lust" was staring back at me on the board and I felt like a complete tool.

I turned around and tried to think of something to say. "You want your audience to hang on every word that comes out of your mouth." I glanced at Penny's full lips. I tried not to picture them around my cock. But it was impossible. It was like they belonged on me. "It's kind of like in a relationship. You want that instantaneous lust you sometimes get." *What the fuck am I talking about?*

I couldn't tear my eyes away from Penny sitting there in my sweater. She was going on a date with another man, so why the hell was she teasing me like this? She clearly wasn't as innocent as I originally thought. I realized all my students were staring at me, probably wondering where the hell I was going with this lust topic. Hell if I knew.

"I don't necessarily mean it in a sexual way," I said. "Although, there is a reason that sex sells."

A heard a few girls laugh and one definitely gave me sex eyes. But not Penny. She was just staring back at me. Didn't she realize she was torturing me?

"You want to capture your audience's attention. You want them to yearn for more. And that, in my opinion, is the hardest thing about giving an effective speech. Because you can't force lust. It has to come naturally." I wanted to cringe at what I was saying. If I didn't get fired for sleeping with a student, I'd probably be fired just for being shitty at my job soon enough. I needed to end this class before I turned it into a sex education class or something else completely inappropriate.

I cleared my throat. "Anyway, something to ponder over the weekend." *Please don't.* If I was lucky none of my students had been paying attention. Hopefully they were too excited about their weekend plans to realize I was lusting over the beautiful redhead in the back row. "Class dismissed."

I watched as Tyler started talking to Penny. I tried not to think about the fact that he wasn't the only guy I was competing with for her attention. Who the hell was the other guy? Was he a student? Was he older like me? Something about that made me angrier than the thought of Tyler with her.

Penny stood up and pulled her backpack over one shoulder. Her hips swayed as she walked up to the front of the classroom. I was pretty sure no one else on earth could look so seductive in rain boots. The rest of the class had filtered out. This was our moment to be alone. Our one moment. But instead of stopping, she tried to pass by my desk without a word.

Not happening. "Miss Taylor, if you would, please wait a moment."

She froze in place. I couldn't tell if she looked excited or scared that I was speaking to her.

My eyes trailed down her body. "You're wearing my sweater."

"I've been told I look good in it."

I pressed my lips together. Not just good. Sexy as sin. Enticing. *Untouchable.* I hated that last thought. It made me feel sick to my stomach. "You have a date this weekend." I hoped that came out casual. Because in reality I wanted to rip the guy's head off.

She gulped, her throat making this adorable squeaking noise. "And how was yours?" she asked. The adorableness was gone, she was staring at me rather accusatorily.

"Hmmm?" I raised my left eyebrow. What the hell was she talking about?

"I have another class I need to get to."

"So do I." For some reason my heart started racing. I didn't want her to leave. All weekend I'd just be thinking about who the fuck had their hands on her.

"Well then." She turned.

"Penny?" The tips of my fingers brushed the back of her wrist before I even realized I'd reached out to her. Her skin felt like fire against mine. All the warmth and light from her, invading my senses. I took the deepest breath that I had in weeks. And all I smelled was cherry blossoms. She smelled just like spring.

I watched her shiver, but then she continued retreating from me.

I knew she felt that connection too. How was she walking away right now? How was she going on a date with someone else? *Because you're her professor. You're too old for her.* Everything about the two of us together was wrong.

Before she left, she turned her head and said, "Have a good weekend, Professor Hunter."

It was like she knew my weekend was going to be hell. Because she wasn't going to be a part of it.

Chapter 12

Saturday

I looked down at my phone one more time. For some reason, I had this hope that Penny would text me. She'd say she cancelled her date and show up outside my apartment in nothing but lacy black lingerie, holding a bottle of whipped cream.

There was a lot wrong with that scenario. Everything down to the fact that she had no idea where I lived. And the fact that the autumn air was too cold to prance around in just lingerie. *Oh, and the fact that I'm her professor.*

Breathe. This week had been slow torture. Penny had invaded all my senses. My appointment with Dr. Clark tomorrow couldn't come soon enough. I needed to actually tell him about Penny. The secret was driving me insane. Or maybe it was just the temptation that was killing me. Either way, he'd know what to do.

He'll tell you to stop.

But I ignored a lot of Dr. Clark's advice. If I did everything he said, I'd probably be going to a family dinner at my parents' on Sundays instead of seeing him. Which would be unbearable. I doubted they'd even let me join them for a meal. Not that I wanted to. Fuck them. Fuck everyone in New York. That city nearly killed me. I couldn't go back to a city that felt like it suffocated me.

Dr. Clark didn't really understand. And just because he told me to do something didn't mean I had to. I eyed the yoga mat collecting dust in the corner of my closet. Proof that I wasn't taking my therapy sessions seriously enough.

I glanced at my phone one more time and then pulled on my running shoes. I needed to get some fresh air. Maybe then I'd come back and lie in corpse pose until I died of sex deprivation.

***

I wasn't sure why I even tried to sleep anymore. Tonight was especially impossible. I couldn't stop thinking about Penny with someone else. That perfect smile. Her laugh. The blush that crept across her cheeks when she was embarrassed. All for someone else.

I opened my eyes and stared at the ceiling again. Maybe I needed to put a poster up there. Something motivational for slumber like, "Shut your damn eyes and go to sleep you idiot." Anything along those lines would do.

But the poster wasn't there, so my mind stayed focused on Penny. Was she inviting her date back to her place? Was he kissing her goodnight? Or was she inviting him in for more? The thought of her wanting anyone else was the hardest pill to swallow. Because I certainly didn't. She was all I could think about.

I couldn't just lie here all night thinking about the what-ifs. I needed to get some fresh air. Another run would be good. But my body didn't move. I was exhausted, mentally and physically. So why the hell wouldn't my brain turn off?

Breathe.

I could hear Dr. Clark's voice in the back of my head. He'd say that yoga would help me sleep. I was pretty sure fucking Penny was the only way I'd ever sleep again. As soon as I thought it, my phone buzzed.

The list of people who would be texting me at midnight was pretty slim. My brother being one option. And the other…

I lifted up my phone and stared at the text. The perfect, beautiful, text I'd been waiting for from Penny.

"Any chance I can get a lift?"

I smiled. But then I immediately frowned. If she needed a lift, that meant she was drunk. The thought of her being too wasted to walk herself home was one thing. But the thought of her being drunk and the guy she was out with not walking her home? Not okay. Who the hell was this asshole? I was furious. But also grateful. Because maybe if he'd been a good guy, they'd still be together right now. And I couldn't stand the thought of someone else touching her. Even if it was as innocent as holding hands. Her hands were only mine to hold. The thought made me pause. I shook my head. I was sleep-deprived. I didn't know what I was thinking.

"Where are you?" I texted back.

My phone bleeped immediately. "Outside of Kildare's."

"I'll be right there." I was already climbing out of bed, pulling on the nearest clothes: a pair of dark jeans and…I looked around for my shirt from earlier. But all I could find was a zip-up gray hoodie. *Screw a shirt*. There wasn't time.

I went to the bathroom and splashed water on my face. Even though I couldn't fall asleep, I was exhausted. The last thing I wanted was to endanger Penny even more. I brushed my teeth, hoping that the mint flavor would help zap my brain awake. Or maybe I did it because I wanted to kiss her.

Breathe. She was drunk. She was calling me for help. The last thing I was going to do was kiss her. I'd save that for a night that she'd remember. Because I wanted that memory to be seared into her brain forever.

I made my way down to my car as fast as I could. Main Street was pretty empty as I pulled out of the parking garage. Most students were probably still out at parties. If she had called me at one o'clock it would have been a different story. I would have had to drive 10 miles per hour to dodge drunk students. But since it was empty, I sped down the road fast enough for a cop to cite me for reckless driving.

Kildare's was close enough to my apartment that I could have walked. But she'd asked for a lift. And I didn't mind the idea of her being so close to me. Or the fact that no one would even see us together. *Stop. She's drunk for God's sake.*

It started to drizzle, the rain hitting my windshield like it was pouring because of how fast I was going. I saw her in the distance, sitting on the curb without an umbrella, seemingly not caring an ounce that she was getting wet. She was even smiling. *Definitely drunk.*

I pulled the car to a stop right in front of her. She stood up and all I could do was stare at the way her black dress clung to her. It was probably that tight before it was wet, but somehow knowing that she was soaked made it that much more seductive. The hemline barely covered her ass and the neckline plunged to her belly button. There was black mesh material over her cleavage so that she wasn't completely exposed. And a slit up the side that would have been sinful if it were any higher.

But then I saw the broken stiletto in her hand. My eyes wandered down her legs. There was blood dripping down her knees. What the hell happened? I leaned over and opened the car door from the inside. She climbed inside and shut the door.

I wanted to ask her who the fuck left her on the curb like this. I wanted to ask her a million questions really. But I was distracted by the fact that she didn't smell like a brewery. The sweet smell of cherry blossoms invaded the car. Had she even been drinking?

"Did I wake you?" she asked sweetly.

That was how she was going to start this conversation? She was fucking bleeding. I needed a second to calm down, or else I'd snap at her when what I really wanted to do was kill whoever had been with her. I put the car in drive and focused on the road for a minute. She'd asked me a question. But I didn't have an appropriate answer. No, I hadn't been sleeping. I'd been lying in bed wishing I was fucking her instead. But I couldn't exactly tell her that. "Yes," I finally said.

The rain was picking up. In the silence, the drops began to splash loudly on the windshield. I gripped the wheel tighter.

"You live near here?" she asked.

Was she seriously not going to tell me what the hell had happened tonight? The small talk made me feel like it was bad. Worse than the millions of things running through my head. "Yes."

"Where?"

I stopped at a red light and leaned across her to open the glove compartment. All I wanted to do was turn my head and kiss her. I told myself it wasn't a possibility because she'd be drunk. But she wasn't. I didn't smell any alcohol on her breath. The only smell was those damn cherry blossoms. Everywhere. I smelled her everywhere.

But just because she wasn't drunk didn't mean she was in any state to make good decisions tonight. And even if she was, I certainly wasn't. I was furious. She had been sitting alone on the curb bleeding. I grabbed a tissue and placed it gently on one of her cut knees. Ignoring her question, I asked, "Do you want to talk about what happened?"

"I fell, that's all," she whispered. Her gaze dropped to my lips.

I'd been dreaming of being alone with her. But not like this. Not when rage was pulsing through my veins. I let go of the tissue and sat back in the driver's seat.

She blotted her knees with the tissue.

"That's all?" I asked, my eyes never leaving her face.

She lifted her stiletto from her lap and shrugged.

That wasn't the whole story. We both knew it. And I was going to get to the bottom of it. When the light turned green I stepped on the gas. "You enjoyed your date then?"

"No."

I was going to kill whoever she was with. My knuckles were turning white because I was gripping the steering wheel so tight. I tried to take a deep breath as we drove on in silence. We were almost back to her dorm and I had zero answers. Just more questions.

"Is that what you wanted to hear?" she asked.

"I don't desire for you to be unhappy, Miss Taylor." I just wish it was me she was choosing to pursue happiness with. I could feel her eyes on me, but I didn't look over at her. I'd resolved not to kiss her tonight because I knew she'd been drinking. But now? I felt my resolve disappearing the farther I drove. And my anger. Tasting her was all I could think about. This was my chance. Possibly my one and only chance.

"Why did you give me your number, Professor Hunter?"

I pulled to the curb outside of her dorm and turned the car off. "You seem keen on putting yourself in dangerous situations." I glanced at her clingy dress and then got out of the car. I needed to walk her to her door. To make sure she didn't fall again. To make sure nothing else bad ever happened to her.

I ran through the rain and opened her door. She stepped out slowly like she wasn't ready for this moment to be over.

And I wasn't either. Instead of turning to walk her to the door I just stood there, staring at her. The dream that had plagued me since we'd met seemed to be playing in slow motion. It was pouring and I was waiting for something to happen. Waiting for a sign that she wanted the same things I did. A sign that it was okay to touch her. Any sign that what I wanted wasn't wrong.

"Professor Hunter..."

Fuck. I needed her. I needed her so badly. I leaned down and placed my hands on the car on either side of her. Our mouths were less than an inch apart. I needed to warn her to stay away from me. I needed to tell her she was about to make a mistake. But I could feel the heat of her breath in the rain, alluring and sweet. Instead of saying anything, I drew a fraction of an inch closer.

"I can't seem to stop thinking about you," she whispered.

That sign would do. I grabbed the back of her neck and let my lips meet hers. *Fuck.* Her kiss was full of passion, passion that she had been holding back just as much as I had. And there wasn't any trace of alcohol on her tongue. She was making this decision clearly. She wanted this just as badly as me.

I pressed my body against hers and lightly pushed her so that her back was on the cold, wet steel of the car. I leaned into her, feeling the friction of her hips against the front of my jeans. Her hand wandered beneath the back of my hoodie, skimming over my skin.

I felt the same heat as I did when I touched her wrist. The warmth of perfection a stark contrast to what I was. And I didn't want to stop kissing her. I never wanted to stop kissing her. *Never.* I wanted to push her skirt up right here in front of her dorm. Feel her wetness. Fuck her senseless. I didn't know how to stop. I felt all my self-control slipping away with each swirl of her tongue. Every ounce of control seeped out of me. And that wasn't good. That wasn't good at all.

Her hands rose higher up my back. Her skin against mine a delicious feeling that I suddenly wasn't sure I knew how to live without.

Fuck. I couldn't do this. Just because I was broken didn't mean I needed to break her. I groaned as I pulled my lips away from her. "Penny, you need to try to stop." *Because I can't. I can't stop.* And the thought was terrifying. I stepped back and lifted the hood of my hoodie over my head. *I can't stop.* I rubbed my forehead as I walked around the car. *I can't stop.* I glanced at her once more before climbing back in my car.

Fuck! I sped off without looking back. I could feel myself slipping. Slipping back into my old habits. I wasn't going to revert to the man I was before I moved here. I couldn't. I slammed my hand against the steering wheel. I was supposed to get her out of my system. Instead I'd just gotten my first taste of perfection. And I was greedy for more.

Chapter 13

Sunday

I ran my fingers along the leather armrest. It was easier to stare at the crease that the repetitive gesture made than to make eye contact with Dr. Clark. Besides, I'd already decided what to do about Penny. I no longer needed to discuss it.

"Your phone isn't attached to your hand today," Dr. Clark said, finally breaking the silence.

How insightful. I was in a foul mood, but it wasn't his fault. I plastered a fake smile onto my face and then let it fall. Putting an act on for my therapist wasn't helping me. Clearly. "Nope."

"Did you hear back from the woman you were interested in? Your colleague?"

"It's not going to work out."

He shifted in his chair, his notebook settling on his lap. "And why is that?"

"Because you were wrong…I'm not ready to date."

He gave me a hard stare. "And why is that?"

I hated when he repeated himself. It made me feel like a petulant child. I took a deep breath instead of snapping at him. "She broke up my routine too much. You're the one who always says my routine is so important."

"But your routine shouldn't be used as an excuse to stop living, James."

I shook my head.

"Don't you think you could add one or two date nights a week to your routine? Most couples hang out on

Friday and Saturday nights when they're first dating. You can easily adjust your schedule to accommodate change."

And where would I take my student? To the bar down the street? Dr. Clark didn't understand. I looked down at the leather armrest again. It wasn't just about the change of routine. That wasn't it at all. It was the feeling that I wasn't in control. I'd fucking kissed her outside her dorm building. Anyone could have seen us. For a second I had forgotten what we were. A professor and his student. It was like I lost all reason around her. And that wasn't acceptable behavior. Not for someone like me.

"Tell me what you're thinking," Dr. Clark said. "That's why you're here."

I ran my hand down my face. What was there left to say? I'd already decided to stop pursuing Penny. End of discussion.

He wrote something down in his notebook, the scribbling sound of the pen against the paper slowly driving me insane. "Did you two go on a date?"

He wasn't letting this go easily. "Not exactly. I gave her a lift home the other night."

"And how did you feel when you were alone with her?"

I thought about Penny's broken heel and the blood dripping down her knees. *Infuriated.* And then I thought about how she smelled like cherry blossoms and how beautiful her blue eyes were. *Intoxicated.* "Conflicted."

"Now we're getting somewhere. What were you conflicted about?"

Whether to turn the car around and kill whoever had ditched her on the side of the road. Or to lean over and kiss away any bad memories of her night. Whether or not I should cross the line of our relationship in the classroom. Whether or not our different ages would be an issue. I was conflicted about every single thing. "All of it. She's out of my league."

Dr. Clark laughed. "I doubt there are many women who'd consider themselves out of your league. I'll ask you again…why were you conflicted? Does this have to do with Isabella?"

"No." I shook my head. Sometimes Dr. Clark seemed really dumb. "It has nothing to do with her."

"We haven't talked about her since our first few sessions."

"Because there is nothing left to say."

"Do you think you're over her?"

Why was he pressing this? "My relationship with Isabella was built off obligation, not love." Our parents had pretty much arranged for us to be together since we were born.

"But you went along with it for years."

"You know perfectly well I wasn't happy."

He shook his head like he didn't believe me. It didn't matter if he did or not. Isabella was nothing to me. And none of my hesitancy about Penny had to do with Isabella. If I liked Isabella at all, I'd still be in NYC with her. I'd still be sharing a bed with her. I wouldn't want to throw up at the mention of her name.

Dr. Clark jotted something else down in his notebook and then looked back up at me. "It just seems logical that you might be sabotaging your relationship with this new woman because you still have feelings for Isabella."

That definitely wasn't it. I had been waiting impatiently for this session. But now that I was here it seemed pointless.

"Maybe it's your whole life in New York that's making you sabotage your fresh start here. You left all your friends and family behind. Don't you think that might be holding you back from embracing your new life here?"

I shook my head.

"Then what did you feel conflicted about when you were driving your colleague home?"

I was done talking about this.

"You know the answer." His voice was stern. "You're paying me to talk through your issues with you. If you won't talk to me, then what are you doing here, James?"

I pressed my lips together.

"Tell me why you're conflicted."

What the hell did he want me to say?

"You were conflicted being alone with this woman because…"

"I'm not a good person! Is that what you want to hear? I'm not a good person. And she deserves better than someone like me."

"James." He put his notebook and pen down. "Only a good person would even consider his own morality in the context of starting a new relationship. Don't you see?"

His point was moot. Because what I said was what really mattered. Penny was everything good in the world. Even her touch radiated warmth. And me? My soul was dark. I was barely holding on. A man like me didn't deserve Penny's light.

Dr. Clark leaned forward. "You worked hard to turn your life around. You're allowed to let go of your past. You're allowed to give yourself a break."

"She's too good for me."

"You took a job as a professor to give back. We both know you don't need the money. You're doing good things here."

"Doing one positive thing in my whole life doesn't make me a saint."

"Positivity attracts more positivity."

I hated when he talked about the universe giving back what I put out. "It's done. I told her it was over." *I begged her to stay away, because I wasn't sure I was strong enough to.*

Dr. Clark shook his head and lifted his pen back up. "I think that was a mistake."

"And coming here was a fucking mistake." I stood up to go.

"When was the last time you had a drink?" he said to my back.

I froze.

"When was the last time you even *wanted* a drink?"

I hadn't consumed a single sip of alcohol since I'd met Penny. I hadn't even thought about it.

"Sit back down, James. We can figure out what's bothering you together. That's why I'm here."

I turned back toward him and shoved my hands in my pockets. Why did I always fight being honest with him? He was literally being paid hundreds of dollars an hour to listen to me. With no repercussions. "When I'm with her, I feel my self-control slipping. And I don't like that feeling."

"You don't need self-control around a consenting adult."

"It's not just sex. I feel myself being drawn to her all the time. It's easier to breathe when she's beside me."

Dr. Clark smiled. "Falling in love isn't a disease, James."

"I'm not falling in love with her."

"What you just described…the smile on your face…"

I didn't realize I was smiling. I quickly cut it out. "I don't know how to let go without feeling like I'm slipping."

"And I'll say it again…slipping into love isn't a disease."

"It feels the same to me."

"You're allowed to let go of your past. You're allowed to embrace change. You're allowed to be happy."

He wasn't getting it. I'd told him the truth and he didn't understand. "I think I just need some fresh air."

"I'll see you next Sunday then?"

I nodded and left the room. Even though I was still resigned to keep Penny at arm's length, there was at least one thing Dr. Clark had said that resonated with me. I needed to let go of my past. And even though I felt like I had, there was still the issue of the unsigned documents.

When I got home, I called my lawyer to set up a few meetings in New York. Then I packed a suitcase and sent off emails to cancel my next few classes. For Comm I moved up the speeches that were supposed to start next week so that I wouldn't have to teach on Wednesday and Friday. This was going to be an exhausting trip. And I needed time to get Penny out of my system.

As I headed out the door, I pressed on my brother's name in my phone. The elevator dinged open and I stepped on.

He answered after a few rings. "If you're going to yell at me again, you might as well hang up the phone now," Rob said. "I don't want you to ruin my vibe."

His vibe? What the hell was he talking about? "Sorry about our last call, Rob." I wasn't really. He had kept pestering me about what students I was hooking up with. It was before classes had started, and at the time I'd just been annoyed that he didn't understand that I was actually here because I loved teaching. If he asked me now? That was a different story. Because now I was guilty.

"Okay…" he said. "So you're not going to rip my head off for being irresponsible again?"

"Are you acting like an irresponsible idiot?"

"No?"

I smiled. That meant he absolutely was. "Then how could I possibly lecture you?" The elevator doors opened and I pulled my suitcase into the parking garage.

"Exactly," Rob said. "So what's up with you? I'd ask about the co-eds, but…I know that your dick is in your pants and you're having zero fun."

Kind of. "I'm coming up to New York for a few days to meet with my lawyer. Can I stay with you?"

"I'm not in the city."

"Where are you?"

"Costa Rica. Man, you should come here instead. The babes are aplenty and some of them have already graduated. Just the way you like them."

God. "What are you doing in Costa Rica?"

"The question is why aren't you in Costa Rica? Come on! We'll have so much fun! We haven't taken a trip together in ages."

"My lawyer is in New York. My spur of the moment vacation is specifically to see him. I can't come to Costa Rica on a whim."

"You can do whatever you want on a whim. You're just too lame to."

I shook my head as I put my suitcase in the car. "When are you coming back to New York?"

"That depends…. How long can you stay in Costa Rica on vacation?"

"Do you have a visa?"

"No. Do I need one?"

I laughed. "If you wanted to stay for a longer time. But without one you can probably stay a max of three months, depending on their laws. You should look into that."

"I trust you. Three months. So…I'll be here for two and a half more months."

Of course. "Have fun with that. Let me know when you're back home."

"Will do. Sink your dick into a sexy student for me."

"Stay out of trouble," I said without acknowledging his comment.

He laughed. "I can't make any promises. Later." Rob hung up the phone.

I slid into the driver's seat. Costa Rica. For a three-month vacation. With absolutely nothing to do. It sounded like my worst nightmare.

Chapter 14

Wednesday

I rolled my suitcase into my office and stashed it in the corner. I'd gotten back to campus without much time to spare before my first class. Waiting to the last minute to do anything wasn't my style. But the more distance there was between me and Penny, the easier it was to convince myself I was doing the right thing by giving her up.

She'd sent me a simple text while I was away: "I hope that everything is alright, Professor Hunter." And that alone was enough to prove I was doing the right thing. I'd cancelled class because I was a dick. And she was worried about me. *Me.* She was supposed to be off going to parties and having the time of her life. Not wondering how her miserable professor was doing.

Despite the fact that my resolve had grown regarding Penny, I hadn't gotten much else out of my trip to New York. The documents were still unsigned. And I was still waiting. How was I ever supposed to get a fresh start if I was still chained to that city? Always waiting. I pictured standing in the rain with Penny on Saturday night right before I kissed her. Waiting to know if I was making the right decision. Waiting to know if she wanted me as much as I wanted her.

I took a deep breath and ran my hand down my face. My fingers stopped on the scruff I'd grown in the past few days because I'd forgotten to pack a razor. If I was lucky, Penny would hate my beard. It would be a hell of a lot easier to stay away from her if she suddenly wasn't attracted to me. Because she would stop looking at me like she wanted me to bend her over and... *Breathe.*

Today was going to be my new start to the semester. I'd keep my head focused on my classes and my students on an educational basis only. This was my job. How hard could it be to stick to the rules? Every other professor at this school did. I stopped outside my Comm class and took another deep breath. *Stay focused.* All I needed to do was keep my head on my work and my dick in my pants.

As I walked into the room, I didn't even glance in Penny's direction. And I wouldn't have to, because today I was going to be sitting amongst my students staring at the front of the classroom. "It's presentation day!" I said and pumped my fist into the air.

Most of the class groaned.

"It's not going to be that bad." My eyes were begging me to look at the back of the classroom even though my mind was telling them to stop. I clenched my hand in a fist. *Breathe.* "Okay, first up is Raymond Asher. Let me just fix this." I grabbed a podium from the corner and placed it in the middle of the room. "And I'll get out of your way." My eyes scanned the desks, looking for an empty one in the front row. But...there was only one empty desk in the whole classroom. The one in front of Tyler Stevens. In such close proximity to Penny that I knew I'd be able to smell her cherry blossom perfume. *Fuck me.*

I made my way to the back of the classroom. At least I hadn't been forced to sit behind Penny. That would have made it impossible to focus on the presentations. I dropped my satchel on the floor and slid into the empty desk. Luckily the student next to me was drinking a cup of some crazy coffee concoction with whipped cream and it was all I could smell. *I got this.*

Raymond walked up to the front of the class and started talking. He casually grabbed the sides of the podium and leaned in a bit. It looked like he had done this hundreds of times. He gave a funny presentation about his grandfather who was apparently "clearly better than any of Professor Hunter's grandparents" and deserved a proper shout-out. *Fair enough.* The kid was a regular entertainer. I jotted down a few notes. If the rest of the presentations were this good, it was going to be an easy semester. I was just starting to feel less on edge when Tyler started whispering behind me.

"Crap, he stole my idea," Tyler said. And even though I could hear him clearly, I had a feeling he wasn't talking to me.

Penny laughed. I closed my eyes for a second. *Breathe.* I called the next name on my roster. Unfortunately Raymond was the only one in class that didn't seem nervous to be standing in front of everyone. Almost all the speeches were about siblings, parents, friends, or significant others. I wrote down my notes about each presentation, hoping they'd be helpful. There was definitely room for improvement.

The minutes ticked by slowly. And the coffee scent in the room eventually dissipated and I could smell Penny's perfume. It felt like it was all around me. The minutes ticked by even slower. Slow breathing didn't exactly help when all I could smell was her.

Finally the minute hand clicked to the ten. "Great job today," I said instead of calling the next name. "Class dismissed." I finished writing my notes for the last presentation as the students started filtering out.

"I'll see you at lunch, Penny," Tyler said.

My hand froze. I continued to look at the paper on my desk, but I couldn't help but tilt my head a little to the left.

I needed to know what she was going to say. I needed to hear her confirm that she had a date with Tyler Stevens. That she was moving on just like I'd told her to. The thought wasn't as comforting as it should have been.

"Don't be late, I have a class at two," she responded.

"I wouldn't dare." Tyler laughed and I heard his footsteps diminish as he walked out the back door.

So that was it. I'd told her to stay away, and she'd listened. But as the class emptied in front of me I could still smell her. She was still sitting there, watching me. I turned and put my papers into my satchel. Maybe she needed closure to fully enjoy her date with Tyler. That's what I wanted, right? For her to be happy with someone better suited for her? Besides, if she didn't start dating someone else, I was worried I'd try to pull her back in. And I couldn't do that. I needed to push her away.

"I'm sorry about the other night, Miss Taylor. I was out of line," I said without looking at her. I continued to shove the rest of my papers in my satchel.

"I'm not sorry."

I shook my head, even though it killed me. She wasn't sorry. She liked it. I knew that. I knew that from the way she'd kissed me back. And the way her hands roamed my skin. I wasn't sorry either. But I'd always been a great liar. "You don't need to be. It was my mistake."

"I mean that I'm not sorry that it happened."

I finally turned to look at her. Sitting at this desk reminded me of what it was like to be a student. It made me feel like her equal. And for just a moment, I wished I could go back and do it all differently. She still had her whole life in front of her. I'd already squandered away a chunk of mine. I wasn't going to let her do the same thing. And certainly not because of me.

"Enjoy your lunch date, Miss Taylor. I will see you in class on Friday." I stood up and walked away. If she didn't realize I was doing this for her now, she eventually would. She'd look back at this moment and be thankful that she never took things further with her professor.

***

All the Comm presentations from today were graded and my other classes didn't have anything left for me to go over. I'd already run five miles, lifted weights in the apartment gym to avoid running into any students, and eaten dinner.

And now? I had nothing to do and I was obsessing over whether or not Penny's lunch date had gone well. It wasn't what I should have been dwelling on. I needed something else to occupy my time with.

I thought about calling one of my friends from New York. But there was a reason why we'd drifted apart. And none of those guys were good for me to hang out with. They were replicas of my little brother. Right now I wasn't interested in going out, getting wasted, and having a one night stand. I wasn't going to slide back into my old ways.

I leaned back in my chair in my apartment's office. It was the only room in the house that I'd actually taken the time to make my own. It was just as big as my bedroom and there were windows overlooking Main Street to one side. All the furniture was modern and my desk was positioned near the window to get the best view. Two of the walls were covered in floor to ceiling bookcases. There was a whiteboard on the other wall. If I'd been inspired to do anything, it would have been full of mathematical equations. But the whiteboard was blank. There was even a dartboard and a little basketball hoop above the trash can that I spent a lot of time failing to hit.

I lifted a picture frame off my desk. It was of me and my siblings at my company's launch party. We all looked younger and were smiling so hard. A conversation with Rob was easy if unproductive. But with my older sister Jen? I'd gone back home and I hadn't called her. Because I already knew what she'd say: "Sure, I'm having dinner with Mom and Dad tonight and you can join!"

The last thing I wanted to do was rekindle a relationship with my parents. I wasn't as forgiving as Jen. But they also hadn't fucked her life up as much as they had mine. Regardless, I couldn't call her either. She'd just be pissed that I hadn't visited her. And further pissed that my heart was so cold. I knew I was a disappointment. I didn't need anyone else reminding me.

I set the picture back down. I remembered that launch party like it was yesterday. Was that really the last time I'd smiled like that? *Dr. Clark says you smile when you talk about Penny.* But he also thought I was talking about a colleague. Not one of my fucking students. I pushed the thought aside. I loved teaching. But I didn't love idle nights like this. I looked over at my empty whiteboard.

I needed something to focus on so that I wouldn't think about Penny. I stood up and walked over to the board. *Something. Anything.* I folded my arms across my chest and stared at the blank board. Instead of an idea popping into my head, there was nothing. I felt as empty as the whiteboard. Completely and utterly empty.

Chapter 15

Friday

It was harder to focus on the speeches today. I wasn't sure if it was because I could feel the distance between myself and Penny, or if it was the fact that she would be going up to the podium soon and I'd have to look at her. I wouldn't have a choice. And whatever distance had been put between us might disappear as soon as I got my first proper look at her since last weekend.

I'd been doing better. Thinking about her less and less. At least...trying to. And I was worried that as soon as she was in front of me, I'd feel like I was starving to taste her again. I imagined us standing together in the rain. Pushing her against the car. Pressing her full lips against mine.

Breathe. I jotted down a few notes and then glanced at the next name on my roster. *Great.* My favorite student. *Not.* "Tyler Stevens."

Like Raymond, he didn't look at all nervous when he reached the podium.

He looked over at Penny and started talking. "I've gotta be honest with all of you. I'm going to be incredibly sappy for the next few minutes, because I have met THE most amazing girl. She's sweet and funny and super cute."

I had been hoping he'd make a fool of himself. Trip on his way to the podium. Stumble over his words. But no luck. And to make matters worse...he was definitely addressing Penny. His eyes were locked on her. It was like he was claiming her in front of the whole class. It was what I wanted and yet...I also wanted to rip his head off.

"And she is quite inspirational," he said. "Let me give you some examples. She usually says no when I ask her on a date."

The whole class started laughing.

"But it's okay, because she does laugh at all my jokes. She also kneed me in my junk that one time."

Everyone laughed again. But all I could think about was why. Why had she kneed Tyler in the crotch? What had he done to her? It must have been something inappropriate. Something she didn't want. I glared at him.

"But she's apologized. So that was nice of her. As you can see, she's a handful. Wow, now that I think about it, is she really that inspiring? I know it sounds crazy, but I really think so. And hey, at least she's inspiring me to be persistent."

His speech garnered a good applause. He walked confidently back to his seat. *Cocky asshole.* After he sat down, I heard him whisper, "You're up, Penny. By the way, your face is bright red."

I finished my notes on Tyler's stupid speech. For the first time all morning, I didn't need to look down at my roster. "Penny Taylor."

She slowly walked past me. But she didn't make it very far before she tripped over a backpack in the aisle and fell sideways into someone's desk. The desk screeched a few inches to the right and the girl sitting there looked like she had just been woken up. I was surprised she didn't scream.

The whole class started laughing. But I cringed. I'd just thought that I wanted Tyler to trip down the aisle, but now that Penny had, I wanted to give everyone a failing grade that laughed at her.

"I'm so sorry," she said and rushed up to the podium. The screeching sound seemed to echo as the girl moved her desk back where it belonged.

The majority of the class was still laughing at her. I looked down at my paper for a second. *Breathe.* I didn't want to snap at the entire class. Honestly, if it had been anyone else I probably would have laughed too.

I finally looked up at her. She was wearing jeans and a tank top and her hair was straight instead of unruly. And she was wearing more makeup than usual. *She's trying to impress you.* I felt myself breathe easier than I had all week. But then I noticed just how pale and nervous she was. Her hands were clutching her paper so tightly I thought she might rip it. My most nervous student. The shyest one. She could start speaking in Spanish and I doubt I'd be able to give her anything less than a B. Didn't she see that she had nothing to worry about? But still she just stood there, a deer in headlights. *Say something, Penny. Anything.* I smiled at her, hoping it would encourage her to start her speech. That everything would be okay.

"Okay so that was embarrassing," she said. "Anyway, I...," her throat caught.

Keep going. You're okay.

"I have been inspired by so many people that it's hard to choose just one. Which got me thinking that we actually choose the people that are going to influence our lives. It's our choice. We're able to choose who is going to influence us because we choose which strangers become more than acquaintances. We get to choose that. So really, aren't we all as individuals the ones that inspire ourselves the most?

"Acquaintances come in and out of your life all the time. And yes, we can certainly be influenced by mere acquaintances, because some are a positive force and others are a negative energy. Sometimes I think that pain is what defines you; the way you react to adversity. I actually have been inspired by many strangers in my life. The elementary school bullies. They helped me grow. They made me stronger. The professor who gave me my first D last semester."

A few students laughed at her joke. But even though it was funny, I wasn't laughing. Yes, she was shy and nervous. But her speech was thought-provoking. Clever. Different than anyone else's angle, that was for sure.

"I've learned to study harder," she said with a smile. "Acquaintances can be impactful. But there's usually a reason that they remain at a distance. Whether it's because you're uncomfortable with the idea of befriending them, or they just hate you." She shrugged. "I'm stronger because of the acquaintances that have come in and out of my life.

"But it's the people that become more than acquaintances that really inspire us. The people we choose to grow with. Sometimes it's best to remain strangers. But more often than not, if you choose to let them in, they'll inspire you in more ways than you can possibly imagine."

Me. She was talking about me. And in that moment, I wasn't sure I'd ever felt more relief. I did want her to go on a date with Tyler. I did want her to try to move on. But if she had tried? And decided to pursue me anyway? Wasn't that enough?

She was standing at the podium staring at me. I realized I hadn't written a single thing down. I glanced at my roster and called the next name so that Penny would be free to leave the front of the class.

She looked down as she walked, probably terrified of tripping over anything. I couldn't take my eyes off her. Right before she passed my desk, she glanced up.

Nervous and shy. But talking about me for her speech? I raised my left eyebrow. More than anything she was naughty. Very, very naughty. It felt like she was challenging me. And I'd never backed down from a challenge before.

"You decided to talk about me too, huh?" Tyler whispered when she sat down. "I liked it."

Tyler Stevens may have been great at giving speeches, but he was rather dense. Penny's speech had nothing to do with him. She hadn't even glanced his way the entire time. But Penny also didn't correct him. Which probably meant she wasn't closing the door on the possibility of being with him quite yet. The ball was in my court. And I was done messing around. If Penny wanted me after I'd warned her to stay away? That was her decision. I was nothing if not respectful of women's choices.

She wanted this. And clearly I needed this. Just the thought of letting myself have her had my dick straining against my pants. Fuck it. Fuck everything. I could only tell myself no so many times.

After the last speech, I dismissed the class. And I waited. I knew she'd come to me. There was a plan forming in my head on how to get her alone again. But it definitely involved her always coming to me.

Once the class emptied out, she stepped in front of my desk.

"Did you enjoy my speech, Professor Hunter?" she asked.

I looked up at her. "Miss Taylor, you'll have to wait until Monday for your grade, just like the other students."

She looked down. I saw the flush of her cheeks. As much as I liked seeing her embarrassed, I wasn't trying to dismiss her. I was tiptoeing around the game that she'd started. I lightly touched her elbow.

She looked back up.

"But I will say that it was rather enlightening."

We stood like that for a few seconds too long. Her blinking shyly at me. My fingers brushing her skin. I let my hand fall to the desk. And as soon as I did, a chill ran down my spine. I tried to ignore the feeling as I stood up. It's not like I'd have to go long before I got to touch her again. To feel her warmth. Because there was no going back now. Not when she was blatantly flirting with me in class. Not when she was staring at me like *that*. Begging me with just her eyes.

I leaned forward as I went to grab my satchel. When my head was level with hers, I paused. Our faces were only a few inches apart. One bend and we'd be reenacting our first kiss. But teasing her was half the fun.

I flashed her a smile instead. "Have a good weekend, Penny," I said, grabbed my satchel, and exited the room. I had her right where I wanted her.

Chapter 16

Monday

I'd skipped my weekly therapy session. All I could think about was how Penny had looked at me after class on Friday. During her speech. Pretty much every time I'd ever seen her. I'd tried to keep my distance. But what was the point when she didn't want me to? We were both consenting adults. I was done taking the high road. And I couldn't look Dr. Clark in the face and lie anymore. Not when I knew what I was about to do.

Besides, the more I thought about it, the more I realized what my infatuation with Penny was. A game. I'd win it and then I'd be able to walk away. I didn't need to talk to Dr. Clark about that. He'd just tell me I was making a mistake. That I deserved someone good. Yadda, yadda. Something about the universe giving back what I put out. Complete and utter bullshit. Because I knew that I didn't deserve anything other than the hell I was living. If I had changed, and if I was suddenly a good man, I wouldn't be thinking about a student.

Actually, there were a lot of things I wouldn't be doing if my therapy sessions had helped at all. I wouldn't be alone every night. I wouldn't be bitter about the life I'd left behind. I wouldn't be terribly unhappy.

I tried not to think about any of that as I climbed the stairs up to my Comm classroom. If my plan worked out the way I presumed it would, I'd have a moment of relief from my dismal thoughts. I'd be focused on Penny. Her warmth. Her smile. Her moan. She'd be the reprieve I desperately needed.

I smiled to myself as I opened the classroom door. All I needed to do was get through today and tomorrow and then she'd be beneath me. I took a deep breath, but not to clear my thoughts. For the first time since I'd met Penny, I allowed myself to embrace them. And for some reason, not warring over my desire for her helped clear my head.

"So I have the grades here," I said and lifted a stack of papers out of my satchel. "You'll get them at the end of class. The main problem that I saw with the first speeches was the amount of eye contact."

I grabbed the podium from the corner and placed it in front of the class. "Okay, I'm going to give you two examples, and I want you to tell me which speech is better." I pulled out a piece of paper from my pocket and began reading it word for word without looking up:

"My older sister always inspired me growing up. She did everything first, fearlessly. And I admired her for that. Her insane courage was something that I lacked, but reveled in. She always pushed the boundaries and knew what she wanted. And she was determined enough to go after all her dreams. I just wished she had rubbed off on me a little more. Don't get me wrong, I love being your teacher. But I like to follow the rules. I like to play it safe. Because of her, though, sometimes I feel compelled to take those risky chances. Sometimes I make huge, stupid mistakes and don't look back. She inspired me to be strong."

For one of the first times this semester, I was actually sticking to the lesson plan. And I didn't think it had anything to do with my ode to my sister. This speech was for Penny. She was my risky chance. She was the mistake I was about to make, and I wasn't going to look back.

"Okay, let me try that again. And let's see if you can see a difference." I gave the same speech, but only looked down once. For most of it, I gazed around the room. I made gestures with my hands. I delivered my joke a little louder and smiled. I paused as the class laughed so they'd be able to hear my next point. And since they thought I was hilarious today, probably because I was actually doing my job well, I added to the end: "Not physically strong. I'm pretty sure I could bench press two of my sister." I smiled as the class erupted in laughter again. Another point to make was that a little improv never hurt anyone.

"So, which speech was better?" I asked.

A hand shot up in the front of the room.

"Yes, Miss Lang?" I was also finally remembering the students' names. I was completely in my element.

"The second one. In the first one, you didn't make any eye contact. And you were pretty monotone throughout."

"Right. Was there anything else about the second one that was better?"

Another hand shot up.

"Mr. Potter?"

"You emphasized different parts of the speech and also had more personality during it. You used hand gestures and stuff."

"Right." I pointed at him to further emphasize his point. "So how many of you preferred the first speech over the second one?"

No one raised their hands.

"So why did half of you give me a speech like that first one, if you can so easily tell that the second one is better?"

Again, no one raised their hands. I turned around and wrote "fear" in all caps on the chalkboard. "Not everyone was lucky enough to have a sister like mine growing up, to help teach you how to be fearless. It's completely normal to get up here and stutter and have your knees shake. But what's there to be scared of? Me? Certainly not. Like I told you before, I'm a fairly easy grader."

I was true to my word. Most of the class had gotten As and Bs even though the delivery of their speeches needed vast improvement.

"So are you scared of your peers? You shouldn't be. You'll never see the majority of them ever again after you graduate. And chances are, they aren't even listening. They're probably daydreaming about their next class or that guy or girl they have a crush on. Not that I'm encouraging this behavior. We should all be listening to each other's speeches so you can get ideas on how to improve your own. But I'm getting sidetracked. My advice for you all for your next speech is simple. Stop worrying so much. Take a walk on the wild side and be fearless."

I walked away from the podium and lifted the stack of papers on my desk. "As soon as you get your grade, you can leave. If you have any questions about it, feel free to email me or stop by my office hours. I went easy on everyone this time, but make sure to take the advice I give to heart and try to improve for the next project. And most importantly, don't forget to make eye contact."

I began to wind around the classroom handing out the papers. Every now and then I'd have to call out a name that I wasn't sure of, but for the most part, I could put faces to the names on my roster now. Finally I walked to the back of the room and placed Penny's paper face down on her desk.

When I said most students received As and Bs, I meant all of them except one. Well, technically Penny did receive an A. It was marked as such in the database. But that wasn't what I'd written on her paper.

I smiled to myself as I handed out the rest of the grades and thought about what Penny was currently reading…and hopefully fuming over.

OBSESSED

Student: Penny Taylor
Topic: Yourself/Acquaintances
Miss Taylor,

It didn't seem like you were properly prepared for this presentation, despite being one of the last students that had to present. You stumbled over your words. You failed to make sufficient eye contact with the audience. You failed to harness your audience's attention. And the general lack of confidence you portrayed left your audience wanting.

You only loosely followed the topic of the presentation, and the topic that you did choose did not seem constant. Your examples were scattered and unrelated. The presentation as a whole was unfocused. You failed to nail your point home, Miss Taylor, mainly because it was unclear what that point even was.

Grade: C-

All of it was nonsense. Penny had given the best speech of anyone in the entire class. A unique, thought-provoking topic. Which was why she truly did receive an A. If she looked closely enough, she'd see the original grade beneath the whiteout.

I glanced at her reading the page as I pulled my satchel over my shoulder. She definitely looked pissed. My eyes ran down her body. A tight black tank top tucked into a turquoise skirt. Tomorrow I'd finally get to see what she looked like underneath all that. I'd dreamed of it too many times to count. I should have known we'd be together eventually. Because every dream always ended the same. With me deep inside of her and my name on her lips.

I left the classroom before she had a chance to storm up to me right now. I'd waited long enough for her, but one more day was worth it. *Just one day.* I could already picture her storming into my office hours. This time I'd lock the door behind her.

Chapter 17

Monday

This was by far the best day of the semester. The air was turning crisp as fall descended upon campus. The sun was shining. And tomorrow afternoon I was going to get to fuck Penny Taylor.

I smiled to myself as I walked along the brick path to Lerner Hall. I had a break between classes and I usually spent the time holed up in my office. For a moment I thought about stopping and grading some papers outside in the nice weather. But then it would be open season for students to approach me. I preferred being unapproachable.

A mid-morning coffee sounded good though. At least I'd get to spend a little more time outside. I took a detour and stopped by the quaint little coffee shop where I'd met Penny on the first day of classes. God she was beautiful. Even with coffee stains down her shirt she was gorgeous. I glanced around the shop as the barista handed me the to-go cup. It wasn't the first time I'd stopped by hoping to run into Penny again. But she was never here. It seemed like she didn't make a habit of coming to this coffee shop. Which made our meeting that first day even more momentous to me. Chance. A lucky roll of the die. *Fate.* I shook away the thought. There was no such thing as fate.

I left a generous tip and walked back outside. The 10:10 classes had started now and campus was a bit emptier. I could probably grade papers under a tree in peace. But for some reason, I still didn't stop. It was like I was being drawn to my office. A nagging feeling in the back of my mind that I was supposed to be there. I picked up my pace.

Maybe I had forgotten about a meeting? That was probably it. I was used to someone taking care of my schedule for me. And I hadn't been sleeping well. Something could have easily slipped through the cracks.

I pushed through the doors of Lerner Hall and took the stairs two at a time. When I rounded the corner toward my office, I saw her. Penny was standing outside my office door. It was like my body knew she was there. Like I was drawn to her. But she wasn't supposed to be here right now. She was supposed to storm into my office hours *tomorrow. Unpredictable.* I glanced at the scowl on her face. *Hot.*

"Can I help you, Miss Taylor?"

She stayed by my office door, pulling me closer, like we were opposite ends of two magnets. When I reached her, she held up the paper with her grade on it.

"Yeah, what the hell is this?" she asked.

I lowered my eyebrows. I'd wanted her to come, but I didn't want her to make a scene. I kind of thought she'd come beg me to change her grade. And I'd show her exactly how she could convince me... *Breathe.*

"My office, now." I pulled my keys out of my pocket and unlocked the door. She stormed past me and I took another deep breath and followed. Just because I'd expected her to stop by tomorrow when she'd had time to cool off, it didn't mean this was going to go down any differently. I knew without a doubt that when I left this room before my next class, I'd have fucked her out of my system.

I closed the door behind us and locked it slowly, hoping she wouldn't hear the click. I was the one in control of this situation, not her. Which was important because she was pulsing with too much anger to think straight. I strolled over to my desk, trying to remain unphased by her anger. She was always sexy. But when there was fire in her eyes? I was seconds away from ripping off her clothes without her saying another word. I shook away the thought. I needed to stay in control. She had to agree to my terms. She had to beg me for it. I took a slow sip of my coffee and placed it down.

"What can I do for you?" I asked with an easy smile. It was my turn to torture her. Because she'd been driving me insane for fucking weeks.

She was still standing near the door. Her hands were on her hips. A cute pout on her full lips. "You said you were tired of hearing everyone talking about the same people in their lives. You said to think outside the box. That's what I did. This," she held the paper up again, "is bullshit, Professor Hunter."

My dick stirred when she called me by my title. "Please take a seat," I said.

She ignored me and walked behind my desk. "You failed to harness your audiences' attention," she quoted from the paper in her hands. "I was one of the last people to go, and I still made them laugh!"

She was enticing when she was all smiles and sultry looks. But when she was pissed off…it did something to me. I tried to take another steadying breath. "Penny…"

"It was unclear what your point was," she quoted again. "My point was that I choose who gets a chance at inspiring me. I said that several times, Professor Hunter. Maybe you weren't listening." She glared at me.

Oh, I was listening. "Penny…"

"And this C- used to be an A. I can see it through the whiteout. You changed my grade. You changed it because you overheard Tyler say that the speech was about him.

Well it wasn't about him. It was about you." She poked me hard in the middle of my chest.

Her hands on me felt like heaven. I swallowed hard, willing her to continue with her outburst, resisting the urge to grab her arm and pull her whole body against me.

"I don't know why I ever let you kiss me," she said. "Is this a game to you, Professor Hunter?"

I thought it was a game. It's exactly what I had been thinking before she showed up here unannounced. A game I was about to fucking win. But when she was looking at me like she wanted to devour me, it didn't feel like a game. It felt real. Raw. Tantalizing. I was supposed to get her out of my system. But what if this made it worse? What if I couldn't get enough? Because there were a whole lot of things I wanted to do to her perfect body... *Breathe.* All I could smell was her cherry perfume. And I could feel myself leaning closer. I so badly wanted to taste it on her skin. She was going to ruin me.

"Penny, I'm fully aware that this isn't a game. This is my career that we're talking about." *My fresh start.* I was jeopardizing everything for her. But I wasn't second-guessing it. I needed her. Right. Fucking. Now.

"And this is my G.P.A." She crinkled the paper in her fist and threw it on the ground.

I knew she was a good girl. That this contradictory behavior was caused by me. *For me.* The reason why she was standing here begging me to kiss her didn't matter. All I knew was that I was transfixed by her. I just didn't realize that she was equally transfixed by me until this moment. The heat in her gaze. The desire written all over her face.

I'd played this scenario out in my head over and over again. But I never expected her to make the first move, and that turned me on even more. I think I was as surprised as her that she was about to initiate this. She was inching forward. She was going to kiss me in…three…two…one…

She reached up behind my neck and pulled my head down. Without hesitation, I tilted my head the rest of the way down and kissed her back. When our lips touched I felt more relief than when she first fell into my arms. I kissed her like I was greedy for air. Her exhales ignited something inside of me. She made me feel alive for the first time in years.

For a moment it didn't matter that I was her professor. All that mattered was that I was a man. And she was the most beautiful woman I'd ever met. I could have just kissed her for hours. But that wasn't the plan. And I needed to stick to the plan if I was going to come out of this whole.

I placed my hands on the small of her back and let them drift to her ass. As if I had given her permission to touch me now too, her fingers dipped below the collar of my shirt. A soft moan escaped her throat. I loved her hands on me almost as much as I loved the weight of her ass in my hands. But that moan? That trumped everything. I squeezed the toned flesh of her ass hard and lifted her up.

She wrapped her legs around me as I shoved her back against the adjacent wall. I knew I was being rough with her, but I couldn't control myself. I needed her. I'd needed her for weeks. She was all I could think about. Thoughts of her consumed my days and nights. All I wanted to do was unzip my pants right here and take her against the wall. But it couldn't be over yet. I needed this moment to last longer. I buried my face in her neck and breathed in her heavenly cherry scent, trying to slow myself down. I traced my lips along her collarbone as her perfume engulfed me.

Her skin pebbled under my lips, goosebumps rising to the surface. God she was responsive. I kissed the side of her neck again.

She slid her fingers into my hair like she'd been desperate to do it forever, the slight pull making me lift my head. We locked eyes for a moment and everything felt so right. But it was also wrong. So fucking wrong. And I needed to make sure we were on the same page. We had to be before I let this get any further. Not that I was sure I could stop. I was too tangled up in her.

"I told you to stop thinking about me," I said. My breathing was heavy. There was no possibility of turning back. I pressed my body even more firmly against hers, knowing she could feel what she was doing to me. I was hard as a rock for her. She'd been teasing me for weeks. I wanted her to know what she caused.

And she didn't back down at all. "I can't possibly."

I glanced at her swollen lips. "You're infuriating, Penny." *What am I going to do with you?*

She stared at me with all the conviction in the world. "Then punish me, Professor Hunter."

I groaned at her words and pulled her off the wall. I couldn't wait another second to taste her. To feel her pussy clench around my cock. My elbow hit a filing cabinet and sent a vase toppling off the top. It smashed against the ground, but neither of us flinched. Holding her firmly against me with one hand, I shoved the contents on my desk to the floor with my free arm. A stapler and a container of pens crashed to the floor. Papers slowly drifted to the ground as I dropped her down on top of my now empty desk. I'd pictured this moment with her a lot. And in all my favorite fantasies, I took her on my desk. Her skirt rising up her thighs. Her looking at me just like that. *Fuck.*

I reached up her skirt, grabbed her thong, and pulled it down her thighs in one swift movement. I bent down and kissed the inside of her knee as her thong slid down her legs and onto the floor. She moaned as my lips trailed up her inner thigh. Her skin was soft and her body was toned and tight. She was perfection. I stopped at the top of her thigh. Her pussy was glistening with need even though we'd barely done anything. She'd be coming on my tongue in a few minutes, but not yet. Not until I got to see her perfect tits. The things I wanted to do with them...

I pulled her to a seated position and grabbed the sides of her tank top. She raised her hands over her head without an ounce of hesitation and I slowly lifted it off of her, my palms running along her smooth skin.

Her breasts were heavy and full in her bra, straining the straps on her shoulders. I undid the back hinge with one hand and threw the fabric across the room. Fucking heaven. Her nipples were hard, demanding attention. I thought I could kiss her forever. But I could definitely rest my head on her chest for the rest of my days.

I licked my lips as I tugged my sweater off. She reached forward and clumsily undid the buttons on my dress shirt. It was the first bit of nerves I'd seen. But I didn't think she was second-guessing what was happening. I was pretty sure she was just nervous around me. She was as desperate as I was. Had she fantasized about this every night too? Had she played out this scenario for weeks? I knew without a doubt that she had. I pictured her touching herself as she thought about me. And I wondered how many times she'd already moaned my name.

She pushed my shirt off my shoulders, her hands pausing briefly on my biceps, before shoving the fabric the rest of the way down. She was staring at me like she worshipped me. There were stars in her eyes and we'd barely touched. *Just wait until I'm inside of you.* The thought made me even harder.

Her throat made this adorable squeaking noise as I pushed her naked back onto my desk. My hand splayed between her perfect breasts. I knew she could feel my erection on her leg, trying to break free of my jeans. I'd had this scene in my head for weeks. But I wasn't sure how far she thought this would go.

I watched her reach out. She ran her hands down my abs and stopped at the waistband of my pants.

I need you. You have no idea how fucking much I need you, baby.

There was only a moment of hesitation before she unbuttoned and unzipped my pants. That was the confirmation I needed. I leaned over and sucked on one of her nipples as I squeezed the other. *Fucking perfection.* Her nipple grew even harder underneath my tongue. I could spend hours just worshipping her tits. But if I didn't taste her within the next few minutes, I was going to lose my mind.

I brought my lips to her ear. "You're going to want to scream," I whispered. "But don't make a sound." I knelt down in front of her and traced my lips along the inside of her other thigh. Slowly torturing her like she'd done to me for weeks. There was a drop of wetness on the top of my wooden desk right beneath her pussy. She needed me just as much as I needed her. And there was nothing stopping me now.

I thrust my tongue inside of her, tasting her for the first time. Her hips rose, greedy for more. Greedy for everything I had to offer. But not as greedy as I was for her. God, she tasted as sweet as she smelled. I pressed her thighs down, spreading them even wider as I let my tongue explore her. *Delicious.* I circled my tongue, hitting all of her walls. Her moans were driving me insane. I moved my lips to her clit as my fingers slid up her thigh. I wanted to feel how tight she was. But I needed her to know that this wasn't going to be more than this moment. It couldn't be.

I stood up and leaned down to whisper in her ear. "Just this once, Penny." I bit her earlobe as I pressed down firmly on her clit with my thumb.

She gasped. And her hips rose, wanting more.

Not yet. Not until I let you.

I pushed her hips down more forcefully. "Do you understand?"

"Yes," she replied breathlessly.

I grabbed her thighs and pulled her to the edge of my desk. I pressed one finger into her wetness. She was so fucking tight. And she writhed under my touch. Just one finger and it looked like she'd never been so pleased in her life. I grew even harder. She'd been hanging out with college pricks that didn't know how to properly please a woman. She deserved to be worshipped. I was about to show her everything she had been missing out on.

She moaned when my tongue encircled her clit again. I let another finger slide into her. So tight. I guess she'd been hanging out with small college pricks. She was going to grip my cock like it had never been gripped before.

I moved my hand painstakingly slowly. I didn't want this moment to end. But I knew she was close. Those soft moans falling from her lips coming more frequently. I picked up the pace, my tongue in perfect tune with my fingers. I needed her sated and ready if she was going to handle the erection trying to break through the fabric of my pants.

She started to pulse against my fingers and my dick grew even harder. *That's right, baby. Come for me.* And then she broke. Her whole body shook as I took her over the edge with just my fucking fingers. I was about to change her whole world.

She moaned as I removed my fingers. I was greedy for that sound. I wanted it again and again. My thumb drummed against her clit as I leaned toward her.

"I know how to please, Penny," I said and licked her juices off my fingers. *So fucking sweet.* She looked like she was about to beg me for my cock. But I was going to give it to her on my terms. I walked around the desk, trailing my fingers along her naked torso, over her perky breasts. I lifted her arms above her head.

I needed her lips around my cock. I'd wanted it ever since meeting her in that coffee shop. She'd been teasing me. Tempting me. Torturing me. It was time for her to deliver what she'd been promising.

"But you asked me to punish you." I pulled on her hands and her back slid across my desk. Her head dropped off the edge so that she was looking at me upside down. Her slender neck was just begging me to fill it with my cock.

I let my boxers fall to the ground and brought my erection to her lips. She opened up her mouth, inviting me in. Her eagerness to do exactly what I wanted just made me harder.

Her tongue swirled across my tip, licking up my pre-cum like she was dying of thirst. *Jesus.* She licked the underside of my cock slowly and swirled her tongue as she explored. Slow. Torturously slow. It was like she thought she was the one in control. Still teasing me when she was the one naked on my desk? *I don't think so.* I let my fingers sink into her hair and thrust into her mouth. I groaned when she tightened her lips.

I thought her tongue was a Godsend. But her lips? They tightened even more as her mouth rode my cock.

Her lips were magic. I gripped her hair harder as I thrust in and out of her mouth faster. She was going to make me blow my load down her throat, but I couldn't stop. Not yet. I just needed a distraction so that all the sensation wasn't focused on her perfect mouth.

I leaned over and squeezed one of her perky breasts. I needed to taste her again or I was going to go crazy. I climbed up on the desk, leaned over her, and sucked on her clit. Her moaning with my cock in her mouth was an even more satisfying sound than just her aroused moan. I landed a few strokes of my tongue against her wetness that had her shivering beneath me.

I was the one that needed the distraction so I wouldn't cum, but her greedy pussy had her forgetting that she was giving me head. I moved my hips, taking back the control, fucking her mouth. She took all of it. Every inch.

When I thought she couldn't be any sexier, she grabbed my ass, pulling my cock farther down her throat. *Shit.* I was going to cum without even fucking her.

I landed one more stroke on her delicious cunt before pulling my cock out of her mouth. I needed to fuck her right this second. I climbed off the desk and spun her around so that her ass was on the edge of my desk again. My eyes gravitated back to her perfect face. Her cheeks were more flushed than when she was embarrassed in class. Her chest rose and fell as her eyes raked over my abs. I'd never seen her sexier. God, I was going to explode inside of her. And she was going to milk my cock with her delicious pussy and beg me to never stop.

I grabbed a condom out of my wallet before I lost all sense. She was everything I thought she'd be and more. *Responsive. Greedy.*

"Professor Hunter," she panted.

Perfection. "I've wanted you ever since you fell into my arms at that coffee shop." I slid the condom in place, grabbed her hips, and quickly thrust myself inside of her. *So fucking tight.*

She moaned. Maybe she wanted roses and a kiss on the cheek. But this wasn't going to be slow and loving. I needed to fuck her out of my system. So I was fast and rough. I was in complete control of her body and she didn't protest at all. She wanted it dirty and raw. Kinky as hell. She was a fucking miracle.

I dug my fingers into her hips and her back arched. I fucked her faster. Deeper. Harder. God, I was afraid I'd never be able to stop. Her face flushed even more. I'd never be able to look at her again without thinking her blush was due to fucking instead of embarrassment. She closed her eyes and I found my gaze wandering to the freckles under her eyes and across the bridge of her nose. I stared at the way her red hair splayed across my desk. The way her tits bounced with each thrust. For a second it felt like I was dreaming. Real life never felt this good. This perfect.

She clenched around my cock and I knew she was close. But I wasn't ready for it to be over. Not now. Not ever.

"Please," she begged.

No. I couldn't give her what she wanted. I couldn't let this end. It was a one-time thing and I was still desperate for more. "I asked you to be quiet."

I pulled out of her and flipped her so that her stomach was pressed against my desk and her perfect ass was in the air. I trailed my fingers up over her ass and then pulled her skirt down. It pooled on the floor at her feet. The view of her had been perfect before. But now? It was like a schoolgirl porno brought to life, and hell if it didn't turn me on even more. This had never been a fantasy of mine. But now it was the only thing I ever wanted to see.

I cupped her ass in my hands as I admired the way her hips dipped into her skinny waist. I'd never seen a sexier scene. I wanted to sink into my desk chair and just stare at her. See how long I could get her to lie there with her ass jutting in the air and her naked breasts pressed against my desk. But I was starving. Starving for her.

I pushed her legs apart, grabbed her hips tightly, and thrust inside of her again.

She gasped from the entrance.

And for just a moment I didn't feel like fucking her. I didn't want to hurt her. I wanted to make her feel better than she ever had before. I moved my hips slower, sliding in and out of her wetness. My fingertips traced the back of her thighs. She deserved more than what I could give her. So much fucking more.

"Professor Hunter," she moaned.

Fucking hell, Penny. It was like she was begging to be fucked. I grabbed her hair and pulled her head back. She tensed around my cock and I groaned. I was trying to give her what I thought she needed. Didn't she see that? Slow. Loving. I slid my free hand along the arch of her back, admiring the dimples right above her ass cheeks.

She pushed back against the desk, taking my cock deep inside her once again. *Fuck.*

I grabbed her breasts and squeezed them. They fit perfectly in my hands. Their weight just right. I ran my thumbs along her nipples. *Let me worship you.*

She arched her back so that she was no longer pressed against the desk. She reached one arm back and ran her fingers through my hair again, digging her fingertips into my scalp. Her hips swayed, riding my cock even though I wasn't moving.

I couldn't be gentle with her. Not when she so clearly loved when I was rough. She was begging for me to fuck her senseless. It's what I wanted too. I kissed her raised arm gently, trying to savor each moment. One day she'd want someone sweet and kind. But right now she was naked in my office. She may have been a good girl. But she wanted to be bad. And I could give her bad all day. It was all I knew.

I pushed her back onto the desk. "Stay still," I said. I'd give her what she wanted. I held her down and spanked her hard. *You like that? Is that what you want, you dirty girl?*

I slapped her other ass cheek harder. I'd claim every inch of her body. I'd fuck her until she couldn't walk. I thrust back into her harder than before. Her hips dug into the edge of the desk. My fingernails dug into her flawless skin, marking her. *Ride my dick.* She loved the sensation of pain and pleasure. *Come, you little slut.* I spanked her again and I felt her clench around me.

I groaned and reached down to find her clit. *Come right now. Come with me.*

"Yes!" she moaned.

I stroked her clit possessively and felt her starting to come. Her pussy clenched around me. Over and over. *Fuck!* I broke, my dick pulsing. I dug my fingertips into her hips as her whole body shuddered. *Fuck yes.* I kept thrusting in and out of her. Slower. "Mmmmm."

I blinked. I didn't even realize that noise had come out of my own throat.

I stared down at Penny's naked back. That was it. All of my fantasies culminating in one mind-blowing orgasm. I sighed. Now it was over. It had to be. I pulled out and gently turned her over. I should have started to get dressed, but instead I just stared down at her. Slender waist, curvy hips, perfect tits. I bit my lip so I wouldn't press them against hers again. *Now you have to stop.* I ran my hand through my hair where her fingers had been earlier. It felt better when she did it. *You have to stop.*

I took a deep breath. We were a one-time thing. And we were done. "Penny."

"Professor Hunter." Her chest rose and fell with each breath. She was staring at me like she always did, with lust in her eyes. That's all it was. And lust wasn't lasting.

I pulled off the condom and tossed it in the trash. I needed to get out of this office. I needed to walk away. I looked around for my shirt.

"I like being punished," she said.

Fuck me. "I like punishing you." I wasn't going to lie to her. She was fucking amazing. I pulled my jeans back in place and buttoned my shirt. I focused on rolling up my sleeves instead of looking at her. I didn't want it to end. But it was already over. The sooner I left, the better. I glanced at my sweater. It was too hot for it. Too hot in here. I needed to walk away.

"I have a class that I must get to or I'd be tempted to have you again." I couldn't have her again. I knew that. We were done before we ever started. I lifted my satchel over my shoulder. A quick exit was my best move here. Squash whatever it was she was thinking this could be. Because she was thinking she wanted more…it was written all over her beautiful face. "By the way, you gave a fair argument. I'll reconsider your grade." *End of negotiations.* It was just like any other business deal I'd made in the past. Unpersonal. We'd exchanged something we both wanted. A better grade. Her body. It was done. Now I'd be able to move on.

But I found my eyes lingering on her exposed breasts. So perfect. It was a shame that I'd never get to see them again. Hold them in my hands. Suck on her nipples. Cum all over them. I found myself getting hard all over again. *What the fuck.*

Breathe. "Please lock the door when you leave." I let my eyes linger on her body for one more moment, soaking in every inch of her. Locking the image away for a rainy day. And then I walked out of my office and closed the door behind me.

A one-time thing. How many times had I told myself that before? My thoughts should have shifted to my next class. But all I could think about was how I'd left her naked and alone in my office. And the fact that my craving for her wasn't satiated in the least. One taste of her and suddenly I was starving.

Part 2

Chapter 18

Monday

When I came back to my office after class, it looked like a tornado had just swept through it. Papers were scattered all over, some soaked in the coffee that had spilled on the floor. A broken vase lay on the ground in fragments. *Just this once*. So why did a part of me wish she'd been waiting here, naked, for me to come back?

I took a deep breath as I started to clean up the mess we'd made. Her scent was everywhere, driving me insane. *Just this once*. She'd agreed to it. We were on the same page. But looking at the desk, thinking of what we'd done, made me want her all over again.

I collapsed in my chair after my office looked presentable again. And that's when I saw her note.

Professor Hunter,

Thank you for listening to my argument. But I don't think I've learned my lesson. You might need to show me that again.
P.S. I borrowed your sweater.

I ran my thumb along the words. I could show her again and again and again. My dick stirred at the thought. But that wasn't going to happen. Just because I'd given in to the temptation didn't mean I wasn't in control of the situation. And now it was time to move on. *Just this once*. I wouldn't be tempted again.

***

I stared at my whiteboard that had been blank yesterday. Now it was filled with ideas. Too many possibilities to bring to fruition. It was like a switch had gone off in my mind. I was able to think clearer. I was able to breathe easier, no yoga necessary.

It was because of Penny. I wished it wasn't. But she was the only thing in my life that had changed. Maybe she was my muse. I folded my arms across my chest as I stared at the board. My muse? It was a ridiculous thought. And yet...I'd been more productive tonight than I had been since moving to Delaware. I continued to stare at the whiteboard without focusing on any one idea. There were several things that I could run with. Distractions that I clearly needed since my mind kept wandering back to Penny naked on my desk.

But I didn't want to be distracted. Clearly. Or the scene of her beneath me wouldn't be running through my mind on repeat. And I wouldn't be dying to repeat what we'd done. I mean...Penny and I had gotten away with sneaking around once. We could do it again...

I squinted my eyes at the board. Her letter indicated that she didn't want it to be a one-time thing. Did I? Really? It wasn't a question I needed to ask myself. I already knew the answer was no. But it didn't matter what I wanted. We were done. Over. That was the beginning and the end of it.

Dr. Clark's advice popped into my head. He'd said I deserved something good. Penny was everything good. I pulled my cell phone out of my pocket and clicked on my thread of messages with Penny. She was graduating in the spring. It wasn't like she'd be off-limits for long. We could sneak around for two semesters. We could...

What are you thinking?

But that was the problem. I couldn't stop thinking about her. I felt more like myself tonight than I had in ages. I felt…good. And good things attracted good things, according to Dr. Clark. My own therapist encouraged me to date Penny.

I ignored the fact that Dr. Clark didn't know Penny was a student and typed out a message. "I see that you've taken another one of my sweaters." *Breathe.* I stared at the text. *Fuck breathing when I could be breathing in the smell of Penny's skin instead.* I pressed send before I could change my mind. I could picture Penny curled up in bed wearing my sweater. Her cheeks still flushed from earlier. Maybe she couldn't focus on her work either because all she wanted to do was talk to me.

I wanted to reprimand myself. But I didn't have the energy or patience to pretend I wasn't going to pursue her. I'd lost all reason as soon as I sent the text. No, I'd lost all reason when I decided to fuck her. Of course once wouldn't be enough. Since when had once ever been enough for me?

Her text came a minute later: "I was a bit chilly after you left me naked and alone in your office, Professor Hunter."

I wanted her naked in my office all the time. "I apologize for my abrupt departure. But you barged into my office at a rather inconvenient time." Messing up my plans. I smiled at the thought. I wouldn't have changed a thing, though. My routine was rigid and boring. She brought spontaneity into my life. Hell, she brought life into my life.

"And when would be a convenient time?" she texted back.

I'd told her just this once. I had the perfect out. The only problem was that my plan backfired. I didn't fuck her out of my system at all. She'd crawled under my skin. She was still all I could think about. For just a moment while I had been working tonight, I'd thought I was cured. But as soon as I'd put the marker down? All my thoughts had gone back to her. Which meant one thing. I wasn't in control of this situation. And that was dangerous.

I needed to stop. I knew it. But instead, I texted her again. "It would be most convenient after you graduate in the spring."

The minutes ticked by. Was she considering that proposal? Did she really want to wait for months to reenact our tryst? It wasn't what I actually wanted. What I wanted was for her to be right in front of me, on her knees, worshipping my cock again. Everything would have been easier if she wasn't a student. But would I have wanted her as badly if she wasn't? There was something about the way she said Professor Hunter that did something to me. I raked my hands through my hair. I was a sick fuck.

"What happened to just this once?" she replied.

I rarely ever did anything just once. I thought I was getting better. I thought I could handle it. But I didn't realize how fucking fantastic she'd be. I didn't realize that she'd clear my mind enough to actually think for a few hours, only to reel me back in. I was consumed by her. It was terrifying. But I fucking loved the high.

I texted her back before I could talk myself out of it. "We can discuss it over dinner. I will pick you up on Saturday at 8." A date. I was going on a date with one of my students.

"I'll be waiting," she texted back.

I smiled and looked up at my whiteboard again. Just hearing from her had helped clear my head once more. It was time to start working on one of these ideas. Because I was probably going to be fired soon.

Chapter 19

Wednesday

I felt Penny's eyes on me as I entered the classroom. The class grew quiet. For just a second, I wondered if they had been talking about me. About what I'd done. I glanced at Penny out of the corner of my eye. She looked perfectly content. And sexy as hell. She wouldn't look so calm if her classmates had just been talking about us. My office door had been locked. No one knew. Besides, I didn't care anymore. I'd tried to tell myself to cancel my plans with her ever since I'd made them. But I'd never been good at telling myself no.

Her eyes scanned me from head to toe. I was more dressed up than usual. I was even wearing a tie. And I wondered if she was imagining the things I could do to her with just a tie.

Breathe. I pulled my satchel off over my head and placed it on my desk. It would be easy to stand here and envision all the ways I wanted Penny Taylor, but I had a class to teach. *For now.*

"I only had a few people complain to me about their grades, so I'm glad that we're all on the same page," I said. "I think we'll all be seeing even better speeches for the next assignment. Speaking of which, have any of you read ahead in the syllabus to find out what the next speech is about?"

Only one person raised their hand. Which was funny, because I knew for a fact that Penny had read the syllabus. But she was much too shy to volunteer an answer in class.

Yet bold enough to storm into my office and kiss me. I tried to hide my smile.

"Yes, Miss Snyder?"

"We're supposed to tell you about why we chose our majors."

"Precisely. There's usually a pretty personal reason why we choose the majors that we do. Whether it's about who you want to become, impressing your parents, or maybe just not knowing what the heck you want to do after you graduate. I find this topic to be quite beneficial for seniors, because maybe a look inside that true reason will help you decide which jobs you should be starting to apply to. So today let's go around and state what your majors are and one thing you love about them. Raymond, you're up."

I sat down in my chair. I was having a hard time focusing on what my students loved about their majors. Even though it had been some time, it was easy to picture myself in their shoes. I'd known exactly what I wanted to do. I'd always known. But I'd let my parents make all the decisions regarding my future for me. I still resented them for that. I looked down at my hands. I resented them for everything I'd become.

Taking a job in teaching was the first decision I'd ever made just for me. Walking out on my ex was the second. And the third?

"Penny Taylor," I called when the shmuck that always sat next to her sat back down. She was the third thing I'd ever done for myself. And it really felt like the third time was a charm.

"I'm majoring in marketing," she said.

Marketing? I sat up a little straighter. How was that possible?

"And mostly I love the creativity behind it." She sat back down.

No flirtations today, not that the topic had left room for much. But I wasn't sure I would have registered the fact that there was an innuendo even if there had been. *Marketing?* I taught lots of marketing classes. I should have had her in one of my classes by now. The odds that we hadn't run into each other before this semester were slim.

Fate. The term rolled in my head again for the second time this week. If I'd had her in a class last semester, I never would have pursued her. I hadn't been ready for a relationship. I was barely ready now. She'd fallen into my lap at the perfect time. Quite literally. I remembered how she'd fallen into my arms in the coffee shop. How for just a second it had been a little easier to breathe. I tried to shake away the thought. There was no such thing as fate.

I stuck to my lesson plan as best I could, distracted the whole time. Penny was all I seemed capable of focusing on anymore. I had a million questions for her. I wanted to know everything. And I felt like an idiot for not even knowing her major.

When I dismissed class, Penny dillydallied in the back of the room as the class emptied. Once it was just the two of us, she came straight up to my desk.

"I'm surprised to hear that you're majoring in marketing, Miss Taylor."

Her gaze dropped to my lips. If we were alone in my office, I wouldn't hesitate to kiss her. But I was glad she didn't come any closer to me right now. A student could come in for the next class at any moment. Although it pleased me to know she was thinking the same thing I was.

"Why does that surprise you?" she asked.

I stood up and pulled my satchel over my shoulder. "I'm just surprised that it's taken us this long to run into each other, since I'm a marketing professor."

"I guess we weren't supposed to meet until now," she said.

"I take it you're a believer in fate then?"

She nodded. "And you?"

I took a step closer to her. "I don't know what I believe. But I know what I want." *You. Again.*

She looked adorably nervous. She knew exactly what I was thinking. "I'm going to be late for my next class, Professor Hunter."

God I loved when she called me that. "I'm not stopping you." But I'm pretty sure I was. Neither of us wanted to move. Because then we'd have to wait two days to see each other again. I wasn't sure why I'd picked Saturday for our date. Maybe I was hoping I'd be able to talk myself out of it by then. That I could convince myself I could resist her. Staring at her right now, I knew that wasn't a possibility. I could barely keep my hands to myself when she stared up at me with her big blue eyes. How could she still look so innocent after everything I'd already done to her?

"Why are you so dressed up?" she asked.

"I have a work function after I'm done classes today." *Kind of. Not really.* But I couldn't tell her the truth. It was part of the surprise for Saturday.

"Oh?"

Her lips made the perfect "o" at the expression. And for a second all I could think about was them wrapped around my cock again. For fuck's sake. This was where I should warn her away. Try again to push her away. Toward someone more suitable. But I didn't want those lips on anyone but me. I'd already tried to keep her away. And I didn't have the self-control to deny myself any longer. Well, at least until Saturday.

I glanced down at my watch. "You don't want to be late, Miss Taylor. And neither do I." If I didn't leave soon, I'd end up spoiling the surprise of what we were doing on Saturday. Or kissing her. Or fucking her again. I smiled at her, shoved my hands in my pockets so I wouldn't reach out and pull her close, and strolled out the door.

Saturday couldn't come soon enough.

Chapter 20

Wednesday

I walked out of Lerner Hall and looked around for Ian's old Jeep with terrible gas mileage. I'd been pestering him to trade it in for ages, but he always refused. Something about nostalgia. To me, that wasn't a good enough excuse for the carbon footprint.

So when I spotted him leaning against a Tesla, I was more than a little surprised. "You finally upgraded?"

Ian lifted his gaze from the phone in his hand and smiled. "You like the haircut?"

I laughed and gestured to the car.

"Well, now I'm just insulted," he said. "But the car is pretty sweet."

"I thought for sure you'd just get another Jeep."

He shrugged. "I'm bored and have lots of money to spend. Both your fault."

Instead of giving me a handshake or a hug, he opened the passenger door for me. Other than Rob and Ellen, he was the closest thing I had to a friend. But Rob was my brother. Ellen was my housekeeper. And Ian was the head of my security detail. I didn't have any friends left. The only reason Ian was here was because I was still paying his salary despite the fact that I didn't need security in Delaware. Eventually I'd go back to New York and I'd still be employing the best head of security in the state. He was here out of obligation. Not because he missed me.

"You didn't have to come all the way down here," I said as I climbed into the car. He really didn't. All of this could have been done over the phone.

"You're still paying me. And I was bored, remember?" He smiled and closed the door.

"Does that mean you're enjoying your time off?" I asked as he slid into the driver's seat.

"If I was enjoying my time off do you think I'd jump at the chance to drive two and a half hours to see the likes of you?"

I laughed. "Fair point."

"And since I was coming down anyway, I brought that background check you wanted." He reached around to the back seat, grabbed a folder, and plopped it on my lap.

For a few minutes we were quiet as he put the car into drive and made his way through Main Street traffic.

"She's young," he finally said.

I looked down at the folder in my hands. I wasn't even sure if I wanted it anymore. Knowing everything about Penny, even if there were some skeletons in her closet, wouldn't change my mind about pursuing her. "Not that young." I put the file into my satchel without opening it.

"Is she one of your students?" he asked.

Maybe he'd judge me. But probably less than my psychologist would. I wasn't going to give up Penny. I wasn't even sure I could if I wanted to. And at least with Ian I had his signature on a confidentiality agreement. "Yes."

Ian whistled.

At least he didn't shake his head. "Speaking of which, maybe you could dig around to see what the rules are regarding professor-student relationships at the University of New Castle?"

"Like…a relationship relationship?"

"What else would I mean?"

"I don't know…a rebound short-term thing?"

"I'm not sure the dean will care about how serious we are either way." And I didn't have the answer for him. All I knew was that I hadn't had enough of her. Yet.

Ian hit his turn signal. "You probably won't like what I'll find. I think most schools frown on that kind of thing."

I didn't respond. What was there to say?

"Does that mean you're coming back to New York soon?"

"I have no idea."

"I could move down here, you know. I know you don't need as much security outside the city, but I could rent an apartment in your building and keep a low profile. I'd even be able to take care of stalkers."

I laughed. He'd done a similar background check on Kristen Dwyer for me last year. But it wasn't because I liked her. It was because I wanted to make sure her mental state was sound. I didn't want her showing up naked in my apartment with a knife like a crazy person. But she was clean. Certainly cleaner than me. If someone did my background check they'd be a lot more concerned. I eyed my satchel. Maybe there were some reasons to check out Penny's file...

"How's Jen?" I asked. It was better to change the topic than give him any false hope of moving here. I didn't need any security on campus. And it was a breath of fresh air to have time to myself, even if it was a little lonely. Besides, Penny made it significantly less lonely.

"How would I know?"

"I know you give her rides sometimes..."

"Oh. Well. Yeah." He looked a little flustered. "She's fine, I guess. Why?"

Weird answer. "I haven't spoken to her in a few months. She's relentless with trying to get me to patch things up with my parents."

"She may have mentioned that."

Of course she had.

"Are you going to talk to them soon? Pretty sure it's driving Jen crazy that you're fighting with them."

"You're a lot nosier than I remember," I said.

"You're a lot happier than I remember."

I laughed.

"It's because of the girl, right? Penny?"

Dr. Clark had said something similar to me. That I smiled more now. "Yeah, I guess it is."

"You don't think the age difference will matter?"

Penny was 21. That wasn't that young. She was an adult. She could make her own decisions. "It doesn't matter to me."

"Her parents are going to *hate* you."

"It's a little soon for that. I haven't even taken her on a date yet." And I strongly doubted that her parents would hate me. It's not like I was a deadbeat. I had plenty to offer their daughter. Although that background check of mine might be an issue. It would be good to at least see if either of her parents were cops. I was itching to open the folder, but I didn't want to do it with Ian watching me. At least he was only concerned about her age. That was probably a good thing.

"So this is going to be your first date?" he asked.

"Yeah."

"Isn't this a little extreme? Why don't you just take her to a restaurant a few minutes outside town if you're worried about getting caught?"

"That is what I'm doing."

"No...that's what a normal person would do. You're planning on buying a place and making the entire staff sign confidentiality waivers."

"I make everyone sign confidentiality waivers."

"Has Penny signed one?"

"No."

"Are you going to get her to sign one?"

I lowered my eyebrows. "No."

"What if she's trying to exploit you?"

"I'm pretty sure she thinks I'm a poor professor. She's never asked me any questions about Blive Tech or anything else business related." Which was refreshing.

He shook his head. "But you're about to buy her a restaurant for your first date. If she doesn't already know, she's about to. This is why you need me here. I could tail her and figure out what her motivation is."

"Is it so hard to believe that she actually just likes me?"

"Even if she does like you for you, there's still the whole professor thing. You're in a position of power. There's a whole other level of issues with that." He shook his head again. "There are countless opportunities for blackmail. I have to strongly advise you not to go through with this date. Cut things off before they escalate."

"She's not like that, Ian."

"Then for my sake, at least confiscate her phone when she's with you."

"I can't do that. She's not a petulant child."

"She's a college student…so she pretty much is a kid. Just tell her no phones at dinner," he said with a laugh.

I didn't find it funny. "Did you find anything in her background check that was alarming?"

"No. Middle-class family. Only child. She grew up in a normal suburban neighborhood with two working parents. Average life."

Penny was anything but average. "So nothing that screams blackmailer? Great. Can we drop this then?"

He pulled into the parking lot of the first restaurant on the list. "College is expensive, even for middle-class families. Maybe she's being financially resourceful. Just be careful."

The line between good mother and security detail felt blurred. "I'm not in New York anymore. Not as many people know who I am down here. Besides, I'm going to buy one of these restaurants. Which means you can set up security cameras to keep an eye on everything."

That seemed to perk him up. "Consider it dropped. Let's go find the place for your first date. Maybe we can test out the concept for that new security system you sent me the details of the other day. Did you hash out the surveillance issues?"

"I think I have it all set." The security system was what I'd started designing the night after taking Penny in my office. I had so much energy and so many ideas floating around in my head. She inspired something in me. I didn't know why or how, but she had. It was the first good business idea I'd come up with in over a year. And based off Ian's excitement, it was a great idea.

He rubbed his hands together. "Can I spend the night to go over all the details? And then I can spend the day tomorrow setting up the system."

"Only if you brought me a Totonno's pizza."

He laughed. "It's in a cooler in the trunk. I wouldn't have come without one." We both climbed out of his new car. "But aren't we doing food tastings at all these places?"

"There's always room for Totonno's."

"True. And there's a case of beer in the cooler too. And the Mets are playing tonight so we can catch the game later."

It sounded like something I used to do with my friends. I glanced at Ian as we walked across the parking lot. Maybe giving him this paid time off had broken some barrier between us. Because in a lot of ways, he was acting more like my friend than my employee. He really didn't need to come all the way down here. I could have checked out these places myself. New York City was a lonely place. Maybe he felt that as much as I did. "That sounds great," I said. "You can stay as long as you want."

"I knew I could bribe you with pizza."

We both laughed as we walked into the restaurant and looked around. Unlike Penny, it was completely average. And that wasn't going to do. All the décor was even beige. What had Ian been thinking? Penny had been dating boys like Tyler. I needed to show her that she was out of his league. "Nope," I said and turned around.

"But we have a meeting with the owner in just a minute," Ian said.

"Give him my regards, but it's a pass. What's the nicest place on the list?"

Ian brought up the restaurant list on his phone. "There's this old country club ten minutes from here. Definitely upscale. And they're actually looking for a new owner. The current one is retiring. Plus, who are you going to find from the university at a country club?"

"Let's go there next."

"Our meeting there isn't for another hour."

"I hope the food is good then. Because we'll be testing it out."

When we arrived, a valet took Ian's car keys. Ian stared after it longingly, probably worried that it would get dinged. But I had a feeling that the valet had it covered. When we walked inside everything was elegant with gold trim. The chandelier hanging from the vaulted ceiling completed the entrance.

"Hello. Are you here to dine with us this evening?" asked a well-dressed hostess.

"Yes," Ian said. "And we have a meeting with…"

I elbowed him in his side. I wanted to see how they treated normal patrons. Not ones they were trying to sell the country club to. "A meeting with our bosses later," I said. "So we'll definitely need a round of shots."

The hostess laughed. "Very well. We have top-shelf liquor, and I definitely recommend the tequila. I can grab those shots for you as soon as I get you seated." She glanced at the seating chart. "If you'll follow me right this way." She ushered us into the restaurant portion of the country club. "Is this table alright?" she asked.

"It's perfect," Ian said. "And that tequila sounds great too."

"Wonderful. Here are your menus. Your waiter will be right over to tell you about our specials today. And I'll go get you those shots. Enjoy your meal!" She hurried off to grab our drinks.

"Good service," Ian said.

I looked around the room. The dining area was filled with mostly older patrons. Ian was right, there probably weren't any people from the university here. It was far enough away from campus to be inconvenient and a little expensive for students and professors.

The hostess came back with two shots of tequila. I slid mine over to Ian. By the time dinner was over, I was hoping he'd let me take a spin in his Tesla. "Let's go take a look at the golf course," I said, trying to get him to down both of them.

"But we haven't even ordered yet."

"They'll wait." I stood up. "Aren't you coming? You gotta check out where to put surveillance."

"Rich people are so weird."

"Says the guy who owns a Tesla."

Ian laughed. "I like the new you," he said. "You're way more fun."

Life was more fun when you didn't want to jump out the window of your high rise.

Chapter 21

Saturday

I readjusted my glasses and continued to read through the papers I was grading. But my mind kept shifting focus to Penny. We didn't get a chance to talk on Friday because another student had a question for me after class. I thought the distance from Penny might give me some clarity. And in a way it had…just not in the way it should have. Not being allowed to talk to her. Touch her. Taste her. It was driving me slowly insane. I had all the fucking clarity I needed.

It had been a long time since I'd had something to look forward to. It had also been a long time since I'd been on a date. But I wasn't worried about that. It was clear to me that Penny hadn't dated anyone worthy of her. And even though I wasn't worthy, I was very capable of showing her a good time. A better time than some broke college student could. I thought about the blood dripping down her knees when I'd picked her up from her last date.

The edge of the paper in my hand crinkled in my fist. *Shit.* I tried to focus on the paper I was grading, instead of Penny walking alone in the rain. Seriously, what kind of idiots had she been dating? I wasn't a good person. But that didn't mean I couldn't be good to her. She certainly wouldn't be walking around alone on my watch.

"Surveillance is all set," Ian said as he came into my apartment.

I looked up from my papers. "I thought you finished that yesterday?" I welcomed Ian's distraction. Thinking about Penny with other men made my blood boil.

"Yeah…at the restaurant. I put a few test cameras throughout your apartment complex and right outside. I stopped by your office too. And I left some around campus. Don't worry, they're undetectable."

I ran my hand down my face. What he'd just done wasn't legal. It was one thing to have them in my apartment and new country club. I owned those things. But he couldn't just put cameras around campus. "That really wasn't necessary."

"Peace of mind." He set down one of the to-go coffee cups he was carrying down in front of me.

"So where exactly are these cameras?"

"I thought it might be nice to set one up outside Lerner Hall. That way you'll never have a surprise visit from someone you don't want to see." He sat down on the stool beside mine. "Like Isabella."

That did give me a little peace of mind. And if it was just one tiny camera on campus, it wasn't a big deal. "So that's it?"

"I may have put one outside of Sussex Hall too. This coffee is good, right?" He took a long sip like that was somehow going to distract me from what he just said. Penny lived in Sussex Hall.

"You shouldn't have done that."

"Why? I told you I was worried she had ulterior motives for dating you. Let me tail her for a few weeks to make sure. Besides, aren't you curious about who she spends her free time with?"

I could easily dismiss the first part of what he said. But I was curious about who Penny hung out with when she wasn't with me. Besides…wouldn't it be safer if I was watching out for her? She didn't keep the best company. I knew it was wrong, but now I was curious. "If you have information, you might as well tell me."

He smiled as he pulled out his phone. "She left her dorm building around noon today to go to brunch." He pulled up a video on his phone of her leaving her dorm.

It was wrong to look. I didn't want to spy on her. But I couldn't help it when the footage was right in front of my face.

"She was with Melissa Monroe, her roommate. Apparently they were randomly assigned to be roommates last year. They must have hit it off if they're roommates again. They're the same age. Both have birthdays in October. They both have great GPAs. But Melissa's family isn't as well off and her mother is just barely scraping by. She lives in lower Delaware which apparently is called Slower Lower to locals. Which is kind of funny." He laughed to himself.

It was scary how much he could find out about someone in such a small amount of time.

"Anyway, that's her," he said and pointed to the girl next to Penny in the video. There was a boy with shaggy blonde hair on the other side of Penny. "And that's…"

"Tyler Stevens," I said.

"You already know him?"

"He's in my Comm class with Penny. They sit next to each other. Does he live in their dorm too?"

"No. He lives in a frat house off Main Street. He must have been visiting them or someone else."

I stared at the video footage until they left the screen. The three of them looked like friends. They were all laughs and smiles. No hand-holding. But there was something about the video that still pissed me off. Maybe it was because I knew I would never have a moment like that with her. I could never go inside her dorm. I could never walk around campus with her. Or go to brunch at the dining hall. We'd never just be us. Our relationship would always be professor and student first. *What the fuck am I doing?*

IVY SMOAK

"Remove the camera," I said.

"But…"

"I don't want to spy on her." Honestly, I did. And that was the problem. The incredible violation of privacy didn't matter to me. What worried me was that I would watch her. That I wouldn't be able to stop.

"You wouldn't be. *I'm* running surveillance on her. I'll just tell you if anything important happens."

"I don't think…"

"Like if Isabella shows up there," he said before I could continue.

"She wouldn't do that." As soon as I said the words, I didn't believe them. Honestly, Isabella *would* do that. She'd never been one to care about consequences. Only results.

"We have no idea what she will and won't do. You were pretty sure she'd sign those papers, and she hasn't done that yet. You were pretty sure she'd never step foot in Delaware, but she's been to your apartment before. Cutting ties isn't always as seamless as you want it to be. Just look at the surveillance as a way to protect Penny."

I took a deep breath. "Fine. But you can't stay in my guestroom anymore." I pulled a key out of my pocket and tossed it to him. "I'm renting out another apartment in the building for a few months."

Ian smiled. "I can stay?"

"Just don't let anyone see you. I'm trying to keep a low profile. And I didn't buy it, I'm just renting it…so don't piss me off."

He laughed like it would be impossible to piss me off. Maybe he didn't know me as well as I thought he did.

"It'll be like I'm not even here," he said. "Except on game nights. And then I'll be on your couch."

"Deal."

- 144 -

"Great. My furniture should be arriving any minute..." he glanced at his watch and then back up at me.

"What? How did you..."

"I told you I set up cameras in the building. I already knew you were letting me move in. Apartment 3B right?" He put the key onto his keychain. "I'll check in with you later. Unless you're planning on bringing Penny back here tonight and that's the reason you're kicking me out. And if you are...you should consider finally decorating the place. It's a little...cold."

I looked past my kitchen into the living room. Everything was white and pristine. The modern furniture was sleek with hard lines. It really was cold. The only room I'd bothered to decorate was my office because it was where I spent all my time. And I couldn't actually picture Penny in any of the other rooms. She was so full of life, and my apartment was just...empty. It looked the same as it had the first day I moved in.

I could still remember Isabella barging in last semester. She'd looked around and laughed. She'd made some snide comment about how I was nothing without her. But maybe I just liked simple décor. It wasn't like she'd ever taken the time to get to know me. Either way, the thought of Isabella here made the idea of bringing Penny here less enticing. Isabella and Penny were nothing alike. A stark contrast that just made me appreciate Penny more. Maybe I would do some decorating before I invited her over.

I looked back down at the papers I needed to grade. "I don't think I'll be bringing Penny back tonight. So take your time getting settled into your new place." Ian being here would be a good excuse for me not to bring her back. Because as soon as Penny stepped foot in here? The smell of her would be everywhere. I wouldn't be able to get rid of the smell of cherry blossoms. It would be all consuming. And that was a dangerous thing if I wanted to stay in control of this situation.

"Does that mean I can eat dinner here? Ellen made lasagna with my name all over it."

I didn't bother to tell him he could just take the casserole dish to his place. "Yeah, that's fine."

He smiled. "One last thing before I check out my new digs. I emailed you the section of the university's handbook about professional conduct in case you want to read through it yourself. But there was nothing explicitly stated about professor-student relationships. There were things about sexual harassment, favoritism, that kind of thing. But nothing about actually dating an undergrad."

"It's more just a question of ethics then," I said without looking up. "And I'm not concerned about that. I wouldn't be pursuing her if my feelings weren't real." I frowned at my own words. I barely knew Penny. And I knew how problematic it was that I was already saying shit like that. It was easy to second guess everything when she wasn't right in front of me.

"You don't have to justify it to me. Just yourself. And maybe the dean if you get caught. And the press. The press will eat you alive."

"I'm not concerned about that either."

"Why?"

I lifted up the paper I'd been trying to focus on so that Ian would get the hint and leave. "Because she's worth the risk." The feeling she gave me when I was around her was worth losing everything. All the therapy in the world couldn't make me breathe as easily as she could. Tonight was just a test to make sure there was potential for more. Because I desperately wanted more. I wanted all of her.

Chapter 22

Saturday

I pulled up outside Sussex Hall. Eight o'clock was early on campus on the weekends and there wasn't a student in sight. Parties wouldn't start until later. And the dining halls were already closed. It would be a ghost town until later when Main Street would be flooded with drunk students without a care in the world.

That was why I'd chosen this time. For just a few moments, Penny and I could be a normal couple dating on campus. No one would look at us like a professor and his student. Especially at the back entrance of her dorm building. I looked around once more to make sure the coast was clear and put my car into park.

The camera Ian had placed outside the dorm's door was impossible to see. Even though I had designed it and had already seen the angle of the video footage. I smiled to myself. An undetectable high-quality surveillance system. That was the whole point.

Even though this use hadn't been my intention, I was still pleased with the results. There were always consequences to new tech. The list was a mile long with this camera. The world was full of disgusting people. And there wasn't a way to keep it out of their hands if I went through with production. Except for the exorbitant price tag.

I straightened my tie. I wasn't going to think about business tonight. Penny was my sole focus. I needed to figure out whatever was going on between us. Whether it was all in my head. Whether it was real. Whether it could and should be more than a one-time thing.

My body tensed when I heard her dorm door open. But then she appeared with a smile on her face and I breathed a little easier. It didn't matter how the date went. I already knew we would be more than a one-time thing. That number would go up tonight if everything went according to plan.

For just a moment, I watched her walking down the steps, knowing she couldn't see me through the tinted glass of my windows. She was wearing a strapless, summery dress and a brown belt that cinched around her waist. Not that she needed the belt to have a sexy hourglass frame. You could tell she was perfect even when she was wearing one of my sweaters. She took the stairs slowly and I smiled. She probably wasn't used to wearing heels. There was something comforting about the fact that she was just a normal girl. Not one that spent the weekends at red carpet events and elite charity functions, more concerned with climbing social ranks than having fun. She was real. Down to earth. And despite what Ian thought, she wasn't after me because of my money. She liked me for God knows what reason. And I couldn't wait to know more about her.

Before she could reach the car, I looked around to make sure we were still alone and stepped out. She just stared at me as I walked around the car and opened the door for her. I got a whiff of her cherry perfume and remembered the feeling of my lips pressed against her skin. I swallowed hard. It had been too long. I wasn't used to waiting for things that I wanted. And my patience was wearing thin.

"Hi, Professor Hunter."

I grabbed her face in my hands, leaned in, and kissed her. We were supposed to discuss us tonight, but instead all I wanted to do was rip off all her clothes again. *Breathe.*

But even telling myself to focus on my breathing didn't help. Not when all I smelled when I breathed in was her.

I forced myself to break the kiss. "Good evening, Penny." I tilted my head, motioning for her to get in my car. "We should get going. We have a reservation."

She slowly stepped back, like she'd rather be ripping off my clothes too, and got into the car. I closed the door behind her and took another slow breath. I needed to focus on her, not just all the ways I wanted to have her.

I climbed into the car and sped off without opening the conversation back up. I was worried that I didn't have enough willpower to resist her. That we'd end up on the side of the road fucking instead of getting to our destination. And I'd spent a lot of money to make tonight perfect. She deserved that. Besides, I already knew we were compatible in bed. I wanted to know if we were compatible in other ways.

"Where are we going?" she asked, breaking the silence.

"Someplace where we can be alone." I merged onto I-95. The farther I drove away from campus the less wrong this felt. We were just two adults on a date. And there was nothing wrong with that.

"But I haven't had anything to eat."

I lowered my eyebrows. Did she seriously think I wasn't going to feed her? What kind of dates had she been going on? "Yes, I'm taking you to dinner."

She settled into the passenger's seat, looking more relaxed by the minute. "So you wanted to discuss what you meant by just this once?"

I was surprised that she jumped right into the heart of the matter. She kept surprising me. "I meant what I said." That's all we were supposed to be.

"Oh." She turned away from me and stared out the window. "I don't understand why you asked me to dinner then." Her voice sounded small.

I wasn't trying to upset her. I was just being honest. But I'd left off an important detail. "Because I've changed my mind."

"Why?" She turned back to me.

I took my attention away from the road for a second. "Because I can't stop thinking about you, Penny."

"I can't stop thinking about you either."

We drove in silence for a few moments. I tried to focus on the road instead of on her. She was wearing red lipstick which made her look a little older. It was like she was trying to be more sophisticated for me. I wanted to tell her it wasn't necessary. That I liked her exactly how she was. She didn't need to be someone she wasn't for me. That wasn't what tonight was for at all. I just wanted her to be herself.

I tried to concentrate on the road, but it was almost impossible when she was beside me. My gaze kept gravitating back to her, like I couldn't resist. I watched her bite her lip as she looked out the windshield.

She turned back to me. "Did you grow up around here?" she asked.

"No. I'm from New York."

"What made you come here to teach then?"

I gripped the wheel a little tighter. I wanted to know more about her, but I had forgotten that she'd be asking me questions about myself. Personal things weren't something I talked about freely. I was barely honest with my shrink. Let alone a beautiful woman. I thought about the suggestion Dr. Clark had given me – that I'd need to be honest. But I wasn't ready to lose Penny yet. "I needed a change." It was a vague answer, but at least it was true.

"Did you live in the city?"

"Yes."

"I understand why you needed a change then."

I laughed. "Not a fan of New York City?"

"Everything is so loud and busy all the time. And everyone seems so depressed on the subway."

"I wouldn't know, I rarely rode the subway." But I agreed with the first thing she'd said. NYC was loud. And busy. It was easy to get lost in all that.

"I'm sure the taxis aren't much better. And there's not enough grass."

I laughed again. This was a topic she had a strong opinion about. But she hadn't seen *my* New York. I had a feeling a subway and taxi-free experience with a view of Central Park could easily change her mind. Not that I wanted to go back. I'd left for a good reason. "Well it is very different from here. Is this where you grew up?"

"I live about an hour away," she said. "Well, an hour from school. I don't really know where we are now."

I pulled into the country club's entrance without answering her. She'd see for herself soon enough.

A valet quickly came to her door and opened it for her.

"Welcome, madam," he said and put out his hand for her to grab.

I climbed out of the car while he assisted her.

"Hello, Mr. Hunter," the valet said with a huge smile. "I've heard so much about you."

I was sure he had. The whole staff had been briefed about the new ownership transition. And about the importance of this evening. I handed the valet the key. "Thank you."

I put my hand on the small of Penny's back and escorted her inside.

The marble floors had been polished since the last time I'd been here. And the chandelier glistened even brighter. Small cosmetic changes and the place already seemed livelier.

The same hostess that had greeted me the other day walked up to us. "Mr. Hunter. Your table is ready." She seemed nervous to be talking to me this time. I wasn't sure why. I hadn't let any of the previous staff go. I wanted things running as seamlessly as possible. Especially for tonight.

We followed her down the hallway and entered the restaurant. I felt like everyone turned to look at us. Unfortunately I wasn't able to get patrons to sign confidentiality agreements, or else I would have. There were no country club members that also went to the University of New Castle. Ian had confirmed it after I bought the place. But the restaurant was open to the public. Hopefully no one I knew or that knew me was here.

The hostess showed us into the private room in the back that I'd requested. There was a roaring fire and an elegant loveseat to one side. In the middle of the room was a table with a flower arrangement in the center. A bottle of wine and two glasses were already on the table. It was perfect.

"Your waiter will be right with you," she said and walked out of the room, closing the door behind her.

Penny looked up at me. "Where are we?"

"My country club."

She nodded, but I couldn't tell if she understood what I meant or not. Which made me smile. If she knew who I was, she would have known I meant *my* country club. That I owned it and wasn't just a member here. Ian was wrong about her. I'd already known it, but it was nice to confirm it for myself.

I pulled her chair out for her.

She smiled. "No one's ever pulled out a chair for me before." She sat down and stared at me.

Seriously, what kind of people had she been dating? I sat down across from her and tried to push away the thought. "Then you haven't been dating the right people."

"And I've never been to a country club before. Do you come here often?"

"This is actually only the second time that I've been here."

"Oh, so you just joined?"

I found it incredibly comforting that she thought I was just a member here. She liked me for me. Not my money. And I was pretty sure that was a first. "Yes. Earlier this week actually."

The door to the private room opened and our waiter came in with a big smile on his face. "Good evening. My name is Jerrod. It is my pleasure to be serving you tonight, Mr. and Mrs. Hunter."

Well, that was an unfortunate mistake. But all I could do was run with it to avoid an awkward situation. I just gave Penny a small smile, hoping she'd play along instead of correcting him.

She didn't smile back, but her eyes locked with mine. It was like she couldn't look away.

Jerrod started talking about the daily specials, but I was completely focused on Penny. I heard the uncorking of a bottle of wine but didn't look toward it. I was transfixed by her.

I let him know we'd need a minute to look at the menu. But really I just wanted to be alone with Penny. Moments like this with her were few and far between. I wanted to soak up every minute of her without any interruption.

As the door closed behind Jerrod, Penny lifted the menu, hiding her face. But right before she did, I saw the flash of concern. Why was she upset? Wasn't she craving this time as much as me?

"Penny?" I reached over and grabbed her hand.

She lowered her menu. "Professor Hunter, I've never had food that costs this much."

God it was hard to concentrate when she called me that.

"What did you say this place was called? The name isn't even listed on the menu." She picked up her glass with her free hand and took a sip of the wine.

She definitely wasn't after me for my money. So there was no harm in telling her the truth. I was supposed to be honest with her, and this was one of the only things I felt comfortable sharing tonight. Because usually everyone already knew it. "I was thinking Hunter Creek Country Club."

She coughed, choking on her wine. "Professor Hunter, do you own this country club?"

Adorable. "It seemed like a good place for a first date."

She just stared back at me. "What exactly did you do in New York?"

"I was a professor."

"For how long?"

I lowered my eyebrows slightly as I stared at her. She really didn't know? She hadn't heard anything at all? "Less than a year."

"And before that?"

"I owned a startup. Would you mind if I ask you a question?"

"What did you want to know?" She tucked a loose strand of hair behind her ear.

I leaned forward, wishing it was my fingers pushing her hair back. "Everything." I was surprised by my own statement. But it was true. I wanted to know every single thing about her. And why the fuck she was here with a guy like me.

She blushed. "There really isn't that much to know."

"I don't believe that's true. You enjoy challenging me and aren't afraid to speak your mind. I find you unbelievably refreshing."

She took another sip of wine instead of responding, her fingers fidgeting on the stem of the glass. I was making her nervous. And for some reason that just made me more intrigued.

"So why is it that you don't feel like you're interesting?" I asked.

Her throat made that cute squeaking noise as she looked up at me from her glass. "Honestly, you're the first person that's ever made me feel like I'm the only girl in the room. I'm not used to feeling like I matter."

You matter to me. It felt like all the air had gotten sucked out of the room. She was all I could focus on during Comm. I'd messed up so many lesson plans because I was all consumed by her. I couldn't be the first person to realize how intoxicating she was. Could I? But the look on her face made me believe her words. She didn't know how amazing she was. No one had ever told her. I'd tell her over and over again.

I was about to open my mouth when Jerrod came back in to take our order, breaking the spell. Penny looked back down at the menu and bit her bottom lip.

I didn't want her to be nervous around me anymore. And she didn't need to mull over the choices. I'd finally given in and read the last few pages of the file Ian had made on her, skipping over most of the basics. The last page had some random information that I wasn't even sure how Ian had gotten. But I knew for a fact that she liked seafood. I grabbed her hand again. "Penny, I've heard that the crab cakes are wonderful here."

She smiled up at me. "That sounds perfect."

I quickly ordered for us, trying to get Jerrod the hell out of the room again. When the door finally clicked closed, I put my elbows on the table and leaned forward. "When we're together, I can assure you that I don't see anyone else in the room. You always have my undivided attention." I meant every word. I'd tried to stay away from her, and I couldn't do it. No matter what I did, I kept gravitating back to her.

"That must make grading other students' speeches quite difficult."

I laughed. *You have no idea.* "It does."

I thought she'd be happy with the revelation, but she didn't look pleased. A small worry line crossed her forehead, and I was pretty sure if the menu had still been there she would have hidden behind it.

But I'd come prepared for this too. A visit to the bank with a very perplexed teller had gotten me exactly what I needed. I reached in my pocket, pulled out a penny, and slid it across the table. "A penny for your thoughts?"

She smiled up at me. "The last guy that I dated didn't believe in labels. So really, I'm just wondering, where it is that we are? I mean, I'm not trying to pressure you. It's only because I'm curious. I just want to know where you stand on things."

I started laughing. Was she serious? Why did she think we were here? Ian had pretty much told me I was crazy for buying this place for our first date. But I hadn't given it a second thought. I did it for her. To show her that I cared. Maybe there was a part of me that hoped I'd be able to let her walk away after tonight. But that tiny shred of hope disappeared when she'd walked down the steps of her dorm building.

Penny's face turned scarlet.

I hoped she didn't think I was laughing at her expense. "Where I stand on things?" I said when I caught my breath. "Penny, I don't relish the idea of sharing you, if that is what you're referring to."

"I don't relish the idea of sharing you either, Professor Hunter."

The way she said it made me swallow hard. Maybe I was wrong before. Maybe she knew more about me than I thought. The worst things about my past were hard to find, I'd spent a lot of money and resources on burying that information. But a simple Google search would relay a lot. *Fuck.* "What do you mean?" I asked.

"I know that you have a girlfriend. That woman from your office. You were going on a date. It was obvious."

Oh, thank God. I breathed a sigh of relief. "That wasn't a date."

"No?"

"We had a work function that we were both attending. I am not interested in Professor Keen." And I'd made that clear to her. "I am only interested in you. But since you've brought it up, if I were dating Professor Keen, you'd prefer that I'd stop, yes?"

"Yes," she said without thinking it over for a second.

"Then you won't mind me asking you to stop dating Tyler Stevens." I raised my left eyebrow as I stared at her. I'd be lying if I said I hadn't been a little jealous when I saw him exiting her dorm with her. Hopefully he'd spent the night alone in his dirty frat house.

"Tyler and I are just friends."

I leaned back in my chair. Maybe she thought that, but I doubted Tyler did. I'd heard him asking her out. I'd heard her agreeing. Did she not realize she'd already been on a date with him? The expression on her face was innocent enough. Which meant she really did have no idea how alluring she was. "Then I guess neither of us have anything to worry about." But I didn't feel like the subject was settled. Not until Tyler was out of the picture.

Chapter 23

Saturday

"There is one more thing, Professor Hunter."

Jerrod opened the door and brought in our entrees, interrupting her before she could finish her thought.

Penny took a bite of her crab cake like she'd been starving. I smiled, remembering that when she got in the car she hadn't realized I was taking her to dinner. She was probably used to the dining halls closing at 7, as well as dining hall food. I watched the way her lips circled around her fork. Since when had eating been so seductive?

"This is amazing," she practically moaned as she took another huge bite.

I smiled. Isabella only ever ate salads. I literally couldn't picture her eating anything else. I watched Penny take another bite. She really was refreshing. "What is it that you wanted to ask me?"

She finished chewing. "My roommate, Melissa. She can be rather, well, persistent. She always wants me to go out on the weekends and tries to get me to go on double dates and stuff."

"And?" I didn't like where this was going.

"And what am I supposed to tell her?"

"That you're dating someone."

"But she'll want to know who it is."

"So tell her about me. Maybe leave off the professor part though." I smiled at her. One simple lie. How hard could it be to keep our secret?

"You want me to tell her I'm dating an older, wealthy, unbelievably handsome gentleman who is way out of my league?"

You're the one out of my league. "And you'll want to say my name is James, not Professor Hunter. Which you should probably start doing in public as well." As much as I liked what her calling me Professor Hunter did to me.

"She won't believe a word of it."

"Hmmm. You'll have to mention that it's the best sex of your life as well. Maybe you can distract her with those details."

Her face started to flush again.

I was glad I wasn't the only one thinking about how fantastic our sex had been. Was she thinking about reenacting it tonight? It was the only thing on my mind now.

"Thank you for dinner. That was one of the most amazing things I've ever put in my mouth."

Definitely not the only one with sex on my mind. "Certainly not the best, though. Do you need to be reminded?" One of the many benefits of a private room. And I'd already pictured having her in here. More times than I'd care to count. The one constant of my dreams was that Penny was always on the dessert menu.

She smiled at me and my dick hardened.

"I may need a refresher," she said, a smile curling on the corner of her full lips.

This girl was fucking amazing. Flushed cheeks one moment and dirty words the next. I never knew what was going to come out of her mouth. My gaze dropped to her mouth. I needed those lips around my cock.

But Jerrod the cock-blocker walked back in with dessert menus. "Are either of you interested in dessert this evening?" He placed the menus down in front of us.

"I'd absolutely love some dessert," Penny said, but she was staring at me.

Jesus. "Could you give us a while to discuss our options?" I smiled politely at Jerrod, but what I really wanted was to tell him to get the hell out. He took forever to retreat. As soon as he closed the door, I stood up and pulled out her chair.

She started to get up.

"Sit back down," I growled.

Her perfect ass immediately made contact with the fabric of the seat again. And she blinked up at me, daring me to make the next move.

"I already know what I want for dessert," I said and dropped to my knees. Every moment with her was like a fantasy come to life. I slid her lacy thong down her smooth thighs and spread her legs wide.

"But Jerrod will be back in just..."

I leaned down and swirled my tongue around her clit. Her words quickly turned into a moan. I sucked on it once more and let my tongue enter her wetness. *So fucking sweet.* Her delicious cunt had been haunting my dreams. One taste was never going to be enough. The taste of her. The little sounds her throat made as I feasted on her. No, we were never going to be a one-time thing.

Her hips rose, begging me to go deeper. I moved my mouth back to her clit and let my fingers enter her void.

She gasped.

"What were you saying, Penny? That you want me to stop?" I pulsed my fingers faster.

"No. Please, don't."

"Don't what?" She was so wet that I was able to easily slide one more finger in. It had been far too long since we'd been together. I loved her just like this. Eager and ready. Waiting for what only I could give her.

"Don't stop. Please don't stop," she moaned.

I moved my hand faster. She was seconds away from coming all over my fingers. But I wanted to taste her. I was just about to thrust my tongue back inside of her when the door creaked.

Such a cock-blocker. Jerrod was depriving me of my favorite taste in the world. I stood up and lifted my hands over my head like I was stretching. I added a yawn for effect.

Jerrod walked over to us. I wasn't sure if he expected we were up to anything illicit, but if he got much closer, he'd see Penny's panties dangling around her ankles.

She seemed to notice too and quickly tucked her feet under her chair.

"What is it that you decided you wanted again, Penny?" I asked her. I wanted her to respond like she did in class. Something suggestive and sexy as hell that only we'd understand. There was something about the game we were playing that made me hard as a rock. I'd always just taken what I wanted. I'd never had to sneak around. Who knew that being patient was so damn fun?

Her face flushed and her eyebrows pinched together as she looked up at me. It did not look like she was as eager to play along. But then she surprised me.

"I'm actually in the mood for something warm and salty." She raised an eyebrow at me.

I bit my lip, trying not to groan. *Such a dirty girl.* If Jerrod happened to look down, he'd see my erection pressing against my suit pants. Luckily he was the epitome of professionalism and his eyes remained on Penny.

"Well, we have salted caramel squares," he said. "If you'd like, we can heat them slightly. I'll have to ask the chef though. I'm not sure if they'll melt."

"I'd rather have something sweet," I said, my gaze dropping down to Penny's lap.

"Well our lava cake is made from scratch and it is warm and sweet. Best of both worlds then."

"That sounds perfect," Penny said.

I needed Jerrod to leave the room right that second or I was going to cum in my pants instead of down Penny's sweet throat. "We'll split the chocolate lava cake then." I handed Jerrod the menus more forcefully than I meant to.

"Very good choice, sir." He walked back out of the room.

I turned my attention back to Penny. I was going to devour every inch of her. "Your juicy cunt is the most amazing thing I've ever had in my mouth. And I'm not done with it yet." I got back down on my knees, grabbed her perfect ass, and pulled her closer. One long, slow, stroke with my tongue broke her. *Fuck me.* I let her orgasm wash over her and continued to slowly encircle her with my tongue. So sweet. I placed one gentle kiss on her clit and slid her panties back up her legs. I stood up and pulled her to her feet.

"We almost got caught," she said breathlessly.

"We're not out of the clear yet." I needed her smart mouth around my cock before I exploded. I unzipped my pants and undid my boxers, letting my erection spring to life. "I still need to remind you what the best thing that's ever been in your mouth is."

She dropped to her knees as soon as I spoke the words. And a moment later her warm tongue slowly traced around my tip.

Fuck. She wasn't as innocent as she looked. Or maybe she was. I liked the idea that she only acted this way with me. That she got off on the idea of me telling her what to do.

She let her lips slide down my shaft. Going all the way down in one breath. I could feel the head of my dick entering her tight throat. She didn't even gag.

"Penny," I groaned. My fingers intertwined in her hair and I pushed deeper. She didn't seem to mind, so I guided her head up and down my shaft. Faster. I'd been dying to do this. And the real thing was so much better than my dreams.

She moaned around my cock. *You like that?* I moved my hips faster and she moaned again. She loved me fucking her mouth. Obedient. Dirty. Perfect.

I was getting close. And I was going to make her drink every ounce of my cum. My fingers dug into her hair. Faster and faster. She moaned again and the way her lips vibrated around me sent me over the edge.

I came hard. Shot after shot into her greedy mouth. And she drank me down just like I wanted her to, like she was as desperate for me as I was for her.

She pulled back and licked her lips as she locked eyes with me.

Definitely not as innocent as I thought. But I loved every second of it. I wanted to just stand here with her at my feet. Like she was worshipping me. But I wasn't sure I was done worshipping her yet. I zipped my pants and pulled her to her feet.

"Are you convinced now?" I asked.

"There's nothing I'd rather do than that."

"Are you sure about that?" I grabbed her ass and pulled her in close. Her breasts pressed against my chest. I could think of a lot of other things I'd rather do. A lot of them included her perfect tits.

"No." Her reply came out as a whisper.

"Tell me what you want then." I lifted her thighs and she wrapped her legs around my waist. I'd give her anything she wanted. All she had to do was ask. And I had a feeling I knew what she wanted…a redo of our session in my office. My dick deep inside her tight pussy. I could feel myself getting hard again as I set her down on the loveseat in front of the fireplace.

She didn't answer my question. Was she suddenly shy now that my cock was out of her mouth? I'd made her come with one stroke of my tongue after Jerrod finally left us alone. She fucking loved sneaking around with me. It got her off better than any foreplay.

I leaned over her and whispered in her ear. "I think I know exactly what you want. Because you like a little danger. You liked having Jerrod's eyes on you when you were seconds away from coming. You like breaking the rules and the idea of getting caught turns you on even more. And right now all you want is my dick so deep inside of you that you scream."

Again, she met my statement with silence. I needed to hear her say the words. To beg me.

"But I have no intention of giving you what you want," I whispered. "At least, not yet."

"Professor Hunter," she panted as I climbed off the loveseat.

I closed my eyes for just a second. All I could smell was her. The sweet smell of her release. The scent of cherries wafting around the room. I wanted to push her dress up her thighs and fuck her senseless. But not yet. Not here where Jerrod could walk in at any moment. Not in a room where I was pretty sure Ian had set up cameras.

"I think we need some fresh air, Penny." I offered her my hand.

She grabbed it and I pulled her to her feet. She seemed a little wobbly in her heels. Probably because of what I'd just done to her. I smiled and kept her hand in mine as I led her out of the private dining room. It was odd holding her hand. I couldn't remember the last time I'd held anyone's hand. Her skin was warm and soft. I squeezed her hand a little tighter and relished how perfectly it fit in mine.

We exited the restaurant in the back and stepped onto a huge terrace. It was chilly and there were only a few people standing by a fire with glasses in their hands, enjoying an after-dinner drink. I escorted her past them and we made our way down a set of stairs. I wasn't sure what I was doing. All I knew was that I wanted to be as far away as possible from prying eyes. As far away as possible from any cameras Ian had set up. I just wanted to be alone with Penny. I was desperate for it. There were always other students, professors, everyone watching. But tonight it didn't have to be that way. We could just be us. And the farther away we walked, the easier it was for me to breathe.

When we reached a row of golf carts, I leaned into one and turned the key. It sputtered to life. "This will do." I smiled at her.

"Are we allowed to use those? We're going to get in trouble."

I laughed and climbed into the small cart. How much trouble could we get in? I owned the place. It was adorable that she was suddenly worried about breaking the rules when she'd just had her professor's cock in her mouth a few minutes ago. And I wasn't done with her yet. "Get in."

As soon as her ass hit the seat I pressed down on the gas pedal. I hadn't explored the golf course much the other day, so I stuck to the small paths and wooden bridges on the course for a while, driving us farther and farther away from the other patrons. And then I saw it. The perfect place for us to be alone.

I veered off into the grass. We rolled up next to a small waterfall and I cut the engine. Lightning bugs flittered in the dark sky around us. I felt like I was in one of the many dreams I'd had about her. And even though we were surrounded by fresh grass and beautiful flowers, all I could smell was her cherry perfume. This girl was going to be the death of me.

I watched her climb out of the cart and walk over to the little waterfall. Her red hair shimmered in the starlight and her long legs were pale and striking in the darkness. I could still smell her even from a distance, her perfume all over me. I could have sat there staring at her for hours. It's what I wanted to do every time she walked into my class. But I was never able to. Here though? I could stare all I wanted. All we had was time.

I walked up behind her and wrapped my arms around her. But I wanted to do more than look at her. I wanted her in every way. I wasn't sure I could go back to pretending we weren't together around campus. I didn't have that kind of restraint. I wanted her again. And again. And again. I pushed her hair to one side and kissed the back of her neck. Her body tensed for a moment beneath my lips, but then she melted into me.

I slipped one of my hands down the front of her dress and wrapped my fingers around her breast. God, she was perfect.

My other hand crept up her thigh and under her dress.

Her breath caught.

But I had no intention of stopping. I moved her thong to the side and slid a finger inside of her.

She was still soaking wet. So ready for me. She pushed her hips back and let her ass rub against me. It was one of the most erotic things I'd ever experienced and we were still fully clothed. It only took her a minute to get me rock hard.

"Don't pretend for a second that you don't get excited by the idea of someone catching me deep inside of you," I whispered. I slid another finger inside of her and began to pump my hand. "I can feel how much you love it. The way you clench around me. But at least now you can scream as loud as you want and no one will hear over the water." I moved my fingers faster.

She moaned.

"Tell me what you want."

She shook her head like she didn't know what to say. "More."

"More what?" *Tell me you want me to fuck you. Right here in the middle of the golf course.*

She paused, but only for a moment this time. "I want your dick inside of me."

Good girl. I removed my hand and waited for her to turn and face me.

"James," she said as she turned around. So needy. So fucking hot.

It was the first time she'd used my first name. And even though it sounded sweet on her lips, I shook my head. "Oh, Penny." I cupped her chin in my hands and lifted her face so that she'd be looking at me. "We are not in public right now."

Her throat made that adorable squeaking sound.

My thumb slid down to her neck. "You have a lot to learn."

"Then teach me, Professor Hunter."

I'd teach her everything I liked. Every way I wanted her. Every illicit thing I needed to do to her body. I dropped my hand from her face. "Take off your clothes."

She glanced back toward the terrace. "But..."

We were too far away for them to see us in the dark. And she needed to trust me. And listen to me. I didn't like repeating myself. "Take off your dress before I rip it off."

She slowly undid the belt around her waist and pulled the dress off over her head. For a moment she just stood there half-naked in the starlight. And I unapologetically stared. I stared at the way her tits strained to break free from her bra. I stared at the dip in her waist before it widened for her hips. She was perfect. Every single inch of her. I couldn't pull my gaze away even if I tried.

"Take off all of it."

She unhinged her bra, freeing her breasts, and let the fabric fall to the ground. She kept her eyes downcast. I wasn't sure if she was embarrassed, but quickly dismissed the thought when she leaned forward, arching her back like a master seductress, as she pulled her panties off. She was a paradox that I couldn't wrap my head around. Usually I liked order. I liked knowing exactly how someone would react and behave. But not with her. She surprised me, and it was refreshing in every sense of the word.

She reached down to un-strap her high heels.

I rather liked her in them. So I grabbed her before she undid them and lifted her naked body over my shoulder.

"Professor Hunter!" she laughed.

She wouldn't be laughing in a moment. I lightly nipped at her exposed ass cheek as I ducked underneath the leafy limbs of a weeping willow tree. There was only a little light dancing around as the breeze made the branches sway. I lowered Penny to the ground.

She looked like she was about to get down on the grass.

"Don't sit down." I quickly grabbed her hand.
"Why?"
"The fertilizer will give you a bad rash."

She laughed. "Wait are you serious? Why do you know that?"

Because I've gotten that rash. This wasn't exactly the time to talk about my past sexual encounters. I shrugged.

"Professor Hunter!"

"Put your hands on the trunk of the tree."

"Have you had sex on a golf course before?"

"Penny, put your hands on the trunk." I glared at her, hoping she'd realize that I was being serious right now.

She lifted her hands and placed them against the bark.

Good girl. "Spread your legs." My voice came out tight. I was finding it hard to control myself around her.

She slowly spread her legs. The wind blew and she shivered, but kept her legs spread.

Perfection. But I wanted her to arch her back in that sexy way again. "Arch your back," I said and pulled her hair, making her follow my instructions.

The wind blew again and goosebumps rose on her skin. But she didn't even flinch. She could probably only feel how desperately she wanted me. It was exactly how I felt. An ache of desire. And I couldn't wait another second. I'd never been good at waiting. I pulled a condom out of my pocket. As soon as I had it in place, I grabbed her hips and thrust deep inside her greedy cunt.

She moaned. She was probably still sore from the last time I'd been inside of her. And I knew it was only me. She was still so fucking tight. No one else could give her what she wanted. She liked being fucked. Relentlessly. A line of pleasure and pain so blurred she couldn't tell the difference. It's what I craved too. My fingers dug into her hips.

So I gave her what she wanted. And what I needed. I fucked her harder than she probably knew she could take.

"Yes!" she screamed.

Her swollen breasts bounced with each powerful thrust. She pushed her palms against the trunk of the tree and started moving her hips in time with me. *Fuck yes*. My fingers dug into her flesh and she moaned again. She liked it rough and I knew how to give it to her. I reached around her waist and grabbed her clit between my fingers and squeezed. Hard.

She started to clench around my throbbing cock.

God. I rode her release, loving the feeling of her coming on me, her pussy gripping me like a vice.

But I wasn't done with her yet. Not nearly. I pulled out and turned her toward me. She needed to make me come. Before I could thrust back inside of her, she grabbed my tie and pulled my face down to hers.

"James," she said and bit her lip.

Apparently she wanted it even harder, otherwise she would have been a good girl and called me Professor Hunter like I'd told her to. I grabbed her ass, lifted her up, and pushed her back against the trunk of the tree. *So fucking naughty. So fucking perfect.* I raised my eyebrow. *Is this what you want?* I thrust back inside of her wetness. She was so tight I could barely take it.

"What are you trying to do to me?" I groaned. I pushed into her and pinned her in place as my hands wandered away from her ass. Her legs wrapped more firmly around me as I squeezed her tits. First I'd thought that her hand fit perfectly in my mine. Then I thought that her pussy was made to please my dick. And now her breasts? They fit perfectly in my hands. This woman was made to be mine. I rubbed her nipples and she moaned against my neck.

Even the sounds she made drove me insane. I grabbed her arms and raised them above her head. If I had any more sensations, I'd explode too soon. I wasn't done with her yet. My dick moved slowly in and out of her now, savoring the feeling of her around me. And our lips met. Her kiss was as intoxicating as everything else about her. And then it hit me. Everything was too slow. Too intimate. Too heavy. And that wasn't me.

I bit down on her lips and slammed back into her.

"Professor Hunter!" she whimpered.

I went faster and faster, bringing back the rawness and intensity that I knew she wanted and that I needed. I wanted her to be sore tomorrow. I wanted her to know that she was mine even when we were apart.

I felt that low pull in my stomach and our orgasms collided. My cock throbbed again and again, more intense than the first time I'd had her. What the hell was that?

I knew she felt it too. Her whole body was trembling as I pulled her into my chest. My breathing was heavy, rustling her hair. And her ragged breath was warm on the side of my neck. I wasn't sure how long I held her like that. With us both waiting to catch our breath. But eventually, I pulled out and set her down on her feet.

I'd fucked her. But I was very aware of the fact that a lot of parts of tonight had felt like more than that. Wasn't that what I wanted? For this to be more? But I didn't expect to feel like this…whatever this was. I could have held her forever in my arms. Kissed her slowly. And I wasn't sure I knew what I wanted anymore. But as I stared at her in the moonlight, I didn't want to fuck her. I wanted the grass to not be fertilized so I could lay her down gently and… *Breathe.*

I dropped my gaze from her exposed breasts and zipped up my pants. I was still in my full suit, that's how desperately I'd needed her. No self-control. It was like I could feel myself slipping, but I had no will to stop it.

When I looked back up, she had one arm across her chest and her other hand in front of her pussy.

"You have nothing to hide from me," I said and moved her arms to her sides. My breathing was still uneven as I took her in from head to toe. Maybe I had nothing to hide from her either. But I knew that it wasn't as simple when it came to me. She'd be gone as soon as I told her the truth. And I was getting worried that I didn't know how to exist without her.

Chapter 24

Saturday

Penny ran her fingers through her hair. "Do I look okay?" she asked as she stepped out of the golf cart.

"Penny, you look stunning." Truly. She had that just fucked look I was growing increasingly fond of.

"I mean, does it look like we just had sex?" she whispered, even though no one was around.

I looked at the way her tousled hair fell unevenly on her shoulders. Her dress was wrinkled and a little damp from the dew on the grass. She started to smooth the fabric with her hands to no avail.

I tucked a loose strand of hair behind her ear. "Penny, it looks like I just fucked your brains out."

"Professor Hunter!" she lightly pushed on my chest.

"That's how I prefer you to look." I straightened my tie. "Now, I believe I owe you a piece of cake." I lifted her into my arms and carried her back to the terrace. She was so light in my arms. And for a moment, I thought I really could be good for her. I could protect her. I could actually have a positive influence on her life instead of a negative one.

I set her down on her feet and draped my arm across her shoulders as I escorted her back into the restaurant.

She kept her eyes downcast. It seemed like she was embarrassed like she always was in class. Why? Was it because she was worried she had sex hair? Everyone was staring at her because she was gorgeous. And she didn't even realize it. I wanted to help her with that. Because she had nothing...*nothing* to be embarrassed about.

"Let's eat dessert out here," I said and slid into a booth.

Her eyes grew round as she stared at me.

She needed to ignore everyone else. It was just us. Screw the people staring. I wanted her to be so comfortable around me that she stopped carrying about everyone else. And a part of me wanted to make sure her attention was always trained on me. Like mine was trained on her.

Finally, she sat down across from me.

Jerrod came over with a smile. "Ah, I thought I'd lost you two."

"I just wanted to give the Mrs. a tour," I said and winked at Penny. But the game didn't seem as fun anymore. Eventually she'd discover all my demons. She'd leave. Just the thought made my throat feel tight. Maybe we weren't a one-time thing anymore. But each time we were together like this could be the last. She'd run away from me eventually. Everything good did.

"Of course. Did you two still want the chocolate lava cake?"

"Yes, Jerrod. Thank you."

"We kept it warm for you. I'll be right back."

A moment later Jerrod came back carrying the cake and two glasses of water. "Anything else I can get for you?"

"That will be all for us this evening."

"It was a pleasure meeting you both. I hope to see you again soon."

"Have a good night, Jerrod," I said. I took a bite of cake and watched Penny as her lips wrapped around her fork. How was it possible that she could even make eating look sexy?

"There is one more thing we need to discuss," she said.

"And what is that?"

She leaned forward slightly. "My grade."

I smiled. "What about it?"

"You gave me a C- when I deserved an A."

"Penny, it would be very unprofessional of me to give you favoritism." And according to Ian, a surefire way to get fired.

"As unprofessional as what you just did to me on the golf course?"

I set my fork down on the plate. "Touché."

"So you'll change it back?"

"Penny, I've always had it recorded as an A."

Her eyebrows pinched together, creating an adorable v in her forehead. "But. My paper. It said C-."

"And you think if I wanted to whiteout every single word on a sheet of paper I wouldn't just get another one?"

"You were just trying to upset me?" She glared at me.

"No, I was trying to seduce you."

"So everything played out just like you wanted?" There was no longer lust in her eyes. She looked genuinely pissed. And I didn't really understand why. The ruse had worked. We were sitting here because of what I'd done. Regardless, I didn't want to finish our date this way. Even if what I'd said was true. I pulled my wallet out of my pocket.

"No. Not at all. Like I told you before, I can't stop thinking about you. I thought if I let myself give in to the temptation then I could move on. But I'm more addicted to you than ever." The words just slipped out. Addicted to her? I clenched my jaw for a second, but immediately re-laxed because she looked so relieved. She liked that thought. Me being addicted to her. My eyes fixated on her lips again for just a moment. If only she knew.

I set a hundred dollar bill on the table for Jerrod's tip. "I guess I should get you home. Your roommate is probably wondering where you are." *Hopefully.* If Melissa Monroe was a good friend she'd be very worried indeed. But I'd found Penny in perilous situations before that could have been avoided if she'd had a good friend looking out for her. I needed to find out more about Melissa, that was for sure. I helped Penny to her feet.

As we waited for the valet to grab my car, Penny began to shiver. I took off my suit jacket, draped it over her shoulders, and pulled her in close. "Maybe your roommate will find your story more believable if you wear this back to your dorm."

She leaned into me. "I barely believe that I'm dating you, so it'll be hard to convince someone else that it's true."

I rested my chin on the top of her head. Another perfect fit. I could have stood there keeping her warm in my embrace for the rest of the weekend. But the valet pulled up. What little private time we had was over.

We were both quiet as I drove back to campus. It felt wrong that on Monday we'd have to pretend tonight hadn't happened. That she'd have to just be one of my students. It wasn't what I wanted. I moved my right hand to the center console. She immediately slid her hand into mine. We intertwined our fingers and I had a feeling she was trying to hold on to this moment too.

"What will happen if someone finds out that we're dating?" she asked.

"It's frowned upon, but the university's policy isn't explicitly stated in their handbook. It's more a question of ethics than anything else."

"You've looked it up?"

I glanced at her. "Yes."

"So you won't actually get in trouble?"

"That depends on a lot of things."

"Like what?"

"Well, if there was even a whisper of sexual harassment, I would get fired. Or if someone in your class found out about us and thought you were getting favoritism, they could file a complaint. Or..."

"I'm not going to tell anyone, Professor Hunter."

"Then I don't think we have anything to worry about."

"Would you still have pursued me if the university's policy was explicitly against it?"

I'd already started pursuing her before Ian had looked up the university's policy. I couldn't stop myself. And if I had looked it up beforehand and it had been against the rules? I doubted I would have stopped. I'd already tried to walk away. I'd tried to tell myself this was wrong. But here I was anyway. "Yes." I squeezed her hand.

"Even though you could get fired?"

I didn't need this job. But I loved being a professor. I'd taken a lot of risks in business. It was about figuring out if the risks would pay off. And with Penny, I knew she was worth it. Any time I had with her was worth it. I took a long slow breath. One of the easiest ones I'd ever taken. Yes, she was worth this feeling. "I know that you want this just as much as I do. I believe that my ethics are sound, so no one can make me question them." But I knew it wasn't that simple. If we got caught, I wasn't sure if anyone would buy that. This was wrong no matter how right it felt.

We drove in silence for a few minutes.

"What did your startup company do?" she asked.

"Tech."

"What happened to it?"

These were the kind of questions I didn't want to get into. I just wanted to live in the moment rather than being clouded by my past. "I sold it. But I still have a seat on the board."

"Then why are you teaching?"

"For the same reason I left New York. I needed a change."

"And if it wasn't because of how loud and busy the city was, then what was it? A midlife crisis?"

I laughed. "How old do you think I am, Penny?"

"Actually, I thought you were probably a grad student when I met you in the coffee shop. You can't even believe how shocked I was when I found out you were my Comm professor."

I laughed again. When we met, I'd hoped she was a grad student too. If only life had been so simple. "So take a guess," I said.

"Well, professors have to go to grad school and then get their masters to teach, right?"

"Yes, but I didn't do that. I was busy running a company in my early twenties. They granted me an honorary degree at the last university I worked at if I agreed to teach a few entrepreneurship classes in their master's program. I have the same arrangement here."

"So, maybe you're…29?"

"Close. I'm only 27." It was a relief that she guessed that I was older. It made me believe that the age difference didn't bother her. She was only six years younger than me. That wasn't a big deal. In any other situation it wouldn't be a problem at all. The issue we were facing was solely the fact that I was her professor. And that wasn't lasting. In a few months, she wouldn't be in my class anymore.

But she stayed completely silent. Maybe the age difference was a big deal to her. I pulled up outside of her dorm and cut the ignition. "What, you're sad that I'm not older?"

She laughed. "No. No, that's not it. I just..." she paused, searching for the right words.

But I knew exactly what she was thinking. This was going to be hard. She had nothing to worry about though. If our relationship did go public and there was any backlash, I'd take the blame. My life was already fucked up. And I was determined not to fuck hers up too. I leaned in and kissed her. God, her exhales were sweeter than air. "Like I said, you have nothing to worry about."

Chapter 25

Sunday

"So…" Dr. Clark said.

We'd kind of just been staring at each other for a few minutes, waiting for the other person to start talking. I'd almost cancelled today's session as well because my mind was too foggy. I was worried I'd let something personal slip. And that fear was why I'd made myself come. I was pretty sure I wanted to get the secret that I was fucking a student off my chest. Because I needed help figuring out what to do. Because if I was being honest with myself…it was a whole lot more than fucking.

I shrugged back in response. During our last conversation he hadn't understood what I was telling him about my lack of self-control around Penny. He'd dismissed it as a non-issue. But he'd been wrong. I thought I'd figured out a way around the issue. To have Penny once. Only once. And then it would be over. But since I'd seen Dr. Clark, I'd fucked Penny twice. I'd bought a freaking country club so we could date and not get caught. I was out of control. Literally. And Dr. Clark had done nothing to prevent it from happening.

"Are you just going to sit there silently for the next 55 minutes?" he asked.

"What would you like to talk about?"

He started flipping through her notebook. "I don't know, James. We could discuss the fact that you haven't been sleeping? Or talk about your trust issues?" He flipped a few more pages. "Your lack of communication with your family? Your new fear of commitment?" He flipped another page.

I hated his stupid notes. Pages and pages of how fucked up I was in the head. This could take a while if I didn't cut him off. "One of my friends from out of town is visiting."

"Ah. Perfect." He settled into his chair, seemingly happy with the topic. "Which friend?"

Damn it. "Ian."

He pinched his eyebrows together and then glanced back down at his notebook. He flipped a few pages.

I could have just told him what he was searching for. But what was the point? I had another 53 minutes to fill and I wasn't sure I really wanted to talk to him.

"Ian as in the head of your security detail?"

"Yes, but he's on extended leave. So he's just visiting as a friend."

"Interesting. Is he staying with you?"

I shouldn't have brought this up. "I rented an apartment for him in my building."

"Interesting," he said again. "And has he done any work for you while he's been here? Despite the fact that he's on an extended leave and here as just a friend?"

"Technically I'm still paying him so…I don't see the issue."

He shook his head. "The issue goes back to the trust thing I mentioned earlier. A topic we've been stumbling around for months. You only let people who work for you get close to you. Probably because they're the only ones that you can ask to sign confidentiality agreements."

"He's here as a friend. He even calls me James instead of Mr. Hunter now. We watch the Mets and Giants games together."

"But you're still paying him?"

"Yes." I'd already said that. For a shrink, Dr. Clark wasn't great at listening. I drummed my fingers on the armrest of the chair. "I also talked to my brother several days ago." I needed to change the subject. It had been nice hanging out with Ian, but someone like Dr. Clark wouldn't understand. He didn't have a staff and he'd never met Ian or Ellen. So he had no right to judge our relationships.

"And what is he up to?"

"Traveling around Costa Rica without a care in the world."

"And how does that make you feel?"

"Well, I certainly wouldn't enjoy taking three months off to travel."

"Not how you'd feel joining him. How do you feel that he's doing that while you're a professor at the University of New Castle?"

I wasn't sure where he was going with this. "I'm happy where I am."

"You sounded a little resentful when you said he was traveling without a care in the world."

"I'm not resentful of my brother's philandering ways." If Rob wanted to waste his life away that was his choice.

"Hm." Dr. Clark wrote something down in his notebook.

I glared at him. "I said I'm happy where I am and I meant it." *Stop writing things down.*

"Then have you talked to your sister recently?"

"Nope."

"Your parents?"

I didn't like where this was going. I shook my head.

"What about some of your friends from back home? You've mentioned Mason and Matt before…"

"I just told you Ian was visiting."

He jotted something down in his notebook. Really, what the hell was he writing?

"And I talked to Rob," I added. "That counts."

"And that made you feel…"

"Annoyed." I immediately shook my head. Dr. Clark had tricked me. "Or maybe I'm just annoyed with you."

"Why are you annoyed with your brother?" he asked, ignoring my last comment.

"He's still relying on my parents' money. That's the only way he can afford to travel because he's never worked a day in his life. And I don't understand how he can take anything from them. How am I the only one who sees how fucking awful my parents are?"

He gave me a hard stare. He hated when I cursed during our sessions. "Have you ever thought that maybe he takes their money even though he knows that they're not normal, kind, loving parents? Maybe he feels like they at least owe him that."

"I'd never take a cent from them."

"Yes…*you* wouldn't. Because of how *you* rationalize things. But maybe your siblings have minds of their own?"

Touché. "Your point?"

"That just because your siblings still value a relationship with your parents doesn't mean you can't still value a relationship with your siblings. They're not mutually exclusive."

"And I told you I called Rob." What the hell did he want from me?

"But you admitted that the call annoyed you."

I didn't know what he wanted me to say. *I'll be better behaved next time I call my little brother?* "Okay, great. Anything else you want to dissect today?"

"That colleague you mentioned being interested in. Have you seen her again?"

I glared at him. He'd basically just told me Ian wasn't my friend. And that my relationship with Rob wasn't healthy. Did he really want to get into this too? He was probably just pissed I cancelled my session last week and he hadn't gotten paid. To hell with him. And to hell with this. I was done. I didn't need to sit here and get reprimanded like a child.

"You know what?" I said. "As a matter of fact I have. I fucked her last week to try to get her out of my system because you were no help at all, despite the fact that I had real concerns. And it just messed with my head even more. So I had my *employee* Ian install security cameras outside where she lives so I could see who comes and goes out of her place. I had a background check done on her. And then I fucking lost my mind and bought a country club so we could have our first real date there last night. My first actual date in years and I didn't tell her a God damn thing about myself because we both know she won't want anything to do with me when she realizes who I am. Oh, and there were security cameras there too, so I've had the pleasure of replaying parts of our date all morning like a fucking stalker. And now I'm pretty sure I'm addicted to her, so thanks a fucking lot for all your help. It was your job to stop me."

Dr. Clark set down his notepad and pen on the coffee table. "Can we start at the beginning of that?"

I realized I was gripping the armrests of my chair so tightly that my knuckles were turning white. After that pathetic monologue I was planning on leaving and never coming back. But it was like my body was begging me to stay. I needed his help. I was out of my element with Penny. More than anything, I just didn't want to fuck up my chance with her. Because I would fuck it up. That's what I did. "I don't even know what I said first."

He smiled. "You said you had sex with her despite your concerns. We talked about those concerns a few weeks ago. And I meant what I said when I told you that I thought you were ready for a relationship. Especially since you seemed so happy. But you don't look happy now. Is that because of your behavior regarding the video footage?

"Sex is usually one moment and then it's gone," he continued without waiting for a reply. "If you had surveillance of it…I can understand the temptation to replay it. But it's only because the temptation is there. If Ian hadn't installed the cameras it would be a non-issue. So maybe have him uninstall them to avoid this reoccurrence? And while you're at it, delete the footage that you've been replaying. It's a violation of the woman's privacy and what you're most likely feeling is guilt. Plus, that way you can eliminate every temptation."

Every temptation except for Penny herself. She was still the main temptation that I should be resisting. And the footage of her sucking my cock? How could I possibly delete that? It was my favorite movie now. I nodded, but there was no way I was deleting it. Because when all this blew up in my face? I wanted a reminder that for just a few days something good was mine. Something warm and light and kind. Besides, the footage was amazing. Penny on her knees did something to me. I was getting hard just thinking about it.

"Good. And get rid of the surveillance outside her residence too. Watching her comings and goings is no way to start a healthy relationship."

"But that's what I'm trying to explain…nothing about it is healthy."

He held up his hand. "Because of things that you can fix. We get rid of the cameras. And then what problems remain? You bought a country club. So what? You certainly have the necessary means to make whatever purchases you want. As long as you're clear about the why. Which I assume was that you wanted to impress her, right?"

"Maybe, yeah." *No.* It was because I didn't want to get caught fucking one of my students. Maybe. It could have been what Dr. Clark said. Partially. Nope, definitely the not getting caught thing.

"See…there's nothing wrong with that. And you're scared to tell her about your past because you have real, sincere feelings for her. Everyone has those fears. They're universal. I have those fears when I'm dating someone."

"But you haven't done the kinds of things that I have."

He nodded. "That's true. But you're assuming that the woman you're dating is going to judge you. And that's not fair. Have I judged you?"

"You're my therapist."

"Have I judged you?"

I shrugged. "I don't know." He'd certainly written a lot of secretive things down in his damn notebook.

"I haven't. I've listened. I've helped you. Because that's *my* job."

I figured he wouldn't like the fact that I blamed him for all of it. "Sorry about that comment."

"And I'm sorry if you thought I was suggesting that Ian wasn't your friend. That wasn't my intention. I was simply pointing out your trust issues. Maybe you're having issues trusting this woman because she hasn't signed a document promising to never cross you."

I shook my head. I hadn't even thought of giving Penny a confidentiality agreement. Which was odd now that I thought about it. "I think I…trust her." Hadn't I already proven that? I trusted her not to tell anyone about us. And my job was on the line. The new life I'd worked so hard to get. "I want to be able to trust her."

Dr. Clark looked ecstatic. "Then tell her the truth about your past. Tell her everything. Give her the chance to show you she trusts you too. That's what a relationship is."

If only it was that easy. I knew he was right. But I liked Penny. And I didn't want to lose her. I was playing with fire.

"Are you serious about her?" he asked.

"Yes." I didn't even hesitate. "She's a breath of fresh air." *Much needed cherry-scented air.*

Dr. Clark smiled. "So what's preventing you from accepting her as a good thing instead of someone to run away from? Because hiding information from her is running away. What's really holding you back?"

"I know she's good for me." I was creating things for the first time since I'd moved here. I was happier. I felt at peace. But that's how it always went. "I have a way of ruining good things."

"No matter what you do, you won't ruin her. She's a person, not an object."

"You know what I mean." And I wasn't so sure Dr. Clark was right about this. Penny was so…innocent. I could break her. I could easily break her.

"And that's why I told you to get rid of the cameras. Delete the footage. You need to treat her as an equal. No one should have the upper hand."

No one should have the upper hand. His words rolled around in my head. No matter what I did, I'd always have the upper hand. I was Penny's professor for fuck's sake. And I liked having the upper hand apparently. Because I got hard whenever she called me Professor Hunter.

Dr. Clark didn't understand my concerns. He wasn't getting it at all. It wasn't his fault, he hadn't seen me at my lowest. He didn't realize how I could twist goodness. But now he was just bringing up new concerns, which wasn't helping anyone.

I pushed my hair off my forehead. My problems didn't just go away as time passed. Dr. Clark knew that better than anyone. So why was he pretending like I could be different? I shook my head.

"Are you happy when you're with her?" he asked.

Finally an easy question. "I had more fun last night than I've had in years. I can't remember the last time I felt so carefree. She has this way of making everything and everyone around us disappear." Which was terrifying. Because I had a whole class to teach, and it was hard to focus on anyone but her. And I kept kissing her in public even though we could be easily caught. If I wasn't more careful, I'd be the one to ruin this.

"When was the last time you were in love, James?"

"I dated this girl, Rachel, in high school. I was young and stupid, but it felt real at the time. It was probably the closest I ever got."

"There was someone else in high school right? You mentioned her when you first moved here…" he started flipping through his notebook. "Your classmate who passed away? The one that transferred to your school from Delaware?"

My throat started to feel tight. She was the last thing I needed to talk about. And I never should have spoken about her to Dr. Clark. He would never understand. I was somehow an even bigger mess in high school than I was now. "That wasn't love." It couldn't have been. Because that betrayal was too hard to live with. "She was just a friend."

"Just a friend?"

Friendship was a strange thing. Because of how quickly it could change. I thought about my best friends growing up, Mason and Matt. We broke in high school. Everything broke in high school.

I cleared my throat. "Yeah, we were just friends."

"Okay. Just Rachel then. So like ten years ago? What about Isabella?"

I shook my head. "I never loved her." I tried. I wanted to. But it was hard to love someone with as tortured of a soul as yours. Someone who lied more than they told the truth. Someone with a heart full of greed. Someone hateful and cold and cruel. It was like looking in the mirror. It felt like we deserved each other.

Dr. Clark picked his notebook back up. "So remind me what happened with Rachel?"

"I don't know. We were fine one minute and then she was gone. She just picked up and left without even saying goodbye. Turns out she didn't feel the same way about me in the end."

"That must have been hard."

I shrugged. "That was pretty much the start of all my issues. Well...not the start. But it was when I completely stopped fighting my demons. I just gave in to them. I put a lot of my hopes and dreams on her. She used to encourage me. At first." That didn't last long though. We were more toxic than anything. But I needed an escape. Turns out she wasn't it. I didn't know why we were talking about this. It was so long ago. It meant nothing.

"Do you ever think that maybe you should find her? Get some closure?"

"I got all the closure I needed when she left."

Dr. Clark pressed his lips together. "That's not closure. If you're over it, that's great. But it's just a patch on a wound until you know why. Maybe you're having a harder time opening up to this new woman in your life because you're still stuck in the past."

"I'm not having a hard time opening up to her. I'm choosing not to so she'll stay."

"But doesn't that go back to Rachel? She left, so you're scared anyone new will leave too?"

"That's not it." Maybe it was. The only people that could tolerate me recently were hired staff. And they certainly wouldn't if I didn't pay them. I had a way of messing up everything. Pushing people away. Every single good thing in my life eventually left. Or died. I swallowed hard. I'd buried everything that happened in high school in the past. And that was where it was going to stay. That's where it had to stay. "I have no idea why Rachel left. But I know why someone would fucking leave me now. No one in their right mind should be with me."

Dr. Clark flinched when I dropped the f-bomb.

"Sorry," I added.

"Do you love this new woman?"

"I…yeah…I mean no. It's too soon." Sometimes Dr. Clark's lack of segues left me scrambling. But it was a no. I couldn't love Penny. It was too soon. *Right?* "It doesn't matter how I feel anyway. She doesn't even know me."

"And whose fault is that? James, how do you expect to love someone else if you don't even love yourself?"

I realized my knuckles were turning white again as I gripped the leather armrests. Love had a different meaning to me than it did to anyone else. My demons followed me everywhere. They'd never just go away. But Penny? She was as light as air. It's why it was so easy to breathe around her. She was the light to my darkness. And when you lived a life in the dark, it was really fucking easy to fall in love with the light.

There was a knock on the door, signaling the end of our session.

"We can pick this up next week, okay?" He jotted something down in his notebook.

I nodded.

"Oh and what's this mystery woman's name? You've never said."

"Penny." It was weird saying her name out loud knowing I couldn't get in trouble. To my therapist, Penny was a colleague. An appropriate choice. *If only life was that easy.*

Chapter 26

Monday

I walked into the classroom and my eyes immediately gravitated toward Penny. All I wanted to do was walk over to her and pull her into a kiss. Saturday was still fresh in my mind. Honestly, she was all I could think about. And having to keep my distance on campus was proving harder than I ever imagined. This semester was going to be torture.

The way I was thinking about her was borderline obsessive. I wanted to believe Dr. Clark. He didn't think my past would be an issue. But he didn't know me. No one here really knew me. For just a second I let myself stare at Penny unabashedly. Would she run if she uncovered my secrets? Would she fear me?

My thoughts came to a stop when I noticed the rose sitting on her desk. A rose that wasn't from me. We'd just talked about being exclusive. I ran my hand through my hair as I placed my satchel down. And we'd spoken specifically about Tyler. She claimed he was a friend, but clearly that feeling wasn't mutual. Tyler had a dumb smirk on his face as if he had Penny right where he wanted her. *Not a chance in hell. She's mine.*

Breathe. But it was hard to breathe slowly when I was seething. The baggage I carried around already stacked the odds against me. I didn't need some immature frat boy getting in my way too. *Just friends my ass.*

"Speeches start next Monday," I said. "And this time we'll go backwards in the alphabet. So last names beginning with Z through N will go on Monday and M through

A will go on Wednesday." If Penny was going to flirt with other men, I was going to punish her for it. "I don't want nerves to be as big of a factor for this speech. It's important to feel comfortable in this room. So let's all share something a little more intimate today." I was going off my lesson plan yet again. But I needed to make sure that Penny and I were still on the same page. "Oh, I have an idea. I had an amazing date this weekend."

A few girls in the classroom sighed, but not Penny. She was just staring at me intently, probably eager to hear that I'd had a great night with her.

"Romance, dinner. The whole package." I couldn't really go into more detail than that without being inappropriate in more ways than one. "So how about everyone shares what their ideal first date would be. And let's switch things up today and start at the end of the alphabet so we get a feel for how next week's speeches are going to go. Adam Zabek, start us off." If I was competing for Penny's affection, I'd make sure to pull out all the stops. But first I had to figure out what she wanted. I tuned out the first few answers.

"Penny Taylor," I called.

She stood up. "I like piña coladas and getting caught in the rain. And the feel of the ocean and the taste of champagne."

Most of the class laughed.

I smiled and leaned back in my seat. I wasn't sure if she was joking or not, but I'd play along. "Tyler Stevens?"

Tyler stood up. "Hmmm. My ideal first date is probably making love at midnight in the dunes of the cape."

Penny giggled and something in my chest tightened. The thought of his hands on her made me see red. I needed to squash whatever it was that they had. I cleared my throat. "Okay. Let's move past the song lyrics."

When everyone was done, I went back to my lesson plan and started talking about enunciation. It took forever for the class to end. But when it did, I waited patiently for the students to empty out, knowing Penny would come to my desk. When we were finally alone, she grabbed the rose and walked up to me. I wanted her to toss it in the trash. Or laugh about how ridiculous it was. But she did neither.

"I see that you are continuing your relationship with Mr. Stevens, despite my request," I said. I was surprised by the hint of anger in my voice. We'd only been on one date. The possessiveness I was feeling was as surprising as it was unsettling. But I'd never been one to share. When I wanted something, it usually became my sole focus. That was my whole problem.

"I'm not."

I stared at the rose in her hand.

"It's just a friendship rose."

I folded my arms across my chest. *You can't be that naïve.* "Penny, there is no such thing as a friendship rose."

"But we really are just friends."

She didn't seem like she was lying. She really was just naïve and sweet. But I still had to stake my claim. I didn't want her even thinking about another man. And Tyler Stevens was proving to be quite a snake. "I'll be picking you up at 1." I'd clear my schedule for the afternoon. I wasn't going to wait to prove my point. After this afternoon, she wouldn't have any reasons to second guess any of my intentions. Even if I was still confused about them myself.

"Wait, what?"

"I'm taking you on your ideal date."

"But, I can't. I have a class at 2."

I pulled my satchel over my shoulder. "So skip it."

"You're a terrible influence, Professor Hunter."

I was. Of course I was. But I didn't have enough control to stop now. "I don't think you really believe that. I'll see you at 1." I winked at her and walked out of the room.

I was barely down the hall when my phone started to ring. Thinking it was Penny with some smart remark, I pulled it out. But there was an unknown number on my screen. I didn't even recognize the area code. Barely anyone had my cell number though, so it had to be someone I knew. *Hopefully.* My number being leaked to the public would be a nightmare.

I answered the call as I made my way outside. "Hello?" I said instead of offering my name, just in case it was the paparazzi or someone else equally annoying. I didn't want to risk anyone thinking they actually got my number.

"James, fuck, finally," Rob said. "I couldn't remember your new number and I've been stuck in here for days."

"Stuck where?" There was a distance to his voice. I knew he was thousands of miles away, but when he'd called me the other day his voice had been clearer.

"I messed up. You know what…no. I didn't mess up. This fucking country is messed up. It's not my fault."

How many times had I heard that before? "Where are you?" I repeated, but I was worried I knew the answer.

"I was just trying to help."

"Rob, where are you?"

"I think it's called La Reforma or something like that?"

Fuck. I went into Lerner Hall and up the stairs to my office. Only one establishment would have the word reforma in it, but I waited for him to say it. I closed my office door behind me. He was going to make me late for my next class, but I didn't want anyone to overhear my conversation with him.

"They're just holding me because I don't have cash on me to pay the stupid fine," Rob said. "Can you figure out where to send $10,000 to get me out?"

I sunk into my desk chair. "Why'd you get arrested?"

"There's a water shortage here. People are dying. I was doing my part."

He wasn't doing his part if he was rotting away in jail. And I hadn't asked him what cause he was currently aligned with. "But why are you in prison?"

"There was a protest."

A peaceful protest didn't get you locked up owing ten grand.

"It got a little more intense than I realized it was going to be," he added when I didn't respond.

I opened my laptop and typed in "protests in Costa Rica." Tons of news articles popped up. But they weren't about peaceful protests. "A riot?" I asked. "You took part in a fucking riot in a foreign country? What the hell were you thinking? You're lucky you even got a phone call."

"Are you going to bail me out or not?"

I wasn't surprised by the anger in his voice. He didn't need a lecture. Sitting in a foreign prison was probably enough of a wake-up call. "I'll figure it out. Please tell me you're coming home when you get out."

"I don't have a home."

There was an awkward silence. I could invite him here. I certainly had the room. But I was finally learning how to be happy again. I didn't need my brother coming here messing up my fresh start. Rob wasn't exactly a great influence. I sighed. That wasn't true. I was pretty sure I was the bad influence, not him. No, I wasn't sitting in a jail cell right now. But I was fucking my student. I couldn't exactly judge his moral compass when mine was clearly broken.

"I gotta go," he said. "My phone time's up."

Before I could say goodbye, the line went dead. I dropped my forehead into my hands. I was a shitty brother. It would have been easier to hand this task off to Ian. He'd be able to figure out where to wire the money and make sure Rob got out of jail okay. I'd wanted to take the morning to plan out Penny's perfect date. But I had time for both. And Rob always made time for me when I needed him.

Chapter 27

Monday

My brother's chaos had taken longer than I'd realized. The only thing I'd had time to do myself was send Penny a dozen non-friendship roses while I was on hold with some bail bondsman. Luckily Ellen had grabbed everything I needed for my date without even asking any questions. And I knew if someone had given me that shopping list, I definitely would have had a few questions. Dr. Clark hadn't told me to stop dating Penny. And Ian had warned me but then dopped it pretty fast. And now Ellen was picking up things for a date without any questions. I was surrounded by a bunch of enablers. No wonder I wasn't able to stop.

I pulled up outside Penny's dorm just in time. And any ideas of stopping this quickly evaporated. She was standing there in a pair of jean shorts and a tank top and she had a big canvas bag. I smiled. I was pretty sure she'd figured out where we were going.

She looked surprised by the fact that I was in a red convertible with the top down. She knew I had money, so she probably wasn't surprised that I had more than one car. I had a feeling she was surprised by the fact that I had the top down even though there were students milling about that could easily see me. But after my morning, I didn't give a fuck who saw us. No matter what I did, it wouldn't be as bad as anything I'd done back in New York. Or as bad as anything my brother had done in Costa Rica. So who cared? We were just two adults in need of a little more time together. Besides, my sunglasses helped hide my face. And I'd kept a low profile here. No one had ever seen me in this car. No one here knew who I really was.

I leaned over and opened the door for her from the inside.

"New car?" she asked.

It did still have that new car smell I loved. "No. But I haven't driven it much." I let my eyes rake over her body. Her shorts had ridden up when she sat down, exposing even more of her long legs. She was smiling so brightly and I had a feeling that she'd never ditched class before. She wasn't that type of girl. But she'd done it for me. Which made my smile grow as I pulled away from campus.

"So, where are we going?" she asked. The wind was blowing through her hair and I was finding it hard to focus on the road. All I wanted to do was pull over and have my way with her.

"I think you can probably guess," I said.

"Well, it's not raining, so I'm not sure where we could get caught in the rain. But we've been caught in the rain before, so maybe you're skipping that portion. Which means you're probably going the feel of the ocean route. So I'm guessing that we're heading to the beach!"

I smiled at her.

"You should have warned me though. What if I hadn't worn a bathing suit?"

"I was actually hoping you would forget it." I'd been really hoping.

She lightly pushed my shoulder as she laughed.

I pulled onto I-95 and the noise of traffic filled my ears. I pressed down on the gas, cruising between cars to pass them on the highway.

"You're going to get a ticket!" she yelled over the roar of traffic.

I slowed down a little so I wouldn't scare her, but I was still going faster than most of the other cars. I liked to do things fast. But if she needed me to go a little slower, I could. I'd already been trying to do that for her. "You don't break the rules very often, do you?" I asked, even though I already knew the answer. There was something about a good girl that did bad things only for me. Apparently it was my weakness. Because here I was, when I definitely shouldn't have been.

"Not really. But I do sometimes."

"Give me an example."

"You."

I laughed. "Besides for me."

"Well. One time...no, that was okay. Well there was another time...hmmm..."

"Maybe you're right about me then," I said. "I am a terrible influence on you."

"Yeah, you're the worst."

"Then I'll have to learn to behave myself better."

"I guess so."

I tried not to let our playful words get to my head. Because the truth was, I was the epitome of a terrible influence. And I was pushing it aside because I felt alive when I was around her. She was the best thing that had ever happened to me. I stared at the road in front of us. The best thing? Really? I took a deep breath. *Fuck.* I was in so over my head here.

"I don't actually want you to behave around me, Professor Hunter. I like that you're a bad influence on me. I think you're just what I need."

I smiled. She even knew when I needed reassurance. "Penny, I couldn't behave myself around you even if you begged me to." I pressed my foot down harder on the gas and turned on the radio to drown away my thoughts.

***

We arrived at the beach in record time. I drove to the end of the boardwalk and parked on a side street. "Have you ever been here before?" I asked.

"I used to come here every summer when I was growing up." She grabbed her stuff and stepped out of the car.

"All the more special then." I climbed out of the car and grabbed the towel and cooler that Ellen had packed for me. My hand immediately slid into Penny's as we walked toward the boardwalk.

"What about you?" she asked.

"I've come down here a few times."

"So this is where you take all the ladies to impress them?"

I laughed. "No, I've only ever been here by myself."

"You're kind of a loner, aren't you?"

"I guess you could say that I have a hard time trusting people." That's what Dr. Clark said. But I hadn't always been that way.

"Why?" she asked.

I squeezed her hand. But I didn't know how to answer her question. Today was supposed to be her ideal date. Talking about my past was not the fun afternoon I had planned. My phone started buzzing in my pocket as we reached the boards. *Son of a bitch, what now?* I dropped Penny's hand and pulled my phone out of my pocket.

Even though her number wasn't saved to my phone, I recognized it. *Isabella.* It was the only call I'd like less than one from my brother in prison. *Fucking hell.* Not here. Not in front of Penny. I was trying to protect her from this. That was why I'd driven to New York a couple weeks ago, to try to finalize this damn thing. Isabella had already taken enough from me. I wouldn't allow her to ruin what Penny and I had.

"I'm sorry, I have to take this," I said. I walked a few paces away from Penny, hoping she wouldn't be able to hear me, and answered the phone. "This isn't a good time," I said instead of a proper hello.

"It's nice to hear from you too, James." Her voice was laced with honey. But not the real kind. Some cheap high fructose bullshit. "I thought maybe we could meet up to discuss some of these specifics," she said. "It's been far too long since I've seen you."

That was kind of the point. "I don't even know why we're still talking about this." It had almost been a year since we were together. And when we had been together…she'd spent most of the time fucking some other guy behind my back. How long was she going to keep up this act? We both knew we'd never loved each other. We'd both been living a lie. We'd both been stuck in hell together. I glanced over my shoulder to make sure Penny was still far away.

"We're still talking about this because you won't sit down and have a real conversation with me," she said. "I miss you. I think you should come back to New York and stop fooling around in whatever little town you're in. I know we both made mistakes. And I'm sorry, I've told you that countless times. But honestly…the ones I made? Not quite the same as yours, darling. And I always forgave you. Always. That's what love is."

It felt like the hair rose on the back of my neck when she called me darling. And when she mentioned love? I wanted to laugh. Fake. Insincere. Manipulative. No, I didn't want to laugh. None of this was funny. I felt sick to my stomach.

Before I could respond, she started talking again. "Come back to New York this weekend so we can talk in person. I'll make reservations at Per Se. You owe me at least that, James."

Making reservations at her favorite restaurant was the kind of behavior that made her motivations clear. She just wanted to be seen out in public with me to snuff the rumors. Even Ian knew that my favorite restaurant in the city was Totonno's. But Isabella wouldn't be caught dead in a mom-and-pop pizzeria on the other end of Manhattan even if she knew it was my favorite. Because she didn't care about me. She only cared about herself. And I didn't owe her a thing. We'd tortured each other enough. I took a deep breath. Maybe Dr. Clark was right. Maybe I had made progress. Maybe I did deserve something good for once in my life. And Isabella was anything but good. "I told you I didn't care about any of the specifics. Just sign the damn papers." I ended the call and put the phone back in my pocket. *Breathe. Breathe. Breathe.* Just hearing Isabella's voice made me feel like I was trapped again. *Breathe.*

But I wasn't alone anymore. And Isabella was my past. I'd made a lot of mistakes, but being with her was the worst of them all. I was pretty sure it was a mutual feeling, so I had no idea why she was pretending that she was still in love with me. Especially because she never had been in the first place. She was a fucking con artist.

Breathe. I wasn't going to let her ruin the afternoon I had planned. I plastered a smile on my face as I walked back over to Penny. "Sorry about that."

"Is everything okay?"

"Just a business call," I lied. I grabbed her hand again and we took the few steps down to the beach. Her hand felt warm in mine. And there was something so comforting about it. Like she was holding me here in the present. Grounding me.

"Something with your tech company?"

"Well, it's not mine anymore. But yes." I looked out at the ocean. I thought it would be strange being here with someone else since I usually came here to clear my head. But I felt as comforted by the sounds of the waves as always. Penny had this way of making my mind stop reeling.

We walked toward the water. There wasn't anyone on the beach down here this time of year except for the occasional passerby.

"Professor Hunter? You didn't answer my other question."

I ran my hand through my hair. "I'm sorry, what was your question again?"

"Why do you have a hard time trusting people?"

I took a deep breath, my mind returning to my phone call with Isabella. "People have a tendency to wear many different masks. I've been bad at seeing people for who they really are until it's too late." *I don't want to talk about this.* I put my towel on top of the sand and sat down, pulling her on top of me. I needed her body against mine. I needed her to make me forget.

"I barely know anything about you," she said breathlessly.

"You know that I like you and that you like me." I stared into her blue eyes. "What else does anything matter?" I wanted her to believe that as much as I did. Nothing else mattered but this moment.

I lightly tugged her hair so that our faces were only an inch apart. She immediately leaned down and kissed me. I thought it was easy to breathe when I was around her. But when we were kissing? I was pretty sure I could live off her exhales. And every time we kissed I felt myself slipping even more. I wasn't sure how I was ever going to come back from this. And all I could think about was how much I could take.

I rolled over so that she was beneath me. We were all alone on the beach. If I wanted, I could have her right here. And the way her hips moved beneath me made her desire evident. But she wanted romance on her perfect date. I reluctantly gave her one last kiss and then sat up, pulling her into a seated position next to me.

"So I couldn't bring the real thing, but..." I opened the cooler and brought out two bottles of piña colada cocktails. They looked disgusting, but I was sure Ellen had tried her hardest to find something good. "I guess these are the next best thing." I popped off the caps and handed her one of the bottles.

"Cheers," she said and clanged her bottle against mine.

I watched her take a small sip and her eyes lit up. "This is so good."

Thank you, Ellen. I took a pull from the bottle and started coughing. "Ugh! It's disgusting."

"What? It's delicious."

"It tastes like the lovechild of a coconut and a bottle of Nyquil."

She started laughing. It was starting to become one of my favorite sounds.

"You can have mine too. I brought backup for myself." I handed her my bottle and pulled a beer out of the cooler.

"So piña coladas and getting caught in the rain aren't your thing?" She smiled up at me.

"I'm all about getting caught in the rain. But I prefer scotch."

She looked down at her drink. "I like how sophisticated you are."

"Penny, nothing I'm going to do to you here is sophisticated."

She gulped. "What do you have in mind?"

I reached over and touched the strap of her tank top. "Well, I don't think you need this anymore."

She put down her drink and pulled her tank top off over her head. Her bikini pushed her breasts perfectly together. I wanted to press my face between them and never move again. *What happened to romance? Screw it.* I reached over and unzipped her jean shorts. She lifted her hips and I slowly pulled them down her thighs and off her legs.

My eyes roamed from her breasts down her tiny waist. Every inch of her was perfect. And if she wasn't careful, she was going to be filled with every inch of me in a few minutes. I'd make it romantic enough. I stood up and took off my shirt, savoring the feeling of her eyes on me. I offered her my hand and pulled her to her feet.

"Want to go for a swim?" I asked.

"Yes, just let me put some sunscreen on first."

I laughed. "It's almost the end of September. I'm sure you'll be fine."

"Stop being a bad influence for one second. I get burnt crazy easily." She plopped back down and pulled the sunscreen out of her bag.

I knelt and took the bottle from her. "Let me do it for you then. Lie down." As long as my hands were all over her, I was happy.

She lay down on her stomach and I froze. Her back. There were small cuts all over her back. They had to be from the tree's bark on the golf course. I lightly touched her skin. This was what I was worried about. That I ruined everything good that I touched. "Penny, I'm so sorry." I wasn't good for her. I'd ruin her. I'd ruin everything.

"The risks of having sex on a golf course, I guess. It doesn't hurt though."

I wanted to believe that she was fine. But the cuts proved otherwise. I gently started to massage the sunscreen onto her shoulders and arms. "Are you sure it doesn't hurt?" *I'm so sorry.*

"I'm sure."

Her skin was so soft and delicate beneath my fingers, though, and I had a hard time believing her words. My thumb traced along one of the cuts. I'd overindulged in her and this was the proof. But she wasn't squirming from pain. She did seem fine. So sweet and innocent, but tougher than I was giving her credit for.

"You know, when I was younger I used to be so envious of all the girls on the boardwalk that had boyfriends," she said. "I couldn't wait until I was older. Holding hands on the boardwalk seemed like the epitome of romance."

I smiled as I listened to her. So the whole beach thing was real, even if the song lyrics had been a joke. I rubbed the lotion underneath the strings of her bikini and began to massage her lower back. "So did you force your high school boyfriends to take you here? To show all the other girls up?"

"Yes. I mean, no. I'm sorry, what did you say? I wasn't paying attention."

I laughed and continued to massage the sunscreen onto her skin. Knowing that my touch distracted her was satisfying. "So you must have brought all your high school boyfriends here. Turn over." I wanted my hands everywhere on her all at once. There was nothing as soothing as my skin pressed against hers. When I touched her, it was like I stole a little of her warmth. Like maybe she could keep my demons at bay.

"No. I wish." She rolled onto her back and propped herself up on her elbows.

"Couldn't get them to take you here, huh?" I rubbed my hands across her tight stomach. Then dipped them slightly below the top of her bikini bottom. *Not yet.* I moved them back to her stomach.

Her gaze was following the trail of my fingers. "No, I mean I didn't have any boyfriends in high school." She immediately closed her eyes like she was embarrassed.

No boyfriends in high school? I had skipped a lot of the early information in her background check. Had that tidbit been in there? I was having a hard time believing it was even true. How had no one asked her out in high school? Were all those horned up teenagers she went to school with blind to perfection? Maybe she'd actually attended a school for the blind.

When she opened her eyes again, I smiled at her. She had no reason to be embarrassed.

"I wouldn't have guessed that, Penny. But I find it incredibly adorable." My fingers wandered lazily across her collarbone and then right above her breasts. My hands lingered for a moment. I would have taken the opportunity to massage her tits, but I was distracted by her heartbeat. "Your heart's beating so fast." I locked eyes with her.

She sat up, making my hands fall from her skin. "You make me nervous."

It was the opposite feeling she gave me. Whenever I was with her, I felt calm. And hopeful. So fucking hopeful. "Ready for that swim?" I asked.

"It'll take a minute to dry."

"Okay, then do me."

"What?"

I laughed and tossed her the bottle of sunscreen. "Get your mind out of the gutter, Penny. I'm trying to be a good influence here." I lay down on my stomach.

Her warm thighs straddled me and she began to massage my back. Her hands on me felt fucking amazing. Her fingers dipped ever so slightly below the waistline of my shorts.

"You're getting a little frisky there," I teased.

"I just don't want you to get burnt," she said. Her hands moved to my shoulders and then down my arms. I couldn't help flexing my biceps under her touch.

"Okay, roll over."

I followed her instructions and put my hands under my head so I could watch her. I liked her straddling me. I liked everything about this actually. She squirted some more sunscreen into her hands and massaged it onto my chest. Her cheeks were starting to get rosy, and I had a feeling it was from my gaze and not the end-of-summer sun.

She slid her hand down to my abs. Her touch was definitely doing something to me. My cock started slowly pressing harder against her. I knew she thought this was hot too, because she was starting to squirm above me, making me harder.

The tip of her finger slowly traced down my happy trail. She looked up at me and I swallowed hard. She gave me a playful smile.

"Enjoying yourself?" I asked.

"Very much so. I like being responsible."

She dipped her hand below the waist of my shorts, inches away from my hard cock. *Grab me.* She inched her hand a little lower but then immediately pulled back.

"Ready for that swim?" she asked.

What a tease. A beautiful, perfect, exhilarating tease.

Chapter 28

Monday

I grabbed her hand and we both ran down to the water. As soon as her toes touched the icy water, she screamed and stopped in her tracks.

"Oh my God, it's so cold. There's no way I'm going in!"

"You get used to it." I leaned down and splashed water up at her.

"Professor Hunter!" She ran away from me and back up to our towels. She pulled a small football from her bag. "Let's at least warm up some first!" She tossed it at me.

I caught the ball and threw it back. "I never would have guessed you could throw a football." I shouldn't have been that surprised, though. There were a lot of things about her I never would have guessed. We continued to throw it back and forth.

"What? Why?"

"Has nobody ever told you that you're clumsy?" She literally fell into my arms when we first met.

She laughed.

I tossed her the football. "Now try to see if you can run by me." I drew a line in the sand with my toe and stepped in front of it. "That's the goal line."

She ran toward me and did a few side steps, but I quickly caught her and twirled her around. Her laughter was contagious as I spun her in the air. When I put her back down, I kept my arms wrapped around her to keep her from falling over.

"You lost. So now we both have to run in the water as fast as we can."

"Professor Hunter, you're not even wearing a bathing suit. How about a rain check?"

"Yeah, I thought it would be more fun without a bathing suit." I let go of her, unzipped my shorts, and then tossed them into the sand. Her eyes wandered to my gray boxers. "Have you ever been skinny dipping, Penny?"

She looked away from my noticeable bulge. "No."

"Well, I thought you might join me."

"You did, did you?" She glanced around, but no one was nearby.

I pulled her close and kissed her. I wasn't sure why I wanted to be so reckless with her. Maybe it was because she made me feel young again. She moaned into my mouth, deepening the kiss. God, I could get addicted to this feeling.

It seemed like she hadn't lived very much in high school. A little danger never hurt anyone. This was as much for me as it was for her. My hands wandered up her back and untied her bathing suit top.

"Professor Hunter!" she screamed and held the front of her bikini in place. "It's the middle of the day."

"I dare you." *Do this with me.* We were used to breaking the rules together now, weren't we? I just wanted to be free. And what was more freeing than this?

She looked around again. It was still only us on the beach.

If there was one thing to convince her...I pulled off my boxers. And there I was, in the middle of the beach, completely naked, with an erection. I stared at her, daring her to join me.

She finally mustered the courage, pulled her top off over her head, and stepped out of her bathing suit bottom. She was standing naked on the beach beside me.

I was pretty sure my heart was racing as fast as hers now. It felt like she believed in me. That I wouldn't let us get caught. That I really could take care of her. I wanted to be that guy. Maybe I could be one day. But right now...all I could offer her was some fun. I grabbed her hand and we ran screaming into the freezing ocean.

We both dove into a wave before it crashed down on us.

"I can't believe we're doing this," she said as we swam out a little farther. She was shaking. But I wasn't sure if it was because of the cold water or the thrill of what we were doing. This was probably the craziest thing she'd ever done. Besides sleeping with her professor. And even though I had done a lot of crazy things in my life, I'd never felt quite like this before. She was exhilarating.

I hugged her close. Despite how cold it was, I was still hard. She wrapped her legs around my waist.

"Shit it's cold!" she said. Her teeth were chattering. "How do you always get me to do such crazy things?"

I smiled. "Because you trust me." *And I'm starting to trust you too.*

"Well I don't know why. You've convinced me to do so many things that could get us in trouble."

"There's actually something else that I've always wanted to do." I placed my hand on her cheek. She'd experienced a lot of firsts today. I wanted to share one together.

"And what is that, Professor Hunter?"

God I loved when she called me that. "I've always wanted to have sex in the ocean. Are you on birth control?" It was reckless. It was stupid. But I needed to be inside of her.

"Yes."

"And is there anything I need to worry about?"

"You mean do I have any STDs?"

"Yes." She was going to feel so warm. So tight. Even more perfect without a layer of rubber between us.

"No, I don't."

I thrust inside of her without going through all the reasons why I shouldn't. I couldn't control myself around her. And for the first time in my life, I didn't want to. I needed all of her.

She let out a tiny cry. "Professor Hunter. We can't do this..."

If she really wanted to stop, she shouldn't have called me Professor Hunter. I silenced her with a kiss, letting my tongue caress hers as I slowly started to move my length in and out of her. I was right. She felt even better without a condom. And the warmth she provided in a sea of freezing cold water was intoxicating.

She wrapped her arms around the back of my neck and pressed her naked torso against mine. I lightly bit her lip and then deepened the kiss. Her lips tasted salty from the ocean water and I couldn't get enough. My fingers dug into the skin of her ass cheeks as I started to move in and out of her slowly.

"Professor Hunter," she moaned when my lips left hers.

God, you're perfect. The waves splashed around us as I thrust inside of her.

She tightened her legs around me, somehow gripping my cock even tighter. *Fuck.* Her head fell back as I thrust deeper inside of her. I wrapped one arm behind her so that her back would arch in that perfect sexy way. My other hand wandered to her tits and I squeezed each one. Her nipples were so hard, begging for my attention. But I knew something else was begging for it more. My hand swept down her stomach and my fingers brushed against her clit.

Her breathing hitched, causing her to grip my cock tighter. I thrust in and out of her, a little faster, and matched the rhythm with my fingers against her clit.

"Yes!" she screamed, sooner than I thought she would. She loved the thrill of doing this in public. Probably as much as me.

I pulled her back up against my chest and squeezed her firm ass as I guided myself in and out of her, faster and faster. I couldn't get enough of her. God, I felt wild. And free. She made me feel so fucking free. The sound of the waves crashing and the seagulls cawing suddenly disappeared. The only sensation I had was the feeling of myself inside of her warm, tight pussy.

My cock throbbed and my release shot into her. She clenched around me again, like the only thing in the world her pussy wanted was my cum.

I kissed her again as stream after stream of cum entered her. Her body shivered in my arms. I had never felt anything like that before. I felt so connected to her. So in tune with her body. I could stay like this forever, buried to the hilt in her sweetness.

But I saw that we had an audience in the distance. A few boys were gathered around our clothes in the sand. They looked like they were probably in high school, ditching class.

I pulled out of her and she rested her head on my shoulder, oblivious to the fact that we were no longer alone. I kissed the top of her head. "We have an audience," I whispered.

"What?!" She whipped her head around to look at the shore.

The tallest of the three gave me a thumbs up.

I laughed.

"Oh my God," she put her head back on my shoulder, hiding her face.

I held her protectively against me. The kids were harmless enough, but I didn't want anyone else to see her naked. But then they grabbed her bathing suit.

"Oh, shit. Hey!" I yelled at the boys.

I started to let go of Penny so that I could run after them.

"Don't you dare leave me in this ocean!"

I started laughing because there was nothing else I could do. And...it was fucking hilarious. "Penny, I'm so sorry," I was finally able to get out interspersed between my laughter. I couldn't remember the last time I'd laughed so hard.

"Stop laughing! This isn't funny, Professor Hunter! I just bought that." But then she started laughing too.

"I'll buy you a new one."

"Should we make a run for it? It's freezing." She unwound her legs from my waist.

I grabbed her hand and we started to run out of the water. "Oh, wait. The coast isn't exactly clear." I pointed toward the boardwalk. "Boys don't steal bikinis and run away. They stay to look."

She looked mortified. "What do we do?"

A wave crashed down behind us. I lifted her over my shoulder so it wouldn't knock both of us over.

"Professor Hunter, put me down!"

I laughed and walked the rest of the way to shore, keeping my hand on her ass to help cover it. I wasn't going to stay in this water a second longer or we'd probably both catch a cold. One viral ass video never hurt anyone. Besides, the kids were far away and I doubted they had any idea who I was. And if they were snapping photos, my junk was on better display than Penny's ass.

As soon as I put Penny down, she sprinted to our towels and wrapped one around herself. I took my time. There'd been worse pictures of me in tabloids. "Penny, those boys were far away, they could barely see you."

"But they could still see me! And they probably took pictures with their phones. And they...they saw us having...well, you know."

"The highlight of their young lives, I'm sure." I began to dry off with my towel. Before I'd even run the towel through my hair, Penny was fully dressed. Without her bikini top, her nipples were on full display, trying to poke through her shirt. She folded her arms across her chest and sat down. I would have thought she was upset based on her body language, but she was smiling so hard. She was just trying to hide her very sexy nipples from me. Which wasn't necessary at all. I took a deep breath of salt air, wondering if she felt as relaxed as I did. I pulled my boxers and shorts back on but kept my shirt off. I had a feeling she appreciated the view.

I sat down beside her and rubbed her back. "Are you ready for part two of our date?"

"That depends on what we're doing. I'm not exactly dressed to go anywhere."

"Well, how about we go to my place?" I'd told Ian that I couldn't watch the Giant's game with him tonight, so I hoped he wouldn't be camped out on my couch. Rob and Isabella had already tried to ruin this day for me. But I was pretty sure even if Ian was at my place, nothing could dampen my mood. I felt...so relaxed. More so than I did in corpse pose. Or even when I ran.

Penny smiled up at me. "That sounds perfect."
I couldn't have described it any better.

Chapter 29

Monday

We pulled into the parking garage of my apartment complex on the edge of Main Street.

"You live here?"

"Yes." I turned onto the third story of the parking garage and pulled into a space next to the rest of my cars.

"Your neighbors have really nice cars too."

I stepped out of the convertible. "Those are mine."

"Seriously?" She got out of the car and looked around. "All of them? One of them looks like the Batmobile!" She pointed to the one farthest away.

"Yeah. Turns out it's never very convenient to drive though. And it doesn't give me any superpowers." My smile disappeared as she pulled out a hoodie from her bag. She zipped it up and lifted the hood over her head. I shoved my hands into my pockets as I watched her. What was she doing...getting ready for a heist?

"Okay, I'm ready," she said, adjusting her hood lower.

"What, do you think I'm sneaking you in? I don't believe that anyone from the university lives here."

"Well I don't want to get caught. Someone in the lobby might see us."

I laughed and shook my head. "Okay." If this made her more comfortable. I put my hand on the small of her back and led her over to the elevator. I swiped my card in the sensor and the doors opened immediately. We stepped in and I touched the button for my apartment on the top floor. The elevator doors closed.

"Penthouse, huh?"

"I guess you could say that." She knew I bought that country club. But she was still surprised to see all my cars. And surprised that I lived in a nice apartment building. She really had no clue who I was. And she was still standing here with me. With a smile on her face. And I didn't have the slightest idea why.

She looked around the elevator like she had never been in one before. But certainly she had. Maybe just not one with doors on either side that opened directly into apartments.

The elevator stopped. I took out my apartment card, swiped it through the reader, and the doors parted.

She stood there for a moment like she had never seen anything cooler.

I grabbed her hand and escorted her into my place.

"Wow." She walked down the few steps from the elevator and looked around. She was standing in my living room, which was surrounded by windows that overlooked the small college town. I walked over to the fireplace, touched a button, and a flame burst to life. I knew what she was probably thinking as she looked around. There was no T.V., no magazines on the coffee table, and the modern couch looked like no one had ever sat on it. The kitchen to the right had granite countertops and shiny new appliances. And there was a dining area with a vase of fresh flowers in the center of the table. But it looked like no one lived here. It looked like the model home they used for display purposes only. It was cold and uninviting. But I didn't have good memories to fill pictures. Or anything I wanted to share. It was just me here. Alone. Until her...

Ever since Ian told me the place looked cold, I'd been worrying about bringing Penny here. But it was like she brought life to the place when she stepped into my apartment. It wasn't that she didn't fit. She fixed it. She fixed everything.

Her eyes stopped at the flowers on my dining room table. "Oh, Professor Hunter. Thanks for the friendship roses."

I laughed. "You're welcome."

"But really, thank you. How did you know I was going to agree to skip class anyway?"

"I just hoped you would. And I know that I can be pretty persuasive."

"Yes, you can."

She started looking around again and I realized I was being rude by just staring at her. "Okay, so this is the living room." I walked over to her, grabbed her hand, and steered her to the windows all along the back of the apartment. The lights from the small shops on Main Street made the view of the sweet town even lovelier. I wrapped my arms around her.

"It's beautiful," she said.

"You're beautiful," I whispered into her ear.

She laughed. "I'm a mess."

I was sweaty from the beach and my skin was tight from the saltwater. But she looked perfect. And despite the sunscreen and ocean water, I could still smell a subtle scent of cherries on her skin.

She ran her fingers through her hair.

"Well, I was thinking maybe a quick shower could be the rain portion of the date you requested."

"Actually, that sounds perfect. Are you sure that's okay?" She turned around to face me.

Did she think I meant I was just going to let her shower by herself? That wasn't my plan at all. I smiled down at her, already thinking about her naked skin dripping with water. "Come with me." I grabbed her hand and led her to my bedroom, one of the closed doors next to the kitchen. I flipped the lights on.

My bed was in the center. Pristine white sheets just begging for me to get dirty with Penny. I turned on another light and stepped into my walk-in closet. She looked around the large space. There was a whole row of white collared shirts and suit jackets. And below it, all my pants were folded on hangers. Shoes lined the bottom of the closet.

"You really don't need your sweaters back." She was staring at the dozens that were folded on shelves next to my dress shirts.

I laughed. "I'm afraid I don't really have anything for you to change into." I opened up a few drawers.

"Could I just borrow one of those shirts?"

I handed her one of the V-necks from the drawer I had just opened, switched off the light, and led her to the bathroom. There was an elegant bath to the left with a few steps up to it. And attached was a shower with three glass walls. The vanity was to the right and the only things on it were my toothbrush and some toothpaste. If she was still searching for something personal, she wasn't going to find it.

I switched on the shower as she was looking around. Then I came up to her and slowly unzipped her hoodie. She didn't need to hide. Not here. No one would ever find out about us here. I slowly slid the fabric down her arms, pushing her hoodie until it fell to the ground. Only she could make a hoodie sexy. I pulled her tank top up her sides and over her ribcage, trailing my fingers along her soft skin. She lifted her hands in the air and I pulled it off over her head. I undid her shorts and then slowly slid them off her hips. Since her bathing suit had been snatched, she was left completely naked in the center of my bathroom.

Her skin was a little bronzed from our time in the sun, despite her insistence she'd burn. There were more freckles beneath her eyes too, and I found myself leaning in closer to see them better.

"Do you mind if I join you?" I asked. I could already feel myself growing hard again.

She shook her head.

I slowly undressed. I wanted her again. I wanted her here, in my apartment, in my shower. I wanted her to be mine. I stepped into the shower and she followed me.

My hands were on her as soon as she was under the water. The water fell on our heads as we kissed under its constant stream.

I grabbed a bottle of body wash from the ledge and poured some into my hand. "Face the wall," I said. My voice sounded tight, like I was about to lose it. Maybe I would have if she wasn't so good at following my instructions. But she did exactly what she was told. I pushed her lightly so that her breasts were pressed against the tile, then slowly rubbed my soapy hands up the back of her legs, massaging her thighs. I cupped her ass in my hands. God I loved her ass.

My fingers wandered over her plump ass and between her legs. I bet she was soaking wet for me already. Her body was so responsive. As soon as I thought it, she moved her hips back, arching into me.

Not yet. I swept my hands away from her wetness and across her back. I massaged her shoulders and ran my soapy hands up her arms and across her clavicle. It was a sin for anyone to be this perfect. I wanted her all to myself. Again and again. I wasn't sure I could ever tire of her, even though I'd always found it easy to run from one thing to the next in the past.

I pulled her away from the wall just enough so that I could touch one of my favorite parts of her. I massaged her breasts gently, the soap suds lathering on her slick skin. Her tits were heavy and full, such perfection. My erection pressed against the small of her back. *See what you do to me?*

"Professor Hunter," she moaned. "Please."

I loved teasing her almost as much as I loved when she begged. I pulled her underneath the water, washing the soap away. "Is something wrong, Penny?"

"No."

I pushed her back against the tile. "Is there something that you wanted?" I was seconds away from devouring every inch of her. It had been too long since I'd tasted her sweet cunt.

"Yes."

The steam of the shower surrounded her. She looked almost ethereal. And even though she was bad at voicing her desires, I knew what she needed. I leaned over and took one of her nipples in my mouth and bit it lightly. I pinched her other nipple between two of my fingers and she writhed under my touch.

"And what is it that you want?" I left a trail of kisses down her stomach and stopped right where I knew she wanted it the most. I knew it. But I still wanted her to say it. I wanted her to beg me. I wanted her to scream my name.

"You."

"Do you mean like this?" I stroked her pussy with my tongue. *God, the taste of her.*

"Professor Hunter," she moaned.

I knelt before her on the tile floor and lifted her thighs over my shoulders. I needed the perfect angle for what I wanted to do to her. I slid two fingers inside her aching pussy.

She gasped.

"Or maybe you'd prefer that I fuck you with my fingers?" *You dirty girl.*

"Yes!"

I moved my lips to her clit and sucked on it hard. She tried to move, but I pinned her against the shower wall, completely immobilizing her. I wanted to make her come. How many times had I dreamt of having her just like this in my shower? How many times had I jerked off right here thinking about her? I pumped my hand faster, moving my fingers in and out of her. I continued to stroke her clit with my tongue, driving us both crazy.

"Yes!" she screamed again.

I pushed her thighs even farther apart. The position allowed my fingers to go even deeper. I licked and swirled my tongue over her clit, feeling it grow beneath my mouth. I could feel her body start to shudder in my arms. *That's right, baby.* I placed my lips around her clit again and sucked hard.

"Professor Hunter!"

I continued to thrust my fingers in and out of her as she orgasmed. Her pussy walls constricting around my fingers. So fucking tight.

When she was completely spent, I lowered her feet back to the floor. I grabbed the bottle from the ledge and quickly washed myself off. She just stood there, staring at me. I wanted to push her down and shove my cock down her throat. But I loved pleasing her. And she looked so relaxed and sated, like her body could just slide down the sleek tile wall and she could fall asleep in the steam. I wanted her. Desperately. But I also wanted her to feel safe here. I thought about the marks on her back. I didn't want to ever hurt her again.

I turned to leave.

"Don't go." She reached out and let her hands slide down my wet abs. She didn't hesitate to grab my erection. She slowly moved her hand up and down my shaft.

My breath came out as a hiss.

She got down on her knees and stared up into my eyes, letting her tongue stroke up and down my length. *Fuck, just like that.* She brought her lips to my tip and kissed it. And then she licked her own lips in anticipation.

I swallowed hard as I watched her guide my thick cock into her mouth. She slowly slid up and down, torturing me. I forced myself not to grab the back of her head and guide her. I wanted to see what she could do with those lips. *Fuck, and that tongue.*

She tightened her lips and I groaned. This was better than jerking off to her in here. Nothing could compare to her warm mouth. My tip brushed against the back of her throat.

"Fuck."

She tightened her lips in response and went up and down my shaft as fast as she could. Then her lips went all the way to my hilt. I felt that pull in my stomach. I was seconds away from losing it.

Jesus. I pulled out of her warm mouth. She was mine. And I wanted her to know it. I pumped my fist up and down my length and a shot of cum landed on her tits. She just knelt there looking up at me with lust in her eyes.

I aimed another shot a little higher and it hit her chin. She tilted her head back slightly and squeezed her breasts like this was just as arousing to her as it was to me. God she was perfect. My last shot landed on her chest again. She looked so hot, my cum dripping down her chest and stomach and onto her thighs.

"You look so sexy, Penny." I honestly couldn't think of a better sight. And seeing her like that was making me hard all over again. I rinsed off under the water as I looked down at her. If I didn't step out of the shower, I was going to fuck her again. And I wasn't sure she was ready. "I know you don't like when I leave you naked and alone, but I'm going to go make dinner while you finish up if that's alright."

"Okay."

I got out of the shower, quickly dried off, and got dressed. Even though Ellen made fun of the only meal I knew how to make because of the jarred sauce I used...it was the only thing I knew how to make. And I had a feeling Penny would like anything I gave her. Especially if it was accompanied by a side of cum.

I realized I was actually whistling as the pasta boiled. Whistling. I couldn't even remember the last time I'd whistled. God, I was in deep.

Chapter 30

Monday

I was just getting the casserole dish into the oven as Penny stepped out of my bedroom. She was only wearing the t-shirt I had loaned her. It stopped right below her butt. My eyes gravitated away from her long legs and up to her face. She looked younger without makeup. But still just as beautiful. Her skin was flawless, just the hint of rosiness in her cheeks. There was something nice about the way she was completely exposed to me.

"You look breathtaking, Penny. I don't understand how everything I own looks better on you."

Her cheeks grew rosier. When she reached me, I grabbed her hand and twirled her around. I couldn't help but realize how normal this was. And comfortable. I wanted every night to be like this. I could so easily picture coming home to her. The thought should have terrified me. But if anything, it was comforting.

She laughed and sat down on a stool at the kitchen island. "It smells amazing. What are we having?"

"One of the only things I know how to make. Vodka chicken."

"That sounds fantastic. So, if this is the only thing you know how to make, do you usually order out?" She rested her chin in her hands, her elbows on the granite countertops.

"Rarely."

She laughed. "What, do you have a personal chef or something?"

"Yeah." I opened the oven and peered inside. "Almost ready."

"Why do you never volunteer information? It's like I have to force it out of you."

I shrugged. "I'm sorry. I'm not used to people asking me questions that aren't going to be used for articles or something. I've gotten good at giving very vague answers. If you'd like to ask me a few questions, I'll be happy to try and answer them for you." *Don't ask about my past.* I didn't want to ruin our perfect evening. But I knew I'd just invited her to ask me for personal information. This wasn't going to be good.

I grabbed two plates, two sets of silverware, and two glasses as I waited for her first question.

"I can do that." She slid off the stool and grabbed the dishes from me. "Here, or in the dining room?"

"The dining room is good." I never ate in the dining room. I always ate at the kitchen island really quickly or in my office. But I also usually ate alone.

"And now for the last part of your ideal date," I said as she finished setting the table. I uncorked a bottle of champagne and poured her a glass. "I think that covers everything." "Piña coladas. Getting caught in the rain. The feel of the ocean. And the taste of champagne. "So how did I do? Was today worth skipping class for?"

"I'd do anything to spend more time with you. Today was absolutely magical." She held up her glass. "And here's to getting to know each other better tonight."

Fuck. I'm pretty sure my laugh came out nervous as I clinked my glass against hers. I took a large sip of champagne. The feeling that I had with her was enough. I didn't need to know anything else. But it was true. Just because I didn't need to know anything else, it didn't mean I didn't want to. I wanted to know everything about her. But I couldn't offer her everything back in return.

"So," she said and sat down. "How long have you lived in this apartment?"

I sat down across from her. Now that was a question I could answer. "Ever since I started working at the university."

She looked around again. "So why aren't there any decorations? There isn't a single picture anywhere."

"I wasn't sure how long I'd be staying for."

"Why?"

I shifted in my chair. "Like I told you before, I needed a change. But I wasn't sure if the change would be permanent." I came here on a whim. I'd always wanted to visit Delaware. Rumor had it that people were nicer here than in the city. I was finding that to be true.

"Do you still think you'll go back to New York?"

I didn't want to lose her. Whatever this was between us, I didn't want to picture it ending. We had only just started dating.

The timer on the oven went off.

"There's nothing left for me in New York." I got up and went back into the kitchen. I grabbed some potholders and pulled the casserole dish out of the oven. I hoped that was all the questions she had. I just wanted to eat in peace. And stare at her. I could stare at her for hours in silence and be perfectly content. I set the dish down on the table and scooped some out for both of us.

She didn't even pick up her fork. "So, the move is permanent now?"

I'm not leaving you, if that's what you're worried about. I gave her a smile. "I believe so."

"What made you change your mind?"

Apparently she was not content with silence. But this was another easy question. There was only one thing that had changed my mind. "You."

She looked down at her plate and blushed. She laughed like she didn't believe me and then took a bite of the vodka chicken. "This is delicious."

"Thank you."

She looked back up at me.

"Do you have any more questions for me, Penny?" I truly wanted to be able to answer them. For her. I wanted her to know that I was serious about her.

"Only a million more."

I laughed.

"Tell me about your family."

I slowly finished chewing the bite I'd just taken, trying to figure out how to word a response. "Well, I have an older sister and a younger brother."

"Tell me about them."

"My sister lives in New York." I finished off my glass of champagne and poured myself another. I didn't want to talk about Rob. Hopefully he was out of prison by now. That didn't seem like a great first thing to say about him. She already had enough reasons to stay away from me.

"And what does your sister do?"

"She's a writer."

"Has she written anything that I may have heard of?"

"Probably not." She mostly wrote boring articles.

"And what about your brother?"

I wasn't going to get into this. "The last time I heard from him, he was in Costa Rica." *True enough.*

"Wow. What does he do there?"

"Nothing as far as I know. He's been taking time off to travel."

"Well that's fun."

Not the way he was doing it. I needed to call him later to make sure he was okay. I half expected him to show up tonight unannounced and ruin my night. But luckily that hadn't happened yet. I needed this time alone with Penny. Who was I kidding, all I craved was alone time with her.

"And your parents?"

"What about them?" I didn't mean to sound terse, but this conversation was going from bad to worse.

"Well, where are they?"

"I'm not close with my parents." Every question she asked made me feel more and more tense.

"That's a shame."

I laughed. "No, it's not." I shifted in my chair. I needed to divert the conversation back to her. I already knew how fucked up I was. I just wanted to know about her. "And what about your family, Penny?"

"I'm an only child. Growing up, I was really close with my parents. But not as much since I started college."

"And why is that?"

"I don't know. I feel like some of the best things about college are just things you don't really talk about with your parents."

"You mean like me?" Penny didn't feel like a breath of fresh air at all tonight. She was stifling me. I was finding it harder to breathe. I didn't want to talk about family. I wanted to talk about us. What we could be. Before she had a chance to realize I was wrong for her in every way.

"Yeah," she laughed. "I mean, I can't exactly tell them about you. I don't even like to imagine how upset they'd be with me."

"So you're ashamed that you're fucking your Comm professor?" The words just came out of my mouth. I wasn't even sure why I was suddenly so pissed off. I clenched my jaw so I wouldn't say anything else rash.

"That's not really the way that I think about it. I'm definitely not ashamed. I really like you, Professor Hunter."

You don't know me. And if you did, you'd be ashamed. You'd fucking hate me.

"If that's the way that you think of me, then I guess you've gotten all that you want from me." She folded her arms across her chest, putting a distance between us that I didn't like, and looked down at the table.

I'd pissed her off, but fuck. She was pissing me off too. I wanted her to want me without worrying about all this other nonsense. Wasn't that enough? "I knew I wanted you since I first ran into you in that coffee shop. But I wasn't going to pursue you because you're a student. When you showed up in my class it complicated things, though. Every time I saw you, every answer you gave for the daily assignments, and every time we spoke made it impossible for me to get you out of my head. I knew I wanted you. I thought if I let myself give in to the temptation I could move on."

She abruptly stood up. It looked like she was going to flee.

"Penny, sit down." I was trying to open up to her, didn't she see that? I was doing my best. This was hard for me too.

She didn't move, and that just pissed me off more.

"Sit down, or I'll make you sit down." *Breathe.*

Her throat made that adorable squeaking noise. She sat back down in her chair and stared at me.

"I don't understand why you're upset," I said. "We've already talked about all of this. Everything is different now. I couldn't move on. I don't want to move on. You're all that I think about." I ran my hand down my face. "Geez, you have this way of crawling under my skin."

"Why, because I want to know more about you? That's what people that are dating do! I don't know why you always get upset when we try to talk."

"Because I don't want you to know what kind of man I am."

"I think that you're exactly the kind of man that I want."

That couldn't possibly be true.

She grabbed her glass and took another sip of champagne. "Can you please just try to answer a few more questions without exploding?"

I took a deep breath. "I'm sorry." I was. But I couldn't talk about my family right now. Or the fact that I was wrong for her on every level.

"Are your parents wealthy?"

Jesus Christ. I sighed. "Yes. But everything I have is because of the choices I've made. I don't want a cent from them."

She looked a little frightened.

"Penny, do you enjoy pushing all my buttons?"

"You're always so in control. It's a little fun to see you squirm."

I raised my left eyebrow.

"I just feel like you're hiding something from me. And I don't understand why. I told you that I trusted you. Don't you trust me?"

I stared at her. Had she looked me up online? Did she already know everything I was trying so hard to hide? If she did...wouldn't she just say it? *No. She doesn't know. Or else she wouldn't be here.* And that wasn't why she was asking. As Dr. Clark liked to remind me, relationships were built on trust. And I wanted to build a relationship with Penny. Desperately. "I do trust you," I finally said.

"So what happened with your parents? Why are you so mad at them?"

Breathe. "It's complicated."

"Well, you're a professor. You should be good at explaining things. Make me understand."

Fair point. And for the first time since this conversation started, I almost smiled. I sighed. "My whole life they put so much pressure on me. To the point where I felt like I didn't get to make any of my own choices. It took me far too long to realize. And when I finally did, my life was no longer mine at all. I felt like I was drowning. Becoming a professor was the first thing that I decided for myself in a long time."

"So screw them," she said.

I laughed. "Penny, being here, with you...I finally feel like I can breathe again." I didn't want to talk about my past because I just wanted to be here with her right now.

"I feel the same way. You make me feel alive."

That. That right there was what I wanted. It made me feel like I was enough, even though I was so fucking broken. I wasn't good at talking about my emotions. But I could show her. The best way I knew how. "Come with me." I got up and pulled her to her feet. She followed me to my bedroom. My heart was racing. I slowly peeled off my shirt, then my jeans, and boxers.

"Professor Hunter. I'm a little sore."

"Penny, you'd be surprised to find out how many times you can orgasm in a day. Your body can take it. And I want to show you that this is more than just fucking for me too. So I promise to be gentle." I didn't want her to remember that harsh comment I made. I needed to show her this was more.

She lifted the shirt over her head. She was even better than my dreams.

I lifted her into my arms and placed her down on the bed. This was going to be the opposite of the golf course. I was going to worship her body. I'd show her exactly what she deserved.

I kissed the inside of her ankle and traced kisses up the inside of her leg. I lightly nipped her inner thigh and then moved to her other ankle, repeating the process. When I nipped her inner thigh this time, she moaned.

That sound. I wanted her. I needed to be inside of her, filling her, claiming her body. I slowly circled my tongue around her clit. Her hips rose to meet me. Even though she was sore, she wanted me just as desperately.

But this wasn't going to be fast and rough. Not this time. I moved my head and kissed the palm of her left hand. I trailed kisses up her arm, slowly across her shoulder and clavicle, and then down her other arm. My lips landed against her other palm. Teasing her was making me so hard. Each moan from her mouth. Each time her hips moved. *God.* I kissed between her breasts and slowly went down her stomach.

My lips gently sucked on her clit while my hands massaged her inner thighs. When my fingers finally touched her, she was soaking wet. And even though I could have fucked her hard with my fingers, I entered her slowly, lovingly. The moan that fell from her lips was worth the restraint.

I leaned over top of her and kissed her forehead, her nose, and then her mouth. I hitched my fingers, making sure to rub her g-spot. She practically whimpered beneath me and the sound went straight to my dick, hardening it even more. She was panting when I pulled back from our heated kiss. I wanted her to always look at me like that. Like I was everything. I could get high on that look. And I couldn't wait another second to be inside of her. I moved one hand under her ass, lifted her hips, and slowly filled her.

"Oh!"

I bit my lip as I looked down at her, trying hard not to lose control. I liked when I was rough with her. I loved fucking her. But this? I hadn't expected this to feel so good. I pushed firmly against her, the angle letting me go deep. *Jesus.* Was it possible that this was even better than fucking? I felt so connected to her. And the stars in her eyes made me feel like a god.

There was a moment at the golf course that I'd felt this tightness in my chest. And again at the beach today. I felt it again now. This wasn't just fucking. God, this was so much more than that. And I needed her to understand. I needed her to feel it too. Because I couldn't be the only one falling here. I couldn't be the only one losing control. Because if I was…it would be that much harder when I hit rock bottom again.

Her fingers were tentative as they wandered along the muscles in my back. I never loved the feeling of someone's hands on me so much. Like the warmth of her skin could somehow save the darkness in my heart. Like she gave me life.

I kissed her as I began to thrust in and out of her wetness. Slow. So fucking slow. Her fingertips dug into my flesh.

"You're so gorgeous," I whispered into her ear. "Every inch of you." I bit her earlobe and I felt her clench around my hard cock.

"Yes!" she moaned.

I kissed her passionately, riding out her orgasm. When it subsided, I rubbed my nose down the length of hers, a smile on my lips. "I'm not done with you yet. I'll never be done with you." And I meant it. It was terrifying how much I meant it.

I rolled over and pulled her with me so that she was straddling me. I grabbed her ass and guided my cock in and out of her. Her tits bounced with every movement. It was the perfect view. I moved my hands to her tiny waist and then slowly slid them up the sides of her torso, grabbing her luscious breasts in my hands. She started to move her hips, setting the pace as I gave her tits some much needed attention. I rubbed her swollen nipples and then locked eyes with her as I slid one of my hands down her stomach. My fingers found her clit and I began to massage it gently.

"Professor Hunter."

God, whenever she said that it made me that much harder.

Her head dropped back like she had never felt anything so exquisite. She was going to come again.

I pulled her face back down to mine, kissing her, and rolled over again, pinning her to the soft mattress. I thrust my hard cock in and out of her tight little pussy a little faster. In and out. Faster. She wrapped her legs around my waist and grabbed my ass, pulling me against her.

Fuck. I lost control, filling her with my release. She called out my name as she came. I closed my eyes for just a moment. Being buried inside of her was my new favorite feeling. I wanted her in my bed waiting for me every day with her legs spread. Again and again.

I slowly opened my eyes and looked down at her. I was never going to let her go.

Chapter 31

Monday

As soon as I pulled out, Penny sat up in bed, drawing her legs in and hugging them close. It looked like she was about to cry. That moment had been perfect. For me. But it hadn't been for her. What had I done wrong? I'd tried to be gentle with her. To show her that this was more than just fucking. But what if she didn't want more? My heart started racing. What if she finally realized how wrong this was?

I sat up and cupped her chin in my hand. "Penny, what's wrong?" *Let me fix it.*

"Nothing." She blinked faster, pulling her legs tighter to her chest.

I rubbed the side of her chin with my thumb but didn't say a word. I was so fucking lost in her. I couldn't lose her now. I didn't say a word, waiting for her to speak.

"It's just. For some reason, this whole time, it's seemed like I made this all up. Like it's this fantasy and you're not real. And I'm afraid that I'm going to wake up from this amazing dream and you're going to be gone. That you're just going to disappear."

She was just freaking out because she felt it too. It was real and heavy and scary as hell. "I've told you that I'm not going anywhere. There's no reason to be upset about that. Please don't cry." I wiped away one of the tears that had fallen down her cheek.

"But what we just did. I know you said you were going to be gentle. But I expected it to be like the other times.

This whole day just seemed different. More intimate. I don't know. I didn't expect to feel so...so..."

I thought back to her confession at the beach. No boyfriends in high school. I really should have already known all this. "No one's ever made love to you." I meant to ask it as a question, but it didn't come out that way. Because I already knew the truth. It was written all over her face.

"Well, I thought so. But no, not like...not like that."

Not like that. It was the understatement of the century. I'd never felt like this either. Like suddenly I felt less...empty. I stared at her. That's how I'd felt right before I met her...completely and utterly empty. And it was scary how whole I felt with her in my arms even after she stumbled into them the first time. Was that how love was supposed to feel? Because I'd certainly never felt like this before. Dr. Clark had asked me if I was in love with Penny. I was terrified that this was that feeling. But it didn't seem like the right moment to tell Penny that. Not when she looked terrified. I didn't know if she was a flight risk. She never looked so young to me before, sitting there with tears in her eyes.

"I didn't mean to make you uncomfortable." I rubbed another tear off her cheek. I needed to just calm her down. "How many partners have you been with?"

"One."

One? Jesus. She's going to think I'm a monster. All the thoughts I had been feeling. Could she really be feeling them too if she'd only been with one guy? I was in a different stage of my life than her and it had never been so clear. Yet, it didn't make me want her any less. Her confession didn't make this feel any less real to me. I wrapped my arms around her and pulled her down on top of me. And I just held her. She was more innocent than I thought. And it terrified me. I could lose her. I could really lose her for my shitty past mistakes.

"And how many partners have you been with?" she asked.

The question I'd been worried about. I sighed. "A little more than that."

"How many more?"

"Penny, I don't want you to think poorly of me." *I don't want to lose you.*

"More than five?"

I exhaled slowly. How could it be so easy to breathe around her moment, and the next if felt like I was suffocating? As if she controlled my air supply.

"More than ten?"

"I spent a large portion of my college years fairly drunk." *An understatement.*

"More than fifteen?"

"We should probably stop playing this game."

"Professor Hunter, you're a slut!"

I laughed. "You seem to enjoy all my experience."

She cringed. I didn't like picturing her with anyone else. I imagined it was the same for her.

"And what about your one, Penny?" I thought about the video footage of Tyler leaving her dorm. She said they were just friends. Had they always been just friends? I wasn't sure how I'd be able to handle him being in my class, sitting next to her, knowing he'd fucked her. *Breathe.*

"What about him?" She slid off me and onto her side, her head resting in her hand.

"One is rather intimate. Is he someone I should be worried about?" *Please don't be Tyler.* I was already being a shitty professor. And I had a feeling if it was Tyler I'd be giving out an underserved F.

She laughed. "No."

"So you no longer speak to him?"

"No."

I breathed a little easier.

"I doubt that I'll ever talk to him again," she added. "He's an immature asshole."

"And why is that?" I was relieved it wasn't Tyler. But the thought of someone, anyone, treating her badly made my blood boil.

"Why do you want to know?"

"Because I don't want to make the same mistakes with you that he did."

She sighed. "There isn't much to tell. We dated last semester. He didn't speak to me all summer. He made me feel worthless."

"So you broke up with him?" I felt ridiculous asking so many questions about this one guy. She hadn't made me give her details about all the women I'd slept with. But I needed to know everything. I was a hypocrite, and I knew it.

"You can't really break up with someone who you never officially went out with."

I took her hand in mine. Apparently she didn't just date immature guys. She dated idiots. "Penny Taylor, I promise not to make you feel worthless. And I'll try not to act like an asshole." I smiled, intertwining our fingers. The promise of not making her feel worthless would be easy. Because I was the one that wasn't worthy of her. The asshole promise was harder. Because I really was an asshole on most days.

"I don't know, Professor Hunter. From what I've found out about you, it seems like I'm just going to end up as another notch on your bedpost."

I laughed. "That's not who I am anymore." She'd never be a notch. She was quickly becoming everything. All that I thought about. All that I craved. It was such a thin line for me, and I had already crossed it. I wasn't sure I could go back even if I wanted to.

"I thought it was impossible for people to change?"

"I came here for a change. And I think I'm better off because of it." I pulled her toward me so that her head was resting on my chest again. Her leg crossed over me.

Having her in my arms felt so right. And there was something nice about knowing she felt it too. Because I wasn't just fucking my student. I was in deep. I was pretty sure I was in love with her. *I'm in love with my student.* I breathed in her sweet scent. This moment could last forever and it wouldn't be long enough. Because it had been a really long time since I'd felt this whole. And this happy. Hell, that was a lie. I'd never been whole. And I barely even remembered what it felt like to be happy. The smell of cherries surrounded me. Until now. I was pretty sure this was what happiness felt like.

***

I had never slept so well before. There was something about having Penny beside me that calmed me. She looked so peaceful when I woke up. I wanted to wake up to her beautiful face every morning. *Just like this.* For a few minutes I just stared at the way her red hair fell against the pillow and the shadows her eyelashes cast on the freckles under her eyes. She was good and perfect and pure. *And mine.* Somehow she was mine.

I slowly climbed out of bed, making sure not to wake her. I was in a daze as I brushed my teeth and showered. Last night had been perfect. And there was probably just enough time for a repeat before classes started. I came out of the bathroom, but the bed was empty.

"Penny?" I called as I made my way out into the kitchen. But she wasn't there or in the living room. "Penny?" I turned around. She was gone. And for a moment it felt like my heart stopped beating. She'd left. She'd left and I didn't even know the specific reason. Because there could have been a million reasons why. And all of them were my fault.

Part 3

Chapter 32

Tuesday

I grabbed my phone. Penny probably just left because she didn't want to be late for class. That was it. I sent her a quick text: "I would have driven you home. Persuading you to miss two classes would have been way too irresponsible." I smiled. I loved being irresponsible with her.

I stared at my phone for a minute, waiting for her to text me back. But...she didn't. She was probably just getting ready for class.

I put my phone down. She'd text back soon enough. I tried not to think about it as I finished getting ready. But the minutes ticked by and no response came. When I went to grab a pair of shoes, I found all her clothes still in my room. Even her flip flops. I pictured her walking home in my t-shirt and nothing else. Not even a pair of shoes. What the hell? Something was definitely wrong. I shot her another text: "Did you get back to your dorm okay? You left your clothes here..."

Fuck. I ran my fingers through my hair. I had a class to get to. But all I could think about was why? Why had she left? The list was endless. And I'd expected it eventually. But not yet. It couldn't be over yet.

***

"Three pointer!" Ian pretended to make a basket with an invisible ball. "Called it!" He held up his hand for me to high-five.

I lifted my hand and he slapped it. But I wasn't paying attention to the game. My eyes kept gravitating back to my desk where I'd left my phone. We were watching the game in my office and I was hoping it would distract me or my work would distract me, but...nothing did. All day long all I could think about was Penny. She'd never texted me back. I wanted to drive over to her dorm, but I couldn't just show up and try to walk in when someone walked out. Any student could recognize me. And she knew it. She knew there was no way for me to come see her.

"You okay, man?" Ian asked.

"Fine." Ian had sent me the footage of Penny getting safely back to her dorm. But she'd been barefoot in nothing but my t-shirt. The image infuriated me. She'd run. She'd run and I didn't even fucking know why. Was she seriously not going to text me back? She couldn't avoid me forever. I was her fucking professor. I'd see her tomorrow in class. But waiting that long to figure out what was wrong felt like torture.

"You don't seem fine. Check your phone, maybe she's texted back."

I stood up and grabbed my phone. But there were no missed calls or messages. I typed out another text. "Penny, I had a wonderful day with you. And a wonderful night. If there's something that I've done to upset you, I'll fix it. Just tell me what it is."

"Please tell me you didn't just text her again," Ian said.

"Maybe?"

He laughed. "That's an amateur move. You've got it bad."

I did. I had it so bad that I was finding it hard to breathe without her. It was a familiar feeling. This deep need. The kind of feeling I paid Dr. Clark good money to help me avoid. *Fuck!* I ran my hand down my face.

"You really have no idea what you did to piss her off?" he asked. "Oh, nothing but net!"

I let my eyes gravitate back to the screen. "Not a clue." Our night really had been perfect. She was perfect. And I'd fucked it all up.

"Do you want me to figure out where she is right now? I could just…"

"No. Relationships are built on trust."

Ian raised his eyebrow. "Since when have you believed that?"

I shrugged. I didn't. But it was what Dr. Clark wanted me to believe. Besides, if Ian found Penny and she was with another guy? I didn't want to go to jail for killing some limp dicked college student.

Breathe. I stared at the game without really even seeing it. Really, why had she left without even a note? Was it the conversation about how many women I'd slept with? She seemed fine after that. It had to be something else. *Breathe.* But I couldn't seem to focus on my breath no matter how many times I told myself I had to. I clenched my hand into a fist. If I'd still been wearing a rubber band around my wrist I would have snapped the damn thing in half. *Breathe.*

"I have an idea," Ian said.

I looked up at him. God, at this moment I'd do anything if it meant talking to Penny.

"You could text her again," he said with a laugh.

Asshole. "Ha. Ha." Maybe Dr. Clark had a point about employees being different than friends. Because right now Ian was acting more like a friend, and it was driving me nuts.

"Speaking of texts, have you heard from Jen recently?" Ian asked.

"No. Why?"

He shrugged. "No reason."

I stared at him watching the game. Seriously, why did all our conversations always revert back to Jen? Was something going on between Ian and my sister?

"We could fix this situation though."

"I'm not in the mood to talk to Jen right now."

Ian laughed. "I was talking about Penny. I could put one of those cameras in her dorm room…"

I sighed. As tempting as that was, I couldn't take him up on the offer. Partly because I was worried about what I would see. Besides, how was he planning on breaking into her dorm room? I didn't even want to know. "Let's just focus on the game."

"That's what I was trying to do. But your sulking is very distracting. Are you hungry?" He got up and stretched. "Maybe we should go out and watch the game somewhere on Main Street."

That sounded terrible. There were students at the restaurants on Main Street. Students that weren't Penny that I didn't want to talk to.

"Or…I'll go warm up something Ellen made for us?"

I laughed. "You mean *my* dinner?"

"Nah, Ellen knows I always steal food from your fridge. She's been making me leftovers for years."

"She has?" I hadn't known that. How had I not noticed food disappearing from my fridge for years?

"Yeah." He laughed. "I thought you knew."

I didn't. But it was just like Ellen to want to take care of everyone.

"I'll go warm it up. Don't text Penny while I'm gone. Another text would really be the wrong move."

I knew he was right. I glared at my phone, willing for Penny to respond to me. Each minute that ticked by without a response driving me slowly more insane.

Chapter 33

Wednesday

"I'll talk to you after class." That was the text I'd finally gotten from Penny this morning. Any text like that wasn't good news. But at least she'd reached out. And whatever it was? I'd fix it. Because losing her was not an option. One night without her and I was back to not sleeping. I climbed into bed for a minute, but all I could smell was her on my sheets. I'd ended up sleeping a few hours on the couch in my office and my back was aching.

I hated feeling this out of control. I hated feeling this desperate. This was what I'd been trying to avoid. But here I was. It was fucking pathetic. And I couldn't stop.

I walked out into the kitchen. Ellen paused when she saw me, a plate balancing precariously in her hand.

"What?" I snapped, my voice hoarse.

She didn't even flinch. She was used to my moods. "Are you feeling alright?"

No. "Mhm."

She looked so concerned. "Here. Eat something." She put the plate down on the counter. "It's your favorite."

I honestly didn't care what she'd made. The only thing I was craving was Penny. And I couldn't have her because she was hiding from me. "I'll grab something on the way, I'm running late."

She lightly touched my arm. "Are you sure you're okay, dear? Really?"

I knew how I must look. Ellen had been working for me for years. She knew how low I could get. She'd seen me at my worst. I knew exactly what she was asking me.

And I didn't know how to answer her. Because I was just as worried as her.

Ellen's eyes dropped to the dark circle under my eyes.

I pulled my arm away from her. "I'm fine, Ellen."

"You were so looking forward to your beach date. You ran out of here too quickly yesterday for me to see you…but I thought for sure I'd get a glimpse of one of your rare smiles today." She smiled at me, almost like she was encouraging me to mimic the action.

I didn't return it.

"Did something happen on your date?" she asked.

"No. The whole day was perfect." It wasn't a lie. It had been a great night too. But between Penny falling asleep in my arms and me taking a shower in the morning…something had broken. I was used to breaking things. But this one really fucking hurt. I'd told Ellen I was going on a date on Monday. That's all she knew. And I wasn't going to sit here and make her play therapist when I had one of those. A shitty one that didn't prevent me from giving in to temptation. "I gotta go, Ellen."

She didn't say anything else. But I felt her gaze on me as I left. Her very worried gaze. I wanted to be able to tell her that I wasn't slipping again. That I had everything under control. But I didn't. I could barely breathe.

The elevator doors closing made me feel even more claustrophobic. Penny had definitely uncovered something about my past. I just didn't know what it was. My figurative closet was so full of skeletons that I couldn't even close the door. I had no idea if she was angry or terrified of me or both. I practically ran out of the elevator when the doors finally dinged open.

The air was chillier today as I walked to my Comm class. It was like autumn had appeared overnight. Penny had left and taken all the warmth with her. A few leaves were even turning yellow and red. It felt like an ending. But I wasn't going to accept that. This couldn't be the end of us. Not yet. I hadn't had enough.

I took a deep breath when I reached my classroom. I just had to get through one class and then I'd sort this mess out. I adjusted my glasses and walked in. If she didn't realize how much I needed her, she would after today. I looked a mess.

For just a second, we made eye contact. I could feel the pain in her stare. It was the same pain I was feeling. But she immediately dropped my gaze and looked down at her desk. *She can't even look at me?* This was bad.

I cleared my throat. I realized I had been awkwardly standing at the front of the class. "Passion," I said. *Screw the lesson plan.* "Passion is what drives a good speech. Passion drives everything. And it's probably one of the reasons why you chose your majors." The only passion I currently had was sitting in the back row ignoring me.

I picked up a piece of chalk and started writing on the board. "Without passion, there really is no meaning in life." I turned around and locked eyes with Penny again. *There's no meaning without you.* I'd thought teaching was a perfect fit for me. But I didn't even know what living was until I met Penny. I was drowning. I couldn't breathe. It felt like I was choking. *Look at me, Penny. Fucking look at me!* "Today I'd like us all to talk about something that we're passionate about. Ray, kick us off."

Ray stood up. "I'm passionate about any good booty." The class laughed and he began to sit down.

"Ray, don't you dare sit down." I was seconds away from snapping.

Ray laughed awkwardly and continued to stand there.

"Passion is not humorous. Unless your passion is humor. Don't make a joke of my assignments, Raymond."

"I'm not, man."

"That's Professor Hunter to you. Get the hell out of my class." God, I was taking it out on my students. I was losing it.

Ray grabbed his backpack and left the room without turning around. The whole class was silent. I thought I might get fired for dating a student. Now I had to worry about yelling in class? It felt like I was sinking.

I cleared my throat. "*I* am passionate about teaching. That would be an acceptable answer." *And you, Penny. I'm passionate about you. You're fucking everything.* I called the next name and the girl rose to her feet. It looked like she was shaking. Jesus, I was scaring them. I tuned out her answer. Had I completely lost my mind? The last time I'd lost my temper like this was when I punched the dean of the last college I worked at. Again. And again. I raked my fingers through my hair. *Breathe.*

"Penny Taylor," I said.

She rose to her feet and stared directly into my eyes. "I'm passionate about honesty." She quickly sat back down.

I raised my left eyebrow. *Honesty?* Yeah, I had a few secrets. But this wasn't a one-sided thing. I wanted her to be honest with me too. We could start with what she was so upset about. I wasn't great at relationships, but even I knew that communication was a big part of them. I was willing to have this conversation. I needed her to meet me halfway here.

After the last student shared what they were passionate about, I dismissed the class and waited for her to come up to me.

When the class had finally emptied, she got to her feet and walked toward my desk.

"Penny." I put my hand on her arm. I felt that familiar warmth that I'd been craving. And for just a second I was able to breathe a little deeper.

"I'm sorry, Professor Hunter. We need to end this before we make it any worse." She took a step back from me, removing my hand from her.

"End this? Have your feelings for me changed?"

"Professor Hunter, everything's changed."

"You're right, I like you more than ever." I forced a smile on my face, when all I really wanted to do was get down on my knees and beg her to stay.

She shook her head. "I know."

"Then what's the problem?"

"Professor Hunter, I know." She took a slow breath. "I know your secret."

My secret? Which fucking one? I couldn't come clean unless I knew what specifically she was talking about. Because if one thing was making her run? Imagine if she knew them all. It was my worst nightmare.

"The fact that you don't even know what I'm referring to is disgusting," she said.

I felt gutted. So it was one of the bad ones. I was going to eventually tell her everything. Of course I was. But not yet. Not when we were still so new. Not when I could so easily lose her.

I stepped toward her and put my hand on her arm again. "Penny, let's go to my office to talk about this." *Please.*

"I'm not going anywhere with you." She took another step away from me, like being that close to me repulsed her.

"Whatever you think you know, you couldn't possibly understand. Just give me a chance to explain."

"No, I think I do understand. And I'm sorry that I let anything happen between us."

"Don't say that, Penny." I was about to lose my temper again like I had with Ray. But she was dismissing what we had because of what? A criminal record? The fact that I got fired from my last job? My confession of being promiscuous before I moved here? What? Or just the fact that I could go on for an hour might have been the problem. I was a fucking mess. She had every reason to end this. Every reason to run. But I wanted her to stay. I *needed* her to stay.

"You were right to hide what kind of man you are from me. You're not at all who I thought you were. Don't text me, Professor Hunter."

"Penny!" I called after her as she turned and left the room. *Shit.* I grabbed my satchel and ran after her. But I lost her in the crowded hall. *You were right to hide what kind of man you are from me.* I stopped in the middle of the hall, ignoring the students trying to pass me. *You were right to hide what kind of man you are from me.* What stung was that she was right. And I couldn't do anything to change my past. I came here to move on. But it would follow me everywhere. *You were right to hide what kind of man you are from me.*

***

Penny wouldn't answer my phone calls. So I sent her an email instead. She'd have to open it because I sent it from my work email. She'd think it was for class. It was the only way I could figure out how to communicate with her. I'd delete any trace of the email later. But being caught dating a student wasn't my greatest fear right now. Losing her was.

Subject: Our discussion isn't over

Penny,

I wish you wouldn't always feel so compelled to argue with me. I told you that I have done some things in my past that I regret. I am not withholding information from you to be spiteful. I'm doing it to protect you. If you will allow me to come talk to you, I can explain.

-James

I read it over once more and pressed send. And then waited. I went for a run in the apartment's gym so I wouldn't accidentally run into any students. And I waited. I graded some papers. And I waited. I spent another sleepless night in my office. And another.

I knew it was over. But I couldn't accept that. The more time we spent apart, the more I wanted her. I was craving her. I needed one more fix. Just one more fix.

Chapter 34

Friday

I walked into my classroom. If Penny hadn't thought I was a mess on Wednesday, she'd certainly think it today. I'd bothered to put in my contacts this time, but there were dark circles under my eyes. I was exhausted. I hadn't shaved in days. And I had barely bothered to knot my tie. I was a disheveled mess. I was in pain. And I didn't know what to do. I didn't know how to stand here and give a lecture when I just wanted to melt into my chair. Or fucking scream at someone. I really wanted to scream. Which was bad for poor Ray.

Penny didn't make eye contact with me today. She was acting like I meant nothing. And the thought that it was possible that I had been reduced to so little in her eyes was starting to settle. I'd lost her. And I didn't know how to accept that. It was like I was starving. I hadn't known how much I was starving until I met her. And she was all I wanted.

I picked up a piece of chalk and was about to turn to the board when I saw her move in the back row. I watched her grab her things and push out the back door of the classroom. She couldn't even look at me. She couldn't even listen to my voice. Whatever she'd found out repulsed her. Which made sense. The chalk snapped in my hand.

***

Another restless night. I knew I had to give her up. I knew it. But I couldn't. I splashed water on my face.

I'd watched video footage of Tyler going in and out of her dorm after class yesterday. I knew I was supposed to remove the cameras. But what did Dr. Clark know? If I didn't have the cameras, how was I supposed to know she was safe? How was I supposed to know she was okay while I was fucking falling apart?

I splashed more water on my face. I needed to get a grip. It was one thing to sleep with a student. It was another thing to stalk her. I needed to remember that I just liked to fuck her. Nothing more. That's all it ever was.

No. I dried off my face with a towel. Now I was just lying to myself. I'd made love to her in my bed. The sheets still smelled of her, and I kept telling Ellen not to wash them. It was like I no longer knew how to function without Penny beside me. I kept replaying moments with her over and over again in my head. As if the memory of her would somehow steady me. Keep me going. But the problem was that she wasn't just stuck in my head. My body physically ached for her too. Like there was a knife twisting in my chest.

I stared at my reflection in the bathroom mirror. It didn't matter that I'd been trying to be a better man. Because I was still me. Everyone knew my past. It was the price I paid for being in the spotlight for so long. There was no hiding from it. Penny was bound to find out what kind of man I was eventually. For just a moment though…I'd had it all. I threw the towel down on the vanity and walked out to my bedroom.

My phone buzzed in my pocket. I pulled it out expecting a text from Rob saying he was back in the states. But it wasn't a text. It was an email. From Penny. My eyes scanned the message.

Subject: Trying to Protect Me?
Professor Hunter,

I thought that I was naive, but I believe that description fits you better. I don't think that I'm the woman in your life that you should be protecting.
-Penny

What the fuck was she talking about? I typed out a reply.

Subject: You're the Only Woman in My Life
Penny,

I'm not sure what you think you know about me. But I can tell you that I'm falling for you. There is no woman in my life that is more important to me. It's you. I'm coming over now.
-James

She'd finally written to me. She'd just given me a way back in. And I wasn't going to hesitate for another second. I grabbed a jacket out of my closet. I'd wait outside her dorm all night if I had to. She was going to fucking talk to me. Clearly this was some crazy misunderstanding. My phone buzzed again.

Subject: Don't You Dare
Professor Hunter,

Don't waste your time. Even if you come here, I'm not coming out to talk to you.
-Penny

For some reason I was smiling. I wasn't sure if it was because it was the first she'd spoken to me in days. Or because she was being impossible yet cute. I quickly replied as I went to the elevator.

Subject: I Do Dare
Penny,

Stop being so stubborn. I'm leaving now. I'll see you in ten minutes.

-James

I made it to her dorm in record time. I put my car in park. It was dark, no one would be able to see us. Besides, it was a chilly night and most of the students were either out partying or snuggled up in their dorms.

But none of that mattered if she refused to come out. I stared at the door. *Just talk to me.* I needed to know what she knew. I'd done a lot of stupid shit when I was younger. More when I was older. But I was trying here. I was teaching for a reason. I was in Delaware for a reason.

Maybe I can sneak in. How hard could it really be? I just needed to wait for someone to walk out.

I was just about to climb out of the car when the back door opened. And there she was. I breathed a sigh of relief. She folded her arms across her chest as she walked down the steps. When she reached the car, I opened the passenger's side door from the inside.

"Get in the car," I said.

"But I don't want to go anywhere."

For fuck's sake. "I'm not taking you anywhere. I just want to be able to talk to you in private."

She glanced behind her. "There's no one around."

"Penny, get in the car."

She sighed and sat down in the passenger's seat. I breathed in the smell of her cherry perfume. The same smell that had been lingering on my sheets, haunting me.

Her just being here instantly calmed me down. That ache in my chest eased.

I drove my car to the small parking lot by her dorm, pulled into one of the last spots, and cut the ignition. She was here, but for some reason I couldn't look at her. I didn't know what to say, so I just stared out the windshield like an idiot. I had one chance to fix this and I had no idea how. My hands were gripping the wheel so tightly that my knuckles were turning white.

Breathe. And since she was sitting there, it was a little easier. I turned to look at her. God she was beautiful. "I thought you weren't going to come out and see me."

She crossed her arms over her chest and looked out the window. "I figured I owed it to you to hear your side."

The pout on her face was so adorable it was hard to pay attention to what she was saying. I just wanted her lips back on mine. "You're cute when you're upset."

"Why didn't you tell me?" she asked with a stern glare I'd never seen from her before.

"Tell you what?" I swallowed hard. I knew how terrible having to ask her was. How guilty it made me seem.

"How could you possibly not know what I'm referring to? What is wrong with you?"

I took a deep breath. "You looked me up online, didn't you?" I lowered my eyebrows. She'd found everything.

"No! Well, yes. But that has nothing to do with anything. I found your ring, Professor Hunter."

Oh. I nodded my head. *Oh.* I forgot I even had the ring still. What a fucking relief. That's what all this was about? I was so relieved I almost smiled, but then I realized that would be the wrong reaction. This was just a terrible misunderstanding. And I knew exactly what she was thinking.

"So you have nothing to say to that?" she asked.

"It's not what you think." I raked my fingers through my hair.

"And what is it that you think I'm thinking?"

I raised my left eyebrow. Her cherry perfume was everywhere. I finally had her alone again and I didn't want to talk. I wanted to fuck her. I wanted to remind her that she needed me too. But I had to clear the air. This was my one chance and thank God it was just the ring nonsense. "You're probably thinking that I'm a lying cheater that you want nothing to do with."

"Am I wrong?"

"Yes."

"Enlighten me."

"First of all, I never lied to you. I withheld information that I deemed unimportant to our relationship..."

"Unimportant? You're such an asshole," she said, cutting me off. She grabbed the door handle.

"Penny." I put my hand on her shoulder, keeping her in place.

"And you did lie to me. At the country club when you said you didn't relish sharing me, you made me believe that I wasn't sharing you either. You even denied having a girlfriend. If I had known you were married..." her voice trailed off as she started to cry.

It hurt me to see her cry. My body physically ached for her. Was that why my chest had hurt the last few days? Because hers was hurting too? "Penny, please don't cry." I reached over and wiped the tears from her cheek.

"Don't touch me." She pushed my hand away. "How could you do this to me? Why didn't you just tell me then? I trusted you!"

"Because Isabella and I are over."

"What? You're divorced?" She sunk into the passenger's seat. "You still could have told me."

This was exactly why I hadn't told her. Because I needed more time. "It's just a matter of finalizing the paperwork. I would have told you once it was official. I just didn't want to upset you for no reason."

"So you're technically still married right now?"

"Technically, yes, but I've already signed the divorce papers. It hasn't been a smooth process. But I have no connection to Isabella at all. We're done. We've been done for a long time."

She stared at me, waiting for me to elaborate. But I had nothing else to say on the matter. Did she need to hear that Isabella was a lying, manipulative monster? That I'd been tricked into the whole thing? Probably not. None of that mattered now. The woman sitting beside me was the only person I cared about.

"Well, what happened?" Penny finally asked.

I pressed my lips together. How could I describe how little that relationship truly meant? How I was at my lowest of lows and I thought I deserved to be unhappy? "We didn't love each other."

"Then why did you get married in the first place?"

"It's a long story."

She pulled her legs up onto the seat. "I have some time to spare."

I leaned toward her slightly and put my hand on the center console. A peace offering. "Do you really want to talk about this, Penny? All you need to know is that it was a mistake and it's over." I didn't want to hash through all this. There were a million other things I'd rather do. I was so sick of my past lurking behind the shadows. Why couldn't we just be happy right here right now? Why did it feel like no matter what I did, Isabella would always be there to ruin it?

"Please. I need to know." She put her hand on top of mine.

She met me halfway. I squeezed her hand. "Okay." I sighed. I could meet her halfway too. If she wanted to hear this, I'd tell her. It didn't seem like I had much of a choice. "Isabella's parents are good friends with my parents. Ever since we were little, our parents always pushed us together. But I just never clicked with her. She was always so cold.

"In high school, I started dating a girl named Rachel. Whenever Rachel came over to my house, my parents were completely dismissive. It was clear that they didn't think she was good enough to be part of our family. They always made her feel so unwelcome. When I finally confronted them about it, they told me that if I didn't break up with Rachel they wouldn't pay for me to go to college. And I'm not proud of what I did. My life with them was all that I knew. I didn't want to have to be on my own. I didn't know how to live without money. I was young and stupid. I broke up with Rachel the next day. And my parents began to make it clear that I was expected to eventually marry Isabella."

I didn't bother to tell Penny the part where I kept talking to Rachel after I told my parents I stopped. That we used to hang out in secret and I promised we could be together again after I graduated. That I fucking meant every word. That a few years into college Rachel just stopped talking to me. That she never said goodbye.

I looked down at Penny's hand. I rubbed my thumb along her palm. It didn't matter. None of it mattered now. I'd thought I loved Rachel. But I knew the truth now. Compared to Penny? Rachel was just a blip. It meant nothing. It had never been easy to breathe with her. She suffocated me too.

"Isabella was the only one they would ever approve of. They said that it was in my best interest to marry someone that wasn't after my money. I was so unhappy. When I told you that I was drunk most of college, I was serious. I completely lost it. I spiraled to the bottom. But my parents just kept telling me it was what was best. So eventually I just accepted the fact that I had to marry Isabella. Instead of worrying about it, I threw all my time and energy into the tech company I wanted to start. And when it blew up, I asked Isabella to marry me, because that was the next step I was supposed to take."

I could have gone into more detail. But sometimes it was just too damn hard to think about that time of my life. Everything was…fuzzy. I wasn't sober enough to recall a lot of it. But I did remember feeling like I deserved the hell I was living. That Isabella was my punishment.

"Before I even realized what was happening, the wedding was planned, and everyone had been invited. I knew I didn't love her, but I walked down the aisle anyway. And I made promises to her. I vowed to keep those promises. And I did. I tried so hard to make it work.

"But she didn't love me either. She enjoyed dressing up and playing the part of my wife. Isabella loved the lifestyle, but she didn't love me. She was cold when we were alone. We barely talked. I knew she slept around. I tried to ignore it. I wanted for us to work out because our parents wanted us to be together. Neither one of us were happy. But she was still my wife, so I kept trying to make it work. I was always loyal to her. I tried to make her happy. When I decided to sell my company she freaked out. She couldn't believe that I'd rather spend my days doing something meaningful. And she definitely didn't support my decision. It's funny, because my parents told me we should be together because she wasn't after my money. But really, the only reason that Isabella married me was because I had money."

I didn't have anything else to say. I continued to stare down at Penny's hand. It was such a pathetic sequence of events. I was a pathetic man. And it was hard to look back and see that I had no spine. It was harder to see that no one cared enough to help me. To stop me from making the biggest mistake of my life. I had nothing. And no one. Or maybe everyone I thought that should have my back thought I deserved to live in hell too. I'd hurt everyone around me. I didn't deserve to have anyone on my side.

I took a deep breath. I was lying to myself. I barely remembered my wedding day. But I was pretty sure Rob had tried to stop me. Maybe my friends Mason and Matt did too. I couldn't remember. But clearly I hadn't listened. This wasn't my friends' fault. It was mine. It was all mine. I'd been too far gone to even really care that I was throwing my life away.

Penny squeezed my hand and I looked up at her.

"I'm sorry," she said.

"No, I am. I should have told you. Being here teaching, being with you, this is what I've been missing. I don't want this to mess up what we have."

I looked into her eyes as I continued to rub my thumb along her palm. I felt exactly the opposite with Penny than I had around Isabella. And I wasn't going to fuck this up. I needed this one good thing. I needed her. "I've always been told what to do. I've never had to make choices. But I chose you. And when I walked into my bedroom and you were gone it hurt like hell. My whole life has been painful, living in a way that I didn't want to live. But nothing was as painful as you leaving and not talking to me. Seeing you in class was torture."

"I couldn't see you either. That's why I left class yesterday. I could see that you were feeling all the pain that I was feeling. I've never been so heartbroken."

I leaned over and took her chin in my hand. "Don't do that to me again. I'll tell you whatever you want to know. No more secrets." And I meant it. I'd tell her whatever she wanted to know. I'd told her about Isabella and she wasn't running away. Maybe she needed me just as much as I needed her.

"Okay." She was silent for a moment. "When did you file for divorce?"

"Last year I walked in on Isabella having sex with someone else in our bed. I filed for divorce the next day."

"And came here?"

"Yes."

"There's a rumor that you got fired from your last job."

I grimaced. I should have known that would follow me here. "It's not a rumor; it's true."

"What did you do? Have sex with a student?" She laughed awkwardly.

"What? No, Penny. I haven't made a habit of sleeping with students. You're the exception." How could she think that? I wasn't a professor so that I could hook up with college students. I was a professor because I loved teaching. But I'd risk it all for her.

"So, what did you do?"

"The dean of the college was the one that I walked in on having sex with Isabella. It didn't end well."

"Did you have a fist fight or something?"

"Penny, he was in my bed. It's one thing to suspect it; it's another to see it." I didn't care that Isabella was cheating on me. Honestly, it was kind of a relief. I just cared about being so blatantly disrespected.

"You have anger problems, don't you?"

I rubbed my hand down my face and then back up. "I don't think I'd put it that way."

"So what would you call it?" She tucked a loose strand of hair behind her ear. She looked a little apprehensive and a whole lot beautiful. My gaze landed on her lips.

"Passion maybe." I leaned over and kissed her. I was done talking. Any leftover anger she had disappeared when my lips touched hers. She grabbed the collar of my jacket and pulled me closer. I wanted to make her forget the past few days. I wanted to forget everything.

I pulled back from her kiss. "God I missed you."

"I missed you too."

I leaned over her and pressed the button for her seat to recline. I started to climb over the center console and my ass hit the horn.

Penny started laughing as I straddled her. I silenced her with a kiss. Had her lips always tasted this sweet? Being without her for just a few days had nearly driven me mad. My hand slid from her cheek, down her neck, and onto her breast. I squeezed it hard before letting my hand wander down to the waistline of her yoga pants. I needed her right fucking now.

"Professor Hunter?"

"You said there was no one around."

"Shouldn't we go back to your place?"

"You tortured me for almost a week, Penny. I'm not waiting another second. Switch places with me."

She slid to the side and climbed on top of me, bumping into the dashboard. I tried to hold back my laughter. The car was too small. I probably should have driven us back to my place, but my cock needed attention right now.

"Ow," she muttered.

I placed another kiss on her lips as I slid her yoga pants and thong down her thighs. Every inch of me felt alive when my skin was pressed against hers. She was giving me a second chance. I didn't have to let her go. And I needed her. I needed her so fucking badly.

She kicked off her shoes and pants as I pushed my jeans and boxers to the floor of the car. *See what you do to me?*

She leaned over and kissed me. Without hesitation, I grabbed her hips and pulled her down onto my length. *Fucking perfection.* Her pussy was made to take my cock. Every inch. Fucking heaven. She gasped and pressed her hand against the passenger window.

I didn't care if people saw. I didn't care about anything except being inside of her. "Don't put me through that again, Penny." I kissed her neck, tasting her cherry perfume, as I moved her hips faster and faster.

"Never."

My hands slid to her ass and I slammed my cock so deep inside of her. She moaned as my fingers dug into her soft skin. I needed to feel her surrender to me. I needed to know she wasn't going to leave again. I pulled her closer, like I could physically just keep her with me forever. I sucked the side of her neck a little harder. I'd never felt the need to mark someone's skin. But Penny and I couldn't go public. I at least wanted everyone to know she was taken.

"Promise me," I said.

"I promise," she said breathlessly.

The angle in the car was awkward, but the sensation of being inside her was all that mattered. Complete and utter perfection. And she would never walk away from me again. I'd tell her whatever she needed to hear. But I was done playing games. "You're mine," I growled and thrust myself deep inside of her again. It was hard to read Penny sometimes. But not when we were like this. I'm pretty sure when I was deep inside of her it was the only time I was in control. And I fucking loved controlling her body.

"Yes! I'm yours!" she moaned.

The windows were soon completely fogged up besides for her handprint. I continued to guide her hips, going faster and faster. I was unraveling. I was going to fucking explode inside of her.

"Come for me, Penny." I lifted my hips slightly, pressing my erection into her g-spot.

"Professor Hunter!" She clenched herself around me, her pussy gripping me like a vice.

And I let go. My dick pulsed inside of her, again and again. Filling her up. Claiming her.

She collapsed on top of me. I kissed the top of her head and wrapped my arms around her. This time I wouldn't fuck it up.

Chapter 35

Sunday

"Dr. Clark will see you now," said the receptionist.

I made my way into the room, closed the door, and sat down. I was done playing games. I'd told Penny about Rachel, Isabella, and how lost I was in college. I'd told her I'd gotten fired from my last job for punching the dean. It wasn't everything, but it was a pretty good fucking start. And she chose to stay. She chose me. And I needed to choose her too.

"Good afternoon, James," Dr. Clark said with a smile. "How was your week?"

This was it. I just needed to get this off my chest and I could move forward. With Dr. Clark's help, hopefully. He might also throw me out. But no matter what his reaction, it wouldn't change a thing. I was all in with Penny. Now that I had her back in my life again, I wasn't going to let her go. "My week has been fantastic, thanks for asking. Also, I'm dating a student."

His smile faded. "Excuse me?"

"Penny's a student. She's a senior in my Comm class. We met for a moment before classes started and I couldn't get her out of my head. Trust me, I tried. I really fucking tried. But...I'm done trying. I think you're right. I think I'm in love with her."

"That's...that's a lot, James." He started writing in his notebook.

I tried not to cringe. I knew he wasn't writing it down to show the dean or anything. But I hated that there was personal information about me in his notebook. Information that could potentially hurt Penny if it came to light.

"Can you not…please don't write that down."

He stopped writing and looked up at me. "Very well." He placed the notebook down. "I was making a note about how you lied in previous sessions about Penny's identity. You led me to believe she was a colleague. How did you expect me to help you when you weren't being honest with me?"

I wasn't expecting that to be the problem he had with all this. Did he not hear that I was dating a student? Lying was the least of my problems. I'd made a huge step with that last night. And I wasn't planning on stopping today. I just needed to get it all off my chest. "I couldn't be honest with you when I wasn't being honest with myself. I was trying to resist her." I tried as hard as I could. But it was impossible.

He nodded. "And when you're being honest with yourself…how do you feel?"

"She's all I can think about. We had a little disagreement last week and she wasn't talking to me and it felt like I was drowning. But when I'm with her I forget about my past. I forget about all of it. I want to be better for her. She's given me a reason to start…living."

Dr. Clark smiled. "That's wonderful."

"It is? I thought you'd be a little more…judgmental."

"James." He shook his head. "I just want you to be happy."

I was. I was so fucking happy. I was pretty sure I was grinning like an idiot right now. Just talking about Penny made me feel lighter.

"But I am curious about what the dean thinks about all this."

"I haven't told him," I said. "Penny will graduate soon enough. It's better for her if we wait."

"Better for her or for you?"

I didn't need to think that over. "Her. I don't want to jeopardize her college experience just because she chose to date me."

"That's very mature of you."

I laughed. "Do you usually think I'm not mature?"

"Honestly, when it comes to real relationships, it seems like you don't have that much experience. Also there's the fact that you lied to me. That was rather immature."

"I thought you'd tell me I had to stop seeing her." And I knew I couldn't. This whole time…I just knew I couldn't stay away from Penny. We went from if to when faster than I even had time to process what I was doing. I was done for as soon as she fell into my arms in that coffee shop.

"I may have suggested you stop seeing her. But I also may not have. Like I've been saying during our last few sessions…you seem happy when you're with her. I don't see anything wrong with that."

He'd probably think it was wrong that I got off when Penny called me Professor Hunter. But that was a conversation for a different day. I had no idea why her calling me that made me instantly hard. Right now I didn't care though. I just wanted to enjoy myself for once in my life.

"Have you told her about your past yet?"

"That's what our disagreement was about. She found my wedding ring when she slept over. But I told her about the divorce. Why I married Isabella in the first place. I told her about Rachel and how I lost it in college and hit rock bottom. I even told her about how my parents controlled my life and that I got fired from my last teaching job."

"That's all a good start. But it's not everything." He stared at me, willing me to continue my admissions.

"I'll get there." Geez, a person could only handle so many confessions in one day. I'd tell Penny everything soon. Slowly. So she wouldn't run away screaming.

"Was that all you told her about hitting rock bottom?"

I tried to think back to the conversation. "Yeah, but I think she got the gist. A few nights ago I also told her I was drunk most of college and had a lot of sexual partners. She knows I used to be a mess."

"James, that's not the whole story and you know it. You have to tell her everything. We already talked about this. Just because she's a student doesn't mean she can't handle the truth. You trust her, right? Or else you wouldn't have risked your job to be with her?"

I didn't even need to think about it. "I do trust her."

Dr. Clark threw his hands in the air. "Now that's a reason to celebrate. You trust someone new! James, that's a big deal."

I smiled.

"Did you have her sign a confidentiality agreement?"

"Nope."

"That's good," he said. "That's a really good step. You trust her!"

I laughed. It was strange having someone so excited about something I did. It was the affirmation most kids got from their parents. But I never got that from mine. "I do." Trust seemed like such a simple concept. But it was hard for me. I couldn't help but smile.

"Now, since you lied to me for weeks, I get all the details. Tell me all about her."

I smiled. I could do that. This was the easiest therapy session of my life. Once I started talking, it was like I couldn't stop. I sounded like a sappy idiot, and I didn't give a shit.

Dr. Clark looked almost as happy as I was. Until I let something slip about the cameras I was using to spy on her.

"James, we talked about this. You have to remove the cameras."

"Yeah, I'm on it. I'll tell Ian to do it later today." It was a lie. I had no intention of ever removing the cameras. Penny was mine. And I needed to keep her safe.

He gave me a hard stare. "Are you actually going to tell Ian that?"

"It's honestly not even my fault. This was all his idea."

Dr. Clark shook his head. "You just told me that you trusted Penny. If you trust her, you should allow her her privacy."

"I don't have cameras in her dorm room or anything. I'm not a creep."

"She might view it differently."

"I'll add it to my list of things I still need to confess to her." Honestly, Penny kinda loved the thrill of being almost caught. I bet she'd love that I watched her. I thought about how our waiter kept interrupting us at the country club. She was into that. God, I loved how naughty she was.

"James?"

I looked back at Dr. Clark. I think I must have missed something he said, because he was staring at me intently. "Sorry, what was that?" I asked.

"When you first came in you said you thought you were in love with her."

"Yeah."

"Do you feel differently around her than you did with Rachel?"

"It's not even comparable." I knew now that I never loved Rachel. I'd loved the idea of her when we first met. She felt like an escape from my life. But she just wanted to be a part of it. I was pretty sure she loved money, not me. And I certainly hadn't loved her.

He nodded. "And what about Isabella? Do you feel differently around Penny than you did with Isabella?"

I laughed. "Dr. Clark, I never loved Isabella. She's a psychopath."

He raised his eyebrows.

"Sorry, that was probably insensitive to your line of work."

"No, that's not it," he said. "I'm curious as to why you think she's a psychopath. You think she's crazy because she cheated on you?"

I laughed. "No. She cheated on me because she didn't love me either. I think she's crazy because she was legit locked up for a while at some psych ward after high school."

Dr. Clark's eyebrows pulled together. "You never told me that before. Why was she seeking treatment?"

"She was always a little...cold. And cruel. But she kind of lost it senior year of high school and got a little...murdery. I don't know. We were never really close. She was only in my circle because our parents were friends. That was the only reason. There was just always something off about her. But when she got out of that place, she seemed calmer. Not nicer. Just...different."

"So...not murdery?"

"Yeah." In high school I wouldn't have been at all surprised if Isabella committed homicide. For a while Matt even thought she had. But Isabella didn't seem as crazy now. She was just a fucking bitch.

"Interesting. Was she on any medication or any-thing?"

I tried to remember. "There was something she took every day." I could picture the plastic orange pill container. "I don't know what it was." I'd never cared enough to look.

"Are you at all concerned about how she's going to re-act to the news that you're dating someone else?"

"She should be signing the divorce papers any day now. And like I've said, she never loved me either. I hon-estly don't expect to ever hear from her again. We've always lived very separate lives. The break is going to be clean and easy."

Dr. Clark nodded. "Well, that's good."

It was good. As soon as Isabella signed the papers, I'd never have to see her again. I was thrilled for that moment. I just wanted it all behind me.

"Sorry, we got a little off topic there for a moment," Dr. Clark said with a chuckle. "So, a student, huh?"

I didn't know what to even say.

"I'd feel negligent if I didn't at least advise you to re-consider. This could ruin your fresh start here."

"I think she is my fresh start."

He smiled. "Like I said...I just needed to say it. You never really take my advice though, do you?" He laughed. "I mean...how's the yoga going?"

"I take some of your advice."

"Well, maybe just ignore what I said. It's good to see you happy."

It felt good to be this happy.

"What I was leading up to before I got distracted was...you said you thought you were in love with Penny." He stared at me. "So...are you or are you not?"

I knew that I wasn't worthy of Penny's love. I knew that. But that knowledge had no effect on how I felt. And there wasn't a doubt in my mind now. "I love her. I'm in love with her."

Chapter 36

Monday

I locked eyes with Penny as I walked into the classroom and smiled. I wasn't sure I had ever started a day being this excited about something. Someone. But then I noticed the expression on her face. She looked fucking pissed. At me. *What did I do now?* All I wanted to do was speak with her. To figure out what it was that was bothering her. But I couldn't. I couldn't do anything about it right now. It killed me to see her upset. It killed me more that my position made it impossible to fix it.

I cleared my throat. I just needed to get through this class and then I could talk with her in private. "Okay, time for speeches. I'm excited to learn why all of you chose your majors." I pulled the podium to the middle of the room and made my way to the seat in front of Tyler. I smelled Penny's cherry perfume everywhere, which made it almost impossible to focus on the class. I pulled out my papers to grade the speeches with. "Adam Zabek, you're up."

Adam and a few other people went and then it was Penny's turn. Would she let me know what was wrong in her speech? Somehow let me know? The flirting in her answers was usually subtle. She could give me a hint now. *Let me in.*

"Penny Taylor," I said. I hoped it came out the way I'd called all the other names. And not like I was in the middle of fucking her brains out. I was getting used to groaning her name instead of saying it like this.

"Good luck, Penny," Tyler said.

Fucking Tyler. Friendship rose my ass.

"Thanks," she said.

I watched her make her way to the front of the room. Her jeans hugged her ass perfectly. And she didn't even trip on anything, which was a relief. If any students laughed at her again, I was pretty sure I'd lose it. Especially today when she already seemed upset about…something. No, not just something. She was definitely upset with me.

She gripped the sides of the podium. And just stood there. She just stood there awkwardly staring down at her notes.

Say something. Tell me what's wrong. Say anything, Penny.

Someone in the front row cleared their throat.

She finally looked up and locked eyes with me. And I was pretty sure she looked even angrier than she had when I first walked into the room.

"I am currently majoring in marketing. And for some reason I'm having a really hard time remembering why I chose it." She lifted her paper off the podium and waved it around. "I have a whole list of reasons on here why marketing is a great major, but I'm not sure how much of that I can believe anymore."

Am I marketing in this weird metaphor?

"Because sometimes you think you know something, but actually you have no idea what it's really like. Marketing is like that. It's a complete lie. I mean, we're all taught that marketing is sexy, right?" Her cheeks flushed. "But it's really not. Marketing is ugly on the inside. Hideous, really."

Ouch. I wanted to believe that she really just hated her major. But when she was looking at me like that? It was me. I was definitely marketing in this scenario. Her words echoed around me. There wasn't any hiding from her words. *Hideous on the inside.* I told her the truth and that's what she thought? What the fuck? Where was this coming from? I thought we were on the same page. We were in a good place when I saw her on Saturday night. A great place. What the hell happened between then and now? It was impossible to sit here and listen to this. I wanted to make it right. But all I could do was bite my tongue.

"Marketing lures you into getting something that you don't really need or want," she continued. "A product can't cheat on you. A product can't lie to you. But a marketer can."

It felt like she'd slapped me across the face. I'd just opened up so much to her.

"And a marketer doesn't blink an eye when they lie and cheat. They hook you in and sell you awful products that you don't even want. You know what? I'm actually thinking about changing my major because of this assignment. Because I can't for the life of me think of a reason to continue pursuing marketing. Because marketing is a fucking joke."

"That's enough!" I slammed my fist on the desk. *Jesus.* What the hell was I doing? I couldn't talk to a student that way. But she wasn't just a fucking student. She was Penny. She was mine. I was losing her. And I couldn't do anything about it right here.

"Marketing can go to hell." She grabbed her paper and ran out of the room.

"Penny!" Tyler yelled from behind me.

The whole class was silent. *What the hell do I say now?* A chair squeaked across the floor. A pen dropped. I could feel my pulse ricocheting around my body. I did the only thing I could do. I called the next name on my roster. "Tyler Stevens."

What the hell just happened?

Tyler made his way to the front of the room. The last thing I wanted to do right now was listen to his speech. I wanted to run after Penny. I needed to run after her.

"I chose to major in economics because a major in business seemed like a logical choice," Tyler said. "A safe choice. And I added on a second major of finance because it was easy to get both at the same time." Tyler laughed even though what he just said wasn't funny.

I looked up from the blank sheet of paper on my desk.

He was glaring at me. It looked like he wanted to wring my neck. "But fuck the safe choice," he said.

Had all my students lost their minds? I was about to tell him to watch the language, but he started talking again.

"I think I really chose the majors I did so that one day I can be rich." He shook his head, still staring daggers at me. "Because rich guys can get whatever girl they want, even if he's a manipulative piece of shit."

Oh fuck.

"Because apparently women love rich assholes."

He knows. He knows I'm sleeping with Penny. Christ. I looked back down at the blank paper in front of me. Was it just him that knew? Did the whole class know after Penny's outburst? After Tyler's too? The room was completely silent. I quickly called the next name so that Tyler wouldn't continue his rant.

My heart was pounding faster than it did after running for miles. Seriously, how many people knew? Was it already all over social media? I knew the repercussions of all this. My job was finished. But I wasn't even worried about that right now. I just needed to speak with Penny. I needed to make this right.

Time ticked by slowly, the speeches taking forever. I focused on writing up Penny's grade. Because if I didn't focus on something I'd get up and run after her. And I couldn't do that. If my students hadn't put it together that I was sleeping with her, they'd put it together then. *Breathe.*

Student: Penny Taylor
Topic: Marketing
Miss Taylor,

You don't know how much it pains me to see you hurt. Just give me a chance to explain. I can't lose you.

As for your speech, I am in awe of you. Your passion is inspiring. Even though you strayed off topic, the whole class could learn a lot from you. And the fact that your passion is for me makes everything more real for me. I feel the same way about you. Minus the anger.

But it is usually best not to cry and curse during presentations, Miss Taylor.
Grade: A-

Right before class was over, I heard the back door open. I glanced behind me. Tyler was gone. So was all of Penny's stuff. *Fuck.*

"Class dismissed," I said after the last speech. I tried to call Penny as I gathered my things, but she didn't answer. Did she even have her phone? I pressed on Ian's number.

"What's up?" he asked after the second ring.

"I need your help finding Penny." I maneuvered through the crowded hallway and pushed the door to get outside. A light rain had started to fall.

"Already on it. She was just standing outside her dorm in the rain for a long time. She must have lost her keycard, but someone eventually walked out so she could get in. Everything okay?"

"Is Tyler there too?"

"Yup, he got there a few minutes ago. Penny's room-mate let him in."

Shit. There were students everywhere. I couldn't move fast enough without causing attention. And there was a chance it was only Tyler who knew. *Maybe. Hopefully.* I ran to my car instead. "Cancel my classes for the rest of the day."

"Is there something…"

I hung up the phone before he finished what he was going to say. Maybe Tyler was just an unhinged crazy person. But it seemed more likely that he knew what was going on with me and Penny and was pissed off. And I wasn't going to let him swoop in and steal her out from under me.

When I pulled up to Penny's dorm, Tyler was walking out. *Son of a bitch.* His head was down because of the rain, so I couldn't see his expression. But he wouldn't be leaving if their conversation had gone well. *Right?*

I tried to call her again, but she didn't respond.

Fuck it. I walked up to her dorm and waited in the rain. It was all I could do. And I waited. And waited. People would see me, but I didn't fucking care. I needed to see her. Comfort her. Figure out what that hell was going on.

Finally a student walked out. I grabbed the door before it could close again. Luckily the student didn't seem to recognize me. I wandered through the first floor. Most of the doors had the residents' names on them. Hopefully hers would too. I walked up a set of stairs and kept wandering through the building until I found her room. Penny and Melissa. That had to be her room. I knocked on the door.

There was no response.

"Penny?"

Silence. But she had to be there. Ian would have called me if she'd left.

"Penny, it's me. Can I please come in?" *Please, just let me in.* I pressed my hand against the door, as if that would make me feel closer to her. *Please.*

The door slowly opened. She was standing there with tears streaming down her face, somehow still looking beautiful.

"Oh, Penny." I grabbed her face in my hands and wiped her tear-stained cheeks with my thumbs. All I wanted to do was fix this. I needed her reassuring smile. I needed to know that we were okay.

"What are you doing here?" she asked.

"I needed to see you."

She sniffed. "Don't you have a class?"

She wasn't shoving me out the door. This was good. "I cancelled my classes for the rest of the day."

"But, Professor Hunter..."

"The most important thing right now is that we talk."
I closed the door behind me. "I think it's safe to say that
something is bothering you."

"How did you know which room was mine?"

"Your name is on the door."

"So you walked around the whole building looking at
all the doors for my name? Are you trying to get caught?"

"Everyone's in class. And you're avoiding talking to
me. If you don't tell me what's wrong, it's impossible for
me to fix."

"I don't want you to fix anything." She turned away
from me.

"Penny." I walked over to her and turned her toward
me. "Just tell me what's wrong. I mean, I gathered from
your speech that I'm a lying cheat who's ugly on the inside.
I'd like to know why you think that. Because I thought that
we were in a good place. Unless you were talking about
someone else." If Tyler hurt her, I was going to fucking kill
him.

"On Saturday you asked me if I had looked you up
online and you were really mad. So I was thinking maybe
there was more to find out about you."

"So, you googled me?" I tried to keep my expression
neutral. How much about me really was online? *Probably a
lot.* But not the worst of it.

"I just wanted to make sure you were telling the truth."

"I would never lie to you, Penny." I grabbed both
sides of her face again. Yes, I hadn't told her about Isabella
right away. But I'd never lied. I just withheld information.
There was a difference. And I was in this with her. I was
done holding back. I'd tell her anything she wanted to
hear.

She shook away from my grip. "I found an interview with Isabella that makes it seem like you were lying. And it was only from a few weeks ago."

Was that all? A silly article with my crazy ex? "You can't believe everything you read in tabloids."

"This one seemed pretty convincing."

Jesus, what had Isabella said? "So what did it say exactly?"

"That you two have never been happier. And that the rumors of your split were completely fabricated."

I sighed. How was this supposed to work if Penny believed a tabloid over me? If we were going to be together, our life would end up being in the limelight no matter how hard I tried to protect her from it. "I told you that it hasn't been a smooth process. She won't sign the papers. She's being incorrigible."

"She said in the interview that you were waiting for her to decorate your apartment."

I stared down at Penny's tear-stained face. I knew how bad that looked. My place was so empty. Like I was waiting for my wife to decorate it. "She's lying."

"Then how did she know your apartment hadn't been decorated?"

Breathe. All these accusations stung. I thought I trusted Penny. But when she acted like this…I wasn't sure how I could. I thought about Tyler leaving her building and I crossed my arms over my chest. "Because she's been there before." *But it doesn't matter. It was forever ago. Why the hell are we talking about this? I already told you everything.*

"What? Why?"

"She came a few months after I moved here to talk about our relationship. Or lack of one I guess."

"I don't know if I can trust you."

"And I don't know if I can trust you." I didn't mean to snap, but fuck this. I'd already told her about Isabella. And Penny was the one hiding information from me, not the other way around.

"Why? I haven't done anything wrong."

Breathe. "I saw Tyler Stevens coming out of your building when I pulled up."

"He just came to drop off my stuff that I left in class."

I raised my left eyebrow.

"After I found your wedding ring, I told myself we were over. I was in so much pain. I had never felt so broken before. So I started to think about my relationship with Tyler. I thought maybe it could be more than a friendship. He's always wanted it to be more. It just seemed like the right time."

Fucking hell. I was done with the games. Maybe I was wrong about her. Maybe she wasn't as mature as I thought. I wasn't some college kid looking for a good lay. I was falling for her. I had fallen. And I was in a stage of my life where that actually meant something. Our age difference had never felt like a big gap until this moment. My mind was telling me to walk away. I was too old for this bullshit. But I stayed where I was. I didn't have the strength to walk away. Fuck, all I wanted to do was beg her to forgive me. And I hadn't even done anything wrong. I took a deep breath and leaned against her bed. "You're dating him?"

"No. I thought I wanted to. But I was still confused about you. I've been a mess if you can't tell. I still don't know how I feel. Things seemed easy with Tyler. You just have so much baggage. I think I was just trying to get over you."

"By getting under someone else?" I gripped the side of her mattress. I remembered walking in on Isabella with another man. I was pissed back then. But this feeling right now? This was worse. Because I was pretty sure I was in love with Penny. And she didn't feel the same way. Maybe she never had.

"It didn't go that far, Professor Hunter. And it never will. Tyler found out about you and he wants nothing to do with me."

Fuck. I was hoping I'd been wrong about that. That his speech was about some other rich guy he hated.

Her gaze met mine. "Tyler looked at my phone. He saw that I had missed calls from you."

"You had me in your phone as Professor Hunter?"

"I'm sorry. I don't think he'll tell anyone." It looked like she was about to cry again.

God, she was driving me to madness. But I didn't want to see her cry. I pulled her into my chest. The sweet smell of cherries was everywhere. She'd made a scene in front of the class, did God-knows-what with Tyler, and told him about our relationship. She was a freaking mess. But so was I. And nothing she did could ever be as bad as what I'd done in my early twenties. I continued to hold her in my arms, breathing easier than I had all day. All that mattered was that she was here right now. And I wasn't strong enough to walk away from her. I didn't want to. I couldn't.

"Can I walk you out?" she asked.

What? I pushed her shoulders back slightly and looked down at her. "You want me to leave?"

"No."

"Then I don't want to go."

"But I broke your trust. I had told you Tyler and I were just friends."

"And you were just friends when you told me that. I broke your trust by not telling you about my marriage. Even though I never said I wasn't married."

"So neither of us lied, but we both hurt each other."

I nodded. I was good at hurt. She could hurt me again and again and it wouldn't really phase me. Hurt was all I knew.

"Then I guess we're even?"

I smiled. "Penny, you're hard to control. And I'm used to being in control."

"So what do we do now?" she asked.

It felt like we were in a stalemate. We had both hurt each other and neither one of us knew if we could trust the other. And I hated that feeling. I just wanted to move past this. "Penny, what do you want to do?"

"I don't know."

"You're the one that needs to make a decision. I still want you. I don't care about what happened between you and Tyler. All I care about is what we have."

"I've never felt the way I feel about you with anyone before. You make me feel like I'm living for the first time. But I'm sick of secrets. I don't want to hide that I'm dating you anymore. All the secrets make everything so much harder."

"Who do you feel like you're keeping secrets from?" I asked.

"Melissa."

As soon as she said it, it reminded me of what she'd said about her ex. That they couldn't have broken up because they'd never really dated. Was that what this was all about? Labels? I'd give her any label she wanted if it showed her how much I cared. I'd feel better if we labeled it too. I wanted us to both know where we stood. And I was all in. I'd promised her I wouldn't treat her like her ex had. That I'd never make her feel worthless. I hoped that I hadn't done that. "So tell Melissa that I'm your boyfriend."

She smiled up at me. "Is that really what you want?"

"Yes, I want you to be my girlfriend, Penny. I told you before that I didn't relish the idea of sharing you. I don't want you to be with anyone else *ever again*. Just me." I leaned down and gently pressed my lips against her. She responded like she always did, melting into me. And that was all the reassurance I needed that we were okay. I exhaled a breath that I didn't realize I'd been holding. *We're okay.*

I pulled away and looked around her room. There was a pint of Ben and Jerry's ice cream melting on her desk. And clothes were strewn on the floor. She was...sloppy. I hadn't expected that. "So this is where you live?" I pulled off my suit jacket and draped it over the back of her desk chair.

"It's a dorm room. What did you expect?"

I shrugged. "I haven't been in one for a while. It's a lot smaller than mine was." I looked at the collage of pictures on her bulletin board. She looked younger in several of them, probably pictures of her in high school with old friends. There were also some pictures of her and Melissa around campus. "You're quite popular." I smiled at her.

She laughed. "No, not really."

"Why do you always put yourself down like that?" I reached for her hand. "Don't you see how wonderful you are?"

"No one else sees me the way that you do."

"All I see is you."

Her throat made that adorable squeaking noise.

I looked over her shoulder. My sweater was on her bed. "Do you always make a habit of sleeping with clothing that you've stolen from people?" I lifted my sweater.

Her face flushed. "Just you."

"Just me." I traced my index finger along her jaw line. I wanted to kiss her again, but I wasn't sure that's what we needed. We just needed a moment of peace. Quiet. "This past week has been exhausting."

"Then maybe we should take a nap."

I smiled. That actually sounded perfect. "As you wish." I pulled my tie loose, unbuttoned my dress shirt, and laid both on top of my suit jacket. I slowly unhinged my belt and pulled it free, very aware of Penny's eyes on me. I sat down in her chair and leaned over to unlace my shoes. I kicked them off, along with my socks, and stepped out of my dress pants. I was standing in a dorm room in just my boxers. When was the last time that had happened? I folded my pants and draped them on the back of the chair.

She just stared.

"Are you going to join me?" I asked with a smile.

She quickly undid her pants, slid them down her legs, and pulled off her black t-shirt. She was left in a simple pair of panties and a bra. And she looked seductive as hell.

I picked up the pint of ice cream from her desk and took a bite as my eyes grazed over her body. "Delicious." But I wasn't talking about the ice cream. I was talking about her. "Get in bed." I popped the lid on the ice cream and put it back into the freezer.

She climbed into bed and I joined her. The twin bed was barely long enough for me and definitely too small for both of us together. But I didn't care. I just wanted to be wrapped up in her. I rested my head on the pillow and stared at her in silence for a few minutes. Her lying beside me felt so normal and so comforting. I took a long, slow breath. If she wasn't tired, I could think of a million different things I'd rather do with her than sleep.

"What are you thinking?" I whispered.

"That I'm not that tired." She moved closer and wrapped her legs around me.

"I thought you wanted to nap." I ran my fingers through her hair, pushing it away from her face.

"Not anymore."

"Thank God." I pulled her to me and placed a kiss on her lips.

***

I blinked and slowly opened my eyes. I must have fallen asleep with Penny in my arms. I hadn't slept this well since she'd been in my bed with me. I hadn't really slept at all since then.

She was smiling down at me, her fingers tracing the side of my neck.

I was glad I wasn't the only one having trouble keeping my hands to myself. "Hey," I said and smiled.

"Hey, yourself."

"Were you watching me sleep?" I wasn't sure why, but the idea made me so happy. She was as infatuated with me as I was with her.

"Mhm. Not in a creepy way, though."

I laughed. "I didn't think it was creepy until you said that it wasn't. Now I'm not so sure." I reached out and tucked a strand of hair behind her ear.

"Did you sleep well?"

"Your bed is extremely uncomfortable." She needed to spend more time in mine. I was pretty sure I could find a way to rectify this situation.

"You get used to it."

I raised my left eyebrow. *Yeah right.* "But I do find it easy to fall asleep next to you. You're the only person that seems to be able to make me relax." My hand lazily wandered down her back and landed on her perfect ass.

She laughed. "Melissa is going to be back soon."

"Did you want me to stay and introduce myself?"

"I don't really want you to leave, but I think it's better if I tell Melissa alone."

"Are you kicking me out?" I smiled at her.

"It's nothing personal."

I kissed the tip of her nose and got up. As much as I didn't want to leave, telling her friend in private was the better move. This situation was complicated. Penny wrapped the covers around her as I started to get dressed. When I put on my shirt, she got up and slowly buttoned it for me. God she was sexy. After buttoning one of the last buttons, she pulled my collar and brought my mouth to hers.

"You're making it hard for me to leave," I whispered against her lips.

She laughed and let go of my collar. I finished getting dressed as she pulled on her clothes too. As I knotted my tie, I looked around her room again. I spotted the roses I'd sent her in the trash. "Not a fan of roses?"

"Oh I am. It was just that a domineering professor gave them to me. Or else I would have loved them."

I laughed. She loved that I was domineering. "Before I leave, let me see your phone."

She grabbed it off her desk and handed it to me. I changed my contact information to James in her phone and handed it back to her. *Professor Hunter in her phone?* It had been a ridiculous thing for her to do. But it was also kinky as hell, and I couldn't be mad about that.

"I thought I wasn't supposed to call you James in private?"

No, you're not, baby. "Apparently your phone isn't private."

She bit her lip. If she kept doing that, I'd be on top of her again in a few minutes. I rubbed my thumb along her lower lip to stop her from biting it and gave her a small smile.

"My girlfriends usually call me James."

"That makes it sound like you have more than one girlfriend right now. Am I one of several?"

"Dozens."

She lightly nudged my shoulder.

"No, just you, Penny." *Only you.* I grabbed my suit jacket and draped it over my shoulder. "Let me know how your conversation with Melissa goes."

"I will." She wrapped her arms around my neck and kissed me again. "I'll text you later, James."

My name sounded almost as good as Professor Hunter on her lips. *Almost.*

Chapter 37

Monday

Penny Taylor was my girlfriend. That term made me feel young. The last time I'd officially had a girlfriend was high school. It felt like a lifetime ago. I smiled to myself as I made my way out of her dorm to my car. Hell, she made me feel young. I lowered my head to try to prevent anyone from recognizing me. Although, it would probably be hard to recognize me with a smile on my face.

I climbed into my car, closed the door, and pulled out my phone. I had a million things I needed to do. For a few days there, I'd experienced what life was like without Penny in my life. I didn't want to feel that distance ever again. And now that Penny and I were official, there were some things I needed to take care of. I shot off texts to Ellen and Ian.

Everything was good. I slid my phone back into my pocket. The whole campus didn't know I was dating a student. Just one kid I didn't care about in the slightest. *Freaking Tyler.* And I doubted he'd tell anyone. He clearly hated me, sure. But he liked Penny, and the truth would hurt her more than it would hurt me. Hopefully he was smart enough to realize that.

I took a deep breath. Everything wasn't just good. It was great. I put my car into drive and drove back to my place. I was suddenly full of energy. Sleeping for the first time in days had definitely helped with that. I needed to go for a run and clear my head. Maybe I could even get some work done tonight.

***

I stepped back from my whiteboard with a smile. Fuck, this was good. There was a knock on my door. "Come in."

Ian walked in. "We're all set."

Dr. Clark would not be pleased, because I'd just done the opposite of what he'd recommended. Instead of taking the cameras down, I'd installed more. Talking about how crazy Isabella used to be in therapy the other day had me taking a few extra precautions. Just in case. I didn't think Isabella would show up here. Or act insane. But...I needed to keep Penny safe. I'd just have peace of mind knowing that she was safe at all times. I'd tell her about it soon enough. I wouldn't have done it if I thought it would make her mad. But I had a few other things to bring up next time we talked. Adding "I've been watching you" probably wasn't the best thing to slide in just yet.

"Thanks, Ian. And the tickets?" Penny's birthday was coming up, and based on our conversations...I knew what she wanted.

"The tickets will arrive in about a week. Anything else you need?"

I turned away from the whiteboard. "So...Penny knows about what I used to do. But I don't think she has any idea that I need a security detail when I'm in New York. I just wanted to remind you to..."

"Keep a low profile. I remember. Those were the rules about the apartment you rented me. Say no more, boss. I've got this. She'll never even know I'm here."

It had been really nice having him around. I just didn't want to overwhelm Penny. "I'm not saying you have to disappear or anything. But you're welcome to go back to New York if you want. I'm still paying you either way."

He shrugged. "I'll stick around. You never know when something might come up. Besides…I like my new place. Delaware is growing on me."

"Me too." Well, not really Delaware. But Penny. I was pretty sure I could be anywhere with her and be happy.

"Important question though. Am I still allowed to steal food and watch some of the games with you?"

I laughed. "Of course. Speaking of which…I'm starving."

"I was waiting for you to say something. Ellen made tacos."

My stomach growled. "That sounds perfect." I followed Ian out of my office and down the hall to the kitchen.

Ellen was just putting a plate at the kitchen counter for me.

"This looks great, Ellen." I picked up the plate filled with the most delicious smelling tacos. "But how about you both grab plates and we can all eat together in the dining room."

Ellen raised her eyebrows. "Are you letting us go?"

"What? No!"

"Phew." She put her hand on her chest. "You scared me for a moment, dear. Why do you want us to eat with you? Has someone died?" She grabbed Ian's arm. "Is Robert okay?"

"No, I…" I shook my head. "I mean, yes, Rob's fine, it's not that. He's safely out of prison." Wow, I was a terrible boss. Whenever I was nice my staff thought they were being fired or that someone had died. Geez.

"He was in prison?! What happened?"

"He's fine. It was nothing. We're getting way off track here. I just thought eating together would be…nice. And we can all catch up. It'll be fun."

Ellen looked at Ian.

Ian shrugged. "Don't look at me. He's clearly lost his mind because he's in love."

Ellen put her hand to her chest again. I was getting concerned that she might faint. "Oh. This has to do with why I was buying women's clothing all afternoon? I assumed it was for Jen's birthday."

"Why would I have you unpack a bunch of clothing for Jen in my closet?"

"I don't know, I like when Jen visits."

"Me too," Ian said.

I just stared at both of them.

"I didn't realize Ellen didn't know yet," Ian said. He whistled and started to fill up his plate.

"I was going to tell her during dinner."

"Well, that's wonderful. But it's not that much of a surprise," Ellen said. "It's clear that you're dating someone. I prepped that cooler for your beach date. And I just filled the closet with clothes that wouldn't fit you even if you were a cross dresser."

I wasn't sure whether or not I should be offended by that statement. "But you just said you thought the clothes were for Jen."

She waved her hand through the air. "I was busy all day running errands for you. I just needed a second to put it all together. Especially since you were in such a foul mood after that beach date. I thought it might be over." She shook her head. "I'm getting sidetracked. So you're dating again? That's wonderful, James. But hardly a reason to almost give me a heart attack."

Ian laughed as he handed Ellen a plate and made himself another. "He's definitely dating someone. But it's a little juicier than that."

"Oh, is it a colleague?" Ellen asked as we all sat down.

Ian laughed again.

"Not exactly," I said and glared at him. I honestly didn't know how Ellen was going to react to this. I knew her husband had been older than her but I doubted they met under these circumstances. But she'd find out eventually. "Penny's my student."

Ellen took a big bite of her taco. "That's nice."

What now? "I'm dating my student. I'm going to ask her to move in with me."

"Well I figured that with all the stuff I bought for her today. I hope she likes blue, it's Jen's favorite color."

Ian and I stared at each other for a moment before I looked back at Ellen. "That was not the reaction I was expecting, Ellen."

"Does she make you happy?"

"Yeah, she does."

"Well that's wonderful. Isn't that all that matters? What, did you want me to reprimand you for dating a student? How could I possibly? My husband is ten years older than me and I…" She cleared her throat. "*Was* ten years older." She gave me a weak smile and then looked down at her plate.

I knew slip ups like that were the hardest for her. She'd lost her husband a few months before I decided to move here. I reached out and grabbed her hand and squeezed it. Ellen really was the best. I wasn't sure why I'd been worried about telling her in the first place. She was the kindest person I knew. She'd never judge me.

"I'm fine, James." She patted my hand on top of hers and then pulled away. "Now eat before it gets cold."

"Yes, ma'am," Ian said.

Ellen glared at him.

He knew she hated being called ma'am, and just like that the tension in the air was gone.

"So tell us all about her," Ellen said.

"I can do you one better," Ian said and pulled out his phone. "I have pictures. And I can give you her background check. Hold on a sec, I'll email it to you."

She shook her head. "Men. I meant what is she like."

"Well, her name is Penny. We ran into each other at the coffee shop on Main Street on the first day of classes." I told Ellen a very PG version of the story.

"One last question," Ellen said. "On a scale of one to ten, how much is she like Isabella? Ten being the most like her."

I laughed. Ellen had always hated Isabella. Ian too. It was something the three of us had in common. "Penny's definitely a one on that scale."

"I like her already," Ellen said.

My phone started buzzing in my pocket. I looked down to see that Penny was calling me. "Excuse me for a minute." I walked over to the windows overlooking Main Street. "Hey, Penny."

"Hi."

This was the first time we'd spoken on the phone. Her voice sounded so small and far away. "Is everything alright?" I wasn't opposed to going back to her dorm and reminding her why we should be together.

"Yes, everything's fine. I told Melissa about us."

"How did she take the news?"

"She wants to meet you."

"Well, that's good, right?"

"I guess so." There was a long pause. "She thinks you're a bad boy."

I laughed. That was probably more accurate than either of them realized. "And what do you think?"

"You know I think you're a terrible influence."

She sounded happy now. Maybe she's been worried about calling me for the first time. But this just felt so natural. I could talk to her like this all night. "And I think you like that I'm a terrible influence."

She laughed. "I do."

"I have an idea. How about I take the two of you to my country club tomorrow night so I can get to know Melissa?"

"Um. I think maybe giving it an extra day to let the idea settle in might be better."

"So, Wednesday?"

"Yeah and maybe you could just come here? In case she makes a scene or something. I'm not saying she's going to. I just...she's very outspoken."

I laughed. "You think she hates me."

"I didn't say that."

"I'll win her over, I promise."

"I believe you. She's coming back from her shower now. She probably has more questions for me. I gotta go."

"Good night, Penny."

"Good night, Professor Hunter."

It was like she knew those words would tease me, making me think of nothing but her for the rest of the night. But that was already going to happen.

Chapter 38

Wednesday

It had been a while since I'd been able to walk into my Comm class without being in a bad mood. But today was a crisp fall day and everything was falling into place. I felt grounded. I walked into the room and was even happier when I saw that Tyler wasn't sitting next to Penny. He'd moved up a seat, leaving the one next to *my girlfriend* empty for me. Geez, that term really did make me feel young again. I couldn't help but smile. Penny was mine. And now Tyler was out of the picture. I wasn't sure my mood could improve any more.

I moved the podium to the middle of the room. "So, the first day of speeches was interesting," I said.

Several students laughed and I gave Penny a reassuring smile.

"I'm hoping that today will be a little more toned down. But I guess we shall see. First up, Heather Matthews."

I made my way to the back of the room. I smiled as I sat down next to Penny. She looked equally excited by the new seating arrangement. I pulled out a stack of papers and began writing as Heather started talking. But I wasn't writing about her speech. The paper said, "I wish we were alone right now." I folded it in half and slid it onto Penny's desk. I turned my attention back to Heather. I needed to try to focus.

Penny slid the paper back on my desk. I looked down at her note: "And what would you be doing to me if we were alone?"

I exhaled slowly and tried to keep my head where it belonged: on the speeches. But it was impossibly hard when Penny was biting the end of her pen. *Fuck me*. When Heather was done, I quickly scribbled another note to Penny: "Come to my office during lunch and find out. And stop biting your pen. That's not what belongs in your mouth." I placed it down on her desk.

A moment later she lowered her pen. I flashed her a smile and then tried to be a good professor. Well, as good as I could be. Because I was pretty sure falling for one of my students wasn't good professor behavior.

When class finally ended, I was surprised to see that Tyler didn't move. He waited patiently until he, Penny, and I were the only people left in the classroom. This wasn't going to be good. It was tempting to pull Penny out of the back of the classroom. But if Tyler had something to say to me, it was better to get this over with. Tyler finally rose from his seat and turned around.

"Mr. Stevens," I said. I tried to keep my voice even. I fucking hated the kid for trying to hook up with Penny. But I needed to keep a level head. He knew about us. He could make this whole thing blow up.

"What you're doing is wrong," Tyler said.

"Not everything is so black and white," I said calmly. He couldn't possibly understand. He probably thought I was just fucking Penny. But it was so much more than that. Our relationship wasn't defined by us being a professor and student. I got how it looked. It would be hard to convince anyone otherwise. That was why it was important to keep things quiet for the next several months.

"In this case, it is."

"I beg to differ."

He glared back at me. "This isn't going to end well."

I hadn't expected that. "Are you threatening me?"

Tyler laughed. "No, I would never threaten my professor. I'm fully aware of where the line is, unlike some of us." He shook his head, walked past us, and exited through the back door.

Breathe. "Penny, is that something I should be worried about?" It felt like there was a ticking time bomb on our relationship. I was hoping Tyler would be levelheaded and understand the consequences for Penny if this came out. But he didn't seem levelheaded at all. He was unwound. And a little vengeful.

"I don't know. I asked him not to tell anyone."

Breathe. I'd learned a long time ago that it was pointless to fixate on things out of my control. "Then there's no use dwelling on it." There was nothing I could do. We just had to wait to see if Tyler was an asshole. My hopes weren't high. I leaned in and gave her a swift kiss on the lips while the room was still empty.

"Do you still want me to come to your office for lunch?"

"Of course." I held out my hand to help her to her feet.

"Is 12:30 okay?"

"Sounds good. I'll pick us up something." I looked over my shoulder to make sure the room was still empty and then kissed her again. I meant for it to be a quick kiss, but it swiftly turned hard. Fierce. Possessive. When I drew back she blinked up at me with stars in her eyes. I lifted her hand and kissed it. "Until later."

***

I tried to focus on grading the rest of the speeches from today. But my mind kept wandering back to Penny. It always did that whenever I worked in this office. Because I'd had her right here before. Right on this desk. *"Then teach me, Professor Hunter."* I was pretty sure those were the sexiest words I had ever heard. I was getting hard just thinking about it.

There was a knock on my office door. *Finally.* Penny was standing there with the biggest smile on her face. I looked both ways, grabbed her arm, and pulled her into my office. As soon as the door was closed, I pressed her back against it. "Penny."

"Professor Hunter."

Could she feel how much I already wanted her? I leaned forward, running the tip of my nose down the length of hers. "I thought you were going to start calling me James?"

"It's hard to break a habit. And besides, we are in your office."

So true. I was actually hoping it would be a hard habit for her to break. I smiled and pulled away. "We should probably eat."

"Oh."

It's okay. My mind isn't on food either. But I didn't want her to think I only wanted one thing from her. I'd loved just talking to her last night. I could control myself for a few minutes so we could eat. *Probably.* I walked over and sat down behind my desk. "I picked up sandwiches from Capriotti's. I wasn't sure what you'd like, so I just got two of my favorite."

"And what is your favorite?"

How had she made those words sound so seductive? "Turkey, lettuce, provolone cheese, and mayo." I hoped that was okay.

"That sounds delicious." She sat down across from me, grabbed one of the sandwiches, and unwrapped the paper. "It's actually exactly what I would have ordered." She took a bite. "So good."

I laughed. "We have more in common than I thought."

"Apparently so." She slowly chewed. "Can I ask you something?"

"Of course." Fuck, not more questions. I wanted to be honest with her. But that didn't mean it was easy for me to divulge information.

"I failed my speech, didn't I?"

I breathed a sigh of relief. "You'll have to wait until tomorrow to find out just like everyone else. No favoritism, remember?"

"I thought you were joking. So I really don't get special treatment?"

I shook my head. But it wasn't true. How could I not show her favoritism? I clearly wasn't very professional.

"None at all? I really think there should be certain perks to dating a professor."

"Well, that depends on what you have in mind. I think maybe there could be. I'm sure you could persuade me if you really wanted to."

She put her half-eaten sandwich down on the paper. "This is good. But I'm actually hungry for something else."

I lowered my eyebrows. Screw lunch, I just wanted her too. She stood up and walked around my desk, trailing her index finger along the wood.

"I've had dreams about what you did to me on this desk." She leaned against it and gripped the edge in her hands.

I swallowed hard. I'd had the same dreams. Over and over again. I'd been thinking about it right before she knocked on my door. And all I could think about was one thing. "It would be better to relive it." I lightly brushed the inside of her thigh with my fingertips.

"That's not exactly what I had in mind." She lifted her foot and pushed it against my chair, rolling it back from my desk. And then she knelt down in front of me.

Fuck, this is going to be fun. I was already getting hard.

She ran her hands up my thighs and slowly unbuttoned my jeans. I couldn't wait to shove my cock down her tight throat.

"You're going to want to scream. But don't make a sound." She repeated the words back to me that I'd told her that first time. She was so fucking sexy.

"Penny."

She unzipped my pants. Opened the flap on my boxers. Pulled out my rock-hard cock.

All for you, baby.

She locked eyes with me as she brought her lips to my tip.

Fuck. She was so hot just like that. With her lips pressed against my tip. Right where that sweet mouth of hers belonged.

And then she slowly lowered her mouth and brought her lips around me.

I groaned. Her mouth was a miracle.

She swirled her warm tongue around my shaft and sucked all the way down.

I gripped her hair in my fist and shoved my cock deeper, hitting the back of her throat. She moaned and the vibrations of her mouth felt like heaven.

A knock sounded on the door.

"Shit," I said under my breath. I quickly zipped up my pants. I thought Penny would get up, but she started to climb underneath my desk to hide instead. "No, Penny, don't..."

"Hello, James." The office door squeaked as Ben, another professor, walked in.

I cleared my throat and tried not to look down at Penny hidden beneath my desk. "Ben, I was just in the middle of lunch." *Shit, the extra sandwich.* I pulled her sandwich over to my side of the desk. If Ben had any sense, he'd know there was someone here. Two sandwiches and two drinks meant two people.

"Well don't let me bother you." He walked over and plopped down in the chair across from me. "Hungry today, James?"

I laughed.

And then I felt Penny's hand run up my thigh. She grabbed my zipper.

"No," I said firmly. I grabbed her hand and moved it away from my erection. But she immediately unzipped my pants with her other hand. And then I felt her warm mouth on me again. All the way down. *Jesus.* I couldn't stop the shard exhale that escaped my throat.

"Really? Two sandwiches is normal for you?" Ben asked.

"No," I groaned. *Stop it.* "I mean, yes." I took a bite of my sandwich and groaned again as Penny's lips tightened. Hopefully the sandwich muffled the noise. "Yes, I'm quite hungry today."

"What kind of sandwich is it?"

"Turkey, from Capriotti's." I shifted forward in my chair, hoping to make Penny stop, but it just pushed my hard cock deeper down her throat. I bit the inside of my cheek so I wouldn't groan again.

"It looks good."

So good. Penny really did love the possibility of getting caught, the dirty little thing. She was probably so wet right now. The thought made me want to bury my cock deep inside her aching pussy. She slid her lips up and down my shaft faster, licking and sucking every inch of me.

"It's fucking fantastic," I said, my voice tight as I tried to restrain myself from cumming down Penny's throat right in front of our audience.

"I'll have to try one," Ben said.

"Yes!" I cleared my throat. How was I supposed to have a conversation when she was worshipping my cock? I couldn't even look at Ben. God, how had he not called me out yet? I was pretty sure I'd groaned like five times during this conversation. Penny tightened her lips around my shaft. *Jesus.* "You have to." What was I talking about? Oh right, the sandwiches. "They're irresistible." *Fucking irresistible.*

Ben nodded. "I will then. I've heard lots of good things about Capriotti's. But I don't want to disturb your lunch, James. I just had a quick favor to ask."

Penny's mouth moved faster and faster.

"Oh," I said. I meant to say it as a question, but it came out as more of an exclamation. "What's the favor?" I tried to say a little more calmly.

"It's for my class. I was just wondering if you could come and talk to them about some of the catalysts that made your company explode. So they can see how marketing makes all the difference."

Explode? Jesus. Why had he used that term? Penny took my cock all the way to the back of her throat. I slammed my hand against my desk. With my other hand, I grabbed a fistful of her hair and pushed my cock even deeper into her throat. "Fuck," I groaned.

A second later, I exploded in her mouth.

"Are you okay, James?"

"Yes. I'm just excited to talk to your class." I was panting like an idiot. "I'll do it. Just email me the details."

"Thank you, I really appreciate it." Ben stood up. "I think I might go get one of those sandwiches right now."

"I can't recommend it enough." I sighed.

"Have a good afternoon, James."

"You too, Ben."

Ben left, closing the door behind him.

Was she fucking insane? I stood up and pulled Penny to her feet. "Your mouth is a miracle, Penny. But I will get you back for that," I growled.

"And when will that be?"

"When you least expect it." I leaned in and kissed her, pressing her ass against the edge of the desk. She was in so much trouble. "I forgot how much doing naughty things in public gets you off. You're probably dripping wet, wanting me more than you ever have before."

"I am. I want you so badly."

I smiled and pulled her leggings down just a bit so I could touch her, pushing her thong to the side. "Just like I thought." I pressed my finger against her, teasing her. "You're so wet for me, Penny." I brushed the tip of my nose against hers and kissed her like I'd been starving. I bit her lip and plunged a finger inside of her. In and out. A torturous rhythm. "I didn't realize that my cock in your mouth turned you on so much."

"Everything about you turns me on."

I slid another finger inside of her and she moaned softly. I began to pulse my fingers faster, deeper. She was always so ready for me. As desperate for my touch as I was for hers. I was so wrapped up in her. I pressed my thumb against her clit. *Come for me, baby.* I curved my fingers slightly, hitting that spot that she loved.

"Yes!" she screamed and shattered around my fingers. So fucking hot. I pulled my fingers out of her juices and slid them into my mouth. Sweet as sin.

Her eyes wandered down to my erection that was already straining against the zipper of my pants again.

"I only have a few minutes before my next class," I said.

"Then you better fuck me fast."

I raised my left eyebrow. Where had this woman been hiding all my life? "Penny, I know I can make you come in sixty seconds. Turn around and place your hands on the desk."

She followed my instructions. I hooked my thumbs around her waistband and slid my hands down her ass and thighs, pulling her panties and leggings down to her knees. I pushed her forward so that her torso was on top of my desk and her ass was jutting in the air, waiting for me. *Perfection.*

I ran my fingers down her spine. "This is going to be fast and rough, just the way you like it." I could barely control myself as I made short work of my zipper. I needed to fill her. I needed to show her just how much I liked when she was bad. I slapped her ass hard and thrust my cock inside of her.

She gasped. I wasn't sure if it was because she was shocked that I'd spanked her. Or that she just fucking loved it.

I slid in and out of her slowly at first, waiting for her to adjust to my cock. In a few seconds she was gripping the other side of my desk, pushing her ass against me, begging for more. *I'll give you more.*

I slammed into her and began pumping relentlessly, fucking her harder than I ever had before. Her pussy made me forget about everything.

I leaned forward and brushed her cheek with my knuckles. "You only have thirty seconds left, Penny. If you don't come, then you'll just have to wait."

"I'm so close," she moaned.

I pulled her hair, making that sexy arch in her back appear. *You're so fucking sexy.* I gripped her hair tighter and used it as leverage as I thrust faster. She started to clench around me.

"That's right," I growled. "Come for me, Penny."

I felt her start to orgasm, the pulsing of her pussy nearly driving me insane. God she was good at listening to instructions. I thrust in and out of her faster, riding her high. I gripped both sides of her waist and a moment later I filled her. Nothing felt as good as cumming in her tight pussy. I groaned and pulled out of her. If I didn't have to get to my class, I could stare at her for hours, sated and spent on my desk. I zipped my pants.

She slowly rose and turned around.

There were red lines on her flesh from the pressure of being fucked hard against my desk. Those marks were the only thing I could see. After the golf course, I'd told myself I wouldn't hurt her again. What the fuck had I just done? I knelt down in front of her and kissed each of her hip bones. *I'm sorry.* For just a moment I let my nagging thoughts return. She was too good for me. I'd ruin her. What if I already was ruining her?

I tried to dismiss the thoughts as I pulled her thong and pants back up. I placed another kiss on each of her hip bones. *I'm sorry.* But my thoughts didn't matter. I couldn't walk away from her. I didn't have that kind of willpower. "I'll be by your place at 8."

"What?"

"To meet Melissa, remember?" I stood and placed her hand gently on my cheek. "That's tonight, right? I'll bring dessert."

"Oh." She just stared at me.

"Brownies or something, Penny." I traced her lips with my thumb. "Not me this time." Although, I was hoping that's where the night would lead. I had a lot of stuff I wanted to talk to her about. I just needed to get through meeting her roommate first. It seemed like Melissa wasn't a huge fan of me. Penny wanted us to meet in her dorm because she was worried that Melissa would be *outspoken*. But I was great at winning people over when properly motivated. And Penny was the ultimate motivation. As well as the perfect reward.

She smiled. "Sorry, I'm having a hard time thinking straight."

I smiled back at her. "I don't think I'll ever get enough of you," I whispered.

She stared at me with so much love in her eyes. We hadn't talked about love at all. But I felt it.

"I know that I'll never get enough of you," she said.

There were no longer any doubts in my mind about the fact that I loved her. Only the ones swirling around that she shouldn't love me back.

Chapter 39

Wednesday

"Those are the brownies?" I asked Ellen. I was kind of thinking she'd make them look a little…fancier. Something flashy that could help win Melissa over. They looked so basic. "I thought there'd be like icing, or nuts, or something."

"You're trying to make a good first impression, right?"

I nodded.

"All you need is chocolate. Women love chocolate. You can't go wrong. Trust me." She placed some foil over the pan.

I didn't exactly have anyone else to go to for advice here. So I'd take Ellen's word for it. It wasn't like I was about to call Jen and ask her to corroborate Ellen's hunch about chocolate. Besides, I knew Penny loved chocolate. So she'd at least like them. And Ellen did make the absolute best brownies. "Thanks for this," I said.

"Anything else you need before I head out for the night?"

"Nope, that's it."

"Good luck." She patted my arm, leaving me alone in the kitchen.

A nervous pit of energy had landed in my gut. What if Melissa absolutely hated me? How important was her opinion to Penny? I tried to shake the thought away. *I've got this.* I pulled on my jacket and grabbed the brownies. Ellen's cooking would easily win her over if I couldn't.

The drive over to Penny's dorm was quick at this time of night. I pulled into an empty spot and stepped out of my car. I was meeting Penny's best friend. It was important that she liked me. And unfortunately, she probably already had a bad view of me, just like Tyler did. I needed to sway her opinion.

I texted Penny to let her know I was outside. It was raining yet again, steam coming off the pavement that would make it hard for anyone to recognize me. For just a second it reminded me of the daze I'd lived in during high school and college. Always surrounded by smoke. It was like I could hear Rob, Mason, and Matt's laughter around me. God, Penny really did make me feel young if I could remember us all laughing. I shook away the thought. I needed to call Rob to see how he was doing. It was always easier to talk to him when I was in a good mood. Since he was perpetually in one.

Penny opened the door. She looked like an angel, standing at the top of the steps, surrounded by the steam off the pavement. My angel. My second chance.

There was no one around, so I stepped inside and kissed her. It had only been a few hours since we'd been together, but all I wanted was more. "Penny," I whispered.

"James."

She sounded out of breath. I just wasn't sure if it was because of me or because she was nervous about me meeting Melissa. "Is she excited to meet me?"

"I think so."

"You don't seem very confident." I gave her a smile, hoping it would make her less nervous too.

"It's just that she can be kind of intense. Please just remember how much I like you."

Intense. Good to know. That's why I was here. In case Melissa made a scene. But now that I was thinking about it…she could do a lot more damage for me in a dorm than she could in a restaurant. I hadn't thought this through very well. Everything would be fine though. I was good at winning people over. "I'm sure it won't be that bad. I brought brownies." I held up the pan of brownies that Ellen had sent with me.

"I'd rather have you."

Penny was full of surprises tonight. But the last thing I wanted was an erection when I walked into her dorm room. "Maybe later. Right now, I promised to meet your friend." I put my hand out for her and guided her up the stairs to her room. Penny slowly opened the door.

"So you're the elusive Professor Hunter?" Melissa asked a little too loudly without even introducing herself. Was she trying to get us in trouble? This was not a great start. It was like Melissa was looking for a fight. *I should have insisted on a restaurant…*

Penny quickly closed the door behind us so no one could hear.

I took a deep breath and then flashed Melissa a smile. "Please, call me James. And you must be Melissa." I put my hand out for her to shake.

She hesitated for a long moment before shaking my hand. That was telling, if her tone hadn't already been. She'd already made up her mind. She didn't approve of me. Again I found myself wondering how important Melissa's opinion was to Penny. Surely it couldn't be that important or Penny would have told Melissa about us sooner. But I was here now. So that meant something.

Time for a peace offering. "I brought brownies." I lifted the pan in the air. Dessert would help, right? Ellen's cooking always left me in a good mood.

"Yum! Did you bake them yourself?" Melissa asked.

Shit. "No. I doubt they'd be edible if I had."

"You don't cook?"

"Not very often." I scratched the back of my neck. What had Penny told her about me? It didn't seem like she knew very much at all.

Penny wound her arm around mine. "He has a personal chef."

"Very fancy," Melissa said. She crossed her arms in front of her chest. "It's strange, I never pictured a professor in our dorm room."

Yeah, this was not going well at all. "I never pictured myself in a student's room either. It just happened."

Melissa smiled, but it looked very forced. "So, tell me about yourself."

I forgot that this would involve answering questions about my personal life. I took a deep breath. It was better just to get this over with. "Well, I grew up in New York. I lived there my whole life until I moved here last year. I'm sorry, what is it that you want to know exactly? Something specific?" *Breathe.* I could already feel myself closing off. I could do this. Just a normal conversation. Melissa wasn't a reporter. Just a nuisance of a human.

"Where did you go to school?"

"Can I sit down?" I gave Penny a smile. She looked so nervous, but she had no reason to be. No, this night wasn't off to a great start. But seeing Penny's worried face was all the encouragement I needed. She wanted Melissa to like me. I'd make this right. I could be very charming when I needed to be.

"Yes," Penny said. She pulled out her desk chair for me.

I took off my jacket, draped it over the back of the chair, and sat down. Penny jumped onto her bed and sat Indian style. I wished she was closer. I wanted to be able to reach out and touch her. She had this way of calming me down. I took a deep breath instead. "I went to Harvard," I said.

"Your parents are wealthy then?" Melissa asked.

Wow. Okay. I took another deep breath. "My parents are wealthy, but I had a scholarship to Harvard."

"Impressive."

That didn't sound sincere. "Thank you," I said anyway.

"But even so, you're very handsome and your parents are wealthy. Most things in your life must have been handed to you."

What the fuck? Breathe. She didn't know me. That's why I was here. She wasn't even giving me a fair shot. I could be judging her too. I'd helped Penny out of a lot of perilous situations since meeting her. Where had her supposed best friend been then? *Breathe.* "In some regards, yes. Many things that were handed to me I didn't want though. I owe my success to myself, not my family. Do you have another question for me?"

"Well there's one main one. Why is it that you want to date students?"

God, she was terrible. "I don't want to date students." I emphasized the plural. "You seem to have gotten the wrong idea about me. I just want to date Penny."

"So you have never dated any students besides Penny?"

"No, I have not."

"Can you really even date someone if you're married?"

I glanced at Penny. So she had told Melissa some things. I was kind of hoping she'd just talked about my good qualities, even if they were few and far between. I turned back to Melissa. "I'm getting divorced."

"But you're technically still married."

"Melissa, my soon to be ex-wife has been cheating on me for almost as long as we were together. As far as I'm concerned, we are no longer married." Penny knew that I was uncomfortable talking about my personal life. It felt like she set me up, trying to get even more answers out of me. What else could she possibly want to know?

Melissa was finally quiet for a moment. "I'm sorry about your wife. But you are still married. How much longer will your divorce take?" She finally didn't sound accusatory.

"I honestly don't know. I thought she would have signed the papers by now. I've given her everything she wants."

"It seems wrong to pursue a relationship in that situation."

"I have to disagree. There hasn't been anything that's felt so right in my life." That was the truth. And if Melissa didn't see that, I wasn't sure what else I could do or say to change her mind.

"It may feel right, but there are consequences. Won't you get fired if someone finds out about you and Penny?"

"Not necessarily."

"But aren't you thinking about Penny too? If this gets out, no one will believe the grades you've given her. No one will see her as just another student. Even other professors will question her grades. I know that she's just with you, but people may think she's been with other professors too. Her whole college career will be in jeopardy. You may be fine with getting fired, but she still has to go to school here."

"I think that Penny can make her own choices." I could handle the onslaught of questions. But if Melissa thought I didn't care about Penny, she was dead wrong. I had done nothing but think of Penny. That was why I'd tried so hard to push her away. But hearing those words fall out of Melissa's mouth made my chest feel tight. *I'd tried to save her from me.* I looked over at Penny sitting on her bed. The tightness in my chest eased slightly when her eyes locked with mine. "I've thought about all the possibilities. And I'm willing to risk it as long as she is."

"I am." She smiled at me.

Every day it was growing harder to imagine my life without her in it. I saw a future. Did she see it too?

"And you aren't at all concerned about your age difference?" Melissa continued.

"No, it doesn't concern me." It was honestly the least of my concerns, besides for every now and then when Penny's immaturity seemed to show. But really, who cared about six years? After this semester and the next she wouldn't even be my student any longer. "How about we have those brownies?" I suggested.

"Why, because chocolate makes all women's problems go away?" Melissa scoffed.

Jesus. What is with this girl? "I'm just hungry." I shifted in my chair. Melissa was tough to please. "What are you majoring in anyway, criminal justice?"

"I'll get plates," Penny said. She hopped off her bed and found some paper plates from the closet.

Melissa was just staring at me accusingly. "No, political science."

"Do you want to be a lawyer?"

"This isn't really about me, James, it's about you."

"I was under the impression that we were supposed to get to know each other tonight."

"Yes, I want to be a lawyer. Now back to you. I find it hard to believe that you can't find someone to date that's your own age."

"The only person I want to date is Penny. I don't know what else I can say to make you believe me."

Melissa sighed. "Okay."

"Okay?" It was hard to believe that after all those pointed questions.

"I believe you. I'm sorry about all the questions. I'm just looking out for Penny. Dating a professor just isn't like her."

"I would hope not," I said.

"That's a little hypocritical."

"Then I guess I'm a hypocrite." I smiled at Penny. I liked that she was usually good and just bad for me. God I loved when she was bad.

Penny finished cutting the brownies and handed them out.

"These are really good," Melissa said sweetly.

Maybe her onslaught was finally done.

"I'll pass on your compliments." Ellen would appreciate it. I put my half-eaten brownie down on the plate. "So, if Penny isn't the type of girl who dates a professor, what type of girl is she exactly?"

Melissa laughed. "The type of girl who likes to stay in on a Saturday night. She doesn't break the rules. I mean, I thought she was joking when she told me she was dating you."

"I break the rules sometimes," Penny said.

"No you don't. You're ridiculously straight-laced. I basically have to drag you out of the dorm on weekends."

I laughed. I put down my plate, stood up, and sat down next to Penny on her bed. I was tired of being formal around her. And the tension in the room seemed to completely evaporate once I put my arm around her. She wasn't my student in this room. She was my girlfriend.

Melissa smiled at us. "Going from taking no risks to dating a professor is a huge leap. I didn't really understand it. But seeing you two together..." Melissa shrugged. "I get it."

"Well I'm glad we have your approval. Your opinion seems to be very important to Penny, and therefore important to me."

"And I promise not to tell anyone. Your secret is safe with me."

"Thank you, Melissa."

"And let me officially invite you to our birthday party. I'm sure Penny has already told you about it."

A birthday party? "Actually, she hasn't invited me yet." I smiled at her. "Or mentioned it at all." Not that I was upset. We'd been going through a lot. There'd hardly been time to mention parties. But I knew she was turning 22 soon. I even had her gift already in the works. Five years age difference was basically nothing. It was weird that both Ian and Melissa seemed to think it was a big deal. At least Ellen was on my side.

Melissa laughed. "Well, normally I guess you couldn't come. But since it's going to be close to Halloween, we're having a costume party. So as long as you wear a good costume, I think it'll be okay."

How convenient. I flashed Penny a smile. "I wouldn't miss it."

"Can I come over to your place for a bit?" asked Penny.

I rubbed her back. She looked...off. Was it about the party? I was excited that I'd be able to attend with her. But I knew there were two sides to that. I was only able to because I could wear a mask. It would be a while before we could be just us in public. I swallowed hard. I hoped that wasn't weighing on her. I could wait till the spring. But could she? "Of course."

"I'm sorry, I just have one more thing to say before you go," Melissa said.

"Melissa," Penny pleaded.

"No, it's okay," I interjected. "What is it?"

"You better not hurt her."

"I won't." There were still a lot of things that Penny didn't know about me. But I would never hurt her. Not on purpose. The thought made me pause. I tried to push it away.

"Well, you already have," Melissa said. "So your word is hard to believe. I've never seen Penny act the way she did this past week. And you two may have forgotten about that, but I haven't."

She was right. And I really wished she wasn't. "That was just a misunderstanding."

"Maybe if you're more upfront about your baggage, things like that won't happen."

"I won't hurt her," I repeated. I'd changed. Even Dr. Clark saw it. I could be good for Penny. I knew I could.

"That's all I can ask." Melissa finished her brownie. "You two are cute together."

I looked down at Penny. "It's getting late. If you wanted to come over for a while, we better get going." I got off the bed and pulled on my jacket.

Penny dumped the plates in the trash.

"Penny, can I talk to you for a second?" Melissa asked.

"I'll pull the car around," I said. I extended my hand to Melissa. "It was...interesting to meet you, Melissa."

"Good choice of words. I'm sorry if I made you uncomfortable." Melissa shook my hand without hesitating this time.

"Looking out for your friends is a good quality to have." And I meant it. I was glad she was stepping up. "I hope to see you again soon. You're going to make a good lawyer."

I was pretty sure she blushed. I knew I could win her over. I left the two of them alone and made my way back outside.

Chapter 40

Wednesday

I leaned against my car, waiting for Penny to come out. The evening had turned around. But it wouldn't have needed to be turned around if Penny hadn't told her friend I was fucking married. Penny could have at least warned me. She knew I didn't feel comfortable talking about my personal life. Especially anything involving Isabella. And the longer I stood there, the more pissed I got. It was pretty clear that they were talking about me right now. Penny was probably revealing more intimate details, and I wasn't sure how I was supposed to feel about that. I was used to confidentiality agreements and rules. This…this was hard for me to adjust to.

Yes, I'd told my staff and Dr. Clark that I was dating her. But intimate details about her? *You put cameras around campus to watch her. You had Ian run a background check.* I knew all that was bad. But I was going to tell Penny about the cameras. And I'd barely looked at her background check. I glanced down at my watch. Really, what were they talking about right now?

I had a sinking feeling in my stomach. Maybe Melissa was trying to convince her not to be with me. Maybe she was reminding Penny that I wasn't the only man interested in her. *Fucking Tyler.* The more time that ticked by, the angrier I got.

Penny finally came out of her dorm and walked up to my car. I opened the door for her without a word. I needed a minute to calm down.

I climbed into the car and sped off. The silence was even more unnerving than the waiting. Had Melissa said something bad about me once I was gone? Maybe I hadn't won her over after all.

"I'm sorry about all of Melissa's questions," Penny finally said, breaking the silence.

"It's okay." I kept my eyes on the road, gripping the wheel tighter than necessary.

"It doesn't seem like it's okay."

What the fuck do you want me to say? "When I told you to tell her about me, I thought you were just going to say that I was your professor."

"I thought I was allowed to tell her everything? She would have asked questions if I didn't tell her what our fight was about."

"You should have asked me if it was okay."

"I'm sorry."

"I like to keep my personal life private, Penny."

"I know. Even from me." She folded her arms across her chest and looked out the window.

Now she was pissed at me too. Great. I pulled into the parking garage and into one of my spots. She opened the door for herself before I reached it. *Yup, she's definitely pissed. Well, so am I, baby.*

I grabbed her hand and walked quickly toward the elevator, pulling her inside when the doors parted.

"I said that I was sorry. I should have asked you."

"It's not just that," I said.

"Then what is it?"

"Your friend hates me. She didn't even give me a chance. I think that maybe it's because she has someone else in mind for you."

"She doesn't."

"So, she dislikes Tyler too?" I asked.

"This has nothing to do with Tyler. She's just looking out for me."

"I don't think that's true."

"Stop!" She lightly pushed my chest.

I grabbed her hand. Fuck, why was it so hot when we argued? I pushed her back against the elevator wall and lifted her hands above her head. My kiss was possessive and intense, leaving my dick straining against my pants. Every inch of me felt alive. When the door dinged open, I pulled away.

"Oh God," she said.

I smiled at her and she blushed. That fucking blush. I needed her right now. I needed to remind her that I was the only option. I was enough. I tossed my jacket on the floor and pulled off my t-shirt. "You have a way of crawling under my skin."

"I don't mean to."

"Yes, you do."

"Professor Hunter, I need to talk to you."

"I don't want to talk." I walked over to her and pushed her shirt up the sides of her torso, my fingers skimming her soft skin. There was only one thing on my mind. And it certainly didn't involve any more talking. We'd done plenty of that. This was how I knew we were okay.

"But I have something important to tell you."

I pulled her shirt the rest of the way off. Her nipples were so hard that I could see them through her bra. "It can wait." My lips were on hers before she could protest. And whatever she wanted to say dissolved in our kiss. She felt this too. That a sour mood could turn heavenly sweet as soon as our skin touched. From cold to scorching in a matter of seconds.

I pushed her down onto my couch and climbed on top of her, balancing most of my weight on my arms. My tongue swirled around hers as she moved her delicate fingers down my six pack. She traced my happy trail with her fingertips and grabbed my erection through my jeans. I groaned into her mouth.

She fumbled with the button and zipper on my jeans and wrapped her hand around my length. She moved her hand up and down my shaft.

Fuck. "I know that you're angry with me." I unhinged her bra and gently pulled it down her arms, exposing her perky tits.

"No, it's okay," she panted.

I leaned down and kissed the bruise I'd left on her neck. *Mine. All mine.* I moved down, leaving a trail of kisses across her breasts, sucking hard on each nipple. Her skin was so sweet. I swirled my tongue gently around one of her nipples and then kissed down her stomach and past her belly button. She lifted her hips so I could pull off her leggings and thong with one swift movement. And then I spread her knees apart and slid my hands up her silky thighs.

She gulped.

"I want you to be angry. That'll make this even better." I brought my lips down to her clit and sucked hard.

"Professor Hunter!" She arched her back.

God, she knew just what to say to pull me closer. I sucked again in response and let my tongue answer her needs. I pushed her thighs farther apart, shoving my tongue deeper inside of her. So fucking sweet. The taste of her was enough to drive me insane.

"Yes! I need you," she moaned. "Please."

With my free hand I pushed my pants and boxers to the ground. I'd give her what she craved. But first I needed her sweet lips around my cock. I grabbed her hand and pulled her to a seated position, shoving my fingers deep inside of her.

She gasped with pleasure.

That noise. God, that intoxicating sound. I shoved my thick cock into her open mouth and grabbed a fistful of her hair. *Take it. Take all of me. Remember who you belong to.*

Her perfect mouth mimicked what my fingers were doing inside of her, sliding up and down my shaft faster and faster as I moved my hand quicker. She tightened her lips around me and I closed my eyes in ecstasy. My fingers swirled around her wetness and then she grabbed my ass and pushed me all the way into the back of her throat.

Jesus. I groaned and pulled out of her mouth. "I don't want to cum in your mouth. I want your pussy clenched around me, with you screaming my name." I pulled my fingers out of her and she groaned in protest. "Baby, we're not even close to being finished."

I pulled her off the couch and bent her over the armrest. "Spread your legs, Penny." She followed my instructions and then I just stood there, mesmerized, studying her perfect body.

My fingers brushed against the back of her knees and she arched her back. *So responsive.* My fingers ran up her thighs and over her ass. She was so perfect. I slid my hands to her hips and gripped them tightly as I plunged myself inside of her.

"Yes!" she screamed.

My cock pounded relentlessly, filling her, stretching her until I knew she could barely take any more. So carnal. So raw. So fucking right. Despite what anyone else thought, we were right. When we were together everything just made more sense. I grabbed her shoulders and pulled her to a standing position, tilting my cock and hitting the spot she loved.

Penny gasped.

The sensation was too much. I pulled out before either of us could come. *Not yet.* I pushed her back down onto the couch. "Roll over," I demanded.

She turned. "Professor Hunter, I'm so close," she panted.

"I know." I got down on top of her and grabbed her ass, lifting her legs into the air. And I waited.

"Please," she begged.

I wanted her to say it. I wanted the filthy words to fall from her lips. I raised my left eyebrow.

"Please, Professor Hunter. Fuck me!"

Good girl. I thrust myself inside her again. She gyrated her hips, almost making me cum right there. My hands slid to her hips to stop her movement. I gripped her hips firmly as I began to move slowly in and out of her. I rocked back slightly and then pushed myself deeper, all the way to the hilt, filling her with every inch of me.

And she exploded into a million pieces as my hot cum shot into her. Again and again. I collapsed beside her and pulled her tight against my chest. Her heart was racing. She tilted her head back and I kissed her softly, waiting for her heartbeat to slow. I could have fallen asleep right there with her in my arms. Quiet and sated with all my worries at bay.

Chapter 41

Wednesday

"You called me baby," she said.

I looked down at her. Apparently she didn't have sleep on her mind. "I'm sorry, did you not like that?"

"No I did," she said. "You've just always called me Penny. Or Miss Taylor. Everything you say sounds sexy though. You could call me anything."

I smiled. "And you've always called me Professor Hunter."

"I think you like that I keep calling you that," she said.

"You do, huh?" I really fucking did.

"It makes everything sexier. Mysterious and forbidden. Wrong but so right."

"Nothing is wrong about you and me." I tucked a strand of hair behind her ear. "Melissa said something after I left, didn't she? I can tell that something is bothering you."

"No, it's not that." But she didn't offer any more.

I wanted to reassure Penny, but I couldn't do that if she didn't tell me what was wrong. Maybe a distraction was a better idea. And I had a feeling I knew how to get her mind off whatever was bothering her. I'd been waiting all night to be alone with her. "Hold that thought." I slowly rose from the couch.

Her eyes dropped to my cock.

"What, have you not had enough?"

"I'll never have enough of you."

I smiled and zipped up my jeans. "I'll be right back. I have something for you." I walked into my bedroom and grabbed the box Ellen had left wrapped on my nightstand. I almost laughed, remembering what Ellen had said the other day. That she thought all the clothes I'd asked her to pick up were for Jen. I looked down at the box. Why would I buy my sister *this*? That would have been seriously weird. I couldn't help but laugh. Hopefully Penny would find my good mood infectious. When I came back out, Penny was wearing my shirt.

"God you're sexy," I said.

Her face flushed.

"This is when you look the most beautiful. When your hair is mussed up, your cheeks are pink, and you're wearing one of my shirts." I pulled the wrapped box out from behind my back.

"But my birthday isn't for another few weeks."

"It's not for your birthday." I sat down beside her and placed the box in her hands.

"What is it?"

"Open it, baby."

She smiled at me, then pulled the bow loose, and tore into the paper. She lifted the lid and slid the tissue paper to the side. It was a new bikini. It was a deep blue, the same color as the ocean. The fabric was lightweight and softer than her other bikini. Delicate almost. Ellen had sent me a few pictures from the store, and we'd both agreed that it was the nicest one. I shuddered thinking about Ellen looking at bathing suits with my sister in mind. Gross. I shook the thought away. It was perfect for Penny and no one else. And I couldn't wait for her to try it on. She was going to look sexy as hell.

She ran her fingers across the fabric. "You didn't need to do that," she said.

"I wanted to. Besides, it's my fault that we lost your last one."

She laughed. "We didn't lose it. You somehow convinced me to get naked in public and it got stolen."

"I hate to break it to you, but it didn't take that much convincing." I leaned in and kissed her.

"But this is probably the most expensive thing I own now. It's too much." She put the lid back on the box and pushed it back into my hands.

Wait, what? I never expected her to reject it. "Penny, it's a gift."

"I know. I'm sorry, I do love it. But I'm not used to getting extravagant gifts like this."

"Well you better get used to it. I want to be able to buy you things. I want to get you everything you've ever wanted."

She shook her head. "I don't want anything. I just want you."

"That's refreshing to know." Truly. More than she realized. I cupped her chin in my hand. That was the most comforting thing about all this. She liked me before she knew I was rich. It made what was going on between us real. She liked me for me. "I've never met anyone like you." I leaned in and kissed her again. But now I was worried my other surprise for her wouldn't go so well either.

I pulled back and ran my hand through my hair. "Well, don't get mad at me. I didn't realize that you weren't going to like getting presents. I also picked up a few other things for you for whenever you want to spend the night." Well…Ellen did. This was all probably too soon. But after I'd slept in Penny's hard bed a few days ago, I wanted to make sure she didn't have to spend another night being uncomfortable. If that was what she wanted. And I knew what I wanted. To be all in with her. I already was.

"What?" she asked.

I stood up and held my hand out for her. She grabbed it and I pulled her to her feet. I led her past the kitchen, into my bedroom, and flipped the light on in my closet. Ellen had moved a row of my shirts and in their place were a ton of new clothes. For Penny.

She looked so excited as she ran her hand along the jeans, t-shirts, short dresses, skirts, and blouses. And shoes. There were new sneakers, some flats, and a few high heels with varying lengths of stilettos. I was especially excited to see her in those. But I was more excited by the fact that she looked so damn happy.

"I can't accept all of this," she said. "I mean, I can't accept any of this. Please tell me that you can return everything?"

"I can, but I'm not going to."

"Why?"

"Penny, your face lit up when you saw everything. I understand that you aren't used to being showered with gifts. But I want you to have these things, or else I wouldn't have bought them for you. I want you to be comfortable staying here whenever you want."

She blushed. "It's all so nice. But how did you even know my size?"

"I think I know your body pretty well." I put my hand on the small of her back. "And you left your clothes here that one morning."

She cringed.

I opened one of my drawers, not caring to remember how shitty I'd felt walking out of the bathroom and seeing that she'd left. The drawer was filled with lacy panties with matching bras. These with the heels would be especially nice.

"So these are the kinds of things you like me to wear?"

I pulled her into my arms. "I prefer you in nothing at all." Whenever we touched I was filled with so much warmth. I had the strangest realization that this was probably what happiness felt like.

"Professor Hunter, this is all too much. I appreciate the gesture, but I don't need any of this."

I wrapped my arms tighter around her. Her intoxicating smell was everywhere. Yeah, this was what happiness was.

"I feel like a Disney princess. Which makes you the handsome prince that rescued me. But I didn't even realize that I needed rescuing."

I laughed. "If I'm the prince, I certainly hope that you'll be my princess." But honestly, she had it all wrong. She was saving me, not the other way around. Dr. Clark was right. It had been far too long since I'd trusted someone. Penny made it easy.

She smiled up at me. "It's like I moved in without having to actually move any of my things. I guess that is rather convenient."

"It is."

"So you really want me to keep all this stuff?"

"I'm going to want to spoil you. That's something that you're going to have to accept. I want to give you everything. But I bought these things for you mainly because I want you to consider spending more time here. I thought that having these things here would make that easier. Besides, your bed is so uncomfortable," I added.

"I don't mind my bed. Actually I'm really used to it. It's quite comfortable now."

Had I read this all wrong? I hoped my disappointment wasn't written on my face. "I'm not trying to pressure you, Penny. I know I have some things I need to deal with. And I promise that I am dealing with them. I'm just hoping that you'll consider spending more time here. I'm happiest when you're next to me." I traced my thumb along her lower lip.

"You mean like a few nights a week?"

"If that's what you want."

"What do you want?"

"If it was up to me, I'd have you here all the time." *Permanently.* I leaned down to kiss her, but she pulled away.

"I need to talk to you."

Why did she keep pushing me away? "We are talking. And I can't think of a better conversation to have."

"No, I mean I need to tell you something." She grabbed my arms and unwound herself from me. I instantly felt cold. She walked out of my closet and sat down on the bed.

I didn't want to know whatever she wanted to tell me. I could tell it was bad news. I could already feel her slipping away. The distance between us was unsettling. I closed the gap between us and I sat down beside her. "I'll return everything. I didn't mean to make you uncomfortable." I'd fucked up. Clearly.

"It's not that. I love the idea of spending more time with you. I just need to tell you something."

"Okay."

She didn't say anything at all.

"What's wrong, Penny?" I squeezed her hand. Whatever it was...I could fix it. I knew I could fix it.

"I don't want there to be any more secrets between us," she said.

I gazed into her eyes. It didn't feel like she was about to tell me a secret. It felt like she was about to leave. I remembered how much it had killed me when Rachel disappeared. It would be a thousand times worse with Penny. And I'd actually have to watch her walk out of my life. I'd gotten a small taste of that the other day when she'd been angry with me. I didn't want to do that again. My days and nights had been hell. That's why we were here right now. With me practically asking her to move in with me. Because I knew I needed her. I knew what life was like without her.

She straddled me and put her hands on the sides of my face. I let my hands fall to the small of her back. All I wanted to do was pull her closer. *Stop pushing me away.*

"You're so handsome. I still don't know what you see in me." A tear rolled down her cheek.

"I see everything that I've always wanted." I kissed her cheek where the tear had fallen, like I could make it disappear.

"I need to tell you something. And you have to promise that you won't get mad."

"Just tell me." I kissed her other cheek where she'd shed another tear. Tonight had felt like a new beginning to me. But now it suddenly felt like the end.

She leaned in and kissed me. And I found myself trying to savor it. I wanted to remember what it felt like for her to want me. Because she was definitely leaving. How many times had she already tried to push me away? *Please don't go.* But a piece of me knew it was inevitable. Because had I really changed? Was it even possible that I could be a good fit for her? *No.* She was too perfect. Too good. She had so much life left to live.

I moved my hand to the back of her neck and pulled her into me. Everything seemed so simple when we kissed. It was just right. It was perfect.

She moved her head back, breaking the kiss. If I wanted, I was pretty sure I could have her again right now. I could postpone whatever she was about to say. But what was the point? I always knew this day would come. It was like my whole body was slowly turning numb, preparing for the pain. I was used to the pain.

She placed one last swift kiss against my lips. "You have to promise," she said again.

"Okay. I promise that I won't get mad."

"My birthday is on October 15th."

"That's good to know. I'll make sure to clear my schedule." It was already on my calendar.

"No, that's not what's bothering me." She grabbed my hands from her back, moved them to my lap, and held them firmly. "I lied to you."

I could feel my eyebrows draw together. My first thought was Tyler. It was the only thing she'd lied to me about. Had it been more? I let that thought settle for a moment. If she left me for him, it would kill me. But maybe...maybe she deserved someone her own age that could treat her well. I wasn't a good man. I stared into her eyes. I was a monster. *Breathe.*

"I've been lying to you ever since you walked me home from that party. I didn't mean to. At first I just didn't want to get in trouble. But now it's so much more. I don't want to hurt you. I don't want this to be over."

"Penny, I told you that I'm not going anywhere. Just tell me." I squeezed her hands. *Stay. Please just stay. I'll be better. I'll be better for you.*

She took a deep breath. "I'm not a senior."

What? Of course she was. What was she talking about?

"I'm a sophomore. But my birthday is October 15th. I'll be 20 in just a couple weeks."

It felt like she slapped me. "You're only 19?" I didn't realize I'd said it out loud. She was a teenager? *I'm fucking a teenager? Jesus Christ!* I pulled my hands out of hers.

"I'm practically 20."

I ran both my hands through my hair. "Oh God, I've been serving you alcohol. I could have been arrested."

"I know, I'm sorry."

"You're only 19?" I felt like I was choking. I wanted to reach out to her, but I couldn't. Instead I ran my hands down the scruff on my face. "Penny." My voice sounded broken.

"I know that I should have told you."

"You made me feel awful for not telling you about Isabella. And the whole time you were lying to me?" I'd finally trusted someone and she was fucking 19? I was a monster. I was a pervert. I was fucking disgusting.

"I know, I'm so sorry."

"I told you how hard it is for me to trust people. This is why. Because no one is trustworthy. I thought you were different." *I thought you were older.* I'd loved how innocent she was. But she was innocent because she was a child. *I'm a sick fuck.*

"Professor Hunter, please. That's my only secret. You know everything about me now. You can trust me. It's still me. It's just two years difference. Two years is nothing."

"It's not the age. It's that you lied to me." I didn't know if that was true. It was both. I could barely look at her. *I'm disgusting.*

"If I had told you that first night, you could have reported me to the dean. I would have been kicked out of school."

"I never would have done that."

"But it's your job."

"I don't care about my job! I care about you. I had a crush on you. It took every ounce of control I had to not lift up that short, sparkly skirt you were wearing and have my way with you right there in the middle of campus."

"I didn't know that. All I knew was that I was drinking underage and I had a crush on my professor. I was so out of my comfort zone. I didn't know what to do."

"Well you should have told me."

"I know, and I'm sorry."

She reached for my face, but I pushed her hand away. I couldn't let her touch me. She was a teenager for fuck's sake. "I thought you were different. I let myself fall for you, even though I knew better." I was putting the blame on her, but it was on me. It would always be on me.

"I've fallen for you too."

I ran my hand through my hair. "The things I've done to you. If I had known you were a teenager, I wouldn't have..."

"Don't say that. Don't take away what we have. I love you." She was choking on her words. "Professor Hunter, I love you. I love you so much."

I thought I wanted to hear those words. I thought I felt it too. But what the hell did I know? I was a fucking mess. "Penny, you don't know what love is." She was too young. It slowly registered that a 19-year-old was strad- dling me. I pushed her off my lap. There was a certain kind of place in hell for men like me. Jesus, Ian had tried to warn me. Melissa had even tried to warn me. What the fuck was wrong with me? I'd never bothered to ask. I'd just trusted her. Blindly.

"You promised you wouldn't get mad," she said.

"Damn it, Penny! You made me believe that this was real. I let myself dream about a future with you. We only had to wait two semesters. I wanted to be with you. But six? Six semesters?"

Tears started to stream down her cheeks. "Stop using the past tense."

"What do you expect, Penny? You waited a whole month to tell me. Why didn't you just tell me when we first started dating?"

"That's exactly why. Because we had only just started dating. And I'm obsessed with you. I knew you'd be mad. I knew that you'd leave me. I wanted to have you as long as possible."

Obsessed with me? She had no idea what obsession was. I lived and breathed that pain, not her. But her words made me feel sick. Because I was the one that was obsessed with her. And that feeling of losing control terrified me. I wasn't the kind of man she wanted me to be. I was weak. "That's not an excuse. If you had believed what we had was real, telling me your age wouldn't have mattered."

"So what we have isn't real then?"

I felt like I was suffocating. I stood up and rubbed my hands across my face again. "What finally gave you the nerve to tell me the truth?"

"Because it was the only thing holding me back from happiness."

"That's a selfish reason." She was a child. Nineteen. *Fuck!*

"I know. But I never meant to hurt you."

I stared at her. I could see it now. All the times she'd just run away instead of talking to me. Even the way she looked up at me with her big blue eyes. I liked her innocence. But I didn't like her *that* innocent. "Well you did."

"I'm so sorry."

You will be. I could feel myself growing hard. *Damn it, what the hell is wrong with me?* I couldn't be in the same room as her. I was a fucking pervert and I couldn't control myself. I went to my closet and pulled on a shirt. "I'm going out." I needed air. I couldn't breathe. And I didn't trust myself around her.

- 343 -

"Where? Professor Hunter, it's late. Please stay. We can try to work this out. Don't walk away from what we have."

"I'll be at a bar so that you can't follow me. Or do you have a fake I.D. too?"

"No, I don't."

Breathe. Fucking breathe! "Good." I walked out of my bedroom and over to the elevators. I slammed the button with my fist.

She came running out. "Please don't go."

I stepped onto the elevator. "I believe that you know how to let yourself out." The doors slid shut and she was gone. I pressed my hand against the cold metal. And I broke down. I cried. Because I was a fucking idiot. I thought I could have something good. A fresh start. And all I got was a reminder that I was a monster. Penny deserved more than I could ever give her. Every part of me wanted to turn around, get down on my knees, and beg her to stay. But this moment was inevitable. The end of us. This was her chance to move on. To actually be happy. How could anyone be happy with me when it felt like I was drowning every day?

I needed a drink. And not just a few measured sips. I needed a whole damn bottle. Because what was the fucking point? I'd already slipped. I needed to get the hell out of this apartment before I fell apart. Before I caved in and crawled back to her like the pathetic piece of shit I was. For once in my life, I needed to try to be selfless. Walking away was what was best for her in the long run.

As I walked out into the rain, I remembered how fucking pissed off at the world I'd been when I was 19. Because that was when Rachel left me. That year had been the worst of my life.

I had no idea what love was when I was 19. Now I'd given my heart to a teenager. And I'd gotten what I deserved. Because men like me didn't deserve happiness. I was a monster. A streetlight flickered and dimmed above me. I blinked up at it in the rain. I was meant to live in the darkness.

Chapter 42

Friday

I'd tried my best to drink her away. Or rather, I was still trying. But nothing tasted as sweet as her. I lifted the bottle of scotch to my lips again as I sent off the email to cancel class.

It was 7 in the morning and I was shit-faced. Classic. It was like I was reliving my college years.

A month ago, I thought I had complete control over my life. And then Penny slammed into me and turned my world upside down. I was slipping. I could feel myself slipping. Hell, who was I kidding? I'd slipped as soon as Penny and I went from an if to a when. We never should have even been an if. I was a fucking mess. I'd never had control of anything.

There was a knock on my office door.

"Go away." I snapped. Ellen had been bugging the crap out of me. She was worried that I hadn't left my office all of yesterday. But the rest of my apartment smelled like Penny. This was the only place that didn't reek of her delicious perfume.

Another knock and then the door opened. Ian was standing there with a scowl on his face.

It was tempting to throw the bottle at him, but I had a feeling he'd throw it back. And my reflexes weren't exactly great right now. "What do you want?"

"Ellen made an appointment for you with Dr. Clark this morning."

"I'm not going to see him." I saw him on Sundays. Not Fridays. Besides, I had things to do. I turned back to my computer and watched the video feed of Penny's dorm building. I just needed one glimpse of her. Just one.

"Great. I'll have him call you then."

Before I could protest, Ian closed the door. I didn't need therapy. I just needed more to drink. I took another sip of scotch, feeling dizzier than before. I was just tired. So fucking tired.

I wasn't sure how long I'd been staring at my computer screen before my phone rang. Dr. Clark's name flashed across my screen. Better to get this over with now. It took me a second to remember how to answer it. "Dr. Clark." I ignored the way my words were slurred.

"James. I was hoping we could talk. How about I come over in about an hour?"

Now he was making house calls? And how much was he going to charge for that shit? He just wanted more money. He didn't care about me. "No need. We can do this now."

"Do what?"

There was a movement on my screen. I stared at the person exiting Penny's building. Some girl that wasn't her. *Fuck.*

"James, are you there?" Dr. Clark asked.

"Mhm." And just then Penny appeared on the screen. I reached out and touched her. She looked sad. And small. Young. I pulled my hand away and watched her disappear off my screen. A small piece of me hoped that Tyler would be with her. That she'd moved on. I wanted what was best for her. And that wasn't me. And yet…she was alone. She was always alone. And my resolve was slowly breaking. I was slowly breaking. I tried to take a deep breath, but it felt like the air didn't reach my lungs. "You were wrong. About all of it."

"About what exactly?"

I looked down at the bottle of scotch on my desk. It was supposed to numb my pain. But it did nothing. Nothing. I could barely see straight and still all I could feel was this all-consuming need. A need I was all too familiar with. And I couldn't satisfy it with alcohol. Or anything else that wasn't her. I had nothing left to say to Dr. Clark. I was about to hang up when he started speaking again.

"I thoroughly believe that we've made a lot of progress."

"We? There's no we. I'm in this alone. That's the whole point." *I'll always be alone.*

"That's not…"

"Don't give me a lecture about how you care, Dr. Clark. You care about a paycheck, just like everyone else in my life. You can cancel the rest of my appointments on your calendar. I won't be returning."

"James…"

"You should have stopped me. You should have and you didn't. And now I'm worse off than I was before." *I have nothing.* That feeling of emptiness was creeping back into my chest, suffocating me. I didn't realize I'd thrown the bottle of scotch at the wall until I heard the glass breaking. I watched the liquid run down the wall.

"James, are you drinking? You're better than this. You're stronger than this."

No, I wasn't. I hung up and leaned back in my chair, almost tipping the whole thing over. I wanted another drink. Not that it would help. It wasn't what I needed. I knew the difference between want and need better than anyone.

Chapter 43

Sunday

Drinking her away wasn't working. Because I knew what I wanted. Her. But I couldn't have her. She needed to move on. That's what was best for her. For both of us. I didn't want that to be true. I wanted to be strong enough to let her go. But I doubted that I was. Despite Dr. Clark calling a few more times, I'd skipped my therapy session this afternoon because now I was certain I knew the truth.

I ran faster through the falling rain. But exercise didn't help either. Nothing helped. I slowed down as I ran past Penny's dorm building. I knew I was being stalkery. And I didn't really care. *Come out.* I wasn't sure exactly what I was hoping would happen if I saw her. Maybe I could run into her again and we could just start over. *Stop.*

I picked up my pace. I ran mile after mile after mile, trying to make my chest stop hurting. It was like I was running around campus hoping to see her, but she was never there. I stopped outside the coffee shop where we first met, my legs practically giving out. I could so easily picture her inside. Bumping into me and falling into my arms. I'd gotten fucking stars in my eyes. I'd ignored the fact that she'd had a backpack. I'd ignored the fact that she was in my class. I'd ignored every warning. Because I couldn't stay away. I was weak.

I backed away from the coffee shop and started running again. Faster. A weekend of binge-drinking didn't help the burn in my side or the one in my chest. I needed water. I needed to stop. But I couldn't. Because if I stopped, I'd drink again. And I couldn't keep drinking. I could barely even see straight. And nothing numbed the pain.

I picked up my pace.

But even when I ran, I thought about her. What was she doing right now? Was she drinking away the pain? I doubted it. She wasn't weak like me. Maybe she was curled up in her uncomfortable bed watching a silly TV show. Missing me. Crying. Wishing desperately we could start over too. Something in my chest tightened. I wanted to wipe away her tears. I wanted to be the one to comfort her. To make her smile. To fuck away her sadness. *Monster.*

I had to distance myself from her. I had to give her a chance to be happy. Without me. Because I could never be that person for her. I'd make her miserable. I'd ruin her life. I'd ruin her future. Just like I always ruined everything I touched. God, I desperately wanted to touch her again. *Stop.*

I pushed the hood on my jacket back and let the rain fall on me. I forced myself to keep running, trying to rid the image of her beneath me from my mind. Trying to focus on anything but the way she made me feel. The rain started falling faster. And I wished I could just drown in it.

***

I was watching the video feed of Penny's dorm building again. I couldn't control myself. I'd found myself watching it for hours at a time, even though she never seemed to leave. There was no question about it…I was definitely stalking her now. Why was I doing this to myself? I couldn't have her. I couldn't. My mind was a terrifying place when I was craving something I couldn't have.

I was just about to ex out of it when I saw her emerge from the building. I held my breath as she made her way down the steps.

It looked like she'd been crying. She looked…frail. I zoomed in to see her face more clearly. There were dark circles under her eyes like her sleeping habits had become as bad as mine. And yet…she was still perfect. Her age didn't change that. It didn't change the way I felt about her. And she needed me. Clearly she needed me as desperately as I needed her.

Stop. She didn't need me. She needed anyone but me.

I exed out of the video feed and stared at the opened bottle of scotch. Why didn't anything help numb the pain? I always fucking did this. To most people, the high wasn't worth the pain. But to me? It was worth it. My whole life was pain. So a little escape every now and then was most definitely worth it. I grabbed the bottle of scotch and took a sip. Just a little more had to help. Something had to help.

Maybe that was what I needed. Just one more taste of Penny. *Just this once.* I'd tried that before and it hadn't exactly worked. It just made me crave her even more. But maybe it would work this time…

I'd lost it. My stomach was empty except for the booze. And I wasn't thinking clearly. I could not go back to Penny. No matter how badly I wanted to. I couldn't give in to the temptation this time. I downed more scotch.

There was a knock on my door.

"Go away," I mumbled.

The door opened.

I really needed to hire staff that respected me a little bit more. I glared at Ellen as she walked in.

"We need to talk," she said.

"I'm good."

She scoffed. "No. No you are not." She grabbed the bottle of scotch out of my hand. "You are not good."

I stared at the bottle. Couldn't she see that I needed it?

"Look at me," she said.

I continued to stare at the bottle.

She grabbed my chin and forced my gaze to meet hers. "I will not do this with you again. Do you understand me?"

I hated when she pretended to act like my mother. The joke was on her, because my mother didn't give a shit about me. "Whatever you say, Ellen."

"James. I'm throwing this out." She held the bottle out of my reach.

"What? No." I reached for it and nearly fell out of my chair.

She started to walk away.

What the fuck was her problem? I slowly followed her, wishing my legs didn't hurt so damn much from my run. And certainly if I could see in a straight line this would have been easier. By the time I reached the kitchen she was already pouring the scotch down the drain.

The whole counter was filled with empty bottles of liquor. Apparently she'd poured it all down the drain.

"Well, that's just a waste," I mumbled.

She turned around with her hand on her hip. "Enough of this. Sober up and then go ask Penny to forgive you for whatever you did to screw this up."

Why did she assume that I was the one that fucked everything up? "I can't."

"Of course you can. You can start with the words 'I'm sorry' and go from there. You're used to giving speeches. Figure it out."

"I'm not going back to her."

"Why?"

"Because she lied to me!"

Ellen just stared at me. "Then forgive her."

"It's not that simple. She's 19, Ellen." My legs were so tired that they gave out. I slumped down onto the kitchen floor.

"So what? My husband was ten years older than me. And you didn't see me making a fuss."

I'm not making a fuss. "That's not all."

"Then tell me why. Why isn't it as simple as her forgiving you or you forgiving her?"

"Because I'm a monster! And she deserves better than me."

Ellen's face fell. "You are not a monster, James. You are one of the kindest, most generous people I've ever met."

"You only think that because I pay you a small fortune not to leave me."

She sat down next to me on the floor. "That's not why. You've donated so much of your money to good causes. You gave up your lifestyle in New York to come teach and give back here. And you gave Ian a job when no one else would."

"Well that's just because he's the best at what he does."

"No. That's not the reason and you know it. He had PTSD and you were patient with him as he healed. No one else would give him that kindness or that chance."

"I'm sure someone else would have."

"Maybe one day. But you did right away. You are not a monster." She put her hand on my knee. "But you're not a very nice boy when you've been drinking."

I laughed and she smiled.

I slowly shook my head. "But it doesn't matter. Penny is still better off without me."

"That couldn't possibly be true."

"For once in my life, I'm trying to do the right thing, Ellen."

"Right for who? Certainly not for you. You're a mess. And if Penny feels the same way about you too...I bet she's just as miserable.

I pictured the dark circles under Penny's eyes. She looked like she was in pain too.

Ellen patted the side of my face. "And if you don't figure it out soon, I'm leaving. I told you once and I'll tell you again...I'm not doing this with you again." She slowly got up off the floor.

I knew I'd just bitched about needing new staff and hating that she pretended to be my mother. But in truth, I loved Ellen. And I liked that she acted like an actual mother to me. I couldn't lose her.

"And drink some water." She tossed a water bottle at me.

I went to catch it, but my reflexes were delayed, and it hit my chest.

Ellen walked away.

But her words echoed in my head. *And if Penny feels the same way about you too...I bet she's just as miserable.* I was trying to do the right thing. I really was. But what if by trying to do the right thing I was actually doing the exact opposite?

Our relationship had crumbled in part because I thought we were doomed from the beginning. But what if we weren't? If she really did want to be with me...if she was choosing me...that only left the other issues. I'd gotten mad at her about being 19, but I could get over that. Like she said, she'd be 20 soon enough. And as much as I told myself that I was disgusting, there wasn't a single disgusting thing that had happened between us. We fit.

Perfectly. And a few years age difference didn't change anything. Ellen was right…I was just making a fuss.

But that went back to my lie of omission. Penny was furious about the fact that I hadn't told her I was still married to Isabella. And no, Penny couldn't change her age. But I could change this. I could fix it. And maybe once I did, I wouldn't feel like such a monster. I could do this one thing…and maybe…just maybe…feel a little more worthy of her.

I pushed myself up off the floor and went back to my office. I rummaged through the grades I was handing out in class tomorrow, until I found Penny's. I'd written it right after she'd stormed out of my classroom. I'd begged her for a chance to explain. But we'd already worked all that out.

I pulled out a pen. Ellen was right. I didn't care that she was 19. I was caught up in the fact that she was a student for a few more years. But I could wait. I'd waited this long to be happy. What were a few more years? I felt like I'd been trying to convince myself we were wrong. But Ellen was right…we weren't.

What was wrong was that she'd lied and I'd lied. And now I could fix it. I scrawled at the bottom of her grade:

P.S. Now I know how it feels. I just need some time.

I was done running away from a good thing. I'd fix this. I set the pen down and pulled out my phone. There was nothing I wanted to do less than talk to Isabella. But if it meant I'd be more worthy of Penny? It was worth talking to the devil. I clicked on Isabella's number and pulled my cellphone to my ear.

Chapter 44

Friday

My phone started buzzing and I immediately grabbed it off the nightstand. Penny had tried texting and calling a few times. Emailing too. I loved receiving her messages, but I never responded. I wasn't going to approach her again until I could tell her I was officially divorced. I wanted her to know that I wasn't going to lie to her anymore. That would be a new beginning for us. A fresh start.

But my fresh start was taking forever because Isabella wouldn't return any of my fucking calls. Why did she always show up when she was unwanted and disappear when I actually needed to see her? She just liked torturing me.

But it wasn't a message from Penny. Or Isabella calling me back. It was Rob calling.

"Hello?" I said.

"You sound like shit," Rob said.

"Thanks, you too."

Rob laughed.

I wasn't drunk anymore. I'd taken to working out so much that I couldn't move. And yet...I still wasn't numb. Nothing worked. Nothing helped. I couldn't get her out of my system. But knowing that I didn't really need to anymore...knowing I'd be able to have her again soon? That helped. I just needed a bit more time to sort my shit out. It didn't make every day hurt any less though.

I was lying in my bed in the middle of the day now because her scent on my sheets was still lingering. It was the closest I could be to her. And the perfect place to jerk off to the images of her in my head. Well, here and in the shower. I loved that image of her naked in the shower. On her knees with my cum dripping down her chin. It was a vision. I got hard every time I smelled her perfume, stepped in the shower, went to class. Even when it rained I got fucking hard. I'd even gotten hard when my phone buzzed. That's what thinking about Penny did to me. I needed her again. Desperately. *Soon.* I took a deep breath.

"Did you hear what I said?" Rob asked.

I hadn't. "Yeah, great."

There was a long pause.

"So you're fine if I come stay with you in a bit?"

Was that what he'd asked? "Sure." Honestly, it might be nice to have him here. He was always good at distracting me. And I needed all the distractions I could get. Because if Isabella didn't call me back soon, I'd go crawling back to Penny before I deserved her. And I didn't want to do that. I wanted her to know how serious I was about us.

"Don't sound so enthusiastic about it."

I laughed, and it sounded strange in my throat. "When are you coming?"

"Eh. Sometime soon."

How…specific. Whatever. I didn't have any plans. "Great. See you then."

"Are you okay, man? You're being way too agreeable."

"Is that even a thing?"

Rob laughed. "When it comes to you, yes. You sound…off."

I didn't need Rob worrying about me too. Ian and Ellen already stared at me with pity. Or was it fear? I couldn't tell. Either way, I didn't like it. "I'm fine, just dealing with some personal stuff."

"Is the troll still giving you problems with the divorce papers?"

That was one of his favorite topics to discuss. And normally I just ignored him, because the specifics didn't really matter. But they did now. They were the only thing keeping me away from Penny. "Yes, actually. She won't return any of my calls. I want this thing finalized."

"You really gotta just go over her head. Surely Papa Pruitt would love to talk contracts with you. Vom."

Holy shit. I sat up in bed. *Over Isabella's head.* That was my way out of my marriage. Isabella's father was the perfect person to talk to. We could come to some kind of agreement. "You're a genius."

"I really don't hear that enough. Feel free to say it again."

"I gotta go."

"A double complement was asking too much. See you in a few days. Or weeks. Or hours."

That's annoying. "See you then." I hung up the phone. It would only take me a couple hours to get to Mr. Pruitt's apartment if I was the one driving. I emerged from my bedroom, not bothering to shower or change out of my sweats.

"Good heavens, James, where are you going?" Ellen said as she saw me walking toward the elevators.

I looked down, suddenly worried I was still sporting that boner from when I was daydreaming about Penny earlier. I wasn't. The thought of seeing Mr. Pruitt had gotten rid of that. So I had no idea what she was upset about. "I'm driving up to New York. I'm not staying the night or anything. I'm driving there and then back." I just needed to get this thing done. Because as soon as I did...I could have Penny again.

"No you are not."

"Excuse me?"

"You're drunk."

I just stared at her. "No I'm not."

"You've been drunk all week."

It had been a while since Ellen had seen me like this, and she was seriously off her game. Just because I looked depressed didn't mean I was drunk or high off my mind. I was just in…withdrawal. "I haven't had an ounce of liquor since the weekend." Well, technically Monday morning. And maybe a little Wednesday. And just like…one drink this morning. I wasn't spiraling anymore. But seeing Penny in class was fucking torture. All I wanted to do was reach out and touch her. And I couldn't. Not yet.

Ellen didn't need to know that though. The point was I was sober enough to drive right now.

"I'm calling Ian."

"I can drive. I swear. Look." I rubbed my tummy and patted my head at the same time. An act of pure coordination that could only be performed by a sober individual.

She stared at me like I'd lost my mind.

In her defense, I probably had. But I used her sudden shock to bypass her and step onto the elevator.

"James!" she yelled after me.

But the elevator doors were already closing. I breathed a sigh of relief and leaned against the side of the elevator. And then I was picturing pressing Penny's back against the wall of the elevator. *Fuck.* I ran my hand down my face. Images of her haunted me. All I wanted to do was recreate every scene playing out in my head. Again and again. Maybe I'd be able to tonight.

If I could convince Mr. Pruitt that his daughter was better off without me, I'd be free to start things up again with Penny. And convincing him wouldn't be hard. I could just act like I was drunk when I showed up or something.

Or offer him money. I was pretty sure that was the only thing the old man cared about. He'd never liked me very much anyway. He was friends with my parents, not with me.

When the doors opened, I wasn't at all surprised to see Ian standing there with a pair of car keys in his hand.

"Ellen says we're going on a day trip to New York?"

It wasn't worth fighting him. I literally couldn't. Every part of my body was too tired to fight him off. Except for that one part that kept popping up whenever I thought about Penny.

But for the first time since we'd ended things, I finally had something else to focus on. One damn signature would set me free. Free to do whatever I wanted. And I wanted to do Penny. I smiled to myself.

Ian waved the keys in the air.

"Fine." I brushed past him. It would give me time to call Mr. Pruitt in the car. Besides, Ian's car didn't smell like Penny. It was for the best, unless Ian wanted me to have a boner the whole ride. And I was pretty certain he did not.

But as soon as I sat down in his car, I pictured fucking Penny in my car. I'd been desperate for her after our fight. I couldn't wait. I couldn't resist.

Just a few more hours. As soon as I was back in Newark, I'd reach out to her. I'd win her back. I had to. Ian was quiet as he pulled the car out of the parking garage, letting my thoughts wander. The farther away we drove from Delaware, the harder it got to breathe.

Each minute that passed it got more and more obvious. I really didn't care about Penny's age. Or that she'd lied. Or any of it. All I cared about was her. And every mile farther we drove, I missed her more and more. I never wanted to be apart from her again.

***

"Are you sure you want to do this?" Ian asked as he pulled into a spot outside Mr. Pruitt's apartment building.

Mr. Pruitt said he had time to talk at 8 tonight. Ian had driven us around the city in circles as we waited. I had nowhere else I wanted to go while I was here. I just wanted this divorce to be finalized so I could...

What? I smiled to myself as I pictured knocking on Penny's dorm room door. Telling her the good news. Her sinking to her knees. My fingers buried in her red hair.

Yeah. That would work. God, I loved the way she worshipped my cock. I used to think that Delaware was my fresh start. But that wasn't true. It was Penny. I ran my hand down my face. Isabella not signing the papers was the last thing tethering me to New York. I needed to cut ties with the city that had almost killed me. And the woman who I despised.

"I'm sure," I said and unbuckled my seatbelt.

"Do you want me to come up?" Ian asked.

"No. This won't take long." I climbed out of the car and slammed the door. Mr. Pruitt was a dick. But I was pretty sure he hated me as much as I hated him. Surely he'd be happy to oust me from his family. He'd actually sounded a little excited on the phone. Maybe contracts were his Penny. *Breathe.*

The air wasn't fresh here. But it did bring back memories. How many times had Rob and I been forced to go to the Pruitts' place for dinner? Or on holidays and other special occasions? A chill ran down my spine as I opened the door to the lobby. I hadn't been here in years. Isabella and I didn't spend much personal time together. Which meant I hadn't attended her Sunday family dinners. Or any of that nonsense. We lived separate lives. And now I just wanted to make that even more separate. Permanently separate.

I stepped onto the elevator and thought about my approach here. Acting like a drunken fool was definitely tempting. And giving him a check was a nice backup plan. But…maybe honesty would work best with Mr. Pruitt. After all, he was a father. He must want what was best for his daughter. And Isabella certainly didn't love me. I nodded to myself. Lies had messed things up with me and Penny. I was done lying. My fresh start had to be built on honesty. I stepped off the elevator, walked down the hall, and stopped outside the Pruitts' door.

I'd tried to drink Penny away. I'd tried to exercise her away. But all I did was prove how much I needed her. I could feel her in my veins. I wanted to taste her skin again. And breathe in her exhales. The lines between want and need were blurred. But I didn't even care. I'd win her back. I had to. I didn't know if getting my divorce finalized truly made me worthy of her. But what I did know was that I was tired. I was just so fucking tired of hating myself so much. For just a brief moment, Penny had helped me remember what living felt like. What breathing felt like. What being happy felt like. How could I ever stop craving that feeling? Craving her?

I'd found love in a place where it wasn't supposed to be. And no matter what anyone said, a piece of me would always know it was wrong. I knew Penny could have a better life without me. And yet…I couldn't stay away. I wouldn't. Not when I knew she needed me too. And I'd do everything in my power to make her happy. I'd be a good man for her. There was no other choice here. I clenched my hand into a fist and knocked on the door of the devil's father.

As soon as I had Penny back, I'd be able to sleep again. Eat again. I'd be able to stop drinking. I'd be happy. Living life without my girl beside me was torture. I had to end this. I had to win her back. This had to be enough. Because it was all I could offer her as an apology.

And I wasn't strong enough to let her go. I wanted to be. I wanted it desperately. But I'd never been one to resist temptation. It was how I'd wound up in his mess in the first place.

Literally. I wouldn't be standing outside the Pruitts' door if I had my shit together. If I'd been sober enough to put an end to this train wreck sooner. I knocked on the door again, louder this time. Where the hell was he?

I took a deep breath. Standing outside this door reminded me of all the shit I'd been through to get to this point in my life. I just wanted to be happy. With Penny. I felt the corner of my mouth lift. How could happiness be bad? Just thinking about her freely made me breathe easier again. I wasn't sure I could exist without her.

Finally the door opened. But Mr. Pruitt wasn't the one who answered.

And just like that, I couldn't breathe again. I was in hell.

The woman staring back at me might as well have been a stranger. She smiled, the skin on her face stretching oddly thanks to a fresh dose of Botox. "James, darling. You're just in time. Daddy had to step out, but I'm sure we can reach an agreement together. For old time's sake. Here, your favorite." She tried to hand me a drink.

"Isabella." Saying her name out loud made me feel sick to my stomach. I ignored the drink in her outstretched hand. She knew I had a problem. She loved when I was in pain. She loved watching others suffer. She loved watching me drown. And I was drowning without Penny in my life. I couldn't fucking breathe without her.

"It really looks like you could use a drink," Isabella said, lifting the glass higher.

Fuck it. I needed something to get me through this terrible discussion. I grabbed the glass Isabella was offering and swallowed the liquid in one big gulp, feeling the burn down my throat.

"Feeling better?" Isabella's words were slurred.

Or was I hearing them slurred? I tried to shake my head, but I felt dizzy. Dizzier than I should have after one drink. I wasn't exactly a lightweight. "What did you put in here?" I said.

Isabella smiled her wicked smile. "Nothing. You feel better because you're with me." She put her hand on my chest and it was like I could feel her coldness seeping into me. The exact opposite of how Penny made me feel. I tried to push her away but my arms were suddenly really heavy.

"You drugged me, you psychotic bitch."

"Language," she said. "You know I hate when you curse. And I didn't drug you. That would be crazy. And I'm not crazy anymore. You know I got help with that, darling." Her eyes narrowed at me.

She most certainly was still crazy. My vision blurred and then blacked out completely. I knew better than to come here. Once you make a deal with the devil...you can't escape the darkness.

What's Next?

Professor Hunter and Penny know how to melt a kindle.
And I can't stop writing about them!

To get your free copy of a steamy bonus scene about
James and Penny, go to:

www.ivysmoak.com/obsessed-pb

A Note From Ivy

I can't seem to stop writing about these characters! Even though Penny and James are fictional, so much of their lives reflect my own. Much to my husband's dismay…James Hunter is based on him. And I will never stop laughing when he insists he's #TeamTyler.

Because these characters are so tangled up in my real life, they will always hold a special place in my heart. I think when I wrote THE END after This is Love I knew that James and Penny's story would never really be over. Because we're still living it. How could it possibly be over just yet?

I'd been toying with the idea of writing James' point of view for years. I wanted to make sure it was different. That there were still mysteries and unanswered questions with a new telling of the story.

I really hope you loved it! Six years after Temptation has been released, and James Hunter is still my most popular hero because of you guys. Thank you from the bottom of my heart for going on this journey with me! And I can't wait to keep writing his perspective. As long as you keep reading, I'll keep writing. :)

Ivy Smoak

Ivy Smoak
Wilmington, DE
www.ivysmoak.com

About the Author

Ivy Smoak is the Wall Street Journal, USA Today, and Amazon #1 bestselling author of *The Hunted Series*. Her books have sold over 2 million copies worldwide.

When she's not writing, you can find Ivy binge watching too many TV shows, taking long walks, playing outside, and generally refusing to act like an adult. She lives with her husband in Delaware.

Facebook: IvySmoakAuthor
Instagram: @IvySmoakAuthor
Goodreads: IvySmoak

Recommend *Obsessed* for your next book club!

Book club questions available at:
www.ivysmoak.com/bookclub

www.ingramcontent.com/pod-product-compliance
Ingram Content Group UK Ltd.
Pitfield, Milton Keynes, MK11 3LW, UK
UKHW031736060125
3976UKWH00036B/349